THE GODS OF GUILT

ALSO BY MICHAEL CONNELLY

Fiction
The Black Echo
The Black Ice
The Concrete Blonde
The Last Coyote
The Poet
Trunk Music
Blood Work
Angels Flight
Void Moon
A Darkness More Than Night
City of Bones
Chasing the Dime
Lost Light
The Narrows
The Closers
The Lincoln Lawyer
Echo Park
The Overlook
The Brass Verdict
The Scarecrow
Nine Dragons
The Reversal
The Fifth Witness
The Drop
The Black Box

Non-Fiction
Crime Beat

E-books
Suicide Run
Angle of Investigation
Mulholland Dive
The Safe Man

THE
GODS OF
GUILT

MICHAEL
CONNELLY

First published in Great Britain in 2013 by Orion Books,
an imprint of The Orion Publishing Group Ltd
Orion House, 5 Upper Saint Martin's Lane
London WC2H 9EA

An Hachette UK Company

A CIP catalogue record for this book is
available from the British Library.

Printed in Great Britain by Clays Ltd, St Ives plc

The Orion Publishing Group's policy is to use papers that are natural,
renewable and recyclable products and made from wood grown in sustainable
forests. The logging and manufacturing processes are expected to
conform to the environmental regulations of the country of origin.

www.orionbooks.co.uk

For Charlie Hounchell

Part 1

GLORY DAYS

TUESDAY, NOVEMBER 13

1

I approached the witness stand with a warm and welcoming smile. This, of course, belied my true intent, which was to destroy the woman who sat there with her eyes fixed on me. Claire Welton had just identified my client as the man who had forced her out of her Mercedes E60 at gunpoint on Christmas Eve last year. She said he was the one who then shoved her to the ground before taking off with the car, her purse, and all the shopping bags she had loaded into the backseat at the mall. As she had just told the prosecutor who questioned her, he had also made off with her sense of security and self-confidence, even though for these more personal thefts he had not been charged.

"Good morning, Mrs. Welton."

"Good morning."

She said the words like they were synonyms for *please don't hurt me*. But everyone in the courtroom knew it was my job to hurt her today and thereby hurt the state's case against my client, Leonard Watts. Welton was in her sixties and matronly. She didn't look fragile but I had to hope she was.

Welton was a Beverly Hills housewife and one of three victims who were roughed up and robbed in a pre-Christmas crime spree resulting in the nine charges against Watts. The police had labeled him the "Bumper Car Bandit," a strong-arm thief who followed targeted women from the malls, bumped into their cars at stop signs in residential neighborhoods, and then took their

3

vehicles and belongings at gunpoint when they stepped out of their cars to check for damage. He then pawned or resold all the goods, kept any cash, and dropped the cars off at chop shops in the Valley.

But all of that was alleged and hinged on someone identifying Leonard Watts as the culprit in front of the jury. That was what made Claire Welton so special and the key witness of the trial. She was the only one of the three victims who pointed Watts out to the jury and unequivocally claimed that he was the one, that he did it. She was the seventh witness presented by the prosecution in two days but as far as I was concerned she was the only witness. She was the number one pin. And if I knocked her down at just the right angle, all the other pins would go down with her.

I needed to roll a strike here or the jurors who were watching would send Leonard Watts away for a very long time.

I carried a single sheet of paper with me to the witness stand. I identified it as the original crime report created by a patrol officer who was first to respond to the 911 call placed by Claire Welton from a borrowed cell phone after the carjacking occurred. It was already part of the state's exhibits. After asking for and receiving approval from the judge, I put the document down on the ledge at the front of the witness stand. Welton leaned away from me as I did this. I was sure most members of the jury saw this as well.

I started asking my first question as I walked back to the lectern between the prosecution and defense tables.

"Mrs. Welton, you have there the original crime report taken on the day of the unfortunate incident in which you were victimized. Do you remember talking with the officer who arrived to help you?"

"Yes, of course I do."

"You told him what happened, correct?"

"Yes. I was still shaken up at the—"

"But you did tell him what happened so he could put a report out about the man who robbed you and took your car, is that correct?"

4

"Yes."

"That was Officer Corbin, correct?"

"I guess. I don't remember his name but it says it on the report."

"But you do remember telling the officer what happened, correct?"

"Yes."

"And he wrote down a summary of what you said, correct?"

"Yes, he did."

"And he even asked you to read the summary and initial it, didn't he?"

"Yes, but I was very nervous."

"Are those your initials at the bottom of the summary paragraph on the report?"

"Yes."

"Mrs. Welton, will you now read out loud to the jury what Officer Corbin wrote down after talking with you?"

Welton hesitated as she studied the summary before reading it.

Kristina Medina, the prosecutor, used the moment to stand and object.

"Your Honor, whether the witness initialed the officer's summary or not, counsel is still trying to impeach her testimony with writing that is not hers. The people object."

Judge Michael Siebecker narrowed his eyes and turned to me.

"Judge, by initialing the officer's report, the witness adopted the statement. It is present recollection recorded and the jury should hear it."

Siebecker overruled the objection and instructed Mrs. Welton to read the initialed statement from the report. She finally complied.

"'Victim stated that she stopped at the intersection of Camden and Elevado and soon after was struck from behind by a car that pulled up. When she opened her door to get out and check for damage, she was met by a black male thirty to thirty-five YOA—' I don't know what that means."

"Years of age," I said. "Keep reading, please."

"'He grabbed her by the hair and pulled her the rest of the way out of the car and to the ground in the middle of the street. He pointed a black, short-barrel revolver at her face and told her he would shoot her if she moved or made any sound. The suspect then jumped into her car and drove off in a northerly direction, followed by the car that had rear-ended her vehicle. Victim could offer no..."

I waited but she didn't finish.

"Your Honor, can you instruct the witness to read the entire statement as written on the day of the incident?"

"Mrs. Welton," Judge Siebecker intoned. "Please continue to read the statement in its entirety."

"But, Judge, this isn't everything I said."

"Mrs. Welton," the judge said forcefully. "Read the *entire* statement as the defense counselor asked you to do."

Welton relented and read the last sentence of the summary.

"'Victim could offer no further description of the suspect at this time.'"

"Thank you, Mrs. Welton," I said. "Now, while there wasn't much in the way of a description of the suspect, you were from the start able to describe in detail the gun he used, isn't that right?"

"I don't know about how much detail. He pointed it at my face so I got a good look at it and was able to describe what I saw. The officer helped me by describing the difference between a revolver and the other kind of gun. I think an automatic, it's called."

"And you were able to describe the kind of gun it was, the color, and even the length of the barrel."

"Aren't all guns black?"

"How about if I ask the questions right now, Mrs. Welton?"

"Well, the officer asked a lot of questions about the gun."

"But you weren't able to describe the man who pointed the gun at you, and yet two hours later you pick his face out of a bunch of mug shots. Do I have that right, Mrs. Welton?"

"You have to understand something. I saw the man who robbed me and pointed the gun. Being able to describe him and recognize him are two different things. When I saw that picture, I knew it was him, just as sure as I know it's him sitting at that table."

I turned to the judge.

"Your Honor, I would like to strike that as nonresponsive."

Medina stood up.

"Judge, counsel is making broad statements in his so-called questions. He made a statement and the witness merely responded. The motion to strike has no foundation."

"Motion to strike is denied," the judge said quickly. "Ask your next question, Mr. Haller, and I do mean a question."

I did and I tried. For the next twenty minutes I hammered away at Claire Welton and her identification of my client. I questioned how many black people she knew in her life as a Beverly Hills housewife and opened the door on interracial identification issues. All to no avail. At no point was I able to shake her resolve or belief that Leonard Watts was the man who robbed her. Along the way she seemed to recover one of things she said she had lost in the robbery. Her self-confidence. The more I worked her, the more she seemed to bear up under the verbal assault and send it right back at me. By the end she was a rock. Her identification of my client was still standing. And I had bowled a gutter ball.

I told the judge I had no further questions and returned to the defense table. Medina told the judge she had a short redirect and I knew she would ask Welton a series of questions that would only reinforce her identification of Watts. As I slid into my seat next to Watts, his eyes searched my face for any indication of hope.

"Well," I whispered to him. "That's it. We are done."

He leaned back from me as if repelled by my breath or words or both.

"We?" he said.

He said it loud enough to interrupt Medina, who turned and

looked at the defense table. I put my hands out palms down in a calming gesture and mouthed the words *Cool it* to him.

"Cool it?" he said aloud. "I'm not going to cool it. You told me you had this, that she was no problem."

"Mr. Haller!" the judge barked. "Control your client, please, or I'll have—"

Watts didn't wait for whatever it was the judge was about to threaten to do. He launched his body into me, hitting me like a cornerback breaking up a pass play. My chair tipped over with me in it and we spilled onto the floor at Medina's feet. She jumped sideways to avoid getting hurt herself as Watts drew his right arm back. I was on my left side on the floor, my right arm pinned under Watts's body. I manage to raise my left hand and caught his fist as it came down at me. It merely softened the blow. His fist took my own hand into my jaw.

I was peripherally aware of screams and motion around me. Watts pulled his fist back as he prepared for punch number two. But the courtroom deputies were on him before he could throw it. They gang-tackled him, their momentum taking him off me and onto the floor in the well in front of the counsel tables.

It all seemed to move in slow motion. The judge was barking commands no one was listening to. Medina and the court reporter were moving away from the melee. The court clerk had stood up behind her corral and was watching in horror. Watts was chest down on the floor, a deputy's hand on the side of his head, pressing it to the tile, an odd smile on his face as his hands were cuffed behind his back.

And in a moment it was over.

"Deputies, remove him from the courtroom!" Siebecker commanded.

Watts was dragged through the steel door at the side of the courtroom and into the holding cell used to house incarcerated defendants. I was left sitting on the floor, surveying the damage. I had blood on my mouth and teeth and down the crisp white shirt I was wearing. My tie was on the floor under the defense table. It was the clip-on I wear on days I visit clients in holding cells and don't want to get pulled through the bars.

I rubbed my jaw with my hand and ran my tongue along the rows of my teeth. Everything seemed intact and in working order. I pulled a white handkerchief out of an inside jacket pocket and started wiping off my face as I used my free hand to grab the defense table and help myself up.

"Jeannie," the judge said to his clerk. "Call paramedics for Mr. Haller."

"No, Judge," I said quickly. "I'm okay. Just need to clean up a little bit."

I picked my tie up and then made a pathetic attempt at decorum, reattaching it to my collar despite the deep red stain that had ruined the front of my shirt. As I worked the clip into my buttoned collar, several deputies reacting to the courtroom panic button undoubtedly pushed by the judge stormed in through the main doors at the back. Siebecker quickly told them to stand down and that the incident had passed. The deputies fanned out across the back wall of the courtroom, a show of force in case there was anyone else in the courtroom thinking about acting out.

I took one last swipe at my face with the handkerchief and then spoke up.

"Your Honor," I said. "I am deeply sorry for my client's—"

"Not now, Mr. Haller. Take your seat and you do the same, Ms. Medina. Everybody calm down and sit down."

I did as instructed, holding the folded handkerchief to my mouth and watching as the judge turned his seat fully toward the jury box. First he told Claire Welton that she was excused from the witness stand. She got up tentatively and walked toward the gate behind the counsel tables. She looked more shaken than anyone else in the courtroom. No doubt for good reason. She probably figured that Watts could have just as easily gone after her as me. And if he had been quick enough he would've gotten to her.

Welton sat down in the first row of the gallery, which was reserved for witnesses and staff, and the judge proceeded with the jury.

"Ladies and gentlemen, I am sorry that you had to see that display. The courtroom is never a place for violence. It is the place where civilized society takes its stand against the violence that is out on our streets. It truly pains me when something like this occurs."

There was a metal snapping sound as the door to the holding cell opened and the two courtroom deputies returned. I wondered how badly they had roughed up Watts while securing him in the cell.

The judge paused and then returned his attention to the jury.

"Unfortunately, Mr. Watts's decision to attack his attorney has prejudiced our ability to go forward. I believe—"

"Your Honor?" Medina interrupted. "If the state could be heard."

Medina knew exactly where the judge was headed and needed to do something.

"Not now, Ms. Medina, and do not interrupt the court."

But Medina was persistent.

"Your Honor, could counsel approach at sidebar?"

The judge looked annoyed with her but relented. I let her lead the way and we walked up to the bench. The judge hit the switch on a noise-canceling fan so the jury would not overhear our whispers. Before Medina could state her case, the judge asked me once more if I wanted medical attention.

"I'm fine, Judge, but I appreciate the offer. I think the only thing the worse for wear is my shirt, actually."

The judge nodded and turned to Medina.

"I know your objection, Ms. Medina, but there is nothing I can do. The jury is prejudiced by what they just saw. I have no choice."

"Your Honor, this case is about a very violent defendant who committed very violent acts. The jury knows this. They won't be unduly prejudiced by what they saw. The jury is entitled to view and judge for themselves the demeanor of the defendant. Because he voluntarily engaged in violent acts, the prejudice to the defendant is neither undue nor unfair."

"If I could be heard, Your Honor, I beg to differ with—"

"Besides that," Medina continued, running me over, "I fear the court is being manipulated by this defendant. He knew full well that he could get a new trial this way. He—"

"Whoa, wait a minute here," I protested. "Counsel's objection is replete with unfounded innuendo and—"

"Ms. Medina, the objection is overruled," the judge said, cutting off all debate. "Even if the prejudice is neither undue nor unfair, Mr. Watts has effectively just fired his attorney. I can't require Mr. Haller to go forward in these circumstances and I am not inclined to allow Mr. Watts back into this courtroom. Step back. Both of you."

"Judge, I want the people's objection on the record."

"You shall have it. Now step back."

We went back to our tables and the judge turned off the fan and then addressed the jury.

"Ladies and gentlemen, as I was saying, the event you just witnessed has created a situation prejudicial to the defendant. I believe that it will be too difficult for you to divorce yourself from what you just saw as you deliberate on his guilt or innocence of the charges. Therefore, I must declare a mistrial at this time and discharge you with the thanks of this court and the people of California. Deputy Carlyle will escort you back to the assembly room where you may gather your things and go home."

The jurors seemed unsure of what to do or whether everything was over. Finally, one brave man in the box stood up and soon the others followed. They filed out through a door at the back of the courtroom.

I looked over at Kristina Medina. She sat at the prosecution table with her chin down, defeated. The judge abruptly adjourned court for the day and left the bench. I folded my ruined handkerchief and put it away.

2

My full day had been scheduled for trial. Suddenly released from it, I had no clients to see, no prosecutors to work, and no place to be. I left the courthouse and walked down Temple to First. At the corner there was a trash can. I took out my handkerchief, held it to my lips and spit all the debris from my mouth into it. I then tossed it away.

I took a right on First and saw the Town Cars parked along the sidewalk. There were six of them in line like a funeral procession, their drivers gathered together on the sidewalk, shooting the shit and waiting. They say imitation is the sincerest form of flattery, but ever since the movie, a whole contingent of Lincoln lawyers had cropped up and routinely crowded the curbs outside the courthouses of L.A. I was both proud and annoyed. I had heard more than a few times that there were other lawyers out there saying they were the inspiration for the film. On top of that, I had jumped into the wrong Lincoln at least three times in the past month.

This time there would be no mistake. As I headed down the hill I pulled my cell phone and called Earl Briggs, my driver. I could see him up ahead. He answered right away and I told him to pop the trunk. Then I hung up.

I saw the trunk of the third Lincoln in line rise and I had my destination. When I got there I put my briefcase down and then took off my jacket, tie, and shirt. I had a T-shirt on underneath, so I wasn't stopping traffic. I chose a pale blue oxford from the stack of backup shirts I keep in the trunk, unfolded it, and started pulling it on. Earl came over from the klatch with the other drivers. He had been my driver on and off for nearly a decade. Whenever he ran into trouble he came to me and then worked off my fee by driving. This time it wasn't his own trouble he was paying for. I handled his mother's foreclosure defense and got her straightened out without her having to go homeless. That got me about six months' worth of driving from Earl.

I had draped my ruined shirt over the fender. He picked it up and examined it.

"What, somebody spill a whole thing of Hawaiian Punch on you or something?"

"Something like that. Come on, let's go."

"I thought you had court all day."

"I did too. But things change."

"Where to, then?"

"Let's go by Philippe's first."

"You got it."

He got in the front and I jumped in the back. After a quick stop at the sandwich shop on Alameda I had Earl point the car west. The next stop was a place called Menorah Manor, near Park La Brea in the Fairfax District. I said I'd be about an hour and got out with my briefcase. I had tucked my fresh shirt in but didn't bother clipping my tie back on. I wouldn't need it.

Menorah Manor was a four-story nursing home on Willoughby east of Fairfax. I signed in at the front desk and took the elevator up to the third floor, where I informed the woman at the nurses' desk that I had a legal consultation with my client David Siegel and was not to be disturbed in his room. She was a pleasant woman who was used to my frequent visits. She nodded her approval and I went down the hallway to room 334.

I entered and closed the door after putting the DO NOT DISTURB sign on the outside handle. David "Legal" Siegel was lying in bed, his eyes on the screen of a muted television bolted to the upper wall across from the bed. His thin white hands were on top of a blanket. There was a low hiss from the tube that brought oxygen to his nose. He smiled when he saw me.

"Mickey."

"Legal, how are you doing today?"

"Same as yesterday. Did you bring anything?"

I pulled the visitor's chair away from the wall and positioned it so I could sit in his line of vision. At eighty-one years old, he didn't have a lot of mobility. I opened my briefcase on the bed and turned it so he could reach into it.

"French dip from Philippe the Original. How's that?"

"Oh, boy," he said.

Menorah Manor was a kosher joint and I used the legal consultation bit as a way around it. Legal Siegel missed the places he'd eaten at during a near-fifty-year run as a lawyer in downtown. I was happy to bring him the culinary joy. He had been my father's law partner. He was the strategist, while my father had been the front man, the performer who enacted the strategies in court. After my father died when I was five, Legal stuck around. He took me to my first Dodgers game when I was a kid, sent me to law school when I was older.

A year ago I had come to him after losing the election for district attorney amid scandal and self-destruction. I was looking for life strategy, and Legal Siegel was there for me. In that way, these meetings were legitimate consultations between lawyer and client, only the people at the desk didn't understand that I was the client.

I helped him unwrap the sandwich and opened the plastic container holding the *jus* that made the sandwiches from Philippe's so good. There was also a sliced pickle wrapped in foil.

Legal smiled after his first bite and pumped his skinny arm like he had just won a great victory. I smiled. I was glad to bring him something. He had two sons and a bunch of grandchildren but they never came around except on the holidays. As Legal told me, "They need you until they don't need you."

When I was with Legal we talked mostly about cases and he would suggest strategies. He was absolute aces when it came to predicting prosecution plans and case roll outs. It didn't matter that he had not been in a courtroom in this century or that penal codes had changed since his day. He had baseline experience and always had a play. He called them moves, actually—the double-blind move, the judge's robes move, and so on. I had come to him during the dark time that followed the election. I wanted to learn about my father and how he had dealt with the adversities of his life. But I ended up learning more about the law and how it was like soft lead. How it could be bent and molded.

"The law is malleable," Legal Siegel always told me. "It's pliable."

I considered him to be part of my team, and that allowed me to discuss my cases with him. He'd throw out his ideas and moves. Sometimes I used them and they worked, sometimes not.

He ate slowly. I had learned that if I gave him a sandwich, he could take an hour to eat it, steadily chewing small bites. Nothing went to waste. He ate everything I brought him.

"The girl in three-thirty died last night," he said between bites. "A shame."

"I'm sorry to hear that. How old was she?"

"She was young. Early seventies. Just died in her sleep and they carted her out this morning."

I nodded. I didn't know what to say. Legal took another bite and reached into my briefcase for a napkin.

"You're not using the *jus*, Legal. That's the good stuff."

"I think I like it dry. Hey, you used the bloody flag move, didn't you? How'd it go?"

When he'd grabbed the napkin, he had spotted the extra blood capsule I kept in a Ziploc bag. I had it just in case I swallowed the first one by mistake.

"Like a charm," I said.

"You get the mistrial?"

"Yep. In fact, mind if I use your bathroom?"

15

I reached into the briefcase and grabbed another Ziploc, this one containing my toothbrush. I went into the room's bathroom and brushed my teeth. The red dye turned the brush pink at first but soon it was all down the drain.

When I came back to the chair, I noticed that Legal had finished only half his sandwich. I knew the rest must be cold and there was no way I could take it out to the dayroom to heat it in the microwave. But Legal still seemed happy.

"Details," he demanded.

"Well, I tried to break the witness but she held up. She was a rock. When I returned to the table, I gave him the signal and he did his thing. He hit me a little harder than I was expecting but I'm not complaining. The best part is I didn't have to make the motion to declare a mistrial. The judge went right to it on his own."

"Over prosecution's objection?"

"Oh, yeah."

"Good. Fuck 'em."

Legal Siegel was a defense attorney through and through. For him, any ethical question or gray area could be overcome by the knowledge that it is the sworn duty of the defense attorney to present the best defense of his client. If that meant tipping a mistrial when the chips were down, then so be it.

"Now the question is, will he deal now?"

"It's actually a she, and I think she'll deal. You should've seen the witness after the scuffle. She was scared and I don't think she'll be wanting to come back for another trial. I'll wait a week and have Jennifer call the prosecutor. I think she'll be ready to deal."

Jennifer was my associate Jennifer Aronson. She would need to take over representation of Leonard Watts, because if I stayed on, it would look like the setup it was and that Kristina Medina had alluded to in the courtroom.

Medina had refused to negotiate a plea agreement before the trial because Leonard Watts declined to give up his partner, the guy who drove the car that bumped into each of the victims. Watts wouldn't snitch, and so Medina wouldn't deal. Things would be different in a week, I thought, for a variety of reasons: I had seen most of the prosecution's case laid out in the first trial, Medina's main witness was spooked by what had happened in front of her in court today, and mounting a second trial would be a costly use of taxpayers' money. Added to that, I had given Medina a glimpse of what might come if the defense presented a case to a jury—namely my intention to explore through expert witnesses the pitfalls of interracial recognition and identification. That was something no prosecutor wanted to deal with in front of a jury.

"Hell," I said, "she might call me before I even have to go to her."

That part was wishful thinking but I wanted Legal to feel good about the move he had strategized for me.

While I was up I took the extra blood capsule out of the briefcase and dropped it into the room's hazardous-waste container. There was no need for it anymore and I didn't want to risk it breaking open and ruining my paperwork.

My phone buzzed and I pulled it out of my pocket. It was my case manager, Lorna Taylor, calling but I decided to let it go to message. I'd call her back after my visit with Legal.

"What else you got going now?" Legal asked

I spread my hands.

"Well, no trial now, so I guess I have the rest of the week off. I may go down to arraignment court tomorrow and see if I can pick up a client or two. I could use the work."

Not only could I use the income but the work would keep me busy and not thinking about the things in my life that were wrong. In that sense the law had become more than a craft and a calling. It kept me sane.

By checking in at Department 130, the arraignment court in the downtown Criminal Courts Building, I had a shot at picking up clients the public defender was dropping because of conflict of interest. Every time the DA filed a multi-defendant case, the PD could take on only one defendant, putting all others in conflict. If those other defendants did not have private counsel, the judge would appoint counsel to them. If I happened to be there twiddling my thumbs, more often than not I'd pick up a case. It paid government scale but it was better than no work and no pay.

"And to think," Legal said, "at one point last fall you were running five points up in the polls. And now here you are, scrounging around first-appearance court looking for handouts."

As he had aged, Legal had lost most of the social filters normally employed in polite company.

"Thanks, Legal," I said. "I can always count on you for a fair and accurate take on my lot in life. It's refreshing."

Legal Siegel raised his bony hands in what I guessed was an apologetic gesture.

"I'm just saying."

"Sure."

"So what about your daughter, then?"

This was how Legal's mind worked. Sometimes he couldn't remember what he'd had for breakfast, but he seemed to always remember that I had lost more than the election the year before. The scandal had cost me the love and companionship of my daughter and any shot I'd had at putting my broken family back together.

"Things are still the same there, but let's not go down that road today," I said.

I checked my phone again after feeling the vibration signaling I had received a text. It was from Lorna. She had surmised that I wasn't taking calls or listening to voice-mail. A text was different.

Call me ASAP — 187

Her mention of the California penal code number for murder got my attention. It was time to go.

"You know, Mickey, I only bring her up because you don't."

"I don't want to bring her up. It's too painful, Legal. I get drunk every Friday night so I can sleep through most of Saturday. You know why?"

"No, I don't know why you would get drunk. You did nothing wrong. You did your job with that guy Galloway or whatever his name was."

"I drink Friday nights so I am out of it Saturdays because Saturdays were when I used to see my daughter. His name was Gallagher, Sean Gallagher, and it doesn't matter if I was doing my job. People died and it's on me, Legal. You can't hide behind just doing your job when two people get creamed at an intersection by the guy you set free. Anyway, I gotta go."

I stood up and showed him the phone as if it were the reason I needed to go.

"What, I don't see you for a month and now you already have to go? I'm not finished with my sandwich here."

"I saw you last Tuesday, Legal. And I'll see you sometime next week. If not then, then the week after. You hang in and hold fast."

"Hold fast? What's that supposed to mean?"

"It means hold on to what you got. My half brother, the cop, told me that one. Finish that sandwich before they come in here and take it from you."

I moved toward the door.

"Hey, Mickey Mouse."

I turned back to him. It was the name he bestowed on me when I was a baby, born at four and a half pounds. Normally I'd tell him not to call me that anymore. But I let him have it so I could go.

"What?"

"Your father always called the jurors the 'gods of guilt.' You remember that?"

"Yep. Because they decide guilty or not guilty. What's your point, Legal?"

"The point is that there are plenty of people out there judging us every day of our lives and for every move we make. The gods of guilt are many. You don't need to add to them."

I nodded but couldn't resist a reply.

"Sandy Patterson and her daughter Katie."

Legal looked confused by my response. He didn't recognize the names. I, of course, would never forget them.

"The mother and daughter Gallagher killed. They're my gods of guilt."

I closed the door behind me and left the DO NOT DISTURB sign on the knob. Maybe he'd get the sandwich down before the nurses checked on him and discovered our crime.

3

Back in the Lincoln I called Lorna Taylor and by way of greeting she said the words that always put the two-edged sword right through me. Words that excited and repelled me at the same time.

"Mickey, you've got a murder case if you want it."

The thought of a murder case could put the spark in your blood for many reasons. First and foremost, it was the worst crime on the books and with it came the highest stakes in the profession. To defend a murder suspect you had to be at the very top of your game. To get a murder case you had to have a certain reputation that put you at the top of the game. And in addition to all that, there was the money. A murder defense—whether the case goes to trial or not—is expensive because it is so time-consuming. You get a murder case with a paying customer and you likely make your whole nut for the year.

The downside is your client. While I have zero doubt that innocent people are charged with murder, for the most part the police and prosecutors get it right and you are left to negotiate or ameliorate the length and terms of punishment. All the while you sit at the table next to a person who has taken a life. It's never a pleasant experience.

"What are the details?" I asked.

I was in the back of the Town Car with a legal pad ready on the fold-down worktable. Earl was heading toward downtown on Third Street, a straight shot in from the Fairfax District.

"The call came in collect from Men's Central. I accepted and it was a guy named Andre La Cosse. He said he was arrested for murder last night and he wants to hire you. And get this, when I asked him where the referral came from, he said the woman he is accused of killing had recommended you. He said she told him you were the best."

"Who is it?"

"That's the crazy thing. Her name, according to him, is Giselle Dallinger. I ran her through our conflict app and her name doesn't come up. You never represented her, so I am not sure how she got your name and made this recommendation even before she was supposedly killed by this guy."

The conflict app was a computer program that digitized all our case files and allowed us to determine in seconds whether a prospective client had ever come up in a previous case as a witness, a victim, or even a client. At twenty-plus years into this career, I could not remember every client's name, let alone the ancillary characters involved in cases. The conflict app saved us enormous amounts of time. Previously, I would often dig into a case only to find out I had a conflict of interest in representing the new client because of an old client, witness, or victim.

I looked down at my legal pad. So far I had written down only the names, nothing else.

"Okay, whose case is it?"

"LAPD West Bureau Homicide."

"Do we know anything else about it? What else did this guy say?"

"He said he is supposed to have his first appearance tomorrow morning and he wanted you there. He said he was set up and didn't kill her."

"Was she a wife, girlfriend, business associate, or what?"

"He said she worked for him but that's all. I know you don't like your clients talking on jailhouse phones, so I didn't ask him anything about the case."

"That's good, Lorna."

"Where are you, anyway?"

"I went out to see Legal. I'm heading back downtown now. I'll see if I can get in to see this guy and feel it out. Can you get a hold of Cisco and have him do some preliminaries?"

"He's already on it. I can hear him on the phone with somebody now."

Cisco Wojciechowski was my investigator. He was also Lorna's husband, and they worked out of her condo in West Hollywood. Lorna also happened to be my ex-wife. She was wife number two, coming after the wife who bore me my only child—a child who was now sixteen years old and wanted nothing to do with me. Sometimes I thought I needed a flowchart on a whiteboard to keep track of everybody and their relationships, but at least there were no jealousies between me and Lorna and Cisco, just a solid working relationship.

"Okay, have him call me. Or I'll call him after I get out of jail."

"Okay, good luck."

"One last thing. Is La Cosse a paying customer?"

"Oh, yeah. He said he didn't have cash but he had gold and other 'commodities' he could trade."

"Did you give him a number?"

"I told him you would need twenty-five just to get started, more later. He didn't freak out or anything."

The number of defendants in the system at any given time who could not only afford a $25,000 retainer but were willing to part with it were few and far between. I knew nothing about this case but it was sounding better to me all the time.

"Okay, I'll check back when I know something."

"Cheers."

Some of the air came out of the balloon before I even laid eyes on my new client. I had filed an engagement letter with the jail office and was waiting for the detention deputies to find La Cosse and move him into an interview room, when Cisco called with the preliminary information he had been able to glean from human and digital sources in the hour or so since we had gotten the case.

"Okay, a couple things. The LAPD put out a press release on the murder yesterday but so far nothing on the arrest. Giselle Dallinger, thirty-six years old, was found early Monday morning in her apartment on Franklin west of La Brea. She was found by firefighters who were called because the apartment had been set on fire. The body was burned but it is suspected that the fire was set in an attempt to cover up the murder and make it look accidental. Autopsy is still pending but the release says there were indications she had been strangled. The press release labeled her a businesswoman but the *Times* ran a short on it on their website that quotes law enforcement sources as saying she was a hooker."

"Great. Who is my guy then, a john?"

"Actually, the *Times* report says the coppers were questioning a business associate. Whether that was La Cosse it doesn't say but you put two and two together—"

"And you get pimp."

"Sounds like it to me."

"Great. Seems like a swell guy."

"Look at the bright side, Lorna says he's a paying client."

"I'll believe it when the cash is in my pocket."

I suddenly thought of my daughter, Hayley, and one of the last things she had said to me before she cut off contact. She called the people on my client list the dregs of society, people who are takers and users and even killers. Right now I couldn't argue with her. My roster included the carjacker who targeted old ladies, an accused date rapist, an embezzler who took money from a student trip fund, and various other societal miscreants. Now I would presumably add an accused murderer to the list—make that an accused murderer in the business of selling sex.

I was beginning to feel that I deserved them as much as they

24

deserved me. We were all hard-luck cases and losers, the kind of people the gods of guilt never smiled upon.

My daughter had known the two people my client Sean Gallagher killed. Katie Patterson was in her class. Her mom was their homeroom mother. Hayley had to switch schools to avoid the scorn directed at her when it was revealed by the media—and I mean *all* the media—that J. Michael Haller Jr., candidate for Los Angeles County District Attorney, had sprung Gallagher from his last DUI pop on a technicality.

The bottom line is that Gallagher was out drinking and driving because of my so-called skills as a defense lawyer, and no matter how Legal Siegel tried to soothe my conscience with the old "you-were-just-doing-your-job" refrain, I knew in the dark shadows of my soul that the verdict was guilty. Guilty in the eyes of my daughter, guilty in my own eyes as well.

"You still there, Mick?"

I came out of the dark reverie, realizing I was still on the phone with Cisco.

"Yeah. Do you know who's working the case?"

"The press release names Detective Mark Whitten of West Bureau as the lead. His partner isn't listed."

I didn't know Whitten and had never come up against him on a case, as far as I could remember.

"Okay. Anything else?"

"That's all I have at the moment but I'm working it."

Cisco's info had dampened my excitement. But I wasn't going to jettison the case just yet. Guilty conscience aside, a paycheck was a paycheck. I needed the dough to keep Michael Haller & Associates solvent.

"I'll call you after I meet the man, which is right now."

A detention deputy was directing me into one of the attorney-client booths. I got up and headed in.

Andre La Cosse was already in a chair on the other side of a table with a three-foot-high plexiglass divider cutting it in half. Most of the clients I visit in Men's Central adopt a slouch and a laid-back, cavalier attitude about being in jail. It's a protective measure. If you act unconcerned about being locked into a steel building with twelve hundred other violent criminals, then maybe they'll leave you alone. On the other hand, if you show fear, then the predators will see it and exploit it. They'll come for you.

But La Cosse was different. First of all, he was smaller than I had expected. He was slightly built and looked to me like he had never once picked up a set of barbells. He was in a baggy orange jail jumper but seemed to carry himself with a pride that belied his circumstances. He didn't exactly show fear, but he wasn't showing the exaggerated nonchalance I had seen so many times before in these places. He sat upright on the edge of his chair and his eyes tracked me like lasers as I came into the small space. There was something formal about the way he held himself. His hair was carefully feathered at the sides and it looked like he might have been wearing eyeliner.

"Andre?" I said as I sat down. "I'm Michael Haller. You called my office about handling your case."

"Yes, I did. I shouldn't be here. Somebody killed her after I was there but nobody will believe me."

"Slow down a second and let me get set up here."

I took a legal pad out of my briefcase and the pen from my shirt pocket.

"Before we talk about your case, let me ask a couple of things first."

"Please."

"And let me say from the beginning that you can never lie to me, Andre. You understand that? If you lie, I fly—that's my rule. I can't be working for you if we don't have a relationship where I can believe that everything you tell me is the god's honest truth."

"Yes, that won't be a problem. The truth is the only thing I've got on my side right now."

I went down a list of the basics, gathering a quick bio for the

26

files. La Cosse was thirty-two, unmarried, and living in a condo in West Hollywood. He had no local relatives, the nearest being his parents in Lincoln, Nebraska. He said he had no criminal record in California, Nebraska, or anywhere else and had never had so much as a speeding ticket. He gave me phone numbers for his parents and his cell phone and landline—these would be used to track him down in the event he were to get out of jail and not live up to our fee arrangement. Once I had the basics I looked up from my legal pad.

"What do you do for a living, Andre?"

"I work from home. I'm a programmer. I build and manage websites."

"How did you know the victim in this case, Giselle Dallinger?"

"I ran all her social media. Her websites, Facebook, e-mail, all of it."

"So you're sort of a digital pimp?"

La Cosse's neck immediately grew scarlet.

"Absolutely not! I am a businessman and she is—was—a businesswoman. And I did not kill her, but nobody around here will believe me."

I made a calming gesture with my free hand.

"Let's cool it down a little bit. I'm on your side, remember?"

"Doesn't seem like it when you ask a question like that."

"Are you gay, Andre?"

"What does that matter?"

"Maybe nothing but maybe it will mean a lot when the prosecutor starts talking about a motive. Are you?"

"Yes, if you have to know. I don't hide it."

"Well, in here maybe you should, for your own safety. I can also get you moved into a homosexual module once you're arraigned tomorrow."

"Please don't bother. I don't want to be classified in any way."

"Suit yourself. What was Giselle's website?"

"Giselle-for-you-dot-com. That was the main one."

I wrote it down.

"There were others?"

"She had sites tailored to specific tastes that would come up if someone searched with certain words or things they were looking for. That's what I offer—a multi-platform presence. That's why she came to me."

I nodded as though I were admiring his creativity and business acumen.

"And how long were you in business with her?"

"She came to me about two years ago. She wanted a multi-dimensional online presence."

"She came to you? What does that mean? How did she come to you? Do you run ads online or something?"

He shook his head as though he was dealing with a child.

"No, no ads. I only work with people recommended to me by someone I already know and trust. She was recommended by another client."

"Who was that?"

"There is a confidentiality issue there. I don't want her dragged into this. She doesn't know anything and has nothing to do with this."

I shook my head as though *I* was dealing with a child.

"For now, Andre, I'll let it pass. But if I take this case, I will at some point need to know who referred her. And you cannot be the one who decides whether someone or something has relevance to the case. I decide that. You understand?"

He nodded.

"I'll get a message to her," he said. "As soon as I have her okay, I will connect you. But I do not lie and I do not betray confidences. My business and my life are built on trust."

"Good."

"And what do you mean, 'if I take the case'? I thought you took the case. I mean, you're here, aren't you?"

"I'm still deciding."

I checked my watch. The sergeant I checked in with said I would get only a half hour with La Cosse. I still had three separate areas of discussion to cover—the victim, the crime, and my compensation.

"We don't have a lot of time, so let's move on. When was the last time you saw Giselle Dallinger in person?"

"Sunday night late—and when I left her she was alive."

"Where?"

"At her apartment."

"Why did you go there?"

"I went to get money from her but I didn't get any."

"What money and why didn't you get it?"

"She went out on a job and my arrangement with her is I get paid a percentage of what she makes. I had set her up on a Pretty Woman Special and I wanted my share—these girls, if you don't get the money right away, it has a tendency to disappear up their noses and other places."

I wrote down a summary of what he had just said even though I wasn't sure what most of it meant.

"Are you saying that Giselle was a drug user?"

"I would say so, yes. Not out of control, but it's part of the job and part of the life."

"Tell me about the Pretty Woman Special. What does that mean?"

"The client takes a suite at the Beverly Wilshire like in the movie Pretty Woman. Giz had the Julia Roberts thing going, you know? Especially after I had her photos airbrushed. I assume you can figure it out from there."

I had never seen the movie but knew it was a story about a prostitute with a heart of gold meeting the man of her dreams on a paid date at the Beverly Wilshire.

"How much was the fee for that?"

"It was supposed to be twenty-five hundred."

"And your take?"

"A thousand, but there was no take. She said it was a dead call."

"What's that?"

"She gets there and there's nobody home, or whoever answers

the door says he didn't call for her. I check these things out as best as I can. I check IDs, everything."

"So you didn't believe her."

"Let's just say I was suspicious. I had talked to the man in that room. I called him through the hotel operator. But she claimed there was nobody there and the room wasn't even rented."

"So you argued about it?"

"A little bit."

"And you hit her."

"What? No! I have never hit a woman. I've never hit a man, either! I didn't do this. Can't you be—"

"Look, Andre, I'm just gathering information here. So you didn't hit her or hurt her. Did you physically touch her any-where?"

La Cosse hesitated and in that I knew there was a problem.

"Tell me, Andre."

"Well, I grabbed her. She wouldn't look at me and so that made me think she was lying. So I grabbed her up around her neck—with one hand only. She got mad and I got mad and that was it. I left."

"Nothing else?"

"No, nothing. Well, out on the street, when I was going to my car, she threw an ashtray down at me from her balcony. It missed."

"But how did you leave it when you were up in the apart-ment?"

"I said I was going to go back to the hotel and knock on the guy's door myself and get our money. And I left."

"What room was it and what was the guy's name?"

"He was in eight thirty-seven. His name was Daniel Price."

"Did you go to the hotel?"

"No, I just went home. I decided it wasn't worth it."

"It seemed worth it when you grabbed her by the throat."

He nodded at the inconsistency but didn't offer any further ex-planation. I moved off the subject—for now.

"Okay, then what happened? When did the police come?"

"They showed up at about five yesterday."

"Morning or afternoon?"

"Afternoon."

"Did they say how they came up with you?"

"They knew about her website. That led to me. They said they had questions and I agreed to talk to them."

Always a mistake, voluntarily talking to the cops.

"Do you remember their names?"

"There was Detective Whitten and he did most of the talking. His partner's name was something like Weeder. Something like that."

"Why did you agree to talk to them?"

"I don't know, maybe because I did nothing wrong and wanted to help? I stupidly thought that they were trying to find out what happened to poor Giselle, not that they came with what they thought happened and just wanted to plug me into it."

Welcome to my world, I thought.

"Did you know she was dead before they arrived?"

"No, I had been calling and texting her all day and leaving messages. I was sorry about the whole blowup the night before. But she didn't call back and I thought she was still mad about the argument. Then they came and said she was dead."

Obviously, when a prostitute is found dead, one of the first places the investigation goes is to the pimp, even if it is a digital pimp who doesn't fit the stereotype of sadistic bruiser and who doesn't keep the women in his stable in line through threat and physical abuse.

"Did they record the conversation with you?"

"Not that I know of."

"Did they inform you of your constitutional right to have an attorney present?"

"Yes, but that was later at the station. I didn't think I needed an attorney. I did nothing wrong. So I said fine, let's talk."

"Did you sign a waiver form of any kind?"

"Yes, I signed something—I didn't really read it."

I held my displeasure in check. Most people who enter the criminal justice system end up being their own worst enemies. They literally talk their way into the handcuffs.

"Tell me how this went. You talked to them at first in your home and then they took you to West Bureau?"

"Yes, first we were in my place for about fifteen minutes and then they took me to the station. They said they wanted me to look at some photos of suspects but that was just a lie. They never showed me any photos. They put me in a little interview room and kept asking questions. Then they told me I was under arrest."

I knew that for them to make the arrest they had to have physical or eyewitness evidence linking La Cosse to the murder in some way. In addition, something he told them must not have squared with the facts. Once he lied, or they thought he lied, he was arrested.

"Okay, and you told them about going to the victim's apartment on Sunday night?"

"Yes, and I told them she was alive when I left."

"Did you tell them about grabbing her by the neck?"

"Yes."

"Was that before or after they read you your rights and had you sign the waiver?"

"Uh, I can't remember. I think before."

"It's okay. I'll find out. Did they talk about any other evidence, confront you with anything else they had?"

"No."

I checked my watch again. I was running out of time. I decided to end the case questions there. Most of the information I would get in discovery if I took on the case. Besides that, it's a good idea to limit the information you get directly from a client. I would be stuck with whatever La Cosse told me and it might color the moves I made later in the case or at trial. For example, if La Cosse told me he had indeed killed Giselle, then I would not be able to put him on the stand to deny it. That would make me guilty of suborning perjury.

"Okay, enough on that for now. If I take this case, how are you going to pay me?"

"In gold."

"I was told that, but I mean how? Where does this gold come from?"

"I have it in a safe place. All my money is in gold. If you take the case, I will have it delivered to you before the end of the day. Your manager said you needed twenty-five thousand dollars to start. We'll use the New York Mercantile Exchange quote on valuation and it will simply be delivered. I haven't really been able to check the market in here but I'm guessing a one-pound bar will cover it."

"You realize that will only cover my start-up costs, right? If this case goes forward to preliminary hearing and trial, then you're going to need more gold. You can get cheaper than me but you're not going to get better."

"Yes, I understand. I will have to pay to prove my innocence. I have the gold."

"All right, then, have your delivery person bring the gold to my case manager. I'm going to need it in hand before your first appearance in court tomorrow. Then I'll know you're serious about this."

I knew time was fleeting but I silently studied La Cosse for a long moment, trying to get a read on him. His story of innocence sounded plausible but I didn't know what the police knew. I only had Andre's tale and I suspected that as the evidence in the case was revealed, I would learn that he wasn't as innocent as he claimed to be. It's always that way.

"Okay, last thing, Andre. You told my case manager that I came recommended to you by Giselle herself, is that right?"

"Yes, she said you were the best lawyer in town."

"How did she know that?"

La Cosse looked surprised, as if the whole conversation so far had been based on a given—that I knew Giselle Dallinger.

"She said she knew you, that you'd handled cases for her. She said you got her a really good deal once."

"And you're sure it was me she was talking about."

"Yes, it was you. She said you hit a home run for her. She called you Mickey Mantle."

That stopped my breath short. I'd had a client once—a prostitute, too—who would call me that. But I had not seen her in a long time. Not since I put her on a plane with enough money to start over and never come back.

"Giselle Dallinger was not her real name, was it?"

"I don't know. It's all I knew her by."

There was a hard rap on the steel door behind me. My time was up. Some other lawyer needed the room to talk to some other client. I looked across the table at La Cosse. I was no longer second-guessing whether to take him on as my client.

Without a doubt, I was taking the case.

4

Earl drove me over to the Starbucks on Central Avenue and pulled to the curb out front. I stayed in the car while he went in to get us coffee. I opened my laptop on the worktable and used the coffee shop's signal to get online. I tried three different variations before typing in www.Giselle4u.com and bringing up the website for the woman Andre La Cosse was accused of killing. The photos were airbrushed, the hair was different, and a plastic surgeon had gone to work since I had last seen her, but I had no doubt that Giselle Dallinger was my former client Gloria Dayton.

This changed things. Aside from the issue of legal conflict regarding my representing a client accused of killing another client, there were my feelings about Gloria Dayton and the sudden realization that I'd been used by her in a way that was not too different from the way she was used by men nearly all her life.

Gloria had been a project, a client I cared about beyond the usual boundaries of the attorney-client relationship. I cannot say why this came to be, only that she had a damaged smile, a sardonic wit, and a pessimistic self-knowledge that drew me in. I had handled at least six cases involving her over the years. All of them involved prostitution, drugs, solicitation of prostitution, and the like. She was deeply embedded in the life but always seemed to me to deserve a shot at rising above it and escaping. I was no hero but I did what I could for her. I got her into pretrial intervention programs, halfway houses, therapies, and even once enrolled her in Los Angeles City College after she had expressed an interest in writing. None of it worked for long. A year or so would go by and I'd get the call — she was in jail again and needed a lawyer. Lorna started telling me I needed to cut her loose or pass her off to another attorney, that she was a lost cause. But I couldn't do that. The truth was I liked knowing Gloria Dayton, or Glory Days as she was known in the profession back then. She had a lopsided view of the world that matched her lopsided smile. She was a feral cat and she let no one but me pet her.

This is not to say there was anything romantic or sexual about our relationship. There was not. In fact, I'm not even sure we could have properly called us friends. We encountered each other too infrequently for that. But I cared about her and that's why it hurt now to know she was dead. For the past seven years I thought she had gotten away and that I had helped. She had taken the money I gave her and flown off to Hawaii, where she claimed there was a longtime client who wanted to take her in and help her start over. I got postcards every now and then, a Christmas card or two. They all reported that she was doing well and had stayed clean. And they made me feel as though I had accomplished something rarely achieved in the courtrooms and corridors of law. I had changed the direction of a life.

When Earl got back with the coffee I closed the laptop and told him to take me home. I then called Lorna and told her to organize a complete staff meeting for eight the next morning. Andre La Cosse was due in arraignment court on second call, meaning he would make his first appearance sometime between ten a.m. and noon. I wanted to meet with my team and get things going before then. I told her to pull all our files on Gloria Dayton and bring them as well.

"Why do you want Gloria's files?" she asked.

"Because she's the victim," I said.

"Oh my god, are you sure? That's not the name Cisco gave me."

THE GODS OF GUILT

"I'm sure. The cops don't realize it yet, but it was her."

"I'm sorry, Mickey. I know you...you liked her."

"Yeah, I did. I was just thinking about her the other day and considering going to Hawaii when the courts are dark over Christmas. I was going to call her if I got there."

Lorna didn't respond. The Hawaii trip was an idea I had for getting through the holidays without seeing my kid. But I'd dismissed it out of hope that things would change. That maybe on Christmas Day I'd get a call and an invitation to come over for dinner. If I went to Hawaii, I'd miss the opportunity.

"Listen," I said, breaking off the thought. "Is Cisco around?"

"No, I think he went over to where the victim—I mean, Gloria—lived, to see what he could find out."

"Okay, I'll call him. See you tomorrow."

"Oh, Mickey, wait. Do you want Jennifer at the meeting, too? I think she has a couple of appearances in county court."

"Yes, definitely. If she has a conflict, see if she can get one of the Jedi Knights to cover her."

I had hired Jennifer a few years ago directly out of Southwestern Law School and she carried what was then our burgeoning foreclosure defense practice. That had slowed down in the past year, while criminal defense had picked back up, but Jennifer still carried a big caseload. There was a group of regular lawyers on the foreclosure circuit and they had taken to monthly lunches or dinners to swap stories and strategies. They called themselves the Jedi Knights, which was short for JEDTI, meaning Jurists Engaged in Defending Title Integrity, and the fellowship extended to covering each other's court appearances when there were time conflicts.

I knew Jennifer wouldn't mind being pulled away from the foreclosure work to visit the criminal side for a bit. When I hired her, she told me first thing that she wanted a career in criminal defense. And lately she had been suggesting repeatedly in e-mails and our weekly staff meetings that it was time to hire another associate to take over the foreclosure business while she immersed herself more fully in the criminal side. I had been resistant because hiring another associate pushed me closer toward needing the traditional setup with an office, a secretary, a copy machine, and all of that. I didn't like the idea of the overhead or the brick-and-mortar anchor. I liked working out of the backseat and flying by the seat of my pants.

After ending the call with Lorna I put the window down and let the air blow into my face. It was a reminder of what I liked about the way I did things.

Soon enough I put the window back up so I would be able to hear Cisco on the cell phone. I called him and he reported that he was indeed working a door-to-door canvass of the building where Giselle Dallinger had lived and died.

"Getting anything good?"

"Bits and pieces. She kept to herself mostly. Not a lot of visitors. She must've handled her business outside the apartment."

"How about getting into that place?"

"There's a security door downstairs. She had to buzz you in."

Which didn't look good for La Cosse. The police probably assumed that Dallinger knew her killer and had let him in.

"Any record of activity on the door?" I asked.

"No, it's not a recorded system," Cisco said.

"Cameras?"

"Nope."

That could cut either way for La Cosse.

"Okay, when you're finished there, I've got some stuff for you."

"I can come back to this. The building manager's being cooperative."

"Okay, then. We're all going to meet tomorrow at eight. Before that, if you can, I want you to run down a name. Gloria Dayton. You can get a DOB from the files Lorna has. I want to know where she's been for the past few years."

"You got it. Who is she?"

"She's our victim, only the police don't know it."

"La Cosse tell you this?"

"No, I figured it out on my own. She's a former client."

"You know, I could use this as currency. I checked with the morgue and they had not confirmed the ID because the body and the apartment were burned. No usable fingerprints from either. They were hoping her DNA would be in the system or that they could find a dentist."

"Yeah, well, you can use it if it gets you something. I just looked at the pictures on the Giselle-for-you website. It's Gloria Dayton, an old client I thought moved to Hawaii about seven years ago. Andre told me he'd been working with her here for the past two years. I want the full picture."

"Got it. Seven years ago, why'd she go?"

I paused before answering, thinking about the last case I handled for Gloria Dayton.

"I had a case that paid me well and she played a part. I gave her twenty-five grand if she promised to quit the life and start over. There was also a guy. She snitched him off to get a deal. I was the broker. It was just time for her to get out of town."

"Could that have anything to do with this?"

"I don't know. It was a long time ago and that guy went away for life."

Hector Arrande Moya. I still remembered his name, the way it rolled off the tongue. The feds had wanted him bad and Gloria knew where to find him.

"I'm going to put Bullocks on that tomorrow," I said, referring to Jennifer Aronson by her nickname. "If nothing else, we might be able use the guy as a straw man."

"Can you still take the case with the victim being a former client? Isn't that some sort of conflict of interest or something?"

"It can be worked out. It's the legal system, Cisco. It's malleable."

"Understood."

"One last thing. Sunday night she had a trick at the Beverly Wilshire that didn't come through. Supposedly the guy wasn't there. Go poke around over there and see what you can come up with."

"Did you get a room number?"

"Yeah, eight thirty-seven. Guy's name was Daniel Price. This all comes from La Cosse. He said Gloria claimed the room wasn't even rented."

"I'm on it."

After I finished the call with Cisco, I put the phone away and just looked out the window until we reached my house on Fareholm. Earl gave me the keys and headed to his own car parked against the curb. I reminded him about the early start the next day and went up the stairs to the front door.

I put my stuff down on the dining room table and went into the kitchen for a bottle of beer. When I closed the refrigerator, I checked through all the photos and cards held on the door by magnets until I found a postcard showing Diamond Head Crater on Oahu. It was the last card I had received from Gloria Dayton. I took it off the magnetic clip and read the back of it.

Happy New Year Mickey Mantle!

Hope you are doing fine. All is well here in the sun. I hit the beach every day. You are the only thing about L.A. I miss. Come see me one day.

Gloria

My eyes drifted from the words to the postmark. The date was Dec. 15, 2011, almost a year ago. The postmark, which I'd had no reason to ever look at before, said Van Nuys, California.

I'd had a clue to Gloria's subterfuge on my refrigerator for nearly a year but I didn't know it. Now it confirmed the charade and my unwitting part in it. I couldn't help but wonder why she'd bothered. I was just her lawyer. There was no need to lead me on. If I'd never heard from her, I would not have been suspicious or come looking for her. It seemed oddly unnecessary to me and even a bit cruel. Especially the last line about coming to see her. What if I had come over at Christmas to escape the disaster of my personal life? What would've happened when I landed and she wasn't there?

I walked over to the trash can, stepped on the pedal to raise the lid, and dropped the card in. Gloria Dayton was dead. Glory Days was over.

I took a shower, holding my head under the hard spray for a long time. More than a few of my clients had come to a bad end over the years. It came with the territory, and in previous cases I always looked at the loss in terms of business. Repeat clients were my bread and butter, and knowing I had lost a customer never left me with a good feeling. But with Gloria Dayton it was different. It wasn't business. It was personal. Her death conjured a raft of feelings, from disappointment and emptiness to upset and anger. I was mad at her not only for the lie she had perpetrated with me but for staying in the world that ultimately got her killed.

By the time the hot water ran out and I cut off the spray, I had come to realize my anger was misplaced. I understood that there had been a reason and purpose to Gloria's actions. Perhaps she had not so much cut me out of her life as protected me from something. What that was I didn't know, but it would now be my job to find out.

After getting dressed I walked through my empty house and paused at the door of my daughter's bedroom. She had not stayed there in a year and the room was unchanged since the day she had left. Viewing it reminded me of parents who have lost children and leave their rooms frozen in time. Only I had not lost my child in such a tragedy. I had driven her away.

I went to the kitchen for another beer and faced the nightly ritual of deciding whether to go out or stay in. With the early start coming in the morning, I went with the latter and pulled a couple to-go cartons out of the refrigerator. I had half a steak and some Green Goddess salad left over from my Sunday night visit to Craig's, a Melrose Avenue restaurant where I often ate at the bar alone. I put the salad on a plate and the steak into a pan on the stove to warm it up.

When I opened the trash can to dump the cartons, I saw the postcard from Gloria. I thought better of what I had done earlier and rescued it from the debris. I studied both sides of the card once more, wondering again about her purpose in sending it. Did she want me to notice the postmark and come looking for her? Was the card some sort of a clue I had missed?

I didn't have any answers yet but I intended to find them. Taking the card back to the fridge, I clipped it to a magnet and moved it to eye level on the door so I would be sure to see it every day.

5

Earl Briggs got to the house late Wednesday morning, so I was the last to arrive at the eight o'clock staff meeting. We were on the third floor of a loft building on Santa Monica Boulevard near the 101 Freeway ramp. It was a half-empty building we had access to whenever needed it, because Jennifer was handling the landlord's foreclosure defense on a quid pro quo fee schedule. He had bought and renovated the place six years earlier when rents were high and there were seemingly more independent production companies in town than camera crews available to film their projects. But soon the bottom dropped out of the economy and investors in independent films grew as scarce as street parking outside the Ivy. Many companies folded and the landlord was lucky to be running at half capacity in the building. He eventually went upside down and that's when he came to Michael Haller & Associates, responding to one of our direct-mail advertisements to properties that come up on the foreclosure rolls.

Like most of the mortgages issued before the crash, this one had been bundled with others and resold. That gave us an opening. Jennifer challenged the foreclosing bank's standing and managed to stall the process for ten months while our client tried to turn things around. But there was not a lot of call for three-thousand-square-foot lofts in East Hollywood anymore. He couldn't get out from under and was on a slippery slope, renting month to month to rock bands that needed rehearsal space. The foreclosure was definitely coming. It was just a matter of how many months Jennifer could hold it off.

The good news for Haller & Associates was that rock bands slept late. Every day the building was largely deserted and quiet until late afternoon at the earliest. We had taken to using the loft for our weekly staff meetings. The space was big and empty, with wood floors, fifteen-foot ceilings, exposed-brick walls, and iron support columns to go with a wall of windows offering a nice view of downtown. But what was best about it was that it had a boardroom built into the southeast corner, an enclosed room that still contained a long table and eight chairs. This is where we met to go over cases and where we would now strategize the defense of Andre La Cosse, digital pimp accused of murder.

The boardroom had a large plate-glass window looking out on the rest of the loft. As I walked across the big empty space, I could see the entire team standing around the table and looking down at something. I assumed it was the box of doughnuts from Bob's that Lorna usually brought to our meetings.

"Sorry I'm late," I said as I entered.

Cisco turned his wide body from the table and I saw that the team wasn't looking at doughnuts. On the table was a gold brick shining like the sun breaking over the mountains in the morning.

"That doesn't look like a pound," I said.

"More," Lorna said. "It's a kilo."

"I guess he thinks we're going to trial," Jennifer said.

I smiled and checked the credenza that ran along the left wall of the room. Lorna had set up the coffee and doughnuts there. I put my briefcase on the boardroom table and went to the coffee, needing a jolt of caffeine more than the gold to get myself going.

"So how is everybody?" I asked, my back to them.

I received a chorus of good reports as I brought my coffee and a glazed doughnut to the table and sat down. It was hard to look at anything other than the gold brick.

"Who brought that?" I asked.

"It came in an armored truck," Lorna reported. "From a place called the Gold Standard Depository. La Cosse made the delivery order from jail. I had to sign for it in triplicate. The delivery man was an armed guard."

"So what's a kilo of gold worth?"

"About fifty-four K," Cisco said. "We just looked it up."

I nodded. La Cosse had more than doubled down on me. I liked that.

"Lorna, you know where St. Vincent's Court is downtown?"

She shook her head.

"It's in the jewelry district. Right off Seventh by Broadway. There's a bunch of gold wholesalers in there. You and Cisco take this down there and cash it in—that is, if it's real gold. As soon as it's money and it's in the trust account, text me and let me know. I'll give La Cosse a receipt."

Lorna looked at Cisco and nodded. "We'll go right after the meeting."

"Okay, good. What else? Did you bring the Gloria Dayton file?"

"Files," she corrected as she reached to the floor and brought up a nine-inch stack of case files.

She pushed them across the table toward me but I deftly redirected them to Jennifer.

"Bullocks, these are yours."

Jennifer frowned but dutifully reached out to accept the files. She was wearing her dark hair pulled back into a ponytail, her all-business look. I knew her frown belied the fact that she'd willingly accept any part of a murder case. I also knew I could count on her very best work.

"What am I looking for in all of this?" she asked.

"I don't know yet. I just want another set of eyes on those files. I want you to familiarize yourself with the cases and Gloria Dayton. I want you to know everything there is to know about her. Cisco's working on her profile in the years since those cases."

"Okay."

"At the same time, I want you on something else."

She slid her notebook in front of her.

"Okay."

"Somewhere in the most recent file there, you'll find some notes from my former investigator, Raul Levin. They regard a drug dealer and his location in a hotel. His name is Hector Arrande Moya. He was Sinaloa cartel and the feds wanted him. I want you to pull everything you can on him. My memory is that he went away for life. Find out where he is and what's going on with him."

Jennifer nodded but then said she wasn't following the logic of the assignment.

"Why are we chasing this drug dealer down?"

"Gloria gave him up to get a deal. The guy went down hard and we might be looking at alternate theories at some point."

"Right. Straw man defense."

"Just see what you can find."

"Is Raul Levin still around? Maybe I'll start with him, see what he remembers about Hector."

"Good idea, but he's not around. He's dead."

I saw Jennifer glance at Lorna and Lorna's eyes warn her off the subject.

"It's a long story and we'll talk about it someday," I said.

A somber moment passed.

"Okay, then I'll just see what I can find out on my own," Jennifer said.

I turned my attention to Cisco.

"Cisco, what have you got for us?"

"I've got a few things so far. First of all, you asked me to run down Gloria since the last time you had a case with her. I did that and went through all the usual channels, digital and human, and she pretty much dropped off the grid after that last case. You said she moved to Hawaii, but if she did, she never got a driver's license or paid utilities or set up cable TV or purchased a property on any of the islands."

"She said she was going to live with a friend," I said. "Somebody who was going to take care of her."

Cisco shrugged.

"That could be but most people leave at least a shadow of a trail. I couldn't find anything. I think what's more likely is that's the point where she started reinventing herself. You know, new name, ID, all of that."

"Giselle Dallinger."

"Maybe, or that could have been later. People who do this usually don't stick with one ID. It's a cycle. Whenever they think somebody might be getting close or it's time to change, they go through the process again."

"Yeah, but she wasn't in Witness Protection. She just wanted a new start. This seems kind of extreme."

Jennifer cut in on the back-and-forth then.

"I don't know, if I had this record on my name and I wanted to start over somewhere, I'd lose the name. Nowadays everything's digital and a lot of it is public information. Probably the last thing she wanted was somebody in Hawaii digging up all of this stuff."

She patted the stack of files in front of her. She made a good point.

"Okay," I said, "what about Giselle Dallinger? When did she show up?"

"Not so sure," Cisco said. "Her current driver's license was issued in Nevada two years ago. She never changed it when she moved over here. She rented the apartment on Franklin sixteen months ago, providing a four-year rental history in Las Vegas. I haven't had time to go back into it over there but I'll get to it soon."

I pulled a pad out of my briefcase and wrote a few questions I needed to ask Andre La Cosse the next time we spoke.

"Okay, what else?" I asked. "Did you get to the Beverly Wilshire yesterday?"

"I did. But before I get to that, let's talk about the apartment on Franklin."

47

I nodded. It was his report. He could deliver it the way he wanted.

"Let's start with the fire. It was first reported at twelve fifty-one Monday morning when smoke alarms in the hallway outside the apartment went off and residents entered the hallway and saw smoke coming from our victim's door. The fire gutted the living room—where the body was located—and heavily damaged the kitchen and the two bedrooms. The smoke detectors inside the apartment evidently did not go off and the reason for that is under investigation."

"What about a sprinkler system?"

"No sprinkler system. It's an old building and it was grandfathered in without it. Now, from what I was able to pick up over at the fire station, there were two investigations of this death."

"Two?" I asked.

This was sounding like something I could use.

"That's right. Both police and fire investigators signed off on it at first as accidental, with the victim falling asleep on the couch while smoking. The accelerant was the blouse she was wearing, which was made of polyurethane. What changed their minds about that was the coroner's initial survey. The remains were bagged and tagged at the scene and taken to the ME's Office."

Cisco looked at his own notes, which had been scratched on a pocket notebook that looked tiny in his big left hand.

"A deputy medical examiner named Celeste Frazier did a preliminary examination of the body and determined that the hyoid bone was fractured in two places. That changed things pretty quick."

I looked at Lorna and knew she did not know what the hyoid bone was.

"It's a small bone shaped like a horseshoe that protects the windpipe."

I touched the front of my neck in illustration.

"If it's broken, it means force trauma to the front of the neck. She was choked, strangled."

She nodded her thanks and I told Cisco to keep going.

"So they went back out, with arson and homicide investigators, and now we have a full-on murder investigation. They knocked on doors and I talked to a lot of the people they talked to. Several of them heard an argument coming from her apartment about eleven Sunday night. Raised voices. A man and a woman going at it about money."

He referred to his notebook again to get a name.

"A Mrs. Annabeth Stephens lives directly across the hall from the victim's apartment and she was watching out her peephole when a man left following the argument. She said the time was between eleven thirty and midnight because the news was over and she went to bed at midnight. She later identified Andre La Cosse when the cops showed her a six-pack."

"She told you this?"

"She did."

"Did she know you were working for the guy she identified?"

"I told her I was investigating the death across the hall and she spoke willingly to me. I didn't identify myself further than that because she never asked for anything further."

I nodded to Cisco. Being able to finesse the story from a key prosecution witness so early in the game was good work on his part.

"How old is Mrs. Stephens?"

"She's midsixties. I think she was stationed at that peephole a lot of the time. Every building has a busybody like that."

Jennifer chimed in.

"If she says he left before midnight, how do the police account for the smoke detector in the hallway not sounding for fifty more minutes?"

Cisco shrugged again.

"Could be a couple of explanations. One, that it took the smoke some time to work its way under the door. The fire could've been burning in there the whole time. Or, two, he set the fire with some sort of delay or other rig to allow him time to get out and get clear. And then there's three, a combination of one and two."

Cisco reached into his pocket and pulled out a pack of cigarettes and matches. He shook a cigarette out of the pack and then put it inside the folded matchbook.

"Oldest trick in the book," he said. "You light the cigarette and it slow burns down to the matches. The matches go up and ignite the accelerant. Gives a three- to ten-minute head start, depending on the cigarette you use."

I nodded more to myself than to Cisco. I was getting a sense of the state's case against my client and was already working out strategies and moves. Cisco continued.

"Did you know that by law in most states, any brand of cigarette sold in that state has to have a three-minute burn-down rate for unattended smoking? That's why most arsonists use foreign cigarettes."

"That's great," I said. "Can we get back to this case? What else did you get from the apartment building?"

"That's about it at this time," Cisco said. "I'll be going back there, though. A lot of people weren't at home when I knocked."

"That's because they looked through the peephole and got scared when they saw you."

I meant it in jest but it wasn't without a point. Cisco rode a Harley and he dressed the part. His usual outfit consisted of black jeans, boots, and a skin-tight black T-shirt with a leather vest over it. With his imposing size, dress, and the penetrating stare of his dark eyes through a peephole, it was no wonder to me that some people didn't answer their doors. In fact, I was more surprised when he reported the cooperation of a witness. So much so that I took pains to make sure cooperation was fully voluntary. The last thing I ever wanted was a witness backfiring on me while on the stand. I personally vetted them all.

"I mean, maybe you should think about wearing a tie every now and then," I added. "I have a whole collection of clip-ons, you know."

"No, thanks," Cisco responded flatly. "Can we move on to the hotel now or do you want to keep taking shots at me?"

"Easy, big guy, I'm just poking you a little bit. Tell us about the hotel. You had a busy night."

"I worked it late. Anyway, the hotel is where this thing gets good."

He opened his laptop and punched in a command as he spoke, his big fingers punishing the keyboard.

"I managed to obtain the cooperation of the security staff of the Beverly Wilshire without even wearing a tie. They—"

"All right, all right," I said. "No more discussion of neckties."

"Good."

"Go on. What did they tell you over there?"

6

Cisco said it wasn't what they told him at the hotel that was important. It was what they showed him.

"Most public spaces in the hotel are under camera surveillance twenty-four seven," he said. "So they have almost all of our victim's visit to the hotel Sunday night on digital. They provided me with copies for a nominal fee that I will be expensing."

"No problem," I said.

Cisco turned the computer around on the table so the rest of us could see the screen.

"I used the computer's basic editing program and put the various angles together in one continuous take in real time. We can track her the whole time she was there."

"Then play it, Scorsese."

He hit the play button and we started watching. The playback was in black and white and had no sound. It was grainy but not to the point that faces were obscured or unidentifiable. It began with an overhead view of the hotel's lobby. A time stamp at the top said it was 9:44 p.m. Though the lobby was busy with late check-ins and other people coming and going, Gloria/Giselle was easy enough to spot as she strolled through the lobby toward the elevator alcove. She was dressed in a knee-length black dress, nothing too risqué, and looked totally at ease and at home. She carried a shopping bag from Saks that helped her sell the image of someone who belonged.

"Is that her?" Jennifer asked, pointing to a woman sitting on a circular divan and showing a lot of leg.

"Too obvious," I said. "Her."

I pointed to the right of the screen and tracked Gloria. She smiled at a security man who stood at the entrance to the elevator alcove and passed him without hesitation.

Soon the angle changed and we looked down from the ceiling of the elevator alcove. Gloria checked her phone for e-mail while she waited. Soon enough an elevator arrived and she got on.

The next camera angle was from inside the elevator. Gloria got on and pushed the 8 button. As she rode up, she raised the bag and looked inside it. The view we had did not allow us to see the contents.

When she arrived at the eighth floor, she stepped off the elevator and the screen went black.

"Okay, this is where we go dark," Cisco said. "No cameras on the guest floors."

"Why not?" I asked.

"They told me it was a privacy issue. Recording who goes into what room can be more trouble than it's worth when it comes to divorce cases and subpoenas and all of that stuff."

I nodded. The explanation seemed valid.

The screen came back to life again, showing Gloria riding the elevator down. I noted on the time stamp that five minutes had gone by, meaning that Gloria had apparently knocked on the door and waited in the hallway outside room 837 for a significant period of time.

"Is there a house phone up there on the eighth floor?" I asked. "Did she spend all that time knocking on the door or did she call down to the desk to ask about the room?"

"No phone," Cisco said. "Just watch."

Once back on the ground floor, Gloria stepped out of the elevator and went to a house phone that was on a table against the wall. She made a call and soon was speaking to someone.

"This is her asking to be connected to the room," Cisco said.

"She is told by the operator that there is no Daniel Price registered in the hotel and no one in eight thirty-seven."

Gloria hung up the phone, and I could tell by her body language that she was annoyed, frustrated. Her trip had been wasted. She headed back through the lobby, moving at a faster clip than when she had arrived.

"Now watch this," Cisco said.

Gloria was halfway across the lobby when a man entered the screen thirty feet behind her. He was wearing a fedora and had his head down, looking at the screen of his phone. He appeared to be heading toward the main doors as well, and there was nothing suspicious about him other than that his features were obscured by the hat and the downward pose of his face.

Gloria suddenly changed directions and headed toward the front desk. This caused the man behind her to awkwardly change his direction as well. He turned and went to the circular divan and sat down.

"He's following her?" Lorna asked.

"Wait for it," Cisco said.

On the screen, Gloria went to the desk, waited while a guest ahead of her was taken care of, then asked the deskman a question. He typed something on a keyboard, looked at a screen, and shook his head. He was obviously telling her that there was no Daniel Price registered as a guest in the hotel. All the while, the man in the hat sat with his head tilted down and the brim of his hat hiding his face. He was looking at his phone but not doing anything with it.

"That guy's not even typing," Jennifer said. "He's just staring at his phone."

"He's looking at Gloria," I said. "Not the phone."

It was impossible to tell for sure because of the hat, but it seemed clear that Gloria had a follower. Finished at the front desk, she turned and once more headed toward the front doors of the lobby. She pulled a cell phone out of her handbag and hit a speed dial. Before she got to the doors, she said something quickly into the phone and then dropped it into her bag. She then exited the hotel.

Before she was gone, the man in the hat was up and crossing the lobby behind her. He picked up his step once she was through the doors, and this seemed to confirm that Gloria's impromptu turn to the front desk had exposed a tail.

After the man in the hat left the lobby, the camera angle jumped to the outside curb, where a black Town Car like my own had pulled up in front of Gloria at the valet stand. She opened the back door, threw the Saks bag in, and then got in after it. The car pulled away and out of the frame. The man in the hat crossed the valet lanes and left the picture as well, never once raising his head enough for even his nose to be seen.

The playback ended and everyone was silent for a long moment while they reviewed it in their heads.

"So?" Cisco finally asked.

"So she was followed," I said. "I take it you asked about the guy at the hotel?"

"I did and he doesn't work there. They had nobody working undercover security that night. That guy—whoever he is—was an outsider."

I nodded and thought some more about what I had seen.

"He didn't follow her in," I said. "Does that mean he was already there?"

"I've got a loop on him, too," Cisco said.

He turned the computer back to him and punched in more commands, bringing up a second video. He turned the screen back to us and hit play. Cisco provided narration.

"All right, this is him sitting in the lobby at nine thirty. He was there before her. He stays like that until she gets there. I have a side-by-side of that."

He spun the computer back and then set up the side-by-side videos before turning it to us again. The images from separate cameras were synced on the time stamps and we were able to watch Gloria cross the lobby and the man in the hat track her, his hat turning as she passed on the other side of the room. He then waited for her to come back down from the eighth floor and followed her out, after her sudden stop at the front desk.

Show over, Cisco closed his computer.

"Okay, so who is he?" I asked.

Cisco spread his hands, a wing span of nearly seven feet.

"All I can tell you is that he doesn't work for the hotel," he said.

I stood up and started pacing behind the table. I was feeling jazzed. The man in the hat was a mystery, and mysteries always played to the defense's side. Mysteries were question marks, which led to reasonable doubt.

"Do you know if the police have been over to the hotel yet?" I asked.

"As of last night, no," Cisco said. "They've already made their case to the DA. They probably don't care what she was doing in the hours before the murder."

I shook my head. It was foolish to underestimate the state.

"Don't worry, they will."

"Could he have been working for Gloria?" Jennifer asked. "You know, like her security or something?"

I nodded.

"Good question. I'll ask the client when I see him before first appearance. I'll also ask about the Town Car that picked her up. See if she had a regular driver. But there's something about this...this video that is off. It doesn't fit with this guy working for her. It's like he knew there were cameras and he kept his hat on and his head down. He didn't want to be seen on camera."

"And him being there before she arrived," Cisco added. "He was waiting for her."

"He acted like he knew she'd be going up and coming right back down," Lorna seconded. "He knew that there was nobody in that room up there."

I stopped pacing and pointed at Cisco's closed laptop.

"He's gotta be the guy," I said. "He's Daniel Price. We have to find out who he is."

"Um, can I butt in here for a moment?" Jennifer asked.

I nodded, giving her the floor.

"Before we get all hot and bothered about this mystery man in the hat, we have to remember that our client admitted to the police that he was in the victim's apartment with her *after* this guy was or was not following her, *and* that he argued with her and put his hand around her throat. So rather than worrying about what was going on before he was in her apartment, shouldn't we be worried about what La Cosse did or didn't do when he was actually in the place?"

"It's all important," I answered quickly. "But it all needs to be vetted. We need to find this guy and see what he was doing. Cisco, can you widen the search a bit? That hotel sits right at the end of Rodeo Drive. There's got to be more cameras out there. Maybe we can track this guy to a car and get a plate. His trail has not gone totally cold."

Cisco nodded.

"I'm on it."

I checked my watch. I needed to get moving toward downtown and arraignment court.

"Okay, what else?"

No one said anything, then Lorna timidly raised her hand.

"Lorna, what?"

"Just a reminder, today at two you have the pretrial conference in Department Thirty on Ramsey."

I groaned. Another of my stellar clients, Deirdre Ramsey was charged with aiding and abetting and a variety of crimes in one of the more bizarre cases to come my or any lawyer's way in years. She first gained public attention the year before as the unnamed victim of a horrible assault that occurred during a takeover robbery of a convenience store. The first reports were that the twenty-six-year-old had been one of four customers and two employees in the store when two heavily armed and masked men entered to rob the place. The customers and employees were herded into a storage room and locked in while the gunmen used a crowbar to open the store's cash deposit slot.

But then the gunmen reentered the storage room and told all the captives to turn over their wallets and jewelry and take off all their clothes. While one of the men stood guard over the others, the second man raped Ramsey in front of the whole group. The men then fled the store, taking a total of $280 dollars and two boxes of candy besides the personal belongings of the victims. For months the crime remained unsolved. The city council offered a $25,000 reward for information leading to the arrests of suspects, and Ramsey filed a negligence lawsuit against the corporation that owned the store, alleging that the business did not provide adequate protection of its customers. Knowing that the last thing they wanted to see was Ramsey testifying about her ordeal in front of a jury, the corporation's board of directors in Dallas voted to settle the case, paying Ramsey $250,000 for her troubles.

Money is the great destroyer of relationships. Two weeks after Ramsey walked away with the money, investigators on the case took a call from a woman inquiring whether the city council award was still available. When informed that it was, she told a surprising story. She said that the $250K settlement was the true goal of the robbery and that the rapist-robber was actually Ramsey's boyfriend, Tariq Underwood. The rape was part of an elaborate and consensual scam, according to the snitch, a get-rich scheme concocted by Ramsey herself.

As it turned out, the caller was Ramsey's former best friend— that is, until she felt she was unfairly left out of the riches bestowed on Ramsey. Court-ordered wiretaps ensued, and soon enough Ramsey, her boyfriend, and his partner in the robbery were arrested. The Office of the Public Defender took on Underwood's defense, which put it in conflict with Ramsey's, and so her file was shuttled to me. It was a low-cost, low-probability case, but Ramsey refused to plead it out. She wanted to go to trial, and I had no choice but to take her there. It wasn't going to end pretty.

Being reminded of the hearing shot holes in the engine block of my day's momentum. My groan did not go unnoticed by Lorna.

"You want me to try to postpone it?" she offered.

I thought about it. I was tempted.

"You want me to take it?" Jennifer offered.

Of course she wanted it. She'd take any criminal case I'd give her.

"No, it's a dog," I said. "I can't do that to you. Lorna, see what you can do. I want to run with La Cosse today if I can."

"I'll let you know."

Everyone was either grabbing a final doughnut or heading to the door.

"Okay, then, everybody's got their assignments and knows what they're doing on this," I said. "Stay in touch and let me know what you know."

I made another cup of coffee and was the last one out. Earl was waiting with the car in the back parking lot. I told him to head downtown to the courthouse and to stay off the freeway. I wanted to get there in time to talk to Andre La Cosse before they hauled him before the judge.

7

I had fifteen minutes with my client before he would be herded into the courtroom with several other custodies for first appearances before a judge. He was in a crowded holding cell off the arraignment court and I had to lean close to the bars and whisper so the other men in the cell wouldn't hear.

"Andre, we don't have a lot of time here," I said. "In a few minutes you'll be taken into the courtroom to see the judge. It will be short and sweet, the charges will be read and they'll set a date for your arraignment."

"Don't I plead not guilty?"

"No, not yet. This is just a formality. After you get arrested they have forty-eight hours to put you before a judge to get the ball rolling. This will be very brief."

"What about bail?"

"You won't make bail unless that gold brick you sent us is just one of many. You're charged with murder. They will set bail, but on the low end it will probably be two million, maybe two and a half. That's a two-hundred-thousand-dollar bond. You have that much gold? You don't get it back, you know."

He slumped and pressed his forehead against the bars that separated us.

"I can't stand this place."

"I know, but you've got no choice right now."

"You said you could get me into another module?"

"Sure, I can do that. Give me the word and I'll get you on keep-away status."

"Do it. I don't want to go back there."

I leaned in closer and whispered lower.

"Did something happen to you last night in there?"

"No, but there are animals in there. I don't want to be there."

I didn't tell him that no matter where he was placed in the jail complex, he wasn't going to like it. The animals were everywhere.

"I'll bring it up with the judge," I said instead. "Now I want to ask you a couple things about the case before we go in there, okay?"

"Go ahead. You got the gold?"

"Yes, I got the gold. More than we asked for but it will all go toward your defense, and if it doesn't get used, the remainder goes back to you. I have a receipt for you if you want it, but I don't think you want to carry around a piece of paper in Men's Central that shows you've got money."

"No, you're right. Keep it for now."

"Okay. Now the questions. Did Giselle have any kind of security that you know about?"

He shook his head like he wasn't sure but then answered.

"She had a burglar alarm but I don't know if she ever used it and I—"

"No, I mean people. Did she have like a bodyguard or somebody that ran security for her when she went out on calls or dates or whatever you call them?"

"Oh, no, none that she ever told me about. She had a driver and she could call him if there was a problem but he usually just stayed in the car."

"My next question was about the driver. Who was he and how do I reach him?"

"His name is Max and he was a friend of hers. He had a different job during the day and drove her at night. She basically just worked at nights."

"Max what?"

"I don't know his last name. I never even met him. She just mentioned him from time to time. She said he was her muscle."

"But he didn't go in with her."

"Not that I know of."

I noticed another prisoner was hovering behind my client's left shoulder. He was trying to listen in on our conversation.

"Let's move down," I said.

We moved down the bars to the other side of the holding cell. The eavesdropper stayed behind.

"Okay," I said. "Tell me about the phone call you made to the hotel to check out the Julia Roberts client. How did that whole thing go down?"

I checked my watch.

"Quickly," I added.

"Well, he made contact through the website. I told him the prices and—"

"Was this by e-mail?"

"No, he called. From the hotel. I saw it on the caller ID."

"Okay, go on. He called from the hotel, then what?"

"I told him her price and he said that was fine, and so we set it up for nine thirty that night. He gave me the room number and I told him I needed to call back to confirm. He said fine, so I did."

"You called the hotel and asked for room eight thirty-seven?"

"That's right. They connected me and it was the same guy. I told him she'd be there at nine thirty."

"Okay, and you never dealt with this guy before?"

"No, never."

"How did he pay?"

"He didn't. That's why I got in the fight with Giz. She said he didn't pay because there was nobody in that room. She said they told her at the desk the guy checked out that day, and I knew that was bullshit because I talked to him in that room."

"Right, right, but did you discuss payment with him? You know, cash or credit?"

"Yes, he said he was going to pay cash. And that's why I went to Giz's place, to collect my share. If the guy had just paid with a credit card, I would have handled the transaction and taken my share. It was paying with cash that made me want to go collect before she had a chance to spend it all or lose it."

La Cosse's business practices were becoming clearer to me now.

"And this is how you always did it?"

"Yes."

"It was routine."

"Yes, always the same."

"And this guy's voice, you didn't recognize it as a previous customer?"

"No, I didn't recognize it and he also said he was a new customer. What does this have to do with anything?"

"Maybe nothing but maybe everything. How often were you in contact with Giselle?"

La Cosse shrugged.

"Every day by text. We did a lot of it by text, but when I needed a quick answer I would call her on the cell. Maybe a couple times a week we'd talk."

"And did you see her very often?"

"Maybe once or twice a week when we had a cash customer. I'd come by to collect after. Sometimes we'd meet for coffee or breakfast and I'd collect then."

"And she never held back on you?"

"We'd had issues before."

"How so?"

"I pretty much learned with Giz that money was for spending. The longer I left my money with her, the greater the chance it would get spent. I never waited long to collect."

I saw the lineup of custodies who had just had first appearances being shuttled from the courtroom back into another holding cell. La Cosse was about to go out.

"Okay, hold on a second."

I stooped down and opened my briefcase on the tile floor. I took out the document I needed signed and a pen and then stood back up.

"Andre, this is a conflict-of-interest waiver. I need you to sign it if you want me to represent you. It acknowledges that you understand that the victim you are charged with killing was a former client of mine. You are waiving any future claim that I had a conflict of interest while representing you. You are saying right now that you are okay with it. Hurry up and sign it before they see you with the pen."

I passed the document and pen through and he signed it. He did a quick scan of the page as he passed it back.

"Who is Gloria Dayton?"

"That's Giselle. That was her real name."

I bent down to return the document to my briefcase.

"Couple more things," I said as I stood back up. "You told me yesterday that you would make contact with the client who vouched for Giselle when she came to you. Did you do that yet? I need to talk to her."

"Yes, she said fine. You can call her. Her name's Stacey Campbell. Like the soup."

He gave me the number and I wrote it down on my palm.

"You have her number memorized? Most people don't remember numbers anymore because they're on speed dial on their cell."

"If I put everybody's number in my phone, the police would have all of that right now. We change phones and numbers often, and I commit them all to memory. It's the only safe way to do it."

I nodded. I was impressed.

"Okay, we're good, then. Let's go out and see the judge."

"You said a couple more things."

"Oh, yeah."

I reached into my coat pocket and pulled out a short stack of cards. I handed them to him through the bars.

"Put these on the bench over there," I said.

"You're kidding," he said.

"No, people are always looking for good representation. Especially when they get out there and meet the deputy PD who's handling their case along with about three hundred others'. Spread them out a little bit on the bench and I'll see you in the courtroom."

"Whatever."

"And remember, you can talk to whoever you want inside about your lawyer, but don't talk to anybody about your case. No one, or it will come back to bite you on the ass. I promise you that."

"Got it."

"Good."

Arraignment court is the place where the criminal justice system becomes a feeding frenzy, where those who are caught in the net are delivered to market. I stepped out from the holding facility and into a morass of defense lawyers, prosecutors, investigators, and all lines of support staff, all moving in an unchoreographed dance presided over by Judge Mary Elizabeth Mercer. It was her job to make good on the constitutional guarantee to swiftly bring those accused of a crime to court to be informed of the charges against them and assigned counsel if they have not made such arrangements themselves. In practice, this meant that each of the accused had but a few minutes before the judge prior to beginning the long and usually torturous journey through the system.

The attorney tables in first-appearance court were large boardroom-size tables designed so that several lawyers could be seated at once as they prepared for their cases and clients to be called. Still more defense lawyers stood and milled about in the corral to the left of the judge's bench, where defendants were brought in from the holding cells in groups of six at a time. These lawyers would stand with their clients for the reading of the charges and then the scheduling of an arraignment hearing, where the accused would formally enter a plea. To an outsider—and this included those accused of crimes and their families packed into the wooden pews of the courtroom's gallery—it was hard to keep track of or understand what was going on. They could only know that this was the justice system at work and that it would now take over their lives.

I went to the bailiff's desk where the custody call list was on a clipboard. The bailiff had crossed out the first thirty names on the list. Judge Mercer was efficiently moving through the morning shift. I saw Andre La Cosse's name next to the number thirty-eight. That meant one group of six was ahead of his group. And that gave me time to find a spot to sit down and check my messages.

All nine chairs at the defense table were taken. I scanned the line of chairs running along the railing that separated the gallery from the court's work area and spotted one opening. As I made my way to it, I recognized one of the men I would be sitting next to. He wasn't a lawyer. He was a cop, and we had a past history that coincidentally had been brought up that morning at the staff meeting. He recognized me, too, and grimaced as I sat down next to him.

We spoke in whispers so as not to draw the attention of the judge.

"Well, well, well, if it isn't Mickey Mouth, great courtroom orator and defender of douche bags."

I ignored the shots. I was used to it from cops.

"Detective Lankford, long time no see."

Lee Lankford was one of the Glendale PD homicide detectives who investigated the murder of my former investigator Raul Levin. The reasons for Lankford's grimace and insults and the friction that still obviously existed between us were many. First, Lankford seemed to have a genetically bred hatred of all lawyers. Then there was the little rub that came when he wrongly accused me of Levin's murder. Of course it didn't help our relationship when I eventually proved him wrong by solving the case for him.

"You're a long way from Glendale," I offered as I was pulling out my phone. "Don't you guys do your arraignments up there in Glendale Superior?"

"As usual, Haller, you're behind the times. I don't work for Glendale anymore. I retired."

I nodded like I thought that was a good thing, then smiled.

"Don't tell me you went to the dark side. You're working for one of these defense guys?"

Lankford looked disgusted.

"No fucking chance I'd work for one of you creeps. I work for the DA now. And by the way, a seat just opened up at the big table. Why don't you go over there and sit with your own people?"

I had to smile. Lankford hadn't changed in the seven years or so since I had seen him. I kind of enjoyed tweaking him.

"No, I think I'm good here."

"Wonderful."

"What about Detective Sobel? Is she still with the department?"

Lankford's partner back then was the one I communicated with. She didn't carry around a bagful of biases like he did.

"She's still there and she's doing well. Tell me, which one of these fine upstanding citizens they're traipsing out in bracelets is your client today?"

"Oh, mine will be in the next batch. He's a real winner, though. A pimp accused of killing one of his own girls. It's a heartwarming story, Lankford."

Lankford pressed back into his chair slightly and I realized I had surprised him.

"Don't tell me," he said. "La Cosse?"

I nodded.

"That's right. It's your case, too?"

A sneer cracked across his face.

"You bet. And now I'm going to enjoy every minute of it."

DA investigators were used for ancillary duties on a case. The primary investigators remained the police detectives who worked the case from the crime scene on. But when the case was filed and shifted from the police department to the Prosecutor's Office, DA investigators were used to help prep the case for trial. Their duties included locating witnesses, getting them to court, and reacting to defense maneuvers and witnesses and the like. It was a mixed bag of second-tier responsibilities. Their job was to be prepared to do what needed to be done in the run-up to trial.

The great majority of DA investigators were former cops, many of whom were retired like Lankford. They were double dippers, collecting a pension from one department and a paycheck from the DA. Nice work if you could get it. The thing that struck me as unusual was that Lankford had already been assigned to the La Cosse case. The defendant had not even made a first appearance yet and Lankford was on the case and in the courtroom.

"I don't get it," I said. "They just filed on him yesterday and you're already assigned?"

"I'm in the homicide division. We get cases on a rotation. This one's mine and I just wanted to get a look at the guy, see what I'll be dealing with. And now that I know who his lawyer is, I know exactly who I'm dealing with."

He stood up and turned to look down at me. I noticed the badge clipped to his belt and the black leather boots he wore below cuffed suit pants. It wasn't a good look but probably no one wanted to incur his wrath by telling him.

"This will be fun," he said and then he walked away.

"You're not going to wait for him to come out?"

Lankford didn't answer. He walked through the gate and down the center aisle toward the door at the back of the courtroom.

After watching him go, I sat still for a few moments, thinking about the veiled threat and the knowledge that I now had to factor in having an investigator with a hard-on for me working for the prosecutor on the case.

It was not a good start.

My phone buzzed in my hand and I checked the text. It was from Lorna and it was a little bit of good news to balance out the Lankford episode.

The gold brick was real! $52K+ deposited in escrow account.

We were in business. No matter what happened, at least I was going to get paid. I started to forget about Lankford. And then a shadow fell across me and I looked up to see one of the detention deputies standing over me.

"You're Haller, right?"

"Yeah, that's me. What's—"

He showered a stack of business cards down on me. My own cards. The ones I had given La Cosse.

"You pull that stunt again and you'll never be allowed back to see one of your scumbag clients. At least not on my watch."

I felt my face growing red. Several attorneys were watching us. The only saving grace was that Lankford had missed the show.

"Got it?" the deputy asked.

"Yeah, got it," I said.

"Good," he said.

He walked away and I started gathering up the cards. Show over, the other lawyers turned and went back to business.

8

There was only one Lincoln at the curb when I got out of court this time. Everybody else had already split for lunch. I jumped in the back and told Earl to head toward Hollywood. I didn't know where Stacey Campbell lived but I was guessing it wasn't in downtown. I pulled my phone, looked at the number on my hand, and punched it in. She answered promptly with a practiced voice that was soft and sexy and everything I assumed was wanted in a prostitute's voice.

"Hello, this is Starry-Eyed Stacey."

"Uh, Stacey Campbell?"

The soft and sexy left her voice and was replaced by a harder-edged tone that had a tinge of cigarette to it as well.

"Who is this?"

"My name is Michael Haller. I'm Andre La Cosse's attorney. He told me he spoke to you and you agreed to talk to me about Giselle Dallinger."

"The thing is, I don't want to be dragged into court."

"That's not my intention. I just want to talk to someone who knew Giselle and can tell me about her."

There was a silence.

"Ms. Campbell, is there a chance I could come by to see you or meet you somewhere?"

"I'll meet you. I don't want anyone coming here."

"That's fine. Is now okay?"

"I need to get changed and put on my hair."

"What time and where?"

Another silence went by. I was about to tell her she didn't have to put on her hair for me when she spoke first.

"How about Toast?"

It was ten past noon, but I understood that a woman of her occupation might have just gotten up for the day.

"Uh, yeah, that's fine, I guess. I'm trying to think of a place where we could get breakfast."

"What? No, I mean Toast, the place. It's a café on Third near Crescent Heights."

"Oh, okay. I'll meet you there. So about one, then?"

"I'll be there."

"I'll get a table and be waiting."

I ended the call, told Earl where we were going, and then called Lorna to see if she got my two o'clock status conference postponed.

"No soap," she said. "Patricia said the judge wants this thing off his calendar. No more delays, Mickey. He wants you in chambers at two."

Patricia was Judge Companioni's clerk. She actually ran the courtroom and the calendar, and when she said the judge wanted to move the case on, it really meant Patricia wanted to move it on. She was tired of the constant delays I had asked for while I tried to convince my client to take the deal the DA had put on the table.

I thought for a moment. Even if Stacey Campbell showed up on time— which I knew I couldn't count on—there was probably no way I could get what I needed from her and get back to the courthouse in downtown by two. I could cancel the meeting at Toast but I didn't want to. The mysteries and motives surrounding Gloria Dayton had my full attention at the moment. I wanted to know the secrets behind her subterfuge, and diverting to handle another case was not going to happen.

"Okay, I'll call Bullocks and see if she's still up for covering for me on it."

"Why, are you still in first-appearance court?"

"No, heading to West Hollywood on the Dayton case."

"You mean the La Cosse case, don't you?"

"Right."

"And West Hollywood can't wait?"

"No, it can't, Lorna."

"She still has a hold on you, doesn't she? Even in death."

"I just want to know what happened. So right now I need to call Bullocks. I'll talk to you later."

I clicked off before I got a sermon about getting emotionally involved with the work. Lorna had always had issues with my relationship with Gloria and could not understand that it had nothing to do with sex. That it wasn't some kind of whore fixation. That it was about finding someone you somehow shared the same view of the world with. Or at least thought you did.

When I called Jennifer Aronson she told me she was working in the law library at Southwestern and going through the Gloria Dayton files I had given her that morning.

"I'm going case to case and just trying to familiarize myself with everything," she said. "Unless there is something I should be specifically looking for."

"Not really," I said. "Did you find any notes on Hector Arrande Moya?"

"No notes. It's amazing you remembered his name after seven years."

"I remember names, some cases, but not birthdays or anniversaries. Always gets me in trouble. You need to check on Moya's status and—"

"I did that first thing. I started with the *L.A. Times* online archives and found a couple stories about his case. It went federal. You said you made your deal with the DA's Office, but the feds obviously took over the case."

I nodded. The more I talked about a case, the more I remembered it.

"Right, there was a federal warrant existing. The DA must've gotten big-footed because Moya was papered and that gave the feds first dibs."

"It also gave them a bigger hammer. There is a gun enhancement with federal drug-trafficking statutes that made Moya eligible for a life sentence, and that's what he got."

I remembered that part, too. That this guy was put away for life for having a couple ounces of coke in his hotel room.

"I'm assuming there was an appeal. Did you check PACER?"

PACER was the federal government's Public Access to Court Electronic Records database. It provided quick access to all documents filed in regard to a case. It would be the starting point.

"Yes, I went on PACER and pulled up the docket. He was convicted in '06. Then there was the plenary appeal—the usual global attack citing insufficient evidence, court error on motions, and unreasonable sentencing. None made it past Pasadena. PCA right down the line."

She was referring to the Ninth Circuit Court of Appeals. It had a Southern California location on South Grand Avenue in Pasadena. Appeals from Los Angeles–based cases would be filed through the Pasadena courthouse and initially reviewed by a theee-member screening local panel of the appellate court. The local panel weeded out appeals it deemed unworthy and kicked the others for full consideration to a merits panel composed of three judges drawn from the circuit that held jurisdiction over the western region of the country. Aronson's saying that Moya never made it past Pasadena meant that his conviction was "per curiam affirmed" by the screening panel of judges. Moya had struck out swinging.

His next move was to file a habeas corpus petition in U.S. District Court seeking postconviction relief, a long-shot move to vacate his sentence. This was like shooting a three at the buzzer. The motion would be his last shot at a new trial unless startling new evidence was brought forward.

"What about a twenty-two fifty-five?" I asked, using the U.S. Code designation for a habeas petition.

"Yep," Aronson said. "He went with ineffective assistance of counsel — claiming his guy never negotiated a plea agreement — and got blown out on that as well."

"Who was the trial attorney?"

"Somebody named Daniel Daly. You know him?"

"Yeah, I know him, but he's a federal court guy and I try to stay clear of the fed. I haven't seen him work but from what I've heard, he's one of the go-to guys over there."

I actually knew Daly from Four Green Fields, where we both stopped in on Fridays for end-of-the-week martinis.

"Well, there wasn't much he or anybody could do with Moya," Jennifer said. "He went down hard and stayed down. And now he's seven years into a life sentence and not going anywhere."

"Where is he?"

"Victorville."

The Federal Correctional Institution at Victorville was eighty miles north and located at the edge of an air force base in the desert. It was not a good place to spend the rest of your life. It was said up there that if the desert winds didn't dry you up and blow you away, then the constant earthshaking sonic booms of the air force jets overhead would drive you crazy. I was contemplating this when Aronson spoke again.

"I guess the feds really don't fool around," she said.

"How do you mean?"

"You know, a life sentence for two ounces of blow. Pretty harsh."

"Yeah, they're harsh all the way around on sentencing. Which is why I don't do federal defense. Don't like telling clients to abandon all hope. Don't like working out a deal with the prosecution only to have the judge ignore it and drop the hammer on my guy."

"That happens?"

"Too often. I had a guy once…uh, forget it, never mind. It's history and I don't want to dwell on it."

What I did dwell on was Hector Arrande Moya and how a

slick deal I made for a client ultimately landed him in Victorville with a life sentence. I hadn't even really bothered to track the case after making the deal with a deputy DA named Leslie Faire. To me it was just another day in the salt mine. A quick courthouse deal; a hotel name and room number in exchange for a deferral of charges against my client. Gloria Dayton went into a drug rehab program instead of jail and Hector Arrande Moya went off to federal prison forever—and without knowing who or where the tip to the authorities had come from.

Or had he?

Seven years had gone by. It seemed beyond the realm of possibility to consider that Moya had reached out from federal prison to exact vengeance on Gloria Dayton. But no matter how farfetched the idea, it might be useful in the defense of Andre La Cosse. My job would be to make the jury second-guess the prosecution. To make at least one of the gods of guilt think for himself or herself and say, *Hey, wait a minute, what about this guy up there in the desert, rotting in prison because of this woman? Maybe...*

"Did you see any hearings in the docket on a motion to produce a witness or a motion to suppress based on lack of probable cause? Anything like that?"

"Yes, that was part of the first appeal on court error. The judge refused a motion to produce any confidential informants in the case."

"He was fishing. There was only one CI and that was Gloria. What about anything on the docket that is under seal? Did you see anything like that?"

Judges usually sealed records pertaining to confidential informants but the documents themselves were often referenced by number or code on PACER so at least one knew that such records existed.

"No," Jennifer said. "Just the PSR."

The presentencing report on Moya. Those were always kept under seal as well. I thought about things for a moment.

"Okay, I don't want to drop this. I want to see the transcript of that battle over confidential informants and probable cause. You are going to have to go to Pasadena and pull hard files. Who knows? Maybe we get lucky and there is something in there we can use. The DEA or FBI had to testify at some point about how they got to that hotel and to that room. I want to know what they said."

"You think Gloria's name could have been revealed?"

"That would be too easy and too careless. But if there is a reference to a specific CI we might have something to work with. Also, ask for the PSR. Maybe after seven years they might let you have a look at it."

"That's a long shot. Those are supposed to stay sealed forever."

"Doesn't hurt to ask."

"Well, I can head to Pasadena right now. I'll get back to these Gloria files later."

"No, Pasadena can wait. I want you to go downtown instead. Are you still up for sitting in for me on the Deirdre Ramsey case?"

"Absolutely!"

She practically jumped through the phone.

"Don't get too excited," I quickly counseled. "Like I said this morning, the case is a dog. You just have to ask the judge for a little bit more time and patience. Tell him we know it's an STD case and we are close to convincing Deirdre that it's in her very best interest to take the state's offer and get this behind her. And you have to persuade Shelly Albert, the prosecutor, to keep the offer on the table another couple of weeks. That's it, just another couple weeks is all, okay?"

The offer was for Ramsey to plead to aiding and abetting and to testify against her boyfriend and his partner in the robbery. In exchange she'd get a three- to five-year sentence. With gain time and time already served she'd be out in a year.

"I can do that," Jennifer said. "But I'll probably skip the syph reference, if you don't mind."

"What?"

"Syphilis. You called it an STD case. Sexually transmitted disease?"

I smiled and looked out the window. We were cruising through Hancock Park. It was all big houses, big lawns, and tall hedges.

"Jennifer, I didn't mean that. STD is shorthand from my days at the public defender's. It means straight to disposition. When I was with the PD twenty years ago, that's how we divided our caseloads. STDs and STTs—straight to dispo or straight to trial. Maybe now they call them STPs—straight to plea—to avoid confusion."

"Oh, well, now I'm embarrassed."

"Not as much as you'd be if you'd said to Judge Companioni that the case has syphilis."

We both laughed at that. Jennifer had one of the brightest and hungriest legal minds I had ever encountered but she was still gaining practical experience and learning the routine and language of the criminal beat. I knew that if she stuck with it, she would eventually become the state's worst nightmare when she walked into court.

"Couple more things," I said, getting back to business. "Try to walk into chambers ahead of Shelly and grab the seat that will put you on the judge's left."

"Okay," she said hesitantly. "Why?"

"It's a left-brain right-brain thing. People are more agreeable toward people on their left."

"Come on."

"I mean it. Whenever I stand in front of a jury for closing argument, I move as far right as I can get. So for most of them I'm coming from their left."

"That's crazy."

"Try it. You'll see."

"It's impossible to prove."

"I'm telling you. There have been scientific tests and studies. You can Google it."

"I don't have time. What was the other thing?"

"If you start feeling comfortable enough with the judge, tell him that what will really help us put this to bed is if Shelly drops cooperation from the plea agreement. If Deirdre doesn't have to testify against her boyfriend, I think we can make this happen. We're even willing to keep the same sentencing terms, just no co-operation. And tell the judge that Shelly doesn't need it. She has all three of them on wiretaps talking about the whole thing. And she's got the DNA from the rape kit matching to the boyfriend. It's a slam dunk even without Deirdre's testimony. She does not need Deirdre."

"Okay, I'll try. But I was sort of hoping this might be my first criminal trial."

"You don't want this to be your first trial. You want that one to be a winner. Besides, eighty percent of criminal law is figuring out how to stay out of trial. And the other half—"

"Is all mental. Yeah, I get that."

"Good luck."

"Thanks, boss."

"Don't call me boss. We're associates, remember?"

"Right."

I put the phone away and started thinking about how I would handle the interview with Stacey Campbell. We were passing the Farmers Market now and were almost there.

After a while I noticed that Earl kept looking at me in the rearview. He did this when he had something to say.

"What's up, Earl?" I finally asked.

"I was wondering about what you said on the phone. About with people on the left side and how that works."

"Yeah."

"Well, one time—you know, back when I was working the streets—I had this guy come up with a gun to rip off my stash."

"Yeah?"

"And the thing was, back then somebody was going around popping guys for their cash and stash, you know? Just popping them in the head and grabbing it all up. And I was thinking that this was the guy and he was about to do me."

"Scary. What happened?"

"Well, I talked him out of it. I just talked about my daughter just bein' born and all. I gave him my stuff and he just ran away. Then later there was an arrest in those other murders and I saw his picture on the TV and it was the guy. The guy that ripped me off."

"You got lucky there, Earl."

He nodded and looked at me in the mirror again.

"And the thing is, he was on my right and I was on his left when he came up, and I talked him out of it. It's kind of like what you were saying there. Like he agreed with me not to kill my ass."

I nodded knowingly.

"You make sure you tell Bullocks that story next time you see her."

"I will."

"All right, Earl. I'm glad you talked him out of it."

"Yeah, me, too. My moms and daughter, too."

9

I got to Toast early, waited ten minutes for a table, and then kept it while nursing a coffee for forty-five minutes. There was a line of West Hollywood hipsters who weren't happy about me monopolizing a coveted table and not even ordering a meal. I kept my head down and read e-mail until Starry-Eyed Stacey showed up at 1:30 and slid into the chair across from me, enveloped in a strong cloud of perfume.

The hair Stacey had put on was a white-blond spike wig with blue highlights at the tips. It went with her so-pale-it-was-almost-blue skin and the wide stripes of glitter paint on her eyelids. I figured that the hipsters who hated me for taking one of their tables were close to rabid about me now. Starry-Eyed Stacey didn't exactly fit in. She looked like she had escaped from a 1970s glam rock album cover.

"So you're the lawyer," she said.

I smiled all business-like.

"That's me."

"Glenda told me about you. She said you were sweet. She didn't say handsome, too."

"Who's Glenda?"

"Giselle. When we first met in Vegas she was Glenda 'the Good Witch' Daville."

"Why'd she change her name when she came here?"

She shrugged.

"People change, I guess. She was still the same girl. That's why I always called her Glenda."

"So you had already come out from Vegas and she followed?"

"Something like that. We had stayed in touch, you know. She checked to see how tricks were out here and whatnot. I told her to come out if she wanted to and she did."

"And you put her in touch with Andre."

"Yeah, to set her up online and take her bookings."

"How long had you known Andre?"

"Not so long. You think we can get any service around here?"

She was right, the waitress who had so attentively asked me every five minutes if I was going to order something was now nowhere to be seen. My guess was that Stacey had that effect on people, especially women. I got the attention of a busboy and told him to fetch our waitress.

"How did you find Andre?" I asked while we waited.

"That was easy. I went online and started looking at other girls' sites. He was the site administrator on a lot of the good ones. So I e-mailed him and we hooked up."

"How many sites does he manage?"

"I don't know. You gotta ask him."

"Did you ever know Andre to be physically abusive to any of the women he managed?"

She snickered.

"You mean like a real pimp?"

I nodded.

"No. When he wants to get rough, he knows people who can do the rough stuff for him."

"Like who?"

"I don't know any names. I just know he's not that physical. And there were a few times when some guy was trying to chip off his deal and he had to put a stop to it. At least that's what he told me."

"You mean guys trying to take over the online stuff?"

"Yeah, like that."

"You know who they were?"

"No, I don't know names or anything. Just what Andre told me."

"What about the guys who do the rough stuff for him? You ever see those guys?"

"I saw them once when I needed them. Some guy wouldn't pay and I called Andre when the john was in the shower. His guys showed up like that."

She snapped her fingers.

"They made him pay, all right. The guy thought that because he was on some show on cable that nobody ever heard of he didn't have to pay. Everybody pays."

The waitress finally came back to the table. Stacey ordered a BLT on what else?—toast—and a Diet Coke. I went with chicken salad on a croissant and switched from coffee to iced tea.

"Who was Glenda hiding from?" I asked as soon as we were alone again.

Stacey handled the jump cut in direction pretty casually.

"Isn't everybody hiding from somebody or something?"

"I don't know. Was she?"

"She never talked about it, but she looked over her shoulder a lot, if you know what I mean. Especially when she came back here."

This wasn't getting anywhere.

"What did she tell you about me?"

"She said that when she lived out here before, you were her lawyer, but she could never call you again if she took a bust."

The waitress put down our drinks and I waited until she was gone.

"Why couldn't she call me?"

"I don't know. Because it would all unravel, I guess."

That wasn't the answer I expected. I thought that she would say that Glenda could never call me because it would expose her betrayal.

"Unravel? Was that her word?"

"That's what she said, yeah."

"What did she mean by that?"

"I don't know, she just said things. She said it could unravel. I don't know what it meant and she didn't say any more about it."

Stacey was starting to act put out by the questioning. I leaned back and thought about things. Besides offering a few tantalizing words with no further explanation, she wasn't much help. I guess I had been foolish to think Gloria Dayton—if that was even her real name—had confided in another prostitute about her distant past.

All I knew now was that the whole thing depressed me. Gloria-Glenda-Giselle had been inextricably bound to the life. Unable to leave it, and it eventually took everything away from her. It was an old story and in a year's time it would be forgotten or replaced by the next one.

Our food came but I had lost my appetite. I watched Starry-Eyed Stacey put globs of mayonnaise on her BLT and eat it like a little girl, licking her fingers after the first bite. And that didn't lift my spirits either.

10

I sat in the backseat for a long time thinking about things. Earl kept looking at me in the rearview, wondering when I would give him directions. But I didn't know where to go next. I thought about waiting for Stacey Campbell to come out of the restaurant after using the restroom and following her home so I knew where she lived, but I knew Cisco could run her down if I needed her again. I checked my watch and saw it was quarter to three. Bullocks was probably in the middle of things with the status conference in Judge Companioni's chambers. I decided to wait a while before checking in with her.

"The Valley, Earl," I finally said. "I want to go watch practice."

Earl turned the ignition and we were off. He took Laurel Canyon up the mountain to Mulholland Drive. We turned west and after a few curves came to the parking lot entrance for Fryman Canyon Park. Earl pulled into a space, opened the glove box, and handed the binoculars over the seat to me. I took off my jacket and tie and left them on the backseat as I got out.

"I'll probably be a half hour or so," I said.

"I'll be here," he said.

I closed the door and walked off. Fryman Canyon descends the northern slope of the Santa Monica Mountains all the way down into Studio City. I took the Betty Dearing Trail down until it split east and west. This is where I went off the trail and farther down through the brush until I reached a promontory with open views of the sprawling city below. My daughter had transferred this year to the Skyline School, and its campus backed up from Valleycrest Drive to the edge of the park. The campus was on two elevations; the lower level contained the academic buildings, and the upper side was where the sports complex was located. By the time I got to the viewing spot, soccer practice was already under way below. I scanned the field with the binoculars and found Hayley in the far goal. She was the team's starting goalkeeper, which was an improvement over her previous school, where she was second string.

I sat on a large rock I had pulled up from the ground and positioned on a previous visit to the spot. After a while I let the binoculars hang around my neck and I just watched with my elbows on my knees, face in my hands. She was denying everything until one shot with a perfect shape to it got by her, hit the cross bar, and then was put in on the rebound. The bottom line was that she looked like she was having fun and the concentration of the position likely crowded out all other thoughts. I wished that I could do that. Just forget about Sandy and Katie Patterson and everything else for a while. Especially at night when I closed my eyes to sleep.

I could've gone to court to force the issue with my daughter, make a judge order visitation and compel her to stay with me every other weekend and every other Wednesday, like it used to be. But I knew that would only make things worse. You do that to a sixteen-year-old and you could lose her forever. So I let her go and began a waiting game. Waiting and watching from afar. I had to have faith that Hayley would eventually come to realize that the world was not black and white. That it was gray and the gray area was where her father dwelled.

It was easy for me to keep that faith because there was no other choice. But it was not so easy to face the larger question that floated above that faith like a storm cloud. The question of how you can hope and expect someone to forgive you when deep down you don't forgive yourself.

My phone buzzed and I took a call from Bullocks, who had just left the courthouse downtown.

"How did it go?"

"I think good. Shelly Albert wasn't happy about it, but the judge pressed her on the cooperation component of the disposition and she finally caved. So we have a deal if we can sell it to Deirdre."

As it was a status conference in camera, Ramsey hadn't been required to be there. We would have to visit the jail and present the new terms of the offer from the DA.

"Good. How long do we have?"

"Basically forty-eight hours. She's giving us till close of shop Friday. And the judge wants to hear from us on Monday."

"Okay, then we go see her tomorrow. I'll introduce you to her and you sell her on it."

"Sounds good. Where are you? I hear yelling."

"I'm at soccer practice."

"Really? You and Hayley have patched things up? That's fan—"

"Not exactly. I'm just watching. So what's your next move?"

"I guess I go back to the law library and hit those files. I think it's probably too late to go out to Pasadena to pull transcripts"

"All right, well, I'll let you get back to it. Thanks for taking Ramsey for me."

"Happy to. I really liked it, Mickey. I want more criminal."

"I'm sure that can be arranged. I'll talk to you tomorrow."

"Oh, one other thing. You got another second?"

"Sure. What?"

"I sat to the judge's left like you said, and you know, I think it worked. He patiently listened to me every time I spoke, and he kept cutting Shelly off every time she responded."

I could have mentioned that the judge's attentiveness might have had something to do with Jennifer Aronson's being an attractive, energetic, and idealistic twenty-six-year-old and Shelly Albert's being a lifer in the DA's Office who seemed to carry the burden of proof in her slumped shoulders and permanent frown.

"See, I told you," I said instead.

"Thanks for the tip," she said. "Talk to you tomorrow."

After I put the phone away I used the binoculars again to watch my daughter. The coach called the practice at four and the girls were leaving the field. Because Hayley was a transfer, she was treated like a rookie, and she had to gather all the balls and put them in a net bag. During the practice she had been in a goal that faced my position. So I didn't see her back until she started gathering up the balls. My heart lifted when I saw she still had the number 7 on the back of her green jersey. Her lucky number. My lucky number. Mickey Mantle's number. She hadn't changed it and that was at least one connection to me she hadn't changed. I took that as a sign that not everything between us was lost and that I should continue to keep the faith.

Part 2

MR. LUCKY

TUESDAY, APRIL 2

11

There is never just one case. There are always many. I liken
the practice of law to the craft of some of the premier
buskers seen working the crowds on the Venice boardwalk.
There's the man who spins plates on sticks, keeping a forest of
china spinning with momentum and aloft at the same time. And
there's the man who juggles gas-powered chain saws, spinning
them in the air in a precise manner so that he never shakes hands
with the business end of the blades.

Aside from the La Cosse case, I kept several plates spinning as
the calendar changed from one year to the next. Leonard Watts,
the carjacker, got a deal he grudgingly agreed to in order to head
off a retrial. Jennifer Aronson handled the negotiations, just as
she did with Deirdre Ramsey, who took a plea deal and did not
have to testify against her boyfriend in court.

I picked up a high-profile case in late December that was more
of the chain saw variety. A former client and lifelong con artist
named Sam Scales was popped by the LAPD on a scam that
brought new meaning to the words *heartless predator*. Scales was
accused of setting up a phony website and Facebook page in order to solicit donations to cover the burial costs of a child killed
in a school massacre in Connecticut. People from far and wide
gave liberally and Scales was said by the prosecution to have
raked in close to fifty thousand that donors believed was going
toward a murdered child's funeral. The scam worked well until

the parents of the dead child got wind of the effort and contacted authorities. Scales had used a variety of false digital fronts to safeguard his identity but eventually—as in all scams—he needed to move the money to a place where he could access it and put it in his pocket.

And that was the Bank of America branch on Sunset Boulevard in Hollywood. When he strolled in and asked for the money in cash, the bank teller saw the flag on the account and stalled while police were called. It was explained to Sam that the bank did not keep that much money in cash on hand because it was in a high-risk location, meaning the chances of a robbery were higher than at other locations. Scales was told that he could wait for the money to be special-ordered and put on the regular three p.m. armored truck delivery, or he could go to a downtown location where that kind of cash was more readily available. Scales, a con artist who didn't know a con when it was directed at him, elected to special-order the money and return to pick it up. When he came back at three, he was met by two detectives with the LAPD Commercial Crimes Division. The same two detectives who arrested him for the last case I defended him on—a Japanese tsunami aid rip-off.

Everybody wanted a piece of Scales this time—the FBI, the Connecticut State Police, even the Royal Canadian Mounted Police, who jumped in on the case because several of the victims who had given money were from across the border. But the LAPD made the arrest, and that meant the Los Angeles County District Attorney's Office had the first shot at him. Scales called me as he had in the past and I took on the cause of a man so vilified in the media for his alleged crime that he had to be placed in solitary at Men's Central for fear he would be harmed by other prisoners.

What made matters worse for Scales was that the outrage was so great that the district attorney himself, Damon Kennedy, the man who had soundly defeated me in the prior year's election, had announced that he would personally prosecute Scales to the full extent of the law. This of course came after I had signed on as defense counsel, and now the stage was set for Kennedy to once again trounce me on the public stage. I had made inquiries about a disposition—the DA had Scales dead to rights on this one—but Kennedy was having none of that. He knew he had a slam-dunk case and there was no need to deal. He would milk the trial for every last video, print, and digital drop of attention he could wring out of it. No doubt, Sam Scales was going to go down for the full count this time.

The Scales case did not help me personally either. *L.A. Weekly* ran a cover story on "The Most Hated Man in America," and the report provided a trip down memory lane of the many cons Scales had been accused of over the past two decades. My name came up often in these vignettes as his longtime defense attorney, and the overall story cast me as an official apologist for my client. The issue landed a week before Christmas and it made for an icy reception from my daughter, who once again believed her father had publicly humiliated her. All parties had previously agreed that I would be allowed to visit on Christmas morning with gifts for both daughter and former wife. But it didn't go so well. What I had hoped would be the start of a winter thaw in both relationships turned into an ice storm. I ate a TV dinner at home alone that night.

It was now the first week of April, and I was appearing on behalf of Andre La Cosse before the Honorable Nancy Leggoe in Department 120 of the downtown Criminal Courts Building. We were six weeks out from trial on the case and Leggoe was taking testimony in regard to the motion to suppress that I had filed shortly after the preliminary hearing in which La Cosse was held to answer.

La Cosse sat beside me at the defense table. He had been in jail going on five months now and the pallor of his skin was just one indication of the deterioration within. Some people can handle a stint behind bars. Andre wasn't one of them. As he told me often when we communicated, he was losing his mind in captivity.

Through the exchange of discovery materials that began in December, I had received a copy of the video of Andre La Cosse's interview with the lead investigator on the Gloria Dayton murder. My motion to suppress claimed that the interview was actually an interrogation and that the police had used trickery and coercion to elicit incriminating statements from my client. Additionally, the motion claimed that the detective who interrogated La Cosse in a small windowless room at West Bureau ran roughshod over his constitutional rights, not properly administering the Miranda warning regarding his right to an attorney until after La Cosse had made the incriminating statements and was placed under arrest.

During the interrogation La Cosse had denied killing Dayton, which was good for our side. But what was bad was that he had given police evidence of motive and opportunity. He admitted that he had been in the victim's apartment on the night of the murder and that he and Gloria had argued about the money she was supposed to have been paid by the client at the Beverly Wilshire. He even acknowledged that he had grabbed Gloria by the throat.

Of course, this evidence La Cosse had provided against himself was pretty damning, and it served as the core of the DA's case, as demonstrated in the preliminary hearing. But now I was asking the judge to eliminate the interview from the case and not allow a jury to see it. In addition to the intimidation practices employed by the detective in the room, La Cosse had not been read his rights until after he had mentioned that he had been in Dayton's apartment in the hours before her death and that there had been an argument.

Motions to suppress are always the longest of long shots but this one was worth a try. If I got the video of the interrogation kicked, the entire case would change. It might even tilt in Andre La Cosse's direction.

The prosecution, led by Deputy DA William Forsythe, began the hearing with Detective Mark Whitten's testimony about the circumstances of the interview and then introduced the video recording of the session. The thirty-two-minute video was shown in its entirety on a screen mounted to the wall opposite the courtroom's empty jury box. I had already watched it numerous times. I had my video time counts and questions ready when Forsythe finished his direct examination of Whitten and turned the witness and the remote control over to me. Whitten knew what was coming. I had laid into him pretty good when he had testified during the preliminary hearing. This time the assault would take place in front of Judge Leggoe, who was assigned to hear the case after the prelim. There was no jury to play to. No gods of guilt. I remained seated at the defense table, my client in his orange jumpsuit next to me.

"Detective Whitten, good morning," I said as I pointed the remote at the screen. "I want to go back to the very beginning of the interrogation."

"Good morning," Whitten said. "And it was an interview, not an interrogation. As I said before, Mr. La Cosse voluntarily agreed to come to the station to talk with me."

"Right, I heard that. But let's take a look at this."

I started playing the video, and on the screen the door to the interview room opened and La Cosse entered, followed by Whitten, who put his hand on my client's shoulder to direct him to one of the two chairs on either side of a small table. I stopped the playback as soon as La Cosse was seated.

"So, Detective, what are you doing there with your hand on Mr. La Cosse's upper arm?"

"I was just directing him to a seat. I wanted to sit down for the interview."

"You were directing him to that particular chair, though, correct?"

"Not really."

"You wanted him facing the camera because your plan was to draw a confession from him, correct?"

"No, not correct."

"Are you telling Judge Leggoe that you did not want him in that particular seat so that he would be in view of the hidden camera that was in that room?"

Whitten took a few moments to compose an answer. Bullshitting a jury is one thing. But it grows increasingly risky to mislead a judge who has been around the block a few times.

"It's standard policy and practice to place the interview subject in the seat facing the camera. I was following policy."

"Is it standard policy and practice to videotape interviews with subjects who have come to the police department for a 'conversation,' as you put it in your direct testimony?"

"Yes, it is."

I raised my eyebrows in surprise but then reminded myself that it wasn't serving my client well to bullshit the judge either. This would include feigning surprise at an answer I knew was coming. I moved on.

"And you insist that you had not classified Mr. La Cosse as a suspect when he came to the police station to talk to you?"

"Absolutely. I had a completely open mind about him."

"So there was no need to give him the standard rights warning at the top of this so-called conversation?"

Forsythe objected, saying the question was already asked and answered during his direct examination. Forsythe was midthirties and lean. With a ruddy complexion and sandy hair, he looked like a surfer in a suit.

Judge Leggoe overruled the objection and let me go with it. Whitten answered the question.

"I didn't believe it was necessary," he said. "He was not a suspect at the time he voluntarily came into the station and then voluntarily entered that room for the interview. I was just going to take a statement from him, and he ended up saying he had been in the victim's apartment. I was not expecting that."

He delivered the answer just as I am sure he had rehearsed it with Forsythe. I moved ahead in the video to a point where Whitten excused himself from the room to go get my client a soda that the detective had offered. I froze the image of La Cosse left alone in the room.

"Detective, what would have happened if my client had decided while alone in there that he had to use the restroom and got up to leave?"

"I don't understand. We would have allowed him to use the restroom. He never asked."

"But what would have happened if he'd decided on his own to get up from the table at this point here and open that door? Yes or no, did you lock it when you left the room?"

"It's not a yes or no answer."

"I think it is."

Forsythe objected and called my response badgering. The judge told the detective to answer the question the way he saw fit. Whitten composed himself again and fell back on the standard out: policy.

"It is the policy of the department not to allow any citizen unescorted access to work areas of police stations. That door leads directly to the detective bureau, and it would have been against policy for me to allow him to wander through the squad unattended. Yes, I locked the door."

"Thank you, Detective. So let me see if I have this right so far. Mr. La Cosse was not a suspect in your case but he was locked in this windowless room and was under constant surveillance while in there, correct?"

"I don't know if I would call it surveillance."

"Then what would you call it?"

"We roll the camera whenever someone is in one of those rooms. It's standard—"

"Policy, yes, I know. Let's move on."

I fast-forwarded through the video about twenty minutes, to a point where Whitten stood up from his seat and took off his jacket and draped it over the backrest. He then moved his chair in toward the table and stood behind it, leaning forward with his hands on the table.

"So you don't know anything about her murder, is that what you're saying?" he said to La Cosse on the screen.

I froze it right there.

"Detective Whitten, why did you take your jacket off at this point in the interrogation?"

"You mean the interview? I took my jacket off because it was getting stuffy in there."

"But you testified on direct that the camera was hidden in the air-conditioning vent. Wasn't the air on?"

"I don't know if it was on or not. I hadn't checked before we went in there."

"Aren't these so-called interview rooms nicknamed 'hot boxes' by detectives because they are used to sweat suspects and hopefully induce them to cooperate and confess?"

"I've never heard that, no."

"You've never used that phrase yourself to describe this room?"

I pointed to the screen and asked the question with such surprise in my tone that I hoped Whitten would think I had something up my sleeve that he didn't know about. But it was a bluff and the detective parried it by using a standard witness out.

"I don't recall ever using the phrase, no."

"Okay, so you took your jacket off and are now standing over Mr. La Cosse. Was that to intimidate him?"

"No, it was because I felt like standing. We had been sitting at that point for a long time."

"Do you have hemorrhoids, Detective?"

Forsythe quickly objected again and accused me of trying to embarrass the detective. I told the judge I was simply trying to place on the record testimony that would help the court understand why the detective felt compelled to stand during the interview after only twenty minutes. The judge sustained the objection and told me to proceed without asking the witness questions of such a personal nature.

"Okay, Detective," I said. "What about Mr. La Cosse? Could

he stand up if he wanted to? Could he have stood over you while you were sitting?"

"I would not have objected," Whitten answered.

I hoped the judge was aware that Whitten's answers were largely bogus and part of the dance detectives engaged in every day in every police station. They walked a constitutional tightrope, trying to push things as far as they could before having to enlighten the hapless saps who sat across the table from them. I had to make a case that this was a custodial interrogation and that under these circumstances Andre La Cosse did not feel that he was free to leave. If the judge was convinced, then she would hold that La Cosse was indeed under arrest when he entered that interrogation room and should have been Mirandized. She could then throw the entire video recording out, crippling the DA's case.

I pointed up to the screen again.

"Let's talk about what you're wearing there, Detective."

I took Whitten through a full description for the record of the shoulder holster and Glock he was wearing, and then moved down to his belt, eliciting descriptions of the handcuffs, extra gun clip, badge, and pepper-spray canister that were attached to it.

"Your displaying of all of these weapons to Mr. La Cosse was for what purpose?"

Whitten shook his head like he was annoyed with me.

"No purpose. It was warm in there and I took off my jacket. I wasn't displaying anything."

"So you are telling the court that showing my client your gun and badge and the extra bullets and the pepper spray were not a means of intimidating Mr. La Cosse?"

"That's exactly what I'm telling the court."

"How about at this point?"

I moved the video forward another minute to the point that Whitten pulled the chair out from the table and put one foot up on it so he could really loom over the small table and La Cosse, who was shorter and more slightly built.

"I was not intimidating him," Whitten said. "I was having a conversation with him."

I checked the notes on my legal pad and made sure I had covered everything I wanted to get on the record. I didn't think Leggoe would rule my way on this one but I thought I had a shot on appeal. Meantime, I had gotten in another round with Whitten on the witness stand. It better prepared me for trial, when I would really need to go at him.

Before ending the cross-examination I leaned over and conferred with La Cosse as a general courtesy.

"Anything I missed?" I whispered.

"I don't think so," La Cosse whispered back. "I think the judge knows what he was doing."

"Let's hope so."

I straightened up in my seat and looked at the judge.

"I have nothing further, Your Honor."

By prior agreement, Forsythe and I were to submit written arguments on the motion following the witness testimony. Pretty much knowing from the prelim how Whitten would testify, my document was already finished. I submitted it to Leggoe and gave copies to the court clerk and Forsythe. The prosecutor said he would have his response by the following afternoon, and Leggoe said she planned to rule promptly and well before the start of the trial. Her mention of her ruling not interrupting the trial schedule was a strong indication that my motion was going to be a loser. With its rulings in recent years, the U.S. Supreme Court had made new law when it came to Miranda cases, giving the police wider leeway on when and where suspects must be informed of their constitutional rights. I suspected that Judge Leggoe would go along to get along.

The judge adjourned the hearing and the two court deputies came to the defense table to take La Cosse back to the lockup. I asked for the chance to confer with my client for a few minutes, but they told me I would have to do it in the courtroom's holding cell. I nodded to Andre and told him I'd be back to see him shortly.

The deputies took him away and I stood up and started repacking my briefcase, gathering the files and notebooks I had spread out on the table before the hearing. Forsythe came over to sympathize. He seemed like a decent guy and up till now had not—as far as I knew—played games with discovery or anything else.

"Must be hard," he said.

"What's that?" I responded.

"Just banging away at these things, knowing the success rate is what, one in fifty?"

"Maybe one in a hundred. But when you hit that one? Man, that's a sweet day."

Forsythe nodded. I knew he wanted to do more than commiserate on the defense attorney's lot in life.

"So," he finally said. "Any chance we might end this before the trial?"

He was talking about a disposition. He had sent up a balloon back in January and then another in February. I didn't respond to the first one—which was an offer to accept a second-degree conviction, meaning La Cosse would be out in fifteen years. My ignoring the offer brought an improvement when Forsythe came around again in February. This time the DA was willing to call it a heat-of-passion case and let La Cosse plead to manslaughter. But La Cosse would still do at least ten years in the pen. As was my duty, I took the deal to him, and he turned it down flat. Ten years might as well be a hundred if you are doing time for a crime you didn't commit, he said. He had a passion in his voice when he said it. It tipped me toward his corner, toward thoughts that maybe he was indeed innocent.

I looked at Forsythe and shook my head.

"Andre's not getting cold feet," I said. "He still says he didn't do it and still wants to see if you can prove he did."

"So no deal, then."

"No deal."

"Then, I guess I'll see you at jury selection, May sixth."

That was the date Leggoe had set for the start of the trial. She was giving us four days max to pick a jury and a day for last-minute motions and opening statements. The real show would start the following week, when the prosecution began its case.

"Oh, you might see me before that. You never know."

I snapped my briefcase closed and headed toward the steel door to the holding cell. The court deputy escorted me back and I found La Cosse waiting alone in the cell.

"We'll be moving him back in fifteen," the deputy said.

"Okay, thanks," I said.

"Knock when you're ready to come out."

I waited until the deputy went back through the courtroom door before turning and looking at my client through the bars.

"Andre, I'm worried. It doesn't look like you're eating."

"I'm not eating. How could anyone eat when they're in here for something they didn't do? Besides, the food is fucking horrible. I just want to go home."

I nodded.

"I know, I know."

"You are going to win this, aren't you?"

"I'm going to give it my best shot. But just so you know, the DA is still floating a deal out there if you want me to pursue it."

La Cosse emphatically shook his head.

"I don't even want to hear what it is. No deal."

"That's what I thought. So we go to trial."

"What if we win the motion to suppress?"

I shrugged.

"Don't get your hopes up on that. I told you, it's a long shot. You have to expect that we are going to go to trial."

La Cosse lowered his head until his forehead was against one of the bars that separated us. He looked like he was going to cry.

"Look, I know I'm not a good guy," he said. "I did a lot of bad things in my life. But I didn't do this. I didn't."

"And I'm going to do my best to prove it, Andre. You can count on that."

He drew his head up to look at me eye to eye and nodded.

"That's what Giselle said. That she could count on you."

"She said that? Count on me for what?"

"You know, like if anything happened to her, she knew she could count on you to not let it go by."

I paused for a moment. In the past five months La Cosse and I had had limited communication. He was in jail and I was working a full caseload. We spoke when together for court hearings and during occasional phone calls from the pink module, where he was housed at Men's Central. Even so, I thought I had gotten everything I needed from him in order to defend him at trial. But what he had just said was new information, and it gave me pause because it was about Gloria Dayton, who still remained an enigma to me.

"Why did she tell you that?"

La Cosse shook his head slightly, as though he didn't understand the urgency I had put into my voice.

"I don't know. We were just talking once and she mentioned you. You know, like if anything happens to me, then Mickey Mantle will go to bat for me."

"When did she say that?"

"I don't remember. She just said it. She said to make sure to let you know."

With my one free hand I gripped one of the bars and moved closer to my client.

"You told me you came to me because she said I was a good lawyer. You didn't tell me any of this other stuff."

"I had just been arrested for murder and was scared shitless. I wanted you to take my case."

I held myself back from reaching through the bars and grabbing him by the collar of his jumpsuit.

"Andre, listen to me. I want you to tell me exactly what she said. Use her words."

"She just said that if something happened to her, I had to promise to tell you. And then something did happen and I got arrested. So I called you."

"How close was this conversation to when she was murdered?"

"I can't remember exactly."

"Days? Weeks? Months? Come on, Andre. It could be important."

"I don't know. A week, maybe longer. I can't remember because being in this place, all the noise and the lights on all the time and the animals, it wears you down and you start losing your mind. I can't remember things, I don't even remember what my mother looks like anymore."

"Okay, calm down. You think about this on the bus ride and when you're back in your own cell. I want you to remember exactly when this conversation took place. Okay?"

"I'll try but I don't know."

"Okay, you try. I have to go now. I'll be seeing you before the trial. There's still a lot of prep work to be done."

"Okay. And I'm sorry."

"For what?"

"For getting you upset about Giselle. I can tell you are."

"Don't worry about it. Just make sure you eat the food they give you tonight. I want you to look strong for the trial. You promise me?"

La Cosse reluctantly nodded.

"I promise."

I headed back to the steel door.

12

I walked back through the courtroom with my head down, oblivious of the hearing that Judge Leggoe had started following ours. I moved toward the rear exit, pondering the story La Cosse had just told me, that he had reached out to me following his arrest because Gloria Dayton had wanted me to know if something happened to her, not necessarily because she thought I should be his attorney. There was a significant difference in the stories and it helped ease the burden I'd carried for months in regard to Gloria. But did she want me to get this message so I would avenge her, or was it to warn me about some unseen danger? The questions put a new complexion on how I viewed things about Gloria and even myself. I now realized that Gloria might have known or at least feared that she was in danger.

The moment I stepped out of the courtroom and into the crowded hallway I was confronted by Fernando Valenzuela— the bondsman, not the former baseball pitcher. Val and I went way back and once shared a working relationship that was financially beneficial to both parties. But things turned sour years ago and we drifted apart. When I needed a bondsman these days, I usually went to Bill Deen or Bob Edmundson. Val was a distant third on that list.

Valenzuela handed me a folded document.

"Mick, this is for you."

"What is it?"

I took the document and started to unfold it one handed, waving it to get it open.

"It's a subpoena. You've been served."

"What are you talking about? You're running process now?"

"One of my many skills, Mick. Guy's gotta make a living. Hold it up for me."

"Fuck that."

I knew the routine. He wanted to take a photo of me with the document to prove service. Service had been made but I wasn't going to pose for pictures. I held the paper behind my back. Valenzuela took a photo with his phone anyway.

"Doesn't matter," he said.

"This is totally unnecessary, Val," I said.

He put his phone away and I looked at the paper. I immediately saw the styling of the case; *Hector Arrande Moya vs Arthur Rollins,* warden, FCI Victorville. It was a 2241 filing. This was a permutation of a habeas petition that was known by lawyers as a "true habeas," because rather than being a last-ditch effort grasping at legal straws like ineffective counsel, it was a declaration that startlingly new evidence was now available that proved innocence. Moya had something new up his sleeve and somehow it involved me, meaning it must involve my late client Gloria Dayton. She was the only link between Moya and me. The basic cause of action in a 2241 filing was the claim that the petitioner—in this case, Moya—was being unlawfully detained in prison, and thus the civil action directed against the warden. There would be something more in the full filing, the claim of new evidence designed to get a federal judge's attention.

"Okay, Mick, so no hard feelings?"

I looked over the paper at Valenzuela. He had his phone out again and took my photo. I had forgotten he was even there. I could've gotten mad but I was too intrigued now.

"No, no hard feelings, Val. If I knew you were a process server, I would have been using you myself."

Now Valenzuela was intrigued.

"Anytime, man. You've got my number. Money's tight in the bond market right now, so I'm just picking up the slack. Know what I mean?"

"Yeah, but you tell your employer on this that lawyer to lawyer, a subpoena is not the way to…"

I paused when I read the name of the lawyer issuing the subpoena.

"Sylvester Fulgoni?"

"That's right, the firm that puts the F-U in litigation."

Valenzuela laughed, proud of his clever response. But I was thinking of something else. Sylvester Fulgoni was indeed a one-time ball buster when it came to practicing law. But what was unusual about being subpoenaed by him to give a deposition was that I knew he had been disbarred and was serving time in federal prison for tax evasion. Fulgoni had built a successful practice primarily suing law enforcement agencies over color-of-law cases—cops using the protection of the badge to get away with assault, extortion, and other abuses, sometimes even murder. He had won millions in settlements and jury verdicts and taken his fair share in fees. Only he hadn't bothered to pay taxes on most of it and eventually the governments he so often sued took notice.

Fulgoni claimed he was the target of a vindictive prosecution designed to stop his championing of victims of law enforcement and government abuse, but the fact was he hadn't paid or even filed his taxes for four successive years. You get twelve taxpayers in the box and the verdict always comes out against you. Fulgoni appealed the guilty verdict for nearly six years but eventually time ran out and he went to prison. That was only a year ago and I now had a sneaking suspicion that the prison he'd ended up in was the Federal Correctional Institution at Victorville, which also happened to be home to Hector Arrande Moya.

"Is Sly already out?" I asked. "He couldn't have gotten his bar ticket back already."

"No, it's his son, Sly Jr. He's on the case."

I had never heard of a Sylvester Fulgoni Jr. and I didn't recall Sylvester Sr. being much older than me.

"He must be a baby lawyer, then."

"I wouldn't know. I never met the man. I deal with the office manager there and I gotta go, Mick. I've got more goodies to deliver."

Valenzuela patted the satchel he had slung over his shoulder and turned to head down the courthouse hallway.

"Any more on this case?" I asked, holding up the subpoena.

Valenzuela frowned.

"Come on, Mick, you know I can't be—"

"I send out a lot of subpoenas, you know, Val. I mean, whoever gets my business stands to make some pretty good coin month to month. But it's gotta be somebody I trust, you know what I mean? Somebody who's with me and not against me."

Valenzuela knew exactly what I meant. He shook his head and then his eyes lit when he came up with a way out of the corner I had put him in. He signaled me over with his finger.

"Say, Mick, maybe you can help me out," he said.

I stepped over to him.

"Sure," I said. "What do you need?"

He opened his satchel and started looking through the papers in it.

"I gotta go over to the DEA to see this agent over there named James Marco. You have any idea where the DEA is in the Roybal Building?"

"The DEA? Well, it depends if he's on one of the task forces or not. They have them spread around that building and other places in town."

Valenzuela nodded.

"Yeah, he's part of something called Interagency Cartel Enforcement Team. I think they call it ICE-T or something like that."

I thought about that, the intrigue of the subpoena and everything else building inside of me.

"Sorry, I don't know where they're at in there. Anything else I can help you with?"

Valenzuela went back to looking through his bag.

"Yeah, one other. After the DEA, I gotta go see a lady named Kendall Roberts—that's with a *K* and two *l*'s—and she lives on Vista Del Monte in Sherman Oaks. You know where that is by any chance?"

"Not offhand, no."

"Well, I guess I'll have to fire up the old GPS then. I'll see you, Mick."

"Yeah, Val. I'll call you with my next batch of paper."

I watched him go off down the hall and then walked over to one of the benches that lined the hallway. Finding a small open space to sit down, I opened my bag so I could write down the names Valenzuela had just given me. I then pulled my cell and called Cisco. I gave him the names James Marco and Kendall Roberts and told him to find out whatever he could on them. I mentioned that Marco was supposedly law enforcement and possibly with the Drug Enforcement Agency. Cisco groaned. All people in law enforcement take measures to protect themselves by eliminating as many digital trails and as much public information as possible. But DEA agents take it to a whole new level.

"I might as well be running down a CIA agent," Cisco complained.

"Just see what you come up with," I said. "Start with the Interagency Cartel Enforcement Team—ICE-T. You never know, we might get lucky."

I left the courthouse after that and spotted the Lincoln parked on Spring. I jumped in the back and was about to tell Earl to head to Starbucks when I realized it wasn't Earl behind the wheel, because I was in the wrong Lincoln.

"Oh, sorry, wrong car," I said.

I jumped out and called Earl on the cell. He said he was parked on Broadway because a parking cop had chased him off the curb on Spring. I waited five minutes for his arrival and used the time to call Lorna to check on things. She told me nothing worth mentioning was happening and I told her about the subpoena from Fulgoni and that it was scheduled for the following Tuesday morning at his office in Century City. She said she'd put it on the calendar and seemed to share my annoyance with Fulgoni's using Val to drop paper on me. Traditionally, it is not necessary for one lawyer to subpoena another. Usually a phone call and professional courtesy accomplishes the same thing.

"What a jerk!" Lorna said. "But how is Val doing?"

"I guess all right. I told him I'd throw him some of our paper."

"And did you mean it? You have Cisco."

"Maybe. We'll see. Cisco hates process serving, thinks it's beneath him."

"But he does it and it doesn't cost you anything extra."

"That's true."

I ended the call as Earl pulled up in the right Lincoln. We drove over to the Starbucks on Central so I could use the Wi-Fi.

Once I was set up online, I went to the PACER site and plugged in the case number I took off the subpoena. The filing by Sylvester Fulgoni Jr. was indeed a true habeas motion seeking to vacate the conviction of Hector Arrande Moya. It cited gross government misconduct in the actions of DEA Agent James Marco. The filing alleged that prior to Moya's arrest by the LAPD, Marco used a confidential informant to enter the premises of Moya's hotel room and plant a firearm under the mattress. Marco then used the informant to orchestrate the arrest of Moya by the LAPD and the finding of the weapon by the arresting officers. The firearm allowed prosecutors to add an enhancement charge against Moya, making him eligible upon conviction for a life sentence in federal prison. He was indeed sentenced to life following his conviction.

The government had not yet responded, at least as far as I could determine online. But it was early. The filing by Fulgoni was dated April 1.

"April Fool's," I said to myself.

"What's that, Boss?" Earl asked.

"Nothing, Earl. Just talking to myself."

"You want me to go in and get you somethin'?"

"No, I'm good. You need a coffee?"

"No, not me."

The Lincoln was set up with a printer on an equipment shelf on the front passenger seat—I bet those guys in the other Lincolns never thought of that. I printed out a copy of the filing and then closed the computer. When Earl handed the printout back over the seat, I read the motion in its entirety one more time. Then I leaned against the door and tried to figure out what the play was and what my part was supposed to be.

I thought it was pretty obvious that the confidential informant repeatedly mentioned in the document was Gloria Dayton. The inference was clearly that her arrest and my negotiation of a disposition on her behalf were orchestrated by the DEA and Agent Marco. It sure made a good story but I—being one of the players in the story—had a hard time believing it. I tried to recall in as great a detail as possible the case that brought Gloria Dayton and Hector Arrande Moya together. I remembered meeting Gloria at the downtown women's jail and her telling me the details of her arrest. Without any prompting from her I saw the possibility of trading information from Gloria in exchange for a pretrial diversion. It had been wholly my idea. Gloria was not the kind of client who understood or even knew the law. And as far as Marco went, I had never met or spoken to him in my life.

I had to consider, however, that Gloria had been coached to say just enough to get the wheels turning inside her attorney's head. It seemed like a long shot but I had to admit to myself that if the last five months proved anything to me, it was that Gloria had dimensions I didn't know about. Maybe this was the ultimate revelation about her: that she had used me as a pawn for the DEA.

Impatiently I called Cisco again and asked what progress he had made running down the names I had given him.

"You gave me the names less than a half hour ago," Cisco protested. "I know you want this stuff quick but a half hour?"

"I need to know what is going on with this. Now."

"Well, I'm going as fast as I can. I can tell you about the woman but I got nothing yet on the agent. That's going to be a tough nut to crack."

"Okay, then tell me about the woman."

There were a few moments of silence while Cisco apparently collected his notes.

"Okay, Kendall Roberts," he began. "She's thirty-nine and lives on Vista Del Monte in Sherman Oaks. She's got a record going back to the midnineties. A lot of prostitutions and conspiracy to commits. You know, the usual escort stuff. So she's a hooker. Or I should say, she was. Her record's been clean the past six years."

That would have made her active when Gloria Dayton was working as an escort under the name Glory Days. I suspected that Roberts and Dayton knew each other back then, or had known of each other, and that was the reason for the subpoena from Fulgoni.

"Okay," I said. "What else?"

"Nothing else," Cisco said. "What I told you is what I've got. Why don't you call me back in an hour."

"No, I'll just see you tomorrow. I want everybody in the boardroom at nine tomorrow morning. Can you tell the others?"

"Sure. This is including Bullocks?"

"Yes, Bullocks, too. I want everybody there and everybody brainstorming on this latest thing. It could be just what we need on La Cosse."

"You mean the straw man defense—Moya killed Dayton?"

"Exactly."

"Okay, well, we'll all be there in the boardroom at nine."

"And in the meantime you gotta find out who this Marco guy is. We really need it."

"I'm doing my best already. I'm on it."

"Just find this guy."

"Easy for you to say. Meantime, what are you going to be doing?"

It was a good question—good enough to prompt a hesitation on my part before I knew the answer.

"I'm going up to the Valley to talk to Kendall Roberts."

Cisco's rejection of that plan was swift.

"Wait, Mickey, I should be there. You don't know what you're getting into up there with this woman. You don't know who she'll be with. You ask the wrong question and there will be trouble. Let me meet you there."

"No, you stay on Marco. I have Earl and I'll be fine. I won't ask the wrong question."

Cisco knew me well enough to know that one protest was enough, because I wouldn't be changing my mind about going up to brace Roberts.

"Well," he said, "then happy hunting. Call me if you need me."

"Will do."

I closed the phone.

"All right, Earl, let's hit it. Sherman Oaks and step on it."

Earl dropped the car into drive and pulled away from the curb.

I felt my adrenaline surge with the car's velocity. New things were happening. Things that I didn't understand yet. But that was okay. I promised myself that I would soon understand everything.

13

It seemed likely to me that Fernando Valenzuela would deliver his subpoenas in the order in which he had asked me about the names. The Edward R. Roybal Federal Building was just a few blocks from the Criminal Courts Building. He would probably go there first to try to serve the paperwork on James Marco and then head up to the Valley to serve Kendall Roberts. It would not be an easy thing for Val to get to Marco. Federal agents do their best to avoid accepting subpoenas. I knew this from experience. Usually service ended up having to be arranged through a supervisor who would reluctantly accept a subpoena on behalf of the agent in question. The target agent almost never received the subpoena personally.

I believed that the timing of all of this gave me an edge on Val. If Roberts happened to be home, I would be able to get to her long before he did. Of course, I had no idea what getting there first would accomplish, but my hope was that I would be able to talk to Roberts in an unguarded moment, before she knew she was being drawn into some sort of federal case involving an imprisoned cartel kingpin.

I still needed to know more about Roberts than her name. It sounded like Roberts and Gloria Dayton were in similar circles in the 1990s and at least into the beginning of the new century. Cisco's information was a starting point but it wasn't enough. The best way to go into a conversation with a player in a case is to go in with more knowledge than the player has.

I Googled Sylvester Fulgoni Jr. on my cell and then called the number listed. A woman with a deep, smoky voice that seemed more appropriate for taking calls for reservations at Boa than at a law office put me on hold. We were on the 101 Freeway now and in heavy traffic. I figured we were still a half hour from Sherman Oaks, so I wasn't bothered by the wait or the Mexican cantina music playing in my ear.

I was leaning against the window and about to shut my eyes when the voice of a young man announced itself in my ear.

"This is Sylvester Fulgoni Jr. What can I do for you, Mr. Haller?"

I sat up straight and pulled a legal pad from my briefcase up onto my thigh.

"Well, I guess you could start by telling me why you hit me with a subpoena today at the courthouse. I'm thinking you must be a young lawyer, Mr. Fulgoni, because that whole thing was unnecessary. All you needed to do was call me. It's called pro-fessional courtesy. Lawyers don't drop paper on other lawyers — especially not in front of their peers in the courthouse."

There was a pause and then an apology.

"I am truly sorry about that and embarrassed, Mr. Haller. You're right, I'm a young lawyer just trying to make my way, and if I handled it wrong, then I certainly apologize."

"Apology accepted and you can call me Michael. Why don't you tell me what this is about? Hector Arrande Moya? I haven't heard that name in seven or eight years."

"Yes, Mr. Moya has been away a long time and we are trying to improve his situation. Have you had a chance to look at the case the subpoena refers to?"

"Mr. Fulgoni, I barely have time to look at my own cases. In fact, I need to move some things around in order to clear the time you put on this subpoena. You should've left the time of the depo open-ended or at a time convenient to both parties."

"I am sure we can accommodate you if Tuesday morning doesn't work. And please call me Sly."

"That's fine, Sly. I think I can make it. But tell me why I am being deposed for Hector Moya. He was never my client and I had nothing to do with him."

"But you did...Michael. In a way you are the one who put him in prison, and therefore you might also have the key to getting him out."

This time I paused. The first part of Fulgoni's statement was debatable, but whether true or not, it wasn't the kind of thing I wanted a high-ranking cartel man thinking about me, even if he was safely held in a federal prison.

"I want to stop you right there," I finally said. "Saying that I was the one who put your client in prison is not going to engender any help or cooperation from me. On what basis are you making such an outrageous and careless statement?"

"Oh, come on, Michael. It's been eight years. We know the details. You made a deal that got your client Gloria Dayton into diversion and gave the feds Hector Moya tied up in a nice pink bow. Your client is now dead and that leaves you to tell us what happened."

I drummed my fingers on the armrest as I tried to think of the best way to handle this.

"Tell me," I finally said, "how do you know the things you think you know about Gloria Dayton and her case?"

"I'm not going to go there with you, Michael. That is internal and confidential. Privileged, as a matter of fact. But we do need to take your deposition as we prepare our case. I look forward to meeting you Tuesday."

"That's not going to work, Junior."

"Excuse me?"

"No, you're not excused. And maybe you'll see me Tuesday and maybe you won't. I can walk into any court in the CCB and get the judge to quash this in five minutes. You understand? So if you want me there on Tuesday, you'd better start talking. I don't care if it's internal, eyes only, confidential, or privileged, I'm not walking into any depo anywhere with just my hat in my hand. If you want me there, then you need to start telling me exactly why you want me there."

That got his attention and he stammered in his reply.

"Uh, uh, I'll tell you what. Let me get back to you on this, Michael. I promise to call you in a bit."

"Yeah, you do that."

I disconnected the call. I knew what Sly Jr. was going to do. He was going to get Sly Sr. on the phone up at Victorville and ask him how to handle me. It was pretty clear from the call that Junior was doing Senior's bidding. This whole thing was probably cooked up in the rec yard up in Victorville: Sly Sr. going to Moya and suggesting he had a shot at a true habeas motion. From there, Sly Sr. probably handwrote the motion or the instructions to his son in the prison law library. The only question I had about it was how did they know Gloria Dayton had been the confidential informant on Moya?

I looked out the window after the call and saw that we were now making good progress and almost to the Cahuenga Pass. Earl was finding the holes and moving like a scatback through the blockers. That's what he was good at. We were going to get to Roberts sooner than I had thought.

Roberts lived a few blocks from Ventura Boulevard. If you were looking for some sort of status attributed to address, then south of the boulevard was what was preferred in the Valley. After my divorce my ex-wife bought a condo one block south of the boulevard on Dickens, and the distinction had been important to her—and pricey. I, of course, was partially paying for the place, since it also housed our daughter.

Roberts was living a few blocks north of the designation line, in the stretch between Ventura Boulevard and the Ventura Freeway. It was sort of a second-place neighborhood with a mix of apartment buildings and single-family homes.

When we were a block away I saw that we were on a stretch of Vista Del Monte that was lined with homes instead of apartments. I had Earl stop the car so I could get into the front seat.

I first had to unplug the printer and move the platform into the car's trunk.

"Just in case she sees us arrive," I said, once I was in and had closed the door.

"Okay," Earl said. "What's the plan, then?"

"Hopefully we park in front and look official in this car. You go with me to the door and I do the talking."

"Who are we seeing?"

"A woman. I need her to tell me what she knows."

"About what?"

"I don't know."

That was the problem. Kendall Roberts was being subpoenaed in the Moya appeal just as I was. I barely knew what I was bringing to the case, let alone what Roberts had.

We were in luck. There was a red curb and a fire hydrant directly in front of the 1950s ranch house at the address Cisco had given me.

"Park here so she sees the car."

"We might get popped on the hydrant."

I opened the glove box and took out a printed sign that said CLERGY and put it on the dashboard. It worked more often than it didn't and was always worth a try.

"We'll see," I said.

Before getting out of the car, I pulled my wallet out and took my laminated bar card from one of the back slots and slid it into the plastic display window in front of my driver's license. I worked out a quick plan of action with Earl and we then got out. Cisco had said Kendall Roberts's arrest record ended in 2007. My hunch was she was out of the life now and probably clinging to the straight and narrow. I hoped to use that to my advantage— if the woman was even home in the middle of a weekday.

I put on my sunglasses as we approached. My face had been on TV and billboards scattered around town last year in the lead-up to the election. I didn't want to be recognized here. I firmly knocked on the door and then stepped back next to Earl. He had on his Ray-Ban Wayfarers and his standard black suit and tie. I was in my charcoal Corneliani with the pinstripes. Still, standing shoulder to shoulder, both of us wearing shades, I was reminded of the black guy/white guy combo in a popular series of movies I had enjoyed with my daughter during better times. I whispered to Earl.

"What were those movies about the two guys who hunt aliens for a secret govern—"

The door was pulled open. A woman who looked a bit younger than the thirty-nine Cisco reported for Roberts stood in the doorway. She was tall, lithe, and had reddish-brown hair that fell to her shoulders. As far as I could tell, she wore no makeup and didn't need to. She was wearing gray sweatpants and a pink T-shirt that said GOT FLEX? on it.

"Kendall Roberts?"

"Yes?"

I started to pull my wallet out of my inside coat pocket.

"My name is Haller. I'm with the California Bar and this is Earl Briggs. I wonder if we could ask you a few questions about a situation we're investigating."

I flipped my wallet open and briefly held it up so she could see my bar card. It had the Bar's scales of justice logo on it and looked fairly official. I didn't allow her too long a look before flipping the wallet closed and returning it to my inside pocket.

"We won't take too long."

She shook her head.

"I don't understand," she said. "I have nothing…legal going on. There must be some mis—"

"It's not regarding you, ma'am. It involves others, and you are on the periphery of it. Can we come in, or would you like to accompany us to our office in Van Nuys for the conversation?"

It was a gamble offering her another location that didn't actually exist, but I was betting she wouldn't want to leave her home.

"What others?" she asked.

I was hoping she wouldn't ask that until we got inside. But

that was the rub. I was bluffing, trying to act like I knew something about something I knew nothing about.

"Gloria Dayton, for one. You might know of her as Glory Days."

"What about her? I have nothing to do with her."

"She's dead."

I can't say she looked surprised by the news. It might not have been that she knew Gloria was dead, but that she had a knowledge that Gloria's life could lead to a bad end.

"In November," I said. "She was murdered and we are taking a look at how her case was handled. There are ethical questions regarding the conduct of her attorney. Could we come in? I promise we won't take much of your time."

She hesitated but then stepped back. We were in. It was probably against her instincts to let two strangers into her home but she also probably didn't want to keep us— our business—out on the front porch for the neighbors to see and wonder about. I went through the doorway and Earl followed. Kendall directed us to a living-room couch and she took a chair opposite.

"Look, I am very sorry to hear about Glory. But let me just say that I haven't had anything to do with that world in a very long time and I don't want to be dragged back into it. I don't know anything about what Glory was doing or how her case was handled or what happened to her. I had not talked to her in years."

I nodded.

"We understand that and we're not here to drag you back into it," I said. "In fact, we actually want to help you avoid that."

"I seriously doubt that. Not if you come to my house like this."

"I'm sorry but these questions have to be asked. I'll try to be as quick as possible. Let's just start with me asking what your relationship was with Gloria Dayton. You can be open and honest. We know about your record and we know you've been clean a long time. This is not about you. It's about Gloria."

Roberts was silent for a moment while she came to a decision. Then she started talking.

"We covered for each other. We used the same answering service, and if one of us was busy and the other was not, then the service knew to call us. There were three of us, Glory, me, and Trina. We all looked alike and the clients never seemed to notice unless they were repeat customers."

"What was Trina's last name?"

"Why don't you have it?"

"It just hasn't come up."

She looked at me suspiciously but then moved on, probably for the sake of getting the interview over with as quickly as possible.

"Trina Rafferty. She went by the name Trina Trixxx—with a triple *x*—on her website."

"Where is Trina Rafferty now?"

Wrong question.

"I have no idea!" she yelled. "Didn't you hear anything I just said? I am not in the life anymore! I have a job and a business and a life and I have nothing to do with this!"

I held up a hand in a halting gesture.

"I'm sorry, I'm sorry. I just thought you might know. Like maybe you had stayed in touch, that's all."

"I don't stay in touch with any of it, okay? Do you get it now?"

"Yes, I get it and I realize this is digging up old memories."

"It is and I don't like it."

"I apologize and I will try to be quick. So you said there were the three of you and the calls came in to an answering service. If the caller asked for you and you were otherwise engaged, then the call would go to Glory or Trina and vice versa, correct?"

"That's correct. You sound just like a lawyer."

"I guess because I am. Okay, next question."

I hesitated because this was the question that would either get us thrown out or take us to the promised land of knowledge.

"Back then, what was your association with Hector Arrande Moya?"

Roberts stared blankly at me for a moment. At first I thought it was because I had hit her with a name that she had never heard before. Then I saw the recognition in her eyes and the fear.

"I want you to leave now," she said calmly.

"I don't understand," I said. "I just—"

"Get out!" she yelled. "You people are going to get me killed! I have nothing to do with this anymore. Get out and leave me alone!"

She stood up and pointed toward the door. I started to rise, realizing I had blown it with my approach on Moya.

"Sit down!"

It was Earl. And he was talking to Roberts. She looked back at him, stunned by the force of his deep voice.

"I said sit down," he said. "We're not leaving until we know about Moya. And we're not trying to get you killed. We're actually trying to save your ass. So, sit down and tell us what you know."

Roberts slowly sat back down. I did, too, and I think I was as stunned as Roberts. I had used Earl before with the fake investigators move. But this was the first time he had ever spoken a word.

"Okay," he said after everyone was seated again. "Tell us about Moya."

14

For the next twenty minutes Kendall Roberts told us a story about drugs and prostitution in Los Angeles. She said that the two vices were a popular combination in the upscale escort market, with the escort providing the client with both. It more than doubled the profitability of each liaison. And that was where Hector Moya came in. Though normally a middleman who took kilo quantities of cocaine across the border for distribution to lower-level dealers in the network, he had a taste for American prostitutes and always kept a quantity of powder on hand for himself. He paid for these liaisons with cocaine and quickly became a supply source for many of the upscale escorts working in West Hollywood and Beverly Hills.

It became obvious to me in the telling that what I thought I knew about Gloria Dayton was vastly incomplete. It also confirmed my earlier suspicions, that in the last deal I made for her, I had been merely a puppet carefully manipulated by Gloria and others. I tried to keep up the outward pretense of already knowing everything Roberts told us, but inside I felt used and humiliated—even eight years after the fact.

"So, how long did you and Glory and Trina know Hector before he was arrested and went away?" I asked at the end of her story.

"Oh, it must've been a few years. He was around a while."

"And how did you learn of his arrest?"

"Trina told me. I remember she called up and said she heard he got busted by the DEA."

"Anything else you remember?"

"Just that she said we were going to have to find another source if he was in jail. And I said I wasn't interested because I wanted to get out of the life. And pretty soon after that I did."

I nodded and tried to think about what I had learned from her and how it might fit with whatever the Fulgoni play was.

"Ms. Roberts, do you know an attorney named Sylvester Fulgoni?" I asked.

She creased her eyes and said no.

"You've never heard of him?"

"No."

My sense was that Fulgoni needed Roberts as a corroborating witness. Her testimony about Moya would confirm information Fulgoni already had. That pointed toward Trina Trixxx as the likely origin of that information and possibly the source that gave up the name Gloria Dayton. Valenzuela had said nothing about having to serve paper on Trina Rafferty. This might be because Fulgoni already had her on board.

I looked back at Kendall.

"Did you ever talk to Glory about Moya and the bust?"

She shook her head.

"No, in fact, I thought she left the business at the same time. She called me once and said she was in rehab and that she was going to leave town as soon as she got out. I didn't leave town but I quit the business."

I nodded.

"Does the name James Marco mean anything to you?"

I studied her face for a reaction or any sort of tell. In doing so I realized she was really quite beautiful, in an understated way. She shook her head and her hair swung under her chin.

"No, should it?"

"I don't know."

"Was he a client? Most of these guys didn't use real names. If you had a photo I could look at it."

"He wasn't a client as far as I know. He's a federal agent. DEA, we assume."

She shook her head again.

"Then I don't know him. I didn't know any DEA agents back then, thank God. I knew some girls the feds worked. The feds were the worst. They never let them up, you know what I mean?"

"You mean as informants?"

"If they had their hooks in you, then you couldn't even think about quitting the life. They wouldn't let you. They were worse than pimps. They wanted you to bring them cases."

"Was Glory caught like that with Marco?"

"Not that she ever told me."

"But she could've been?"

"Anything's possible. If you were diming for the feds, you wouldn't exactly announce it."

I had to agree with her there. I tried to think of the next question I should ask but I was drawing a blank.

"What are you doing now?" I finally asked. "For a living, I mean."

"I teach yoga. I have a studio on the boulevard. What are you doing now?"

I looked at her and I knew that the ruse was up.

"I know who you are," she said. "I recognize you now. You were Glory's lawyer. You're also the lawyer that got that guy off who then killed those two people in the car."

I nodded.

"Yeah, I'm that lawyer. And I'm sorry for the charade. I'm just trying to find out what happened to Glory and—"

"Is it hard?"

"Is what hard?"

"Living with your past."

There was an unsympathetic tone in her voice as she spoke.

Before I could answer, there was a sharp knock on the door that startled everyone in the room. Roberts leaned forward to get up but I raised my hands and lowered my voice.

"You may not want to answer that."

She froze, half off of her chair, and whispered back.

"Why not?"

"Because I think it's a man with a subpoena for you. He's working for Moya's attorney—Fulgoni. He wants to talk to you and put you on record regarding some of the things we're talking about here."

Roberts dropped back into her chair, her face showing her fear of Hector Arrande Moya. I nodded to Earl and he got up and went quietly into the entry area to check it out.

"What do I do?" Roberts whispered.

"For now, don't answer," I said. "He—"

A louder knock echoed through the house.

"He has to serve you personally. So as long as you avoid him, you don't have to respond to the subpoena. Is there a way out the back? He might sit on the street waiting for you."

"Oh my god! Why is this happening?"

Earl came back into the room. He had looked through the door's peephole.

"Valenzuela?" I whispered.

He nodded. I looked back at Roberts.

"Or, if you want, I could accept service on your behalf and then go see a judge to quash it."

"What does that mean?"

"Trash it. Make sure you're not involved, that there's no deposition."

"And how much will that cost me?"

I shook my head.

"Nothing. I'll just do it. You've helped me here, I'll help you. I'll keep you out of this."

It was an offer I wasn't sure I could make good on. But something about her fear made me say it. Something about her com-

THE GODS OF GUILT

ing to the dreadful realization that she had not outrun the past touched me. I understood that.

There was another knock, followed by Valenzuela calling Roberts out by name. Earl went back to the peephole.

"I have a business," Roberts whispered. "Clients. They don't know about what I used to do. If it gets out, I'll..."

She was on the verge of tears.

"Don't worry. It won't."

I didn't know why I was making these promises. I felt confident I could get the subpoena quashed. But Fulgoni could just restart the process. And there was no way I could control the media. Right now this whole thing was flying below the radar but Moya's appeal contained charges of government misconduct, and if there was a full airing of the allegations, it was bound to draw attention. Whether that interest would extend to a peripheral player like Kendall Roberts was unknown but not something I could prevent.

And then there was the La Cosse case. I wasn't yet sure how I could use Moya and his appeal in my client's defense, but at minimum I knew I could introduce it as a diversion to muddy the waters of the prosecution's case and make the jurors think of other possibilities.

Earl stepped back into the living room.

"He's gone," he said.

I looked at Roberts.

"But he'll be back," I said. "Or he'll sit out there and wait for you. Do you want me to handle it for you?"

She thought for a moment and then nodded.

"Yes, thank you."

"You got it."

I asked for her phone number and the address of her yoga studio and wrote them down. I told her I would let her know when I had disposed of the subpoena. I then thanked her, and Earl and I left. I was pulling out my phone so I could call Valenzuela and tell him to come back so I could accept service, when I saw

I didn't need to. Valenzuela was waiting for me, sitting on the front hood of my Lincoln, leaning back on his hands and holding his face up to the sun. He spoke without turning his face or changing his position.

"Really, Mick? Clergy? I mean, how low will you go?"

I spread my arms wide like a minister in front of his flock.

"My pulpit is the well of the courtroom. I preach to the twelve apostles, the gods of guilt."

Valenzuela casually looked at me.

"Yeah, well, whatever. It's still pretty low and you should be ashamed of your ass. Almost as low as you racing out here ahead of me and hiding in there, telling her not to answer the door."

I nodded. He had it all figured out. I signaled him off the hood of the car.

"Well, Val, Ms. Roberts is now my client and I am authorized to accept the subpoena from Fulgoni on her behalf."

He slid off the car, dragging the wallet chain looped from his belt to his back pocket along the paint.

"Oh, geez, my fucking bad. I hope I didn't scratch it, Reverend."

"Just give me the paper."

He pulled the rolled-up document out of his back pocket and slapped it into my palm.

"Good," he said. "Saves me havin' to sit on this place all day."

He then waved over my shoulder at the house behind me. I turned and saw Kendall looking out the living-room window. I waved as if to say everything was okay and she closed the curtain.

I turned back to Valenzuela. He had his phone out and snapped a photo of me holding the subpoena.

"That's really not necessary," I said.

"With a guy like you I'm beginning to think it is," he said.

"So, tell me, how did it go dropping paper on James Marco, or is he playing hard to get?"

"I'm not telling you shit anymore, Mick. And what you said

before about hiring me to run your paper, that was all bullshit, wasn't it?"

I shrugged. Valenzuela had already been useful to me and I knew I shouldn't burn the bridge. But something about his dragging his chain across the hood of my car bothered me.

"Probably," I said. "I've already got a full-time investigator. He usually handles that stuff."

"No, then that's good, because I don't want your business, Mick. I'll see you around."

He headed down the sidewalk and I watched him go.

"Yeah, I'll see you around, Val."

I got in the backseat and told Earl to get over to Ventura Boulevard and head toward Studio City. I wanted to drive by Kendall Roberts's business. There was no reason to do it other than that I was curious about her. I wanted to see what she had built for herself and what she was protecting.

"You did good in there, Earl," I said. "You saved the day."

He looked at me in the mirror and nodded.

"I got skills," he said.

"That you do."

I pulled my phone and called Lorna to check in. Nothing new had happened since the last call. I told her about the staff meeting I wanted for the next morning and she said Cisco had already informed her. I asked her to make sure she brought enough coffee and doughnuts for five.

"Who's the fifth?" she asked.

"Earl's going to join us," I said.

I looked at him in the mirror. I could see only his eyes but I could tell he was smiling.

After I finished with Lorna I called Cisco. He said he was at a Ferrari dealership on Wilshire Boulevard, about twenty blocks from the Beverly Wilshire. He said the place had multiple security cameras for watching over its expensive fleet at night.

"Don't tell me," I said. "The man in the hat?"

"That's right."

In his spare time Cisco had been pursuing the man in the hat for five months now. It deeply bothered him that he had been unable to find a camera anywhere in the Beverly Wilshire or its immediate surroundings that showed either the man's face or him getting into a car to follow Gloria Dayton.

But Gloria's chauffeur that night had been interviewed and he gave Cisco the exact route he had taken while driving her home from the hotel. Cisco spent all of his spare time on those streets checking businesses and residences with security cameras on the off chance that they picked up the car trailing Gloria home. He had even checked with the transportation departments for Beverly Hills, West Hollywood, and Los Angeles to view traffic cameras along the route. It had become a matter of professional pride to the big man.

I, on the other hand, had long since given up any hope of identifying the man in the hat. To me the trail was dead cold. Most security systems don't keep video for more than a month. Most of the places where Cisco made inquiries told him they had no video from the night Gloria Dayton was murdered. That he was too late.

"Well, you can drop that," I said. "I've got a name I want you to put at the top of your to-do list. I want to find her as soon as possible."

I gave him the name Trina Rafferty and filled him in on my conversation with Roberts about her.

"If she's still a working prostitute she could be anywhere from here to Miami and this might not even be her real name," he said.

"I think she's close," I said. "I think Fulgoni may even have her stashed somewhere. You need to find her."

"Okay, I'm on it. But why the big hurry? Won't she say the same thing Roberts just told you?"

"Somebody knew Glory Days was the CI who set up the Moya arrest. That wasn't Kendall Roberts—at least she says it wasn't her. I think that leaves Trina Trixxx. I think Fulgoni already got to her and I want to know what she told him."

"Got it."

"Good. Let me know."

I disconnected. Earl told me we were coming up on the address for Flex, the yoga studio owned by Roberts. He slowed the car to a crawl as we passed by the storefront studio. I checked the hours printed on the door and saw the place was open eight to eight every day. I could see people inside, all women and all in downward dog positions on rubber mats on the floor. I knew the position because my ex-wife was a longtime yoga enthusiast.

I wondered if Roberts's clients minded being on display to the street and passersby on the sidewalk. Many of the positions in yoga have a subtle or overt sexuality to them and it seemed odd to have a studio where one wall was floor-to-ceiling glass. As I pondered the question, a woman inside the studio walked up to the window and held her hands up to her eyes, pantomiming that she was looking at me through binoculars. The point was clear.

"We can go now, Earl," I said.

He picked up speed.

"Where to?"

"Let's go down the road a bit to Art's Deli. We'll pick up sandwiches and then I'll go see Legal Siegel for lunch."

15

At eight-thirty that night I knocked on the door at Kendall Roberts's home. I had been sitting out in the Lincoln on her street and waiting for her to return.

"Mr. Haller. Is something wrong?"

She was wearing the same outfit from earlier and I assumed she had come from work at the yoga studio.

"No, nothing is wrong. I just came back to tell you that you can forget about that subpoena."

"What do you mean? Did you take it to a judge like you said?"

"Didn't need to. I noticed after I left here that there wasn't a seal on it from the clerk of the U.S. District Court. Moya's case is in federal court. Gotta have that seal or it's not legit. I think the lawyer, Fulgoni, was trying to see if he could get you to come in on the sly, so he doctored up what looked like a subpoena and had his man take it out to you."

"Why would he do that—I mean, want me to come in on the sly?"

I had already been puzzling over this, especially since the subpoena Fulgoni had dropped on me had been legit. Why go through the correct motions on mine and not Kendall's? So far I hadn't been able to figure out why.

"Good question," I said. "If he wanted to keep it quiet, he could have filed the subpoena request under seal. But he didn't. Instead he tried to bluff you into coming in for an interview. I'm probably going to go see him tomorrow and that's exactly what I'll ask."

"Well, it's all confusing...but thank you."

"Confusion aside, we aim to please at Michael Haller and Associates."

I smiled and then felt dumb about what I had just said.

"You know, you could've called me. I gave you my number. You didn't have to come all the way back out here."

I frowned and shook my head like her concern was warrantless.

"It was no problem. My daughter lives nearby with my ex and I swung by there for a bit."

It wasn't exactly a lie. I had indeed driven by my ex-wife's condo building and stared at the lighted windows of her unit. I imagined my daughter in there in her bedroom, doing her homework or on the computer tweeting or Facebooking with friends. I had then driven over to see Kendall Roberts.

"So that means that next Tuesday I don't have to go to that lawyer's office?" she asked.

"No, you're clear," I said. "You can forget about it."

"And I won't have to go to court or testify about anything?"

That was the big question and I knew I had to stop making promises I was not sure I could keep.

"What I'm going to do is see Fulgoni tomorrow and make it clear to him that you're out of it. That you have no knowledge that will be useful to him in this matter and he should forget about you. I think that should take care of it."

"Thank you."

"Anytime."

I didn't make a move to leave and she glanced over my shoulder toward the street where my car was parked again in the red zone.

"So, where's your partner? The mean one."

I started to laugh.

"Oh, Earl? He's off now. He's actually my driver. Sorry again about that today. I didn't know what I was getting into when we came here."

"You're forgiven."

I nodded. There was nothing else to say at that point, but I still didn't move from my position on the front doorstep. The silence became awkward and she finally broke it.

"Is there..."

"Yeah, I'm sorry, I'm just standing here like a goof or something."

"It's okay."

"No, I, uh...you know, the real reason I came back is I wanted to talk about that question you asked. I mean, from earlier today."

"What question?"

She leaned against the door frame.

"You asked me about the past, you know? About how I lived with the past. My past."

She nodded. She remembered now.

"I'm sorry," she said. "I was being sarcastic and that was out of line. I had no business—"

"No, it's fine. Sarcasm or not, the question was valid. But then that guy knocked on the door with the phony subpoena and I, you know, never answered the question."

"So you came back to answer it."

I smiled uneasily.

"Well, sort of. I thought...that the past for both of us was something..."

I started laughing with embarrassment and shook my head.

"Actually, I don't know what I'm saying here."

"Would you like to come in, Mr. Haller?"

"I would love to but you have to stop calling me that. Call me Michael or Mickey or Mick. You know, Gloria used to call me Mickey Mantle."

She held the door wide and I stepped into the entry area.

"I've also been called Mickey Mouth on occasion. You know, because lawyers are sometimes called mouthpieces."

"Yes, I get it. I was about to have a glass of red wine. Would you like one?"

I almost asked if she had something stronger but thought better of it.

"That would be perfect."

She closed the door and we went into the kitchen to get glasses and pour the wine. She handed me a glass and then took up her own. She leaned against the counter and looked at me.

"Cheers," I said.

"Cheers," she said. "Can I ask you something?"

"Sure."

"Your coming here, this isn't some sort of thing you have, is it?"

"What do you mean? What thing?"

"You know with women…like me."

"I don't—"

"I'm retired. I don't do it anymore, and if you went through this whole damsel in distress thing with the subpoena because you thought—"

"No, not at all. Look, I'm sorry. This is embarrassing and I should probably just go."

I put my glass on the counter.

"You're right," I said. "I should've just called."

I was halfway to the hallway when she stopped me.

"Wait, Mickey."

I looked back at her.

"I didn't say you should've just called. I said you *could've* just called. There's a difference."

She took my glass off the counter and brought it to me.

"I'm sorry," she said. "I needed to get that out of the way. You'd be surprised how my former life still affects my current one."

I nodded.

"I get it."

"Let's go sit down."

135

We went into the living room and took the same seats we sat in earlier in the day—across from each other, a coffee table between us. The conversation was stilted at first. We exchanged banal pleasantries and I complimented the wine like the expert oenophile I was not.

I finally asked her how she ended up with a yoga studio and she matter-of-factly explained that a former client from her escort days had loaned her the initial investment. It reminded me of my attempt to help Gloria Dayton but obviously with different results.

"I think for some of the girls, they really don't want to get out," Kendall said. "They get what they need from it—on a lot of levels. So they may talk about wanting out but they never do it. I got lucky. I wanted out, and there was someone there to help me. How'd you end up being a lawyer?"

She had expertly if not abruptly thrown the lead back to me and I responded with the basic explanation about following a family tradition. When I told her my father had been Mickey Cohen's attorney, her eyes showed no recognition.

"Way before your time," I said. "He was a gangster out here in the forties and fifties. Pretty famous—there's been movies about him. He was part of what they called the Jewish Mafia. With Bugsy Siegel."

Another name that did not register with her.

"Your father must have had you late in life if he was running around with those guys in the forties."

I nodded.

"I was the kid from the second marriage. I think I was a surprise."

"Young wife?"

I nodded again and wished the conversation were going in a different direction. I had sorted all of this out for myself before. I had checked the county records. My father divorced his first wife and married his second less than two months later. I came five months after that. It didn't take a law degree to connect the dots. I was told as a child that my mother had come from Mexico, where she was a famous actress, but I never saw a movie poster, a newspaper clipping, or a publicity still anywhere in the house.

"I have a half brother who's an LAPD cop," I said. "He's older. He works homicide."

I didn't know why I said it. I guess to change directions.

"Same father?"

"Yeah."

"Do you guys get along?"

"Yeah, to a point. We never knew about each other until a few years ago. So consequently I guess we're not that close."

"Isn't it funny that you didn't know about each other and you became a defense lawyer and he became a cop?"

"Yeah, I guess. Funny."

I was desperate to get off the path we were on but couldn't think of a topic that would do it. Kendall rescued me with a question that broke new ground but was equally painful to answer.

"You mentioned your ex. So you're not married?"

"No. I was. Twice, actually, but the second one I don't really count. It was quick and painless. We both knew it was a mistake and we're still friends. In fact, she works for me."

"But the first one?"

"We have the daughter."

She nodded, seemingly understanding the lifelong complications and connections a broken marriage with a child produces.

"And your daughter's mother, are you on good terms?"

I sadly shook my head.

"No, not anymore. Actually, I'm not on good terms with either of them at the moment."

"I'm sorry."

"Me, too."

I took another drink of wine and studied her.

"What about you?" I asked.

"People like me don't have long relationships. I got married when I was twenty. It lasted a year. No kids, thank god."

"Do you know where he is? Your ex? I mean, do you keep track of each other? My ex and me, we're in the same business. The law, so I see her in the courthouse every now and then. If she sees me coming in the hall, she usually goes the other way."

She nodded but I didn't detect any sympathy.

"Last time I heard from my ex he wrote me a letter from a prison in Pennsylvania," she said. "He wanted me to sell my car so I could send him money each month. I didn't reply and that was about ten years ago. He's still there for all I know."

"Wow, and here I was all 'woe is me' because my ex-wife turns away from me in the courthouse. I think you win."

I hoisted my glass to toast her and she nodded in acceptance of the win.

"So, why are you really here?" she asked. "Are you hoping that I can tell you more about Glory?"

I looked down at my glass, which was now almost empty. This was either going to be the end of things or the start.

"You'd tell me, right, if there was something I needed to know about her?"

She frowned.

"I told you all I know."

"Then I believe you."

I finished my wine and put the glass on the table.

"Thanks for the wine, Kendall. I should probably go now."

She walked me to the front door and held it open for me. I touched her arm as I passed by. I tried to think of something to say that would leave us with the possibility of another meeting. She beat me to it.

"Maybe next time you come back, you'll be more interested in me than the dead girl."

I looked back at her as she closed the door. I nodded but she was gone.

16

I was trying to talk a final shot of Patrón out of Randy after last call at Four Green Fields, when my phone screen lit up on the bar top. It was Cisco and he was working late.

"Cisco?"

"Sorry if I woke you, Mick, but I thought you'd want me to."

"No worries. What's up?"

Randy hit the bright lights and started blasting "Closing Time" on the sound system, hoping to chase the lingering drinkers out.

I hit the mute button late and slid off the stool to head to the door.

"What the hell was that?" Cisco asked. "Mick, you there?"

Once I was out the door I took the phone off mute.

"Sorry, iPhone malfunction. Where are you and what's going on?"

"I'm outside the Standard downtown. Trina Trixxx is inside doing what she does. But that's not why I called. That could've waited."

I wanted to ask how he had found Trina but noted the urgency in his voice.

"Okay, so then what couldn't wait?"

I muted the phone again and got in my car, pulling the door closed behind me. It had been a stupid move chasing the wine I had shared with Kendall with tequila. But I had felt bad after leaving her place, as though I had fumbled the ball somehow, and I wanted to burn away the thoughts with Patrón.

"I just got a call from a guy who does me favors every now and then," Cisco said. "You know the Ferrari dealership I told you about before?"

"Yeah, the one on Wilshire."

"Right, well, I hit the gold mine there. A lot of video. They keep digital film for a year on the cloud. So we got double lucky."

"Did you see the man in the hat's face?"

"No, not that lucky. Still no face. But we went through the video on the night in question and I picked up Gloria and her driver going by. Then four cars back comes a Mustang and it looks like our guy. He's still wearing the hat, so I'm ninety percent sure he's our guy."

"Okay."

"One of their perimeter cameras shoots east along the front of the lot. I switch to that video and check out the Mustang."

"You got a plate."

"Damn right, I got a plate. So I gave it to this friend of mine and he just called me back after going into work tonight."

By "friend" I knew he meant that he had a source in the cop shop who ran plates for him. A source who obviously worked the midnight shift. This practice of sharing information from the computer with an outsider was against the law in California. So I didn't ask Cisco for any clarification on who provided the information that he was about to share. I just waited for him to tell me the name.

"All right, so the 'stang comes back to a guy named Lee Lankford. And get this, Mick, he's law enforcement. My friend can tell because his address is not on the computer. They protect cops that way. They can put a law enforcement block on the registration of a personal vehicle. But he's LE, and now we have to find out who he works for and why he was tailing Gloria. I already know this, he's not LAPD. My friend checked. Bottom line, Mick, is I'm beginning to think there might be something to our client's claiming he was set up."

I didn't hear most of what Cisco had said after he mentioned the Mustang owner's name. I was off to the races, running with the name Lankford. Cisco hadn't recognized it because he wasn't working for me eight years before when I made the deal whereby Gloria Dayton gave up Hector Moya to the DA's Office, which turned around and gave him up to the feds. Of course, back then Lankford had nothing to do with that deal, but he was skirting around that case like a vulture.

"Lankford is Glendale PD retired," I said. "He's currently working for the DA as an investigator."

"You know him?"

"Sort of. He worked the murder of Raul Levin. In fact, he's the guy who tried at first to pin it on me. And I saw him on this case at La Cosse's first appearance. He's the DA investigator assigned to the case."

I heard Cisco whistle as I started the car.

"So let's talk this out," he said. "We have Lankford following Gloria Dayton on the night she was murdered. He presumably follows her home and about an hour later she is murdered in her apartment."

"And then a couple days later at first appearance, he's there," I said. "He's assigned to the Dayton murder case."

"That's not a coincidence, Mick. There are no coincidences like that."

I nodded, even though I was alone in the car.

"It's a setup," I said. "Andre's been telling the truth."

I needed to get to my Gloria Dayton files but Jennifer Aronson still had them. It would have to wait until the morning staff meeting. In the meantime, I was trying to remember those days eight years ago when I first met Detective Lankford and became his prime suspect in the murder of my own investigator.

I suddenly remembered what Cisco had said at the top of the conversation.

"You're tailing Trina Trixxx right now?"

"Yeah, she wasn't hard to find. I drove by her place to get a feel for it and out she came. I followed her here. Same setup that Gloria had. The driver, the whole bit. She's been inside the hotel for about forty minutes now."

"Okay, I'm heading your way. I want to talk to her. Tonight."

"I'll make that happen. You okay to drive? You sound like you had a few."

"I'm fine. I'll grab coffee on the way. You just hold her until I get there."

17

Before I got to the Standard downtown I got a text from Cisco redirecting me to an address and apartment number on Spring Street. Then I got another text, this one advising me to hit an ATM on the way—Trina wanted to be paid to talk. When I finally got to the address, it turned out it was one of the rehabbed lofts right behind the Police Administration Building. The lobby door was locked, and when I buzzed apartment 12C, it was my own investigator who answered and buzzed me up.

On the twelfth floor I stepped out of the elevator to find Cisco waiting in the open doorway of 12C.

"I followed her home from the Standard and waited until she was dropped off," he explained. "Figured it'd be easier if we took her driver out of the equation."

I nodded and looked through the open door but didn't enter.

"Is she going to talk to us?"

"Depends on how much cash you brought. She's a businesswoman through and through."

"I got enough."

I walked past him and into a loft with views over the PAB and the civic center, the city hall tower lit up and on center display. The apartment was a nice place, though sparely furnished. Trina Rafferty had either recently moved in or was in the process of moving out. She was sitting on a white leather couch with chrome feet. She wore a short black cocktail dress, had her legs crossed in a stab at modesty, and was smoking a cigarette.

"Are you going to pay me?" she asked.

I walked fully into the room and looked down at her. She was pushing forty and she looked tired. Her hair was slightly disheveled, her lipstick was smeared, and her eyeliner was caking at the corners. One more long night in another year of long nights. She had just come from having sex with someone she didn't know before and would probably never see again.

"It depends on what you tell me."

"Well, I'm not telling you anything unless you pay up front."

I had hit an ATM in the Bonaventure Hotel lobby and made two maximum withdrawals of four hundred dollars each. The money had come in hundreds, fifties, and twenties and I split it between two pockets. I took out the first four hundred and dropped it on her coffee table next to the crowded ashtray.

"There's four hundred. Is that good enough to start?"

She picked up the money, folded it twice, and worked it into one of her high-heeled shoes. I remembered in that moment that Gloria had once told me that she always put her cash payments into her shoes because the shoes were usually the last thing to come off—if at all. Many clients liked her to keep her heels on while they had sex.

"We'll see," Trina said. "Ask away."

The whole drive downtown I had considered what I should ask and how I should ask it. I had a feeling this might be my only shot with Trina Trixxx. Once team Fulgoni found out I had gotten to her, they would attempt to shut down my access.

"Tell me about James Marco and Hector Moya."

Her body rocked backward with surprise and then straightened up. She stuck out her lower lip for a few seconds before responding.

"I didn't realize that this is about them. You need to pay me more if you want me to talk about them."

Without hesitation I took the other fold of money out of my

pocket and dropped it on the table. It disappeared into her other shoe. I sat down on an ottoman directly across the table from her.

"Let's hear it," I said.

"Marco's a DEA agent and he had a hard-on for Hector," she said. "He really wanted to get him and he did."

"How did you know Marco?"

"He busted me."

"When?"

"It was a sting. He posed as a john and he wanted sex and coke and I brought both. Then I got busted."

"When was this?"

"About ten years ago. I don't remember the dates."

"You made a deal with him?"

"Yeah, he let me go, but I had to tell him stuff. He'd call me."

"What stuff?"

"Just stuff I would hear or know about—you know, from clients. He agreed to let me go if I fed him. And he was always hungry."

"Hungry for Hector."

"Well, no. He didn't know about Hector, at least not from me. I wasn't that stupid or that desperate. I'd take the bust before I'd give up Hector. The guy was cartel, you know what I mean? So I gave Marco the little stuff. The kind of stuff guys would brag about while fucking. All their big scores and plans and whatever. Guys try to compensate with talk all the time, you know?"

I nodded, though I didn't know if I was revealing something about myself by agreeing. I tried to stay on track with what she was saying and how it fit with the latest permutation of Gloria's case.

"Okay," I said. "So you didn't give Hector up to Marco. Who did?"

I knew that indirectly, at least, Gloria Dayton had given Moya up, but I didn't know what Trina knew.

"All I can tell you is that it wasn't me," Trina said.

I shook my head.

"That's not good enough, Trina. Not for eight hundred bucks."

"What, you want me to throw in a blow job, too? That's not a problem."

"No, I want you to tell me everything. I want you to tell me what you told Sly Fulgoni."

She went through the same body shiver as when I had first mentioned Hector Moya. As though for a second she had been shocked by the name and then was able to reconstitute herself.

"How do you know about Sly?"

"Because I do. And if you want to keep the money, I need to know what you told him."

"But isn't that like attorney-client stuff? Like it's privileged or whatever they call it?"

I shook my head.

"You've got it wrong, Trina. You're a witness, not a client. Fulgoni's client is Hector Moya. What did you tell him?"

I leaned forward on the ottoman as I said it and then I waited.

"Well, I told him about another girl who Marco busted and was putting to work. Like me, only he really had her under his thumb. I don't know why. I think when he caught her she had a lot more on her than I had."

"You mean a lot more cocaine?"

"Right. And her record wasn't as clean as mine. She was going to go down hard if she didn't come up with something bigger than herself, you know what I mean?"

"Yes."

It was how most drug cases were built. Small fish giving up bigger fish. I nodded as though I had full knowledge about how things worked, but once again I was privately humiliated because I had not even known the details of my own client's dealings with the DEA. Trina was obviously talking about Gloria Dayton, and she was telling a story I didn't know.

"So your friend gave up Hector," I said, hoping to keep the story moving so I didn't have to dwell on my own failings in the case.

"Sort of."

"What do you mean 'sort of'? She did or she didn't."

"She sort of did. She told me that Marco made her hide a gun in Moya's hotel room so that when they busted him, they could add charges and send him away for life. See, Hector was smart. He never kept enough in his room for them to make a big case on. Just a few ounces. Sometimes less. But the gun would change everything, and Glory was the one who brought it in. She said when Hector fell asleep after she did him, she took it out of her purse and hid it under the mattress."

To say I was stunned was an understatement. In the course of the past several months I had already accepted the fact that I'd been used by Gloria in some way. But if Trina Rafferty's story was true, the level of deception and manipulation was as masterful as it was perfect, and I had played my part to a T, thinking I was carrying out good lawyering by pulling all the right strings for my client, when all along it was my client and her DEA handler who held the strings—my strings.

I still had many questions about the scenario Trina was outlining—mainly the question of why I was even needed in the scheme. But for the moment I was thinking of other things. The only way this knowledge could be more humiliating would be for it to become public, and everything the prostitute sitting in front of me was saying indicated that this was exactly the direction it was going.

I tried not to show any of the internal meltdown I was feeling. I kept my voice steady and asked the next question.

"When you say Glory, I take it you mean Gloria Dayton, also known at that time as Glory Days?"

Before she could answer, the iPhone on the coffee table started vibrating. Trina eagerly snatched it up, probably hoping she could get in one last booking before crashing for the night. She checked the ID but it was blocked. She answered anyway.

"Hello, this is Trina Trixxx…"

While she listened to the caller I glanced at Cisco to see what

I could read in his face. I wondered if he understood from what had been said that I had been an unwitting participant in a rogue DEA agent's scheme.

"And another man," Trina told her caller. "He said you're not my lawyer."

I looked at Trina. She wasn't talking to a potential customer.

"Is that Fulgoni?" I said. "Let me talk to him."

She hesitated but then told the caller to hold on and handed me the phone.

"Fulgoni," I said. "I thought you were going to call me back."

There was a pause and then a voice I didn't recognize as Sly Fulgoni Jr. spoke.

"I didn't know I was supposed to."

And then I realized I was talking to Sly Sr., person to person from FCI Victorville. He was probably on a cell phone smuggled into the lockup by a visitor or a guard. Many of my incarcerated clients were able to communicate with me on burners—throwaway phones with limited minutes and life spans.

"Your son was supposed to get back to me. How are things up there, Sly?"

"Not too bad. I'm out of here in another eleven months."

"How did you know I was here?"

"I didn't. I was checking on Trina."

I didn't believe that for a moment. It sounded like he had specifically asked Trina about me before she passed the phone over. I decided not to push it—yet.

"What can I do for you, Mr. Haller?"

"Well...I'm sitting here talking to Trina and I'm wondering what I'm going to be doing for you. I got the subpoena and I'm just beginning to put together the angle you're playing for Moya. And I gotta tell you, I have a problem being made to look like a fool—especially in open court."

"That is understandable. But sometimes when one has indeed played the fool, it is difficult to skirt the issue. You have to be prepared for the truth to come out. A man's freedom is at stake."

"I'll keep that in mind."

I disconnected and handed the phone back across the table to Trina.

"What did he say?" she asked.

"Nothing much at all. How much have they promised you?"

"What?"

"Come on, Trina. You're a businesswoman. You charged me just to answer a few questions here. You must be charging something to tell that story in a depo for a judge. How much? Did they already take your statement?"

"I don't know what you're talking about. I haven't been paid anything."

"What about this place? They get you this to keep you close?"

"No! This is my place and I want you to leave. Both of you, get out. Now!"

I glanced at Cisco. I could push it, but it was pretty clear that my eight hundred bucks were spent and she was finished talking. Whatever Fulgoni had said before the phone was handed to me had frozen her. It was time to go.

I stood up and nodded Cisco toward the door.

"Thanks for your time," I said to Trina. "I'm sure we'll be talking again."

"Don't count on it."

We left the apartment and had to wait for the elevator. I stepped back to Trina's door and bent forward to listen. I thought she'd make a call to someone, maybe Sly Jr. But I heard nothing.

The elevator came and we rode down. Cisco was quiet.

"What's up, Big Man?" I asked.

"Nothing, just thinking. How did he know to call her then?"

I nodded. It was a good question. I hadn't thought it through yet.

We left the building and walked out onto Spring Street, which was deserted except for a couple of empty patrol cars parked along the side of the PAB. It was after two a.m. and there was no sign of another human being anywhere.

"You think I was followed?" I asked.

Cisco thought about it for a moment before nodding.

"Somehow he knew we'd found her. That we were with her."

"That's not good."

"I'll get your car checked tomorrow and then put a couple Indians on you. If you have a physical tail we'll know it soon enough."

The associates Cisco used in countersurveillance were so adept at disappearing into the crevices that he called them Indians after the old westerns in which the Indians used to trail the wagon trains without the white settlers even knowing they were there.

"That will be good," I said. "Thanks."

"Where'd you park?" Cisco asked.

"Up in front of the PAB. Figured it was safe. You?"

"I'm around back here. You okay or you want an escort?"

"I'm good. See you at the staff meeting."

"I'll be there."

We headed off in different directions. I looked over my shoulder three times before I made it to my car, parked in the safest spot in downtown. From there I kept an eye on the rearview mirror all the way home.

18

I was the last to arrive at the loft for the staff meeting. And I was dragging. I'd hit the private stash of Patrón Silver when I'd finally gotten home just a few hours before. Between the alcohol consumption, the trip downtown to interview Trina Rafferty, and the disquiet that comes with the knowledge that you are probably being watched, I'd gotten only a couple hours of restless sleep before the alarm sounded.

I grunted a hello to the assemblage in the boardroom and went immediately to the coffee set up on the side counter. I poured half a cup, shot two Advils into my mouth, and took the scalding hot liquid down in one gulp. I then refilled and this time added milk and sugar to make it a little more palatable. That first blast had burned my throat but it helped me find my voice.

"How's everybody today? Better than me, I hope."

Everyone chimed in positively. I turned to find a seat and immediately noticed that Earl was at the table. For a moment I forgot why and then remembered that I had indeed invited him to join the inner circle the day before.

"Oh, everybody, I invited Earl to join us. He's going to take a more active role in some of the work, from the standpoint of investigations and interviews. He'll still be driving the Lincoln, but he's got other skills and I intend to exploit them to the benefit of our clients."

I nodded to Earl and as I did so realized I had not mentioned his elevation to Cisco. Still, Cisco showed no surprise, and I realized I had obviously been helped out there by Lorna, who had kept her husband informed, where I had failed.

I pulled out a chair at the end of the table and sat down, noticing the small black electronic device with three green blinking lights at the center of the table.

"Mickey, you don't want a doughnut?" Lorna asked. "It looks like you should put something in your stomach."

"No, not right now," I said. "What is that?"

I pointed at the device. It was a rectangular black box about the size of an iPhone, only an inch thick. And it had three separate stub antennas sticking out of one end.

Cisco answered.

"I was just telling everyone, that's a Paquin seven thousand blocker. Stops all transmissions by Wi-Fi, Bluetooth, and radio wave. No one will hear what we say in this room outside of these walls."

"Did you find a bug?"

"With one of these things you don't even have to look. That's the beauty of it."

"What about the Lincoln?"

"I have some guys looking at it out back right now. They were waiting for you to arrive. I'll let you know as soon as I know."

I reached into my pocket for the keys.

"They don't need your keys," Cisco said.

Of course not, I realized. They're pros. I took the keys out anyway, put them on the table and slid them down to Earl. He'd be driving the rest of the day.

"Okay, well, let's get started. I'm sorry I'm late. Long night. I know that's not an excuse but…"

I braced myself with another slug of coffee and this time it went down easier and I began to feel it take hold of my bloodstream. I looked at the faces around the table and got down to it.

Pointing to the Paquin 7000, I said, "Sorry for all the secret-agent stuff but I think precautions are necessary. We had some significant developments yesterday and last night and I wanted everybody to be here and to be made aware of what's happening."

As if to underline the seriousness of my opening statement, a power chord from an electric guitar echoed through the ceiling and stopped me cold. All of us looked up at the ceiling. It had sounded like the opening chord tab of *A Hard Day's Night*—the coincidence was not lost on me.

"I thought the Beatles were broken up," I said.

"They are," Lorna said. "And we were promised no band practice in the mornings."

Another chord was strummed and then followed by some improvisational noodling. Somebody pumped a hi-hat on a drum kit and the clash of cymbals almost loosened my fillings.

"You've got to be kidding me," I said. "Shouldn't those guys be hungover or asleep? I know I wish I was still in bed."

"I'll go up," Lorna said. "This makes me really angry."

"No. Cisco, you go up. You already know the update. I want Lorna to hear it and you might get better results up there."

"On it."

Cisco left the room and headed upstairs. It was one of the few times I was pleased that he had worn a T-shirt to work, exposing his impressive biceps and intimidating tattoos. The T-shirt celebrated the one hundred tenth anniversary of Harley-Davidson motorcycles. I thought that might help get the message across as well.

To the rhythm of a bass drum from above, I began updating the others, starting with the subpoena Valenzuela laid on me the morning before and then moving through the happenings of the rest of the day. About halfway through, a terrific crash was heard from above as Cisco put an end to band practice. I finished my story by recounting the late-night meeting with Trina Trixxx and the conclusion prompted by Fulgoni's call from prison that I was under surveillance.

Nobody asked any questions along the way, though Jennifer took some notes. I didn't know if the silence was a testament to the early hour, the implied threat that surveillance meant to all of us, or my fully engaging skill as a storyteller. There was also the possibility that I had simply lost everyone on one of the turns of the convoluted tale I was spinning.

Cisco reentered the room, looking none the worse for wear. He took his seat and nodded to me. Problem solved.

I looked at the others.

"Questions?"

Jennifer raised her pen as though she were still in school.

"I actually have a few," she said. "First of all, you said that Sylvester Fulgoni Sr. called you from the prison in Victorville at two in the morning. How is that possible? I don't think they give inmates access to—"

"They don't," I said. "The number was blocked but I'm sure it was a cell phone. Smuggled in to him or given to him by a guard."

"Couldn't that be traced?"

"Not really. Not if it was a burner."

"A burner?"

"A throwaway phone—bought with no names attached. Look, we're getting off the subject here. Suffice it to say it was Fulgoni and he called me from prison, where someone had obviously reached out to him to inform him that I was speaking at that moment to his star witness Trina Trixxx. That's the salient point. Not that Sly Fulgoni has a phone up there, but that he knows the moves we're making. What's your next question?"

She checked her notes before asking it.

"Well, before yesterday we had two separate things going. We had the La Cosse case and then we had this other thing with Moya that we thought was separate but might be useful to bring in as part of a possible straw man defense for La Cosse. But now, if I'm following you correctly, we're talking about these two things being one case."

I nodded.

"Yes, that's what I'm saying. This is all one case now. What links it for us is obviously Gloria Dayton. But the key thing here is Lankford. He was following Gloria the night of the murder."

"So La Cosse, he was set up all along," Earl said.

I nodded again.

"Right."

"And this isn't just an angle we're playing or a strategy," Jennifer said. "We're saying this is now our case."

"Right again."

I looked around. Three walls of the boardroom were glass. But there was one wall of old Chicago brick.

"Lorna, we need a whiteboard for that wall. I wish we could diagram this. It would make it easier."

"I'll get one," Lorna said.

"And get the locks changed on this place. Also I want two cameras. One on the door, one on this room. When we go to trial, this is going to be ground zero, and I want it safe and secure."

"I can put a guy on the place—twenty-four-seven," Cisco said. "Might be worth it."

"And what money do we use to pay for all of this?" Lorna asked.

"Hold off on the guy, Cisco," I said. "Maybe when we get to trial. For now we'll go with just locks and cameras."

I then leaned forward, elbows on the table.

"It's all one case now," I said again. "And so we need to take it apart and look at all of the pieces. Eight years ago I was manipulated. I handled a case and made moves I believed were of my own design. But they weren't, and I'm not going to let that happen again here."

I sat back and waited for comment but I got only silent stares. I saw Cisco look over my shoulder and through the glass door behind me. He started to get up. I turned around. Across the loft there was a man standing by the front door. He was actually bigger than Cisco.

"One of my guys," Cisco said as he left the boardroom.

I turned and looked back at the others.

"If this was a movie, that guy's name would be Tiny."

The others laughed. I got up to refill my coffee and by the time I returned, Cisco was coming back to the boardroom. I stayed standing and awaited the verdict. Cisco poked his head through the door but didn't come in.

"The Lincoln's been jacked," he said. "Do you want them to take it out? We could find a place for it. Maybe a FedEx truck would be good—keep them running around."

By "jacked" he meant LoJacked, a reference to an anti-theft tracking system. But in this case he was telling me somebody had crawled underneath my car and attached a GPS tracker.

"What does that mean?" Aronson asked.

While Cisco explained what I already knew, I thought about the question of whether to remove the device or leave it in place and possibly find a way of making it work to my advantage against whoever was monitoring my movements. A FedEx truck would keep them running in circles but it would also tip our hand and let them know we were onto them.

"Leave it in place," I said when Cisco finished his explanation to the others. "For now, at least. It might come in handy."

"Keep in mind it could be just a backup," Cisco cautioned. "You still could have a live tail. I'll keep the Indians up on the cliffs a couple days, just to see."

"Sounds good."

He turned in the doorway and signaled to his man with a flat hand, as if running it along the surface of a table. Status quo, leave the tracker in place. The man pointed at Cisco—message understood—and walked through the door. Cisco returned to the table, pointing to the Paquin 7000 as he went.

"Sorry. He couldn't get a call in to me because of the blocker."

I nodded.

"What's that guy's name?" I asked.

"Who, Little Guy? I actually don't know his real name. I just know him as Little Guy."

I snapped my fingers. I'd been close. The others muffled their laughter and Cisco looked at all of us like he knew there was some kind of joke and it was on him.

"Are there any bikers out there who don't have nicknames?" Jennifer asked.

"Oh, you mean a nickname like Bullocks? No, I don't think there are, to tell you the truth."

There was more laughter, and then I turned it serious again.

"Okay, let's look at this thing. We now know what's on the surface. Let's go below. First off, there's the question why. Why the manipulation eight years ago? If we believe what we have been told, then Marco goes to Gloria and tells her to plant a gun in Moya's hotel room so that when he gets busted he gets the firearms enhancement, making him eligible for a life sentence. Okay, we get that. But then comes the hard part."

"Why didn't Marco just bust him once the gun was in place?" Cisco asked.

I pointed at him.

"Exactly. Instead of the easy and direct route, he sets forth a strategy in which Gloria allows herself to get busted by the locals and then comes to me. She drops enough information on me for my eyes to light up and think there is a deal to be made. I go see the DA and make that deal. Moya gets busted, the gun is found, and the rest is history. It still begs the question why go to all that trouble?"

There was a pause while my team considered the complicated setup. Jennifer was the first to dive in.

"Marco couldn't be seen as attached to it," she said. "For some reason he had to be removed from this and wait until it was brought to him. The DA makes the deal with you, the LAPD gets the bust, but then Marco jumps in with the outstanding federal warrant that trumps everything. It looks like it just fell into his lap but he orchestrated the whole thing."

"Which only brings us back to why," Cisco said.

"Exactly," I said.

"Do you think Marco knew Moya and didn't want him to

know he'd set it up?" Jennifer asked. "So he sort of hid behind Gloria and you?"

"Maybe," I said. "But he still eventually got the case."

"What if it was because of Moya?" Cisco said. "He's a cartel guy, and they're the most violent people on the planet. They'll wipe out a whole village just to make sure they get one informant. Maybe Marco didn't want to draw the target on himself for bringing Moya down. This way he just sat back and the case came to him all signed, sealed, and delivered. If Moya started looking for somebody to come down on, it would stop with Gloria."

"That's possible, I guess," I said. "But then if Moya was looking for revenge, why did he wait seven years to hit Gloria?"

Cisco shook his head, unconvinced by either argument. That was the trouble with spitballing ideas. More often than not you found yourself talked into a logic corner.

"Maybe we're talking about two separate things," Jennifer said. "Two things separated by seven years. You have the bust and the unknown reason for how Marco set it up, and then you have Gloria's murder, which may have happened for an entirely different reason."

"You're back to thinking our client did it?" I said.

"No, not at all. In fact, I'm pretty convinced he's a patsy in this. I'm just saying seven years is a long time. Things change. You yourself just asked why Moya would wait seven years to exact vengeance. I don't think he did. Gloria's death is a big loss to him. His habeas suit claims the gun was planted in his hotel room. So he needed Gloria to make his case. Who's he got now? Trina Trixxx and her secondhand account? Good luck putting her before the U.S. District Court of Appeals."

I stared at Jennifer for a long moment and slowly started to nod.

"Out of the mouth of babes," I said. "And I don't mean that in any derogatory way. I'm saying you're the rookie here and I think you just nailed something. Moya needed her alive for the habeas. To tell the court what she did."

"Well, maybe she wouldn't tell the truth and so he had her whacked," Cisco said, nodding afterward to help convince himself.

I shook my head. I didn't like it. Something was missing.

"If we start with Moya needing her alive," Jennifer said, "the question becomes who needed her dead."

I nodded now, liking this logic. I waited a moment, spreading my hands to the others for the obvious answer. None came.

"Marco," I said.

I leaned back in my chair and looked from Cisco to Jennifer. They stared back blankly.

"What, am I the only one seeing this?" I asked.

"So you're choosing a federal agent over a cartel thug as our straw man?" Jennifer asked. "That doesn't sound like a good strategy."

"It's no longer a straw man defense if it is a true defense," I said. "Doesn't matter if it's a tough sell if it's what really happened."

There was a silence as my words were considered, and then Jennifer broke it.

"But why? Why would Marco want her dead?" she asked.

I shrugged.

"That's what we have to find out," I said.

"Lot of money in drugs," Earl said. "It bends a lotta people."

I pointed at him like he was a genius.

"Right there," I said. "If we believe the story that Marco made Gloria plant the gun, then we're dealing with a rogue agent already. We don't know if he breaks the rules to get bad guys or if it's to protect something else. Either way, is it that far a leap to think he might kill to protect himself and whatever his rogue operation is? If Gloria became a danger to him, then I think she was definitely in the crosshairs."

I leaned forward.

"So this is what we need to do. We need to find out more about Marco. And this group he's in—the ICE team. Find out what other cases they've made before and since Moya. See what kind of reputation they have. We look at other cases to see if anything at all looks bent."

"I'll search his name through court records," Jennifer said. "State and federal. Pull out everything I can find and start from there."

"I'll ask around," Cisco added. "I know some people who know some people."

"And I'll take the Fulgoni boys," I said. "And Mr. Moya. They might now actually be assets to our case."

I could feel the stirring of adrenaline in my veins. Nothing like having a sense of direction to get the blood moving.

"Do you think this means it was the DEA who jacked your car?" Jennifer asked. "And not Moya or Fulgoni?"

The thought of a rogue DEA agent monitoring my moves froze the adrenaline into tiny icicles in my veins.

"If that's the case, then Fulgoni calling Trina last night when I was there was just coincidence," I said. "Not sure I believe that."

It was one of the conundrums of the case that would need to be cleared up before we had full understanding.

Jennifer gathered up her notepad and files and started to push back her chair.

"Wait a minute," I said. "We're not finished."

She resettled and looked at me.

"Lankford," I said. "He was tailing Gloria the night she was murdered. If we're looking at Marco, then we have to look for a connection between him and Lankford. We find that and we'll be close to having everything we need."

I turned my attention to Cisco.

"Everything you can find on him," I said. "If he knows Marco, I want to know from where. I want to know how."

"On it," Cisco said.

I looked back at Jennifer.

"Just because we're looking at Marco doesn't mean we take our eyes off Moya. We have to know everything there is to know about his case. It will help us understand Marco. I still want you on that."

"Got it."

Now I turned to Lorna and Earl.

"Lorna, you keep the boat floating. And Earl, you're with me. I think that's it, everybody. For now, at least. Be careful out there. Remember who we're dealing with."

Everybody started to get up. They were all silent as they moved. It hadn't been the kind of meeting that drew any kind of lasting jocularity or camaraderie out of the troops. We were going off in separate directions to conduct a sub rosa investigation of a possibly dangerous federal agent. There weren't too many things more sobering to consider than that.

19

On the way downtown I had to tell Earl to cool it with the single-handed effort to determine if we had a tail. He was weaving in and out of traffic, accelerating and then braking, moving into exit lanes and then jerking the wheel to pull out at the last moment and get back on the freeway.

"Let Cisco handle that," I said. "You just get me down to the courthouse in one piece."

"Sorry, boss, I got carried away. But I gotta say I like all this stuff, you know? Bein' in the meeting and knowin' what's going on."

"Well, like I said, when things happen and I need your help—like yesterday, for example—I'll bring you into it."

"That's cool."

He settled down after that and we made it downtown without incident. I had Earl drop me at the Criminal Courts Building. I told him I didn't know how long I would be. I had no business in court, but the District Attorney's Office was up on the sixteenth floor and I was headed there. After getting out, I looked over the roof of the car and casually scanned the intersection of Temple and Spring. I didn't see anything or anyone out of the ordinary. I did catch myself checking the rooflines for Indians, however. I didn't see anything up there either.

After I made it through the metal detector, I took one of the crowded elevators up to sixteen. I had no appointment and knew I might be in for a nice long wait on a hard plastic chair but I thought I needed to take a shot at getting in to see Leslie Faire. She had been a key player in the occurrences of eight years before, yet she had barely come up for discussion lately. She had been the deputy DA who made the deal that resulted in Hector Arrande Moya's arrest and Gloria Dayton's freedom.

Leslie had done well for herself in the years since that deal was struck. She won a few big trials and chose correctly in throwing her support to my opponent Damon Kennedy in the election. That paid off with a major promotion. She was now a head deputy DA and was in charge of the Major Trials Unit. This made her more of a manager of trial attorneys and court schedules, so it was rare to see her standing for the people anymore. This of course was fine by me. She was a tough prosecutor and I was glad I didn't need to worry about crossing paths with her again in court. I counted the Gloria Dayton case as the only victory I ever scored against her. Of course, it was a hollow victory in my eyes now.

I may have disliked facing Leslie Faire on cases but I respected her. And now I thought she should know what had happened to Gloria Dayton. Maybe the news would make her inclined to help me fill in some of the details from eight years before. I wanted to know if she had ever crossed paths with Agent Marco and, if so, when.

I told the receptionist that I had no appointment but was willing to wait. She said to take a seat while she notified Ms. Faire's secretary of my request for a ten-minute meeting. The fact that Faire had a secretary underscored her lofty position in the Kennedy regime. Most prosecutors I knew had no real administrative help and were lucky if they got to share a pool secretary.

I pulled out my phone and sat down on one of the plastic chairs that had populated the waiting room since before I was a licensed lawyer. I had e-mail to check and texts to write but the first thing I did was call Cisco to see if his Indians had picked up anything on the drive downtown.

"I was just talking to my guy," Cisco reported. "They didn't see anything."

"Okay."

"Doesn't mean they're not there. This was just one drive. We might need to send you out to get a little separation and then we'll know for sure."

"Really? I don't have time to be running all over town, Cisco. I thought you said these guys were good."

"Yeah, well, the Indians that were up in the cliffs didn't have to watch the 101 Freeway. I'll tell them to stick with it. What's your schedule anyway?"

"I'm at the DA's Office now and I don't know how long I'll be here. After this I'm going out to Fulgoni's office to meet Junior."

"Where's he located?"

"Century City."

"Well, Century City might work. Nice wide boulevards out there. I'll tell my guys."

I disconnected and opened up the e-mail on my phone. There were an assortment of messages from clients who were currently incarcerated. The worst thing to happen to defense attorneys in recent years was the approval from most prisons of e-mail access for inmates. With nothing else to do but worry about their cases, they inundated me and every other lawyer with endless e-mails containing questions, worries, and the occasional threat.

I started weeding through it all, and twenty minutes went by before I looked up to change focus. I decided I'd give it a whole hour before giving up on Leslie Faire. I went back to plowing through my e-mail and was able to clear out a good chunk of the backlog, even answering a few of them in the process. I was forty-five minutes into it, with my head down, when I saw a shadow reflect on my phone screen. I looked up and there was Lankford looking down at me. I almost flinched but think I managed to look unsurprised to see him.

"Investigator Lankford."

"Haller, what are you doing here?"

He said it like I was some kind of squatter or other nuisance who had previously been warned to move on and not come back.

"I'm waiting to see someone. What are you doing here?"

"I work here, remember? Is this about La Cosse?"

"No, it's not about La Cosse, but what it is about is none of your business."

He signaled me to stand up. I stayed seated.

"I told you I'm waiting for somebody."

"No, you're not. Leslie Faire sent me out to see what you want. You don't want to talk to me, then you're not talking to anybody. Let's go. Up. You can't use our waiting room to operate your business. You've got a car for that."

That answer froze me. He'd been sent out to me by Faire. Did that mean Faire had knowledge of what was happening behind the scenes on the Gloria Dayton murder case? I'd come to inform her but she might already know more of what was going on than me.

"I said let's go," Lankford said forcefully. "Get up or I'll get you up."

A woman who had been sitting two chairs away from me stood to get away from what she determined was about to become a physical extraction. She sat back down on the other side of the room.

"Hold your horses, Lankford," I said. "I'm going, I'm going."

I slipped my phone into an inside pocket of my jacket and grabbed my briefcase off the floor as I got up. Lankford didn't move, choosing to stay close and invade my personal space. I made a move to go around him but he sidestepped and we were face-to-face again.

"Having fun?" I said.

"Ms. Faire doesn't want you coming back here either," he said. "She's not in court anymore and doesn't need to have anything to do with douche bags like you. Understand?"

His breath was rancid with coffee and cigarettes.

"Sure," I said. "I get it."

I moved around him and out to the elevator alcove. He followed me and watched silently as I pushed the down button and waited. I looked over my shoulder at him.

"This may take a while, Lankford."

"I've got all day."

I nodded.

"I'm sure you do."

I turned back to look at the elevator doors for a moment and then glanced back over my shoulder at him. I couldn't resist.

"You look different, Lankford."

"Yeah? How so?"

"From last time I saw you. Something's different. You get hair plugs or something?"

"Very funny. But, thankfully, I haven't seen your ass since La Cosse's first appearance last year."

"No, somethin' more recent. I don't know."

That's all I said. I turned back to concentrate on the elevator doors. Finally the light went on overhead and the doors opened, revealing a car with only four people on it. I knew it would be packed wall to wall and well over the safety code weight limit by the time it got down to the lobby.

I stepped on the elevator and turned back to look at Lankford. I doffed an imaginary hat in saying good-bye.

"It's your hat," I said. "You're not wearing your hat today."

The elevator doors closed on his dead-eyed stare.

20

The confrontation with Lankford left me agitated. On the ride down I shifted my weight from foot to foot like a boxer in his corner waiting to answer the bell. By the time I reached the ground floor I knew exactly where I had to go. Sly Fulgoni Jr. could wait. I needed to see Legal Siegel.

Forty minutes later I stepped off another elevator onto the fourth floor at Menorah Manor. As I passed the reception desk, the nurse stopped me and told me I had to open my briefcase before she would allow me to go down the hall to Legal's room.

"What are you talking about?" I said. "I'm his lawyer. You can't tell me to open my briefcase."

She responded sternly and without any give.

"Someone has been bringing food from the outside to Mr. Siegel. Not only is it a violation of the health and religious policies of this facility, it is a risk to the patient because it interferes with a carefully considered and scheduled nutrition plan."

I knew where this was headed and I refused to back down myself.

"You're calling what you feed him and what he pays for here a nutrition plan?"

"Whether patients enjoy all aspects of the food here is beside the point. If you want to visit Mr. Siegel, you will be required to open your briefcase."

"If you want to see what's in my briefcase, you show me a warrant."

"This is not a public institution, Mr. Haller, and it's not a courtroom. It is a privately owned and operated medical facility. As head nurse on this ward I have the authority to inspect anyone and anything coming through those elevator doors. We have sick people here and we must safeguard them. Either open your briefcase or I'll call security and have you removed from the premises."

To underline the threat, she put her hand on the phone that was on the counter.

I shook my head in annoyance and brought my briefcase up onto the counter. I snapped open the twin locks and flipped up the top of the case. I watched her eyes scan its contents for a long moment.

"Satisfied? There might be a stray Tic Tac in there somewhere. I hope that won't be a problem."

She ignored the crack.

"You may close it and you may now visit Mr. Siegel. Thank you."

"No, thank *you.*"

I closed the briefcase and walked down the hallway, pleased with myself but knowing I would now need a plan for the next time I actually did want to get food in to Legal. I had a briefcase in a closet at the house that I had taken in barter from a client once. It had a secret compartment that could hold a kilo of cocaine. I could easily hide a sandwich in there, maybe two.

Legal Siegel was propped up on his bed watching an Oprah rerun with the sound on too loud. His eyes were open but seemed unseeing. I closed the door and came over to the bed. I waved my hand up and down in front of his face, fearful for a moment that he was dead.

"Legal?"

He came out of the reverie, focused on me, and smiled.

"Mickey Mouse! Hey, what'd you bring me? Let me guess, tuna-avocado from Gus's in Westlake."

I shook my head.

"Sorry, Legal, I don't have anything today. It's too early for lunch anyway."

"What? Come on, give. Pork dip from Coles, right?"

"No, I mean it. I didn't bring anything. Besides, if I did, Nurse Ratched out there would have confiscated it. She's onto us and made me open my briefcase."

"Oh, that bag of wind—denying a man the simple pleasures in life!"

I put my hand on his arm in a calming gesture.

"Take it easy, Legal. She doesn't scare me. I got a plan and I'll hit Gus's on the way in next time. Okay?"

"Yeah, sure."

I pulled a chair away from the wall and sat down next to the bed. I found the remote in the folds of the bedding and muted the television.

"Thank God," Legal said. "That was driving me nuts."

"Then why didn't you turn it off?"

"Because I couldn't find the damn remote. Anyway, why did you come see me without bringing me any sustenance? You were just here yesterday, right? Pastrami from Art's in the Valley."

"You're right, Legal, and I'm glad you remember it."

"Then why'd you come back so soon?"

"Because today *I* need sustenance. Legal sustenance."

"How do you mean?"

"The La Cosse case. Things are happening and it's getting hard to see the forest for the trees."

I ticked off the cast of characters on my fingers.

"I've got a shady DEA agent out there, a crooked DA investigator, a cartel thug, and a disbarred lawyer. Then I've got my own client in the clink, and the victim in all of this is the only one I really like—or liked—in the first place. To top it all off, I'm being watched—but I'm not exactly sure by who."

"Tell me all about it."

I spent the next thirty minutes summarizing the story and answering his questions. I backed up beyond the last update I had given him and then brought the story forward, going into much finer detail than I had previously given. He asked many questions as I told the story but never offered anything back. He was simply gathering data and holding his response. I took him right up to the confrontation I'd just had with Lankford in the DA's Office waiting room, and the uneasy feeling I had that I was missing something—something right in front of me.

When I was finished, I waited for a response but he said nothing. He made a gesture with his frail hands, as if to throw the whole thing up into the air and let the wind take it. I noticed that both of his arms were purple from all the needles and the prodding and poking they did to him in this place. Getting old was not for the weak.

"That's it?" I said. "Just throw it to the wind like a bunch of flower petals? You've got nothing to say?"

"Oh, I got plenty to say and you're not going to like hearing it."

I motioned with my hand inviting him to hit me with it all.

"You're missing the big picture, Mouse."

"Really?" I said sarcastically. "What is the big picture?"

"Now you see, that's the wrong question," he lectured. "Your first question should not be what but why. Why am I missing the big picture?"

I nodded, going along only grudgingly.

"Then *why* am I missing the big picture?"

"Let's start with the report you just gave on the state of your case. You said it took that rookie shortstop you hired out of the five-and-dime to make you see things the right way at the staff meeting this morning."

He was talking about Jennifer Aronson. It was true that I'd hired her out of Southwestern, which was housed in the old Bullocks Department Store building on Wilshire. It engendered her nickname, but referring to the law school as a five-and-dime was a new low.

"I was only trying to give credit where credit was due," I said. "Jennifer may still be a rookie but she's sharper than any three lawyers I could've hired out of SC."

"Yeah, yeah, that's all well and good. She's a good lawyer, I grant you that. The thing is, you always expect yourself to be the better lawyer and deep down you hold yourself to that. So when all of a sudden this morning it's the team rookie who sees things with clarity, then that gets under your skin. You're supposed to be the smartest guy in the room."

I didn't know how to respond to that. Legal pressed on.

"I'm not your shrink. I'm a lawyer. But I think you gotta stop hitting the booze at night and you gotta get your house in order."

I stood up and started pacing in front of the bed.

"Legal, what are you talking about? My house is—"

"Your judgment and your ability to cut through the obstacles in front of you are, at best, clouded by an outside agenda."

"You're talking about my kid? My having to live with knowing my kid wants nothing to do with me? I wouldn't call that an agenda."

"I'm not talking about that per se. I am talking about the root of that. I'm talking about the guilt you carry over all of it. It is impacting you as a lawyer. Your performance as a lawyer, as a defender of the accused. And in this case, most likely, the wrongly accused."

He was talking about Sandy and Katie Patterson and the accident that took their lives. I leaned down and grabbed the iron railing at the foot of his bed with both hands. Legal Siegel was my mentor. He could tell me anything. He could dress me down lower than even my ex-wife and I would accept it.

"Listen to me," he said. "There is no more noble a cause on this planet than to stand for the wrongly accused. You can't fuck this up, kid."

I nodded and kept my head bowed.

"Guilt," he said. "You have to get by it. Let the ghosts go or they'll take you under and you'll never be the lawyer you are supposed to be. You will never see the big picture."

I threw up my hands.

"Please, enough with the big picture crap! What are you talking about, Legal? What am I missing?"

"To see what you're missing, you have to step back and widen the angle. Then you see the bigger picture."

I looked at him, trying to understand.

"When was the habeas filed?" he asked quietly.

"November."

"When was Gloria Dayton murdered?"

"November."

I said it impatiently. We both knew the answers to these questions.

"And when were you papered by the lawyer?"

"Just now—yesterday."

"And this federal agent you talked about, when was he served?"

"I don't know if he was served. But Valenzuela had the paper yesterday."

"And then there's the phony subpoena Fulgoni cooked up for the other girl from back then."

"Kendall Roberts, right."

"Any idea why he would dummy up paper for her and not you?"

I shrugged.

"I don't know. I guess he knew I'd know if it was legit or not. She's not a lawyer, so she wouldn't. He'd save the costs of filing with the court. I've heard of lawyers who roll that way."

"Seems thin to me."

"Well, that's all I got off the top of—"

"So six months after the habeas was filed with the court they put out their first subpoenas? I tell you, if I ran a shop like that I'd a been out of business and on the street. It's not the timely exercise of the law, that's for sure."

"This kid Fulgoni doesn't know his ass from—"

I stopped in midsentence. I had suddenly caught a glimpse of the elusive big picture. I looked at Legal.

"Maybe these weren't the first subpoenas."

He nodded.

"Now I think you're getting it," Legal said.

21

I told Earl to drop down to Olympic and take me out to Century City and Sly Fulgoni Jr.'s office. I then settled in with a fresh legal pad and started charting timelines on the Gloria Dayton murder case and the Hector Moya habeas petition. Pretty soon I saw how the cases were entwined like a double helix. I saw the big picture.

"You sure you got the right address, boss?"

I looked up from my chart and out the window. Earl had slowed the Lincoln in front of a row of French provincial–style town house offices. We were still on Olympic but on the eastern edge of Century City. I was sure the address carried the correct zip code and all the cachet that came with it, but it was a far cry from the gleaming towers on the Avenue of the Stars that people think of when they imagine a Century City legal firm. I had to think there would be buyer's remorse for any client who arrived here for the first time and found these digs. Then again, who was I to talk? Many was the time I dealt with buyer's remorse when my clients learned I worked out of the backseat of my car.

"Yeah," I said. "This is it."

I jumped out and headed toward the door. I entered a small reception room with a well-worn carpet leading from the front of the reception desk in twin paths to doors to the right and left. The door on the left had a name on it I didn't recognize. The door on the right had the name Sylvester Fulgoni. I got the feeling that Sly Jr. was splitting the space with another attorney. Probably the secretary, too, but at the moment there was no secretary to share. The reception desk was empty.

"Hello?" I said.

Nobody replied. I looked down at the paperwork and mail piled on the desk and saw that on top was a photocopy of Sly Jr.'s court calendar. Only I saw very few court dates recorded on it for the month. Sly didn't have much work — at least work that took him inside a courthouse. I did see that he had me down for a deposition scheduled for the following Tuesday, but there were no notations about James Marco or Kendall Roberts.

"Hello?" I called out again.

This time I was louder but still got no response. I stepped over to the Fulgoni door and leaned my ear to the jamb. I heard nothing. I knocked and tried the knob. It was unlocked and I pushed the door open, revealing a young man seated behind a large ornate desk that bespoke better times than the rest of the office presented.

"Excuse me, can I help you?" the man said, seemingly annoyed by the intrusion.

He closed a laptop computer that was on the desk in front of him, but didn't get up. I stepped two feet into the office. I saw no one else in the room.

"I'm looking for Sly Jr.," I said. "Is that you?"

"I'm sorry but my practice is by appointment only. You'll have to set up an appointment and come back."

"There's no receptionist."

"My secretary is at lunch and I'm very busy at the — wait, you're Haller, aren't you?"

He pointed a finger at me and put his other hand on the arm of his chair like he was bracing himself in case he had to cut and run. I raised my hands to show I was unarmed.

"I come in peace."

He looked like he was no more than twenty-five. He was struggling to produce a reasonable goatee and was wearing a

Dodgers game jersey. It was obvious he didn't have court today, or maybe any day.

"What do you want?" he asked.

I took a few more steps toward the desk. It was gigantic and way too big for the space—obviously a leftover from his father's practice in a better, bigger office. I pulled back one of the chairs positioned in front of the desk and sat down.

"Don't sit. You can't—"

I was seated.

"All right, go ahead."

I nodded my thanks and smiled. I pointed at the desk.

"Nice," I said. "A hand-me-down from the old man?"

"Look, what do you want?"

"I told you. I come in peace. What are you so jumpy about?"

He blew out his breath in exasperation.

"I don't like people barging in on me. This is a law office. You wouldn't want people just—oh, that's right, you don't even have an office. I saw the movie."

"I didn't just barge in. There was no secretary. I called out and then tried the door."

"I told you, she's at lunch. It's the lunch hour. Look, can we get this over with? What do you want? State your business and then leave."

He dramatically chopped the air with his hand.

"Look," I said, "I'm here because we got off on the wrong foot and I apologize. It was my fault. I was treating you—and your father—like we were foes on this case. But I don't think it's got to be that way. So I'm here to make peace and to see if we might be able to help each other out. You know, I show you mine if you show me yours."

He shook his head.

"No, we're not doing this. I have a case and you have whatever the fuck you have, but we're not working together."

I leaned forward and tried to hold eye contact but the kid was all over the place.

"We have similar causes of action, Sly. Your client Hector Moya and my client Andre La Cosse stand to benefit by our working together and sharing information."

He shook his head dismissively.

"I don't think so."

I looked around the room and noticed his diplomas framed on the wall. The print was too small for me to read from a distance but I didn't think I was dealing with an Ivy Leaguer here. I decided to put some of what I was thinking and had charted in the car out there to see how it went over.

"My client is charged with the murder of Gloria Dayton, who figures importantly in your habeas petition. The thing is, I don't think he did it."

"Well, good for you. It's not our concern."

I was beginning to suspect that his use of "our" did not refer to him and Hector Moya. It was a reference to Team Fulgoni—Mr. Inside and Mr. Outside. Only Mr. Outside didn't know habeas corpus from corpus delicti and I was talking to the wrong man.

I decided to go ahead and hit him with the big question. The question that had emerged when I stepped back and looked at the big picture.

"Answer one question and I'll go. Last year, did you try to subpoena Gloria Dayton before she was murdered?"

Fulgoni emphatically shook his head.

"I'm not talking to you about our case."

"Did you have Valenzuela do it?"

"I told you, I'm not talk—"

"I don't understand. We can help each other."

"Then you talk to my father and try to convince him, because I'm not at liberty to discuss anything with you. You have to go now."

I made no move to get up. I just stared at him. He made a gesture with his hands as if pushing me away.

"Please *go.*"

"Did somebody get to you, Sly?"

"Get to me? I don't know what you're talking about."

"Why'd you dummy up the subpoena you had Valenzuela serve on Kendall Roberts?"

He brought a hand up and pinched the bridge of his nose as if trying to ward off a headache.

"I'm not saying another fucking word."

"All right, then I'll talk to your father. Call him right now, put him on speaker."

"I can't just call him. He's in prison."

"Why not? He talked to me last night on a phone."

This raised Sly's eyebrows.

"Yeah, when I was with Trina."

His eyebrows arched again and then flatlined.

"There you go. He can only call out after midnight."

"Come on, man. He's got a cell phone up there. Half my clients do. Big fucking secret."

"Yeah, but at Victorville they've got a jammer. And my dad's got a guy who turns it off for him—but only *after midnight*. And if you've got guys with phones, then you know you never call in. They only call out. When it's safe."

I nodded. He was right. I knew from experience with other incarcerated clients that cell phones were common contraband in almost all jails and prisons. Rather than rely on finding them through constant body cavity and prison cell searches, many correctional institutions employed cellular blockers that eliminated the use of the phones. Sly Sr. obviously had a friendly guard— most likely a guard paid to be friendly—with his hand on the switch during the midnight shift. This was a confirmation that the call from Sly Sr. the night before was coincidence and did not come about because he was having me followed. It meant someone else was.

"How often does he call you?" I asked.

"I'm not telling you that," Sly Jr. said. "We're finished here."

My guess was that Sly Sr. called every night with a to-do list for the following day. Junior did not appear to be much of a self-starter. I was dying to get a look at that diploma so I could see what law school gave him a skin but decided it wasn't worth the effort. I knew lawyers from top schools who couldn't find their way out of a courtroom. And I knew night-school lawyers who I'd call in a heartbeat if it was ever my wrists in the cuffs. It was all about the lawyer, not the law school.

I stood up and pushed the chair back into place.

"Okay, Sylvester, this is what you do. When Daddy calls tonight, tell him I'm coming up to see him tomorrow. I'm going to register at the gate as his lawyer. Moya's, too. You and I are co-counsel. You assure Daddy that I am seeking cooperation of our two camps, not an adversarial relationship. Tell him he better take the interview and hear me out. Tell him to tell Hector the same thing. Tell him not to turn down these interviews or things are going to get uncomfortable for him up there in the desert."

"What the fuck you talking about? Co-counsel? Bullshit."

I stepped back toward the desk and leaned down, two hands on the mahogany. Sly Jr. leaned back as far as he could in his chair.

"Let me tell you something, Junior. If I drive two hours up there and this doesn't go down exactly as I just said it's to go down, then two things are going to happen. One is that the jammer is going to start staying on all night, leaving you high and dry down here without a clue about what to do and what to file and what to say. And second, the California bar is going to take an intimate interest in this little arrangement you've got with Daddy. It'll be called practicing law without a license for Daddy. For you it will be practicing law without knowing the first fucking thing about the law."

I straightened up and made to leave but then turned right back to him.

"And when I talk to the bar, I'll throw in that phony subpoena, too. They probably won't like that much either."

"You're an asshole, you know that, Haller?"

I nodded and headed back to the door.

"When I need to be."

I walked out, leaving the door wide open behind me.

22

The Lincoln was waiting where I had left it. I jumped into the backseat and was greeted by the sight of a man sitting across from me and directly behind Earl. I glanced at my driver's eyes in the mirror and saw an almost apologetic look in them.

I drew my attention back to the stranger. He wore aviator sunglasses, worn blue jeans, and a black golf shirt. He had a dark complexion matched with dark hair and a mustache. My immediate thought was that he looked like a cartel hit man.

The man smiled when he recognized the look in my eyes.

"Relax, Haller," he said. "I'm not who you think I am."

"Then who the hell are you?" I asked.

"You know who I am."

"Marco?"

He smiled again.

"Why don't you tell your driver to take a walk?"

I hesitated a moment and then looked at Earl in the rearview.

"Go ahead, Earl. But stay close. Where I can see you."

What I really wanted was for Earl to be able to see me. I wanted a witness because I didn't know what Marco was about to pull.

"You sure?" Earl asked.

"Yeah," I said. "Go ahead."

Earl got out of the car and closed the door. He walked a few feet forward and leaned against the front fender of the car with his arms folded. I looked across the seat at Marco.

"Okay, what do you want?" I said. "Are you following me?"

He seemed to ruminate on the questions before deciding to answer.

"No, I'm not following you," he finally said. "I came to check out a lawyer who's been trying to paper me and here I see you. You and him, working together."

It was a good answer because it was plausible. It avoided confirmation that Marco had been the one who had jacked my car, and he seemed pleased with it, even though he had not convinced me. I put Marco in his midforties. He carried an aura about him, a sense of confidence and knowledge, like a guy who knows he's two moves ahead of everybody else.

"What do you want?" I asked again.

"What I want is to help you avoid fucking up in a major way."

"And what way is that?"

Marco proceeded as though he had not heard the question.

"Do you know the word *sicario,* Counselor?"

He said it with full Latin inflection. I glanced away from him and out the window, then I looked back.

"I've heard it said, I think."

"There is no real English translation for the word, but it's what they call the cartel assassins down in Mexico. *Sicarios.*"

"Thanks for the education."

"Down there the laws are different than we've got up here. Do you know that they have no legal code or provision that allows a teenager to be charged as an adult? No matter what they do, no charges as an adult and no incarceration beyond the age of eighteen for the crimes they commit as children."

"That's good to know for the next time I'm down there, Marco, but I practice law right here in California."

"Consequently, the cartels recruit and train teenagers as their *sicarios.* If they get caught and convicted, they do a year, maybe two, and then they're out at eighteen and ready to go back to work. You see?"

"I see that it's a real tragedy. No way those boys come out rehabilitated, that's for sure."

Marco showed no reaction to my sarcasm.

"At sixteen years of age Hector Arrande Moya admitted in a courtroom in Culiacán in the state of Sinaloa that he had tortured and murdered seven people by the time he was fifteen. Two of them were women. Three of them he hung in a basement and four he set on fire while they were still alive. He raped both the women and he cut all of the bodies up afterward and fed the remains to the coyotes in the hills."

"And what's that have to do with me?"

"He did all of this on orders from the cartel. You see, he was raised in the cartel. And when he got out of the *penta* at eighteen he went right back to the cartel. By then, of course, he had a nickname. They called him *El Fuego*—because he burned people."

I checked my watch in a show of impatience.

"That's a good story, but why tell it to me, Marco? What about you? What about the—"

"This is the man you conspire with Fulgoni to set free. *El Fuego*."

I shook my head.

"I don't know what you're talking about. The only person I am trying to set free is Andre La Cosse. He is sitting in a cell right now, charged with a murder he didn't commit. But I'll tell you this much about Hector Moya. You want to put the motherfucker away for life, then make the case fair and square in the first place. Don't—"

I cut myself off and raised my hands, palms out. Enough.

"Just get out of my car now," I said quietly. "If I need to talk to you, I'll talk to you in court."

"There's a war, Haller, and you have to choose which side you're on. There are sacrifices that—"

"Oh, now you're going to talk to me about choices? What

about Gloria Dayton, was she a choice? Was she a sacrifice? Fuck you, Marco. There are rules, rules of law. Now get out of my car."

For five seconds we just stared at each other. But finally Marco blinked. He cracked his door and slowly backed out of the car. He then leaned down and looked back in at me.

"Jennifer Aronson."

I spread my hands as if waiting for whatever it was he still had to say.

"Who?"

He smiled.

"Just tell her if she wants to know about me, she can come right to me. Anytime. No need to sneak around the courthouse, pulling files, whispering questions. I'm right here. All the time."

He closed the door and walked off. I watched him as he went down the sidewalk and turned the corner. He didn't go into Fulgoni's office, even though he had claimed that was the reason he was in the vicinity and had spotted me.

Soon Earl got back in behind the wheel.

"You okay, boss?"

"I'm fine. Let's go."

He started the car. My frustrations and feelings of vulnerability got the best of me and I snapped at Earl.

"How the hell did that guy get in the car?"

"He came up and knocked on the window. He showed me the badge and told me to unlock the back. I thought he was gonna put a slug in the back a my head."

"Great, and you just let me jump in the back with him."

"There was nothin' I could do, boss. He told me not to move. What did he say?"

"A bunch of self-deluding bullshit. Let's go."

"Where to?"

"I don't know. Head toward the loft. For now."

I immediately got on the phone and called Jennifer. I didn't want to scare her but it was clear that Marco knew of her efforts to background him and check other cases he had been involved in.

The call went straight to message. As I listened to her recorded voice, I debated whether to leave a full message or just tell her to call me. I decided it would be best and perhaps safest to leave her the message so she got the information as soon as she turned on her phone.

"Jennifer, it's me. I just had a little visit from Agent Marco, and he is aware of your efforts to document his history. He must have friends in the clerk's office or wherever you're pulling records. So I'm thinking you might want to keep what you got on that but switch back to Moya. I'm going up to see him tomorrow in Victorville and I'd like to know all there is to know by then anyway. Let me know that you got this. Bye."

Cisco was next and this time my call went through. I told him of my encounter with Marco and asked why there had been no heads-up from the Indians who were supposedly watching me for a tail. I wasn't too pleasant about it.

"No warning, Cisco. The guy was waiting for me in my fucking car."

"I don't know what happened but I'll find out."

He sounded as annoyed as I was.

"Yeah, do that and call me back."

I disconnected the call. Earl and I rode in silence for a few minutes after that, with me replaying the Marco conversation in my head. I was trying to figure out the motives for the visit from the DEA agent. First and foremost, I decided, was the threat. He wanted to put a chill on my team's efforts to research his activities. He also, it would seem, wanted to steer me away from the Moya case. He probably felt that Moya's conviction and life sentence were relatively safe with the inexperienced Sly Fulgoni Jr. at the helm of the habeas petition. And he was probably right. But hitting me with the description of Moya as the worst thing this side of the devil was just a front. Marco's motives weren't altruistic. I didn't buy that for a moment. All in all, I concluded that Marco was trying to spook me because I had spooked him. And that meant we were pointed in the right direction.

"Hey, boss?"

I looked at Earl in the rearview.

"I heard you telling Jennifer in that message that you're goin' up to Victorville tomorrow. That true? We're goin' up?"

I nodded.

"Yeah, we're going. First thing in the morning."

And in saying so out loud I also sent a silent fuck-you to Marco.

My phone buzzed and it was Cisco, already back with an explanation.

"Sorry, Mick, they fucked up. They saw the guy arrive and get in the car with Earl. They said he showed a badge but they didn't know who he was. They thought it was a friendly."

"A friendly? The guy has to badge Earl to get in the car and they think he's a fucking friendly? They should've called you on the spot so you could call me and stop me from coming out with my goddamn zipper down."

"Already told them all of that. You want me to pull them off now?"

"What? Why?"

"Well, it seems pretty clear we know who jacked your car, right?"

I thought about Marco's claim that he had just happened to see me while he was checking out Fulgoni because of the subpoena. I didn't buy that for a moment. I agreed with Cisco; Marco had jacked my car.

"Might as well save the dough," I told Cisco. "Pull 'em off. They weren't much in the early-warning department anyway."

"You want us to pull the GPS off the car, too?"

I thought about that for a moment and my plans for the next day. I decided I wanted to taunt Marco, show him I was unbowed by his little visit and unspoken threat.

"No, leave it. For now."

"Okay, Mick. And for what it's worth, the guys are really sorry."

"Yeah, whatever. I gotta go."

I disconnected. I had noticed out the windshield that Earl was cutting through Beverly Hills on Little Santa Monica Boulevard on the way to my house. I was starved and knew we were coming up on Papa Jake's, a hole-in-the-wall lunch counter that made the best steak sandwich west of Philadelphia. I had not been there since the nearby Beverly Hills Superior Court was shuttered in the state budget crisis, and I had lost business that would bring me to the area. But in the meantime I had developed a Legal Siegel–type craving for a Jake steak with grilled onions and pizzaiola sauce.

"Earl," I said. "We're going to make a stop for lunch up here. And if that DEA agent is still following, he's about to learn the best-kept secret in Beverly Hills."

23

After the late lunch, I was through for the day. My calendar was clear and I had no further appointments. I considered heading back downtown and seeing if I could line up a visit with Andre La Cosse to go over some things related to the upcoming trial. But the occurrences of the past few hours—from Legal Siegel's lecture to the meet with Sly Jr. and the surprise visit from Marco—led me toward home. I'd had enough for the time being.

I had Earl drive to the loft so he could get his care where he had left it after coming in for the staff meeting. I then drove home, stopping only long enough to change into clothes more appropriate to hiking through the wilds of Fryman Canyon. It had been a long while since I'd seen my daughter in the goal at practice. I knew from the school's online newsletter that there were only a few weeks left in the season and the team was getting ready for the state tournament. I decided to go over the hill to watch and maybe escape from thoughts on the La Cosse case for a while.

But escape was delayed—at least on the ride up Laurel Canyon Boulevard. Jennifer called me back and told me she had received my message and my direction to step back from the search on Marco.

"I'd asked for some court files on other ICE cases because the stuff on PACER seemed incomplete," she explained. "I bet one of those counter clerks called him and told him."

"Anything's possible. So just stick with Moya for now."

"Got it."

"Can you get me whatever you've got by the end of the day? I've got a long drive up to the prison tomorrow and I could use the reading material."

"Will do…"

There was a hesitancy about the way she said it. As though there was something else she wanted to say.

"Anything else?" I asked.

"I don't know. I guess I am still wondering if we are going the right way with this. Moya is a better target for us than the DEA."

I knew what she meant. Casting suspicion on Moya in the upcoming trial would be a lot easier and possibly more fruitful than throwing the light on a federal agent. Aronson was getting at the fine line between seeking the truth and seeking a verdict in your client's favor. They weren't always the same thing.

"I know what you mean," I said. "But sometimes you gotta go with your instincts, and mine tell me this is the way to go. If I'm right, the truth shall set Andre free."

"I hope so."

I could tell she was not convinced or something else was bothering her.

"You okay with this?" I asked. "If not, I can handle it and you just deal with the other clients."

"No, I'm fine. It's just a little weird, you know? Things are upside down."

"What things?"

"You know, the good guys might be the bad guys. And the bad guy up in prison might be our best hope."

"Yeah, weird."

I ended the call by reminding her to get the summaries of her research to me before I hit the road to Victorville the next morning. She promised she would and we said good-bye.

Fifteen minutes later I pulled into the parking lot at the top of Fryman Canyon. I grabbed the binoculars out of the glove box, locked the car, and made my way down the trail. I then left the beaten path to get to my observation spot. Only when I got there, the rock I had positioned had been moved, and it looked like someone had been using the spot, possibly to sleep at night. The tall grass was matted down in a pattern that would fit a sleeping bag. I looked carefully around to make sure I was alone and moved the rock back to the way I'd had it.

Down below, soccer practice was just getting under way. I put the binoculars to my eyes and started checking out the north net. The goalkeeper had red hair in a ponytail. It wasn't Hayley. I checked the other net, and there was another goalkeeper but she wasn't my daughter either. I wondered if she had switched positions and started scanning the field. I checked each player but still didn't see her. No number 7.

I let the binoculars hang from my neck and pulled my phone out. I called my ex-wife's work number at the Van Nuys Division of the District Attorney's Office. The pool secretary put me on hold and then came back and told me Maggie McPherson was unavailable because she was in court. I knew this was not correct, because Maggie was a filing deputy. She was never in court anymore—one of the many things I was held responsible for in the relationship, if it could still be called a relationship.

I tried her cell next, even though she had instructed me never to call the cell during work hours unless it was an emergency. She did take this call.

"Michael?"

"Where's Hayley?"

"What do you mean, she's at home. I just talked to her."

"Why isn't she at soccer practice?"

"What?"

"Soccer practice. She's not there. Is she hurt or sick?"

There was a pause, and in it I knew I was about to learn something that as a father I should have already known.

"She's fine. She quit soccer more than a month ago."

"What? Why?"

"Well, she was getting more into riding and she couldn't do both and keep up with her schoolwork. So she quit. I thought I told you. I sent you an e-mail."

Thanks to the multitude of legal associations I belonged to and the many incarcerated clients who had my e-mail address, I had more than ten thousand messages sitting in my e-mail file. The messages I had cleared earlier in the day while in the DA's waiting room represented only the tip of the iceberg. So many were unread that I knew there could have been an e-mail about this, but I usually didn't miss messages from Maggie or my daughter. Still, I wasn't on firm enough ground to argue the point, so I moved on.

"You mean horse riding?"

"Yes, hunter-jumper. She goes to the L.A. Equestrian Center near Burbank."

Now I had to pause. I was embarrassed that I knew so little about what was going on in my daughter's life. It didn't matter that it had not been my choice to be shut out. I was the father and it was my fault regardless.

"Michael, listen, I was going to tell you this at a better time but I might as well tell you now so I know you got the message. I've taken another job, and we're going to move to Ventura County this summer."

The second impact on a one-two punch combination is supposed to land harder. And this one did.

"When did this happen? What job?"

"I told them here yesterday. I'm giving a month's notice, then I'll take a month off to look for a place and get everything ready. Hayley's going to finish the school year here. Then we'll move."

Ventura was the next county up the coast. Depending on where they moved to, Maggie and my daughter would be anywhere from an hour to an hour and a half away. There were some distances even within Los Angeles County that could take longer to travel because of traffic. But still, they might as well have been moving to Germany.

"What job are you taking?"

"It's with the Ventura DA's Office. I'm starting a Digital Crime Unit. And I'll be back in court again."

And of course it all came back on me. My losing the election had dismantled her career at the L.A. County DA's Office. For an agency charged with the fair and equal enforcement of the laws of the state, the place was one of the most political bureaucracies in the county. Maggie McPherson had backed me in the election. When I lost, she lost, too. As soon as Damon Kennedy took the reins, she was transferred out of a courtroom and into the divisional office, where she filed cases other deputies would take to trial. In a way she got lucky. She could've gotten worse. One deputy who introduced me at an election rally when I was the front-runner ended up with a transfer out to the courtroom in the Antelope Valley jail.

Like Maggie, he quit. And I understood why Maggie would quit. I also understood that she would not be able to cross the aisle to defense work or take a slot in a corporate law firm. She was a dyed-in-the-wool prosecutor and there was no choice about what she would do —it was only where she would do it. In that regard I knew that I should be happy that she was merely moving to a neighboring county and not up to San Francisco or Oakland or down to San Diego.

"So where are you going to look out there?"

"Well, the job is in the City of Ventura, so either there or not too far from it. I'd like to look at Ojai but it might be too expensive. I'm thinking Hayley would fit in real well with the riding."

Ojai was a crunchy, New Agey village in a mountain valley in the northern county. Years back, before we had our daughter, Maggie and I used to go there on weekends. There was even a chance our daughter was conceived there.

"So...this riding is not a passing thing?"

"It could be. You never know. But she's fully engaged for now. We leased a horse for six months. With an option to buy."

I shook my head. This was painful. Never mind my ex-wife, but Hayley had told me none of this.

"I'm sorry," Maggie said. "I know this is tough on you. I want you to know that I don't encourage it. No matter what is going on with us, I think she should have a relationship with her father. I really mean that and that's what I tell her."

"I appreciate that."

I didn't know what else to say. I stood up off the rock. I wanted to get out of there and go home.

"Can you do me a favor?" I asked.

"What is it?"

I realized that I was improvising, running with a half-formed idea that had sprung from my grief and desire to somehow win my daughter back.

"There's a trial coming up," I said. "I want her to come."

"You're talking about this pimp you're representing? Michael, no, I don't want her to sit through that. Besides, she has school."

"He's innocent."

"Really? Are you trying to play me like a jury now?"

"No, I mean it. Innocent. He didn't do it, and I'm going to prove it. If Hay could be there, maybe—"

"I don't know. I'll think about it. There's school, and I don't want her taking time off. There's also the move."

"Come for the verdict. Both of you."

"Look, I have to get going. The cops are stacking up around here."

Cops waiting in the office to file their cases.

"Okay, but think about it."

"All right, I will. I've got to go now."

"Wait—one last thing. Can you e-mail me a picture of Hayley on the horse? I'd just like to see it."

"Sure. I will."

She disconnected after that and I stared down at the soccer field for a few moments, replaying the conversation and trying to compute all the news about my daughter. I thought about what Legal Siegel had told me about moving on past guilt. I realized that some things were easier said than done, and some things were impossible.

24

At seven p.m. that night I walked down the hill and over to the little market at the base of Laurel Canyon. I called for a cab and waited fifteen minutes, reading the community notices on the corkboard out front. The cab took me over the hill and down into the Valley. I had the driver drop me on Ventura Boulevard by Coldwater Canyon. From there I walked the last five blocks to Flex, arriving at the yoga studio shortly before eight.

Kendall Roberts was busy with closing duties at the front counter. Her hair was tied up in a knot on top of her head and there was a pencil stuck through it. The students from the last class were filing out, rolled rubber mats under their arms. I stepped in, got her attention, and asked if I could speak with her after she locked up. She hesitated. I had not told her I was coming by.

"Are you hungry?" I asked.

"I taught four classes back-to-back. I'm starved."

"Have you ever been to Katsuya down the street here? It's pretty good. It's sushi, if you like that."

"I love sushi, but I haven't been there."

"Why don't I go down, get a table, and you come when you're finished here?"

She hesitated again, as though she was still trying to figure out my motives.

"It won't be a late night," I promised.

She finally nodded.

"Okay, I'll see you there. It might be fifteen minutes. I need to freshen up."

"Take your time. You like sake?"

"Love it."

"Hot or cold?"

"Uh, cold."

"See you there."

I walked down Ventura and stepped into Katsuya, only to find the place crowded with sushi enthusiasts. There were no tables available, but I secured two stools at the sushi bar. I ordered the sake and some cucumber salad and pulled out my phone as I began the wait for Kendall.

My ex-wife had come through with an e-mailed photo of my daughter and her horse. The shot showed Hayley with the horse's face leaning over her shoulder from behind. The animal was black with a white lightning-bolt stripe running down its long nose. Both girl and horse were gorgeous. I was proud, but seeing the photo only added to my hurt at the news about the impending move to Ventura County.

I switched over to the message app and composed a text to my daughter. She read her e-mails only once or twice a week and I knew that if I wanted to get a message through without delay I needed to text.

I told her that her mother had sent me the photo of her and her horse and that I was proud of her for pursuing riding the way she was. I also said I had heard about the impending move and that I was sorry she'd be so far away but that I understood. I asked her if I could watch her take a lesson on the horse and left it at that. I sent it off into the air and foolishly thought I might get an answer soon after my phone reported the message delivered. But nothing came back.

I was about to compose another text, asking if she got the first, when Kendall suddenly appeared at the open stool next to me. I put the phone in my pocket as I stood up to greet her, successfully avoiding the embarrassment that second text would have brought me.

"Hi," Kendall said cheerfully.

She had changed clothes at the studio and was wearing blue jeans and a peasant shirt. Her hair was down and she looked great.

"Hello," I said. "I'm glad you could make it."

She kissed me on the cheek as she squeezed by me and onto the stool. It was unexpected but nice. I poured her a cup of sake and we toasted and tasted. I watched her face for a negative reaction to the sake but she accepted my selection.

"How are you doing?" I asked.

"I'm good. I had a good day. What about you? Kind of a surprise to see you come in the studio tonight."

"Yeah, well, I need to talk to you about something, but let's order first."

We studied the sushi list together and Kendall checked off three different variations on spicy tuna, while I went with California and cucumber rolls. Before the election I had started taking my daughter to Katsuya as her palate grew sophisticated and Wednesday-night pancakes stopped being an attraction. Of course my food interests were stunted compared to hers, and I could never wrap my mind around the idea of uncooked fish. But there were always plenty of other things to eat for the nonadventurous.

Sake was another story. Hot or cold I liked it. I was into my third cup by the time one of the sushi chefs finally leaned over and took our order. I think the quick draw on the drink was in part due to my reason for being there and the conversation I felt obligated to have with Kendall.

"So what's up?" she said after expertly using a pair of chopsticks to sample the cucumber salad I had previously ordered. "This is like last night—you didn't have to come all the way out to see me."

"No, I wanted to see you," I said. "But I also need to talk to you more about this case with Moya and Marco, the DEA agent."

She frowned.

"Please don't tell me I have to go there and talk to that lawyer."

"No, nothing like that. There's no depo and I'll make sure it stays that way. But something else came up today."

I paused as I still had not formulated how I wanted to approach her with this.

"Well, what is it?" she prompted.

"The case is kind of dicey because of the people involved. You've got Moya up there in prison and then you have Marco, the DEA agent, down here, trying to protect himself and his cases. And in the middle of this, you have what happened to Gloria and then my client, who they charged with her killing but I don't think did it. So a lot of moving parts in this and then this morning I found out that there's a tracker on my car."

"What do you mean? What's a tracker?"

"Like a GPS thing. It means somebody's tracking me. They know what moves I'm making—at least by car."

I turned on my stool so I could look at her and directly see how she took this information. I could see the significance of it didn't register to her.

"I don't know how long the device has been on there," I said. "But I went to your house twice yesterday. First with Earl and then last night by myself."

Now it started to register. I saw the first inkling of fear move into her eyes.

"What does this mean? Somebody's going to come to my house?"

"No, I don't think it means that. There's no reason to panic. But I thought you should know."

"Who put it there?"

"We're not a hundred percent sure but we think it was the DEA agent. Marco."

At this inopportune moment the sushi chef lifted a large leaf-shaped plate over the counter and put it down in front of us. Five sliced rolls were displayed beautifully with pickled ginger and the hot wasabi paste that my daughter called green death. I nodded my thanks to the chef, and Kendall just stared at the food while considering what I just told her.

"I debated whether to even tell you," I said. "But I thought you should know. Tonight I took precautions. I walked down the hill from my house and caught a cab. They won't know I'm with you. My car's sitting out in front of my house."

"How do you know you're not being followed, too?"

"I've had people working on that all day. It looks like it's just the electronic tracker."

If that brought any measure of comfort to her she didn't show it.

"Can't you just take it off and get rid of it?" she asked.

"That's an option," I said, nodding. "But there are other options. We might be able to use it against them. You know, feed them information that will be confusing or wrong. We're still thinking about it, so for now it's still on there. Why don't you eat some of this?"

"I'm not sure I'm hungry anymore."

"Come on, you worked hard all day. You said you were starving."

Reluctantly she poured a dollop of soy sauce into one of the small dishes and mixed in a dab of wasabi paste. She then dipped a slice of one of the tuna rolls and ate it. She liked it and immediately sampled another. I was useless with chopsticks so I used my fingers to take a slice of California roll. I skipped the wasabi.

Two bites later and I was back to business.

"Kendall, I know I asked you this yesterday but I need to do it again. This DEA agent, James Marco, are you sure you never had dealings with him? He's a dark-haired guy about forty now. Has a mustache, mean eyes. He—"

"If he's DEA, you don't have to describe him. I never had any dealings with the DEA."

I nodded.

"Okay, and you can't think of any reason you might be on his radar in regard to Gloria Dayton, right?"

"No, no reason."

"You told me yesterday that one of the services you provided was to bring cocaine. Gloria and Trina got theirs from Moya. Where did you get yours?"

Kendall slowly finished the piece of California roll she was eating and then put her chopsticks down on the little stand next to her plate.

"I really don't like talking about this," she said. "I think you brought me here so I would feel cornered and have to answer."

"No," I said quickly. "That's not true and I don't want you to feel cornered. I'm sorry if I'm pushing this too far. I just want to be sure you're in the clear, that's all."

She wiped her mouth with her napkin. I had a feeling the dinner was over.

"I need to go to the restroom," she said.

"Okay," I said.

I stood up and pushed my stool back so she would have room for egress.

"Are you coming back?" I asked.

"Yes, I'll be back," she said curtly.

I sat back down and watched her as she made her way to the hallway in the back. I knew she could leave through a rear door and I wouldn't know it for ten minutes. But I had faith.

I pulled out my phone to see if my daughter had answered my text but she hadn't. I thought about texting her again, maybe sending her a photo of the California roll from Katsuya but decided not to push it.

Kendall returned in less than five minutes and slid silently back onto her stool. Before I could speak, she made a statement that she had apparently worked out in the restroom.

"I got the product that I brought to clients from Hector Moya but it was indirectly from him. I bought it from Gloria and Trina at their cost. I never once met their dealer or crossed paths with a DEA agent while I was in that life. It's something I've left behind and I don't want to have to talk about it with you or anybody else again."

"That's perfectly fine, Kendall. I under—"

"When you asked me to dinner I was very happy. I thought... I thought it was for a different reason and I was excited. So that's why I reacted the way I did when you asked about the drugs."

"I'm sorry I messed things up. But believe me, I was excited, too, when you said you would meet me. So why don't we forget about all the work stuff and eat some sushi?"

I gestured toward the platter. Most of our order was still there. She smiled tentatively and nodded. I smiled back.

"Then we need more sake," I said.

25

On the way back home I decided to let the cab take me all the way to my door. I was tired from the work and news of the day and the hike up the trail at Fryman Canyon. I figured even if someone was watching my house and car, he would only be able to puzzle over where I'd been for the last four hours. I paid the fare, got out, and climbed the stairs to the front door.

At the top I paused to look out across the iridescent landscape. It was a clear night and I could see all the way to the lighted towers in Century City. It reminded me that somewhere near those towers in the lowlands was where Sly Fulgoni Jr. made his pitiful stand in the land of law.

I turned and looked over my other shoulder toward downtown. Farther away, the lights seemed less vibrant, having to fight their way through the smog. I could, however, see the glow of lights from Chavez Ravine—a home game for the Dodgers, who had started the season abysmally.

I opened the door and went in. I was tempted to put on the radio and listen to the ageless Vin Scully call the game but I was too tired. I went to the kitchen to get a bottle of water, pausing for a moment to look at the postcard from Hawaii on the fridge. I then went directly to my bedroom to crash.

Two hours later I was on a black horse galloping out of control across a dark landscape lit only by cracks of lightning when my phone woke me.

I was in bed, still fully clothed. I stared at the ceiling, trying to remember the dream when the phone rang again. I reached into my pocket for it and answered without looking at the display. For some reason I expected it to be my daughter, and a tone of desperation infected my hello.

"Haller?"

"Yes, who is this?"

"Sly Fulgoni. Are you all right?"

The deeper timbre in the voice told me I was talking to Sly Sr., calling in from Victorville again.

"I'm fine. How'd you get this number?"

"Valenzuela gave it to me. He doesn't like you too much, Haller. Something about unfulfilled promises."

I sat up on the side of the bed and looked at the clock. It was two ten.

"Yeah, well, fuck him," I said. "Why are you calling me, Sly? I'm coming up to see you tomorrow."

"Yeah, not so fast, smart guy. I don't like you threatening me. Or my son, for that matter. So we need to get a few things straight before you make the long drive up here."

"Hold on."

I put the phone down on the bed and turned on the bed lamp. I opened the bottle of water I had retrieved before going to sleep and drank almost half of it down. It helped clear my head.

I then picked up the phone again.

"You there, Sly?"

"Where else am I gonna go?"

"Right. So what things do we need to straighten out?"

"First of all, this co-counsel bullshit you laid on young Sly. Not going to fly, Haller. Moya's ours and we're not sharing."

"Have you really thought this out?"

"What's to think out? We've got it covered."

"Sly, you're in prison. It's going to reach a point where the paper on this is finished and somebody's got to go to court. And do you really think *young* Sly is going to walk into federal court, go up against government lawyers and the DEA, and not have his head handed to him?"

There was no immediate answer, so I pressed it further.

"I'm a father, too, Sly. And we all love our kids, but young Sly is working off of the scripts you provide him right now. There is no script when you get into a courtroom. It's do or die."

Still no response.

"I didn't have an appointment when I dropped by the office today. I don't know exactly what he was doing but it wasn't lawyer work. He's got nothing on the calendar, Sly. He's got no experience and he can't even answer questions about this case. Those depos you want scheduled for next week? My guess is he'll get the questions—every question—from you."

"Not true. That's not true."

His first objection to anything I had been saying.

"All right, so he'll write some of his own questions. It's still your depo and you know it. Look, Sly, you've got a credible cause of action here. I think this could work but not unless you've got somebody going in there who knows his way around a habeas hearing."

"How much you want?"

This time I paused. I knew that I had him and was about to close the deal.

"You're talking about money? I don't want any money. I want cooperation on my guy. We share information and we share Moya. I may need him on my case."

He didn't respond. He was thinking. I decided to jump in with my closing argument.

"Speaking of Moya, you really want him sitting next to young Sly if this thing goes the wrong way in court? You want him looking at your son when he wants someone to blame after a judge sends him back to Victorville for the rest of his life? I heard some stories today about Moya back in his Sinaloa days. He's not the kind of guy you want near your son when things turn south."

"Who told you those stories?"

"Agent Marco did. He visited me, just like I'm sure he visited Young Sly."

Sly Sr. didn't respond but this time I didn't interrupt the silence. I'd said all I had to say. Now I waited.

But it didn't take long.

"When will you get here?" Sly Sr. asked.

"Well, it's the middle of the night. I'm going to go back to sleep now and sleep late. Maybe eight o'clock and then I'll head up there. I'll process in when I get there, maybe get in to see you before lunch."

"Lunch around here is at ten-fucking-thirty. I used to have a one-o'clock table every day at Water Grill."

I nodded. The little things are missed most.

"Okay, then I'll see you after lunch. First you, then Moya. You remind him that this time I'm on his side. Okay?"

"Okay."

"See you then."

I disconnected the call and switched over to the message app. My daughter had still not responded to the message I had sent her almost six hours before.

I set the alarm on the phone for seven and put it on the nightstand. I stripped off my clothes and this time got under the covers. I lay on my back, thinking about things. My daughter, then Kendall. She had kissed me again when we'd separated outside the door of Katsuya. I felt as though things were changing in me. As though I was closing one door and opening another. It made me sad and hopeful at the same time.

Before drifting off I remembered the black horse racing across the field of lightning. I had been holding on to its neck because there were no reins. I remembered holding fast and hanging on for dear life.

26

I came down the front stairs at exactly eight and found Earl Briggs waiting, leaning against his car parked out front and taking in the view of West Hollywood past the shoulders of Laurel Canyon.

"Morning, Earl," I said.

He took the two Starbucks cups off the hood of his car and crossed the street to the Lincoln. I exchanged the keys for one of the cups and thanked him for thinking of stopping for coffee before we headed off.

The Lincoln had gotten a clean sweep by Cisco the afternoon before. The GPS tracker was still in place but he and his men had found no bugs or cameras on the vehicle.

We headed south to pick up the 10 Freeway east, stopping only to top off the Lincoln's big gas tank. Traffic was grim but I knew it would thin out once we got past downtown and turned north on the 15. From there it was a straight shot north through the Mojave.

Overnight Jennifer had sent me several e-mails with documents from her research attached. I passed the time by reading through these. The first thing to catch my eye was her analysis of Hector Moya's habeas petition and what was riding on it. Moya had already been incarcerated for eight years since his arrest. The life term he received because of the gun enhancement under the federal career criminal statute was the only thing currently keeping him behind bars. He was sentenced to six years for the cocaine found in his possession. The life term was added on top of that.

This meant that Moya's immediate freedom was riding on the outcome of his habeas petition. To me it was an added reason for him to cooperate with me on the La Cosse case and to put his future in more experienced hands than those of Sylvester Fulgoni Jr.

This knowledge also put Marco's visit with me the day before in better perspective. The DEA agent had to have known as he sat across from me in the Lincoln that a violent man he had put away presumably for life could see freedom soon, depending upon the outcome of a couple of court cases he could not control.

I next reviewed the transcript from Hector Moya's trial seven years before. I read two sections, one containing the testimony of an officer with the LAPD warrant enforcement team, and the other containing part of the testimony of DEA agent James Marco. The LAPD cop testified about Moya's arrest and his finding the gun hidden under the mattress in the hotel room. The testimony from Marco contained replies to questioning about the analysis and trace work that was done on the recovered firearm. It was key testimony because it tied the gun to Moya through a purchase in Nogales, Arizona.

About the time we came through the mountains into the Mojave, I grew tired of the reading work and told Earl to wake me when we got there. I then racked out across the backseat and closed my eyes. I'd had a restless sleep after my middle-of-the-night conversation with Sly Fulgoni Sr. and needed to catch up. I knew from prior experience that going into a prison would be exhausting. It was an ordeal that fully taxed the senses. Prison sounds and smells, the drab gray steel set off by the garish orange uniforms of the incarcerated, the mixture of desperation and threat in the faces of the men I'd come to visit—it was not a place I ever wanted to spend an extra minute in. It always felt as if I were holding my breath the whole time I was inside.

Despite the cramped configuration of the backseat, I managed to doze off for almost a half hour. Earl woke me on our approach to the prison. I checked my phone and saw that we had made good time despite the early traffic. It was only ten o'clock and that was when attorney visiting hours began.

"You don't mind, boss, I'm gonna wait outside on this one," Earl said.

I smiled at him in the mirror.

"I don't mind, Earl. I wish I could, too."

I handed him my phone over the seat. There was no way I would be allowed to take it inside, which was ironic, since most prisoners had access to cell phones.

"If Cisco, Lorna, or Bullocks calls, answer it and tell them I'm inside. Everything else let go to message."

"You got it."

He dropped me at the main visitors' entrance.

The process of getting in to see Fulgoni and Moya went smoothly. I had to show a driver's license and my California bar card, then sign one document certifying that I was an attorney, and a second certifying that I was not smuggling drugs or other illegal contraband into the facility. After that I was walked through a magnetometer after removing my belt and shoes. I was placed in an attorney-client room and given an electronic alert to clip to my belt. If I was physically threatened by my client, I was instructed to yank the pager-size device off my belt, and an alarm would sound, drawing guards to the room. Of course, I would still need to be alive to pull it but that detail wasn't mentioned. This had all come about because of one court ruling or another that had prohibited guards from watching over attorney-client meetings in the prison.

I was left alone in the ten-by-ten room to wait. There were a table and two chairs and an electronic call box on the wall next to the door. The waiting was a given. I don't think I had ever made a prison visit where I walked into the interview room and my client was there waiting for me.

It was routine for attorneys to stack interviews with multiple clients at a prison—even when the cases were unrelated. It saved travel and clearance time to get it all done in one visit. But usually the prisoners were brought in on a timetable that suited the prison staff and was based on the schedules and availability of the prisoners. I had asked the visitor center captain to allow me to visit with Fulgoni first and then Moya. He frowned at the request but said he would see what he could do.

Maybe that was why the wait seemed extraordinarily long. Thirty minutes went by before Fulgoni was finally brought into the interview room. At first I almost told the guards escorting him that he had the wrong guy, but then I realized it was indeed Sylvester Fulgoni Sr. Though I'd finally recognized him, he still wasn't the man I recalled from the courthouses and courtrooms we both worked at one time. The man shuffling into the room in leg chains was pale and haggard, hunched over, and for the first time, I realized he must have worn a toupee all those years I knew of him in L.A. No such vanity was allowed in prison. The crown of his head was bald and sharply reflected the overhead fluorescent lights.

He took a seat across the table from me. His wrists were cuffed to a waist chain. We didn't shake hands.

"Hello, Sly," I said. "How was lunch?"

"Lunch was the same as it is everyday here. Bologna on white bread, unfit for human consumption."

"I'm sorry to hear that."

"I'm not. I figure when I start liking it, then I've got a problem."

I nodded.

"I get that."

"I don't know about you, but back in the day I had clients who liked to hide out in prison. Places like this. It was easier than the streets because you got your three squares, a bed, clean laundry.

Sex and drugs readily available if you want 'em. It was dangerous, but the streets were plenty dangerous, too."

"Yeah, I've had a few like that."

"Well, that's not me. I consider this place to be a living hell on
earth."

"But less than a year to go, right?"

"Three-hundred and forty-one days. I used to be able to tell it
down to the hour and minute but I'm a little more relaxed about
that now."

I nodded again and decided that was enough as far as the
pleasantries went. It was time to get down to business. I hadn't
driven all the way up to discuss the pros and cons of prison life or
to figuratively pat Sylvester Fulgoni on the back.

"Did you talk to Hector Moya about me this morning?"

Fulgoni nodded.

"That I did. And you're all set. He'll take the meeting and he'll
take you as co-counsel with young Sly."

"Good."

"I can't say he's too happy about it. He's pretty convinced that
you're in part responsible for him being here."

Before I could say a word in my defense, there was a boom-
ing impact that shook the room and, I assumed, the entire
prison. My hand went to my belt and the alarm as my first
thought was that there was some kind of explosion and prison
break occurring.

Then I noticed that Fulgoni hadn't even flinched and had a
glib smile on his face.

"That was a big one," he said calmly. "They probably have the
B-Two up today. The stealth."

Of course. I now remembered the nearby airbase. I tried to
shake it off and get back to business. My legal pad was on the
table in front of me. I had jotted down a few questions and reminders while I waited for Fulgoni. I wanted to start with the
basics and lead up to the important questions once I had Fulgoni
vested in the conversation.

"Tell me about Moya. I want to know how and when this whole thing started."

"Well, as far as I know, I'm one of two defrocked lawyers in here. The other guy was part of a bank fraud in San Diego. Anyway, it kind of gets known what you did in the world and people come to you. First it's general advice and recommendations. Then some come because they want help with a writ. I'm talking about guys in here long enough to be abandoned by their lawyers because they've exhausted their appeals. Guys who don't want to give up."

"Okay."

"Well, Hector was one of those guys. He came to me, said the government hadn't played fair, and wanted to know what he could still do about it. The thing is, nobody had ever believed him. His own attorneys didn't believe his story and didn't even put an investigator on it, as far as I could tell."

"You're talking about the DEA planting the gun in his room to get the enhancement?"

"Yeah, the enhancement that puts him in here for life. I'm not talking about the powder in the room. He totally cops to that. But he said the gun wasn't his, and it turns out he's been saying that since day one but nobody would listen. Well, I listened. I mean, what else am I going to do in here but listen to people?"

"Okay."

"So that's your start. My son filed the paper and here we are."

"But let's go back to before young Sly filed the habeas petition. Let's go back to last year. See, I'm trying to put all of this together. Moya tells you the gun was planted. Did he tell you Gloria Dayton planted it?"

"No, he said the cops did it. He was arrested by the LAPD after you made the deal with the DA's Office. Remember that? Only he didn't know about any deal until years later—until I told him. All he knew at the time was that the LAPD came through his door with a felony fugitive warrant. They found the coke in the bureau and the firearm under the mattress and that was it. The fugitive beef was for a grand jury no-show. That was nothing compared to the case they had now. He had two ounces of blow in the room and the gun. And then the feds swooped in and scooped the whole thing up and he goes to trial in federal court, where they have the lifetime achievement award. Convenient, huh?"

"Yeah, and I know all of that. I'm talking about the gun. I am trying to track how you went from his story to Gloria Dayton. Your habeas petition says Gloria planted the gun."

"It was simple. I asked the right questions, and then I took two steps back and looked at the big picture. I came at it from the angle of believing Hector Moya. Like I said, nobody had before. But he came to me and said, 'Yes, the powder in that room was mine and I'll do the time for it. But not the gun.' I figured, why deny one and not the other unless you're telling the truth?"

I could think of reasons to do exactly that—lie about one thing and not the other—but I kept them to myself for now.

"So…Gloria?"

"Right, Gloria. Hector said the gun was a plant. Well, I had a case once with a firearm enhancement attached. Same thing, but this was a DEA case from the start. No locals. A straight DEA buy bust and the client swore to me he had no gun on him when the deal went down. I didn't believe him at first—I mean, who goes to buy a kilo with twenty five K in a briefcase and no gun for backup? But then I started looking into it."

"You proved the gun was planted to get the enhancement?"

Fulgoni frowned and shook his head.

"Actually, I was never able to prove it. And my guy went down for it. But the unit that made the bust was something called the Interagency Cartel Enforcement Team, which was run by the DEA and headed up by an agent named Jimmy Marco. He's the same guy who did the swoop and scoop on Moya. So when that name came up in the file I thought there was something to it. You know, that was twice I'd seen this on a case with his name on it. I figured, where there's smoke there might be fire."

I thought for a long moment, trying to put the pieces together and understand the moves Fulgoni had made.

"You had the name Marco but he didn't come into it until after the arrest went down and the locals had found the coke and the gun," I said in summary. "So if Marco was behind this, then you had to figure out how he got the gun in there for the locals to find."

Fulgoni nodded.

"Exactly. So I went to Hector and said, what if the gun wasn't planted by the locals? What if it was already there under the mattress and planted earlier by somebody else? Who was in that room between the time you checked into that hotel and the bust went down? That was four days and I asked him for a list with the names of everybody who'd visited that room in that time frame."

"Gloria Dayton."

"Yes, we zeroed in on her. But she wasn't the only one who had been in that room. There had been at least one other hooker, Hector's brother, and a couple other associates, too. Luckily, we didn't have to vet the housekeepers because Hector kept the do not disturb on his door the whole time. But we zeroed in on Gloria because I had a friend run all the names through the police computer and—bingo!—she happened to get popped one fricking day before they took Hector down."

I nodded. The logic made sense. I would have zeroed in on Gloria as well. I also knew what I would have done next.

"How'd you track down Gloria? She'd changed her name. She moved away and then moved back."

"The Internet. These girls can change names, locations, doesn't matter. The business is based on the visual. Young Sly got her booking photo from eight years ago, when she got arrested on a possession and prostitution beef, and then he went online, checking photos on escort sites. Eventually he found her. She'd changed her hair but that was about it. He printed out photos and brought them up here. Hector confirmed."

I was surprised. Sly Jr. had actually done something that created a significant break in the case.

"And you then, of course, had Junior paper her."

I said it like the next move had been a matter of routine.

"Yeah, we hit her with a subpoena. We wanted to bring her in to put her on the record."

"Who was the process server, Valenzuela?"

"I don't know. Somebody Sly Jr. hired."

I leaned across the table and started increasing the urgency and momentum, hitting him with the questions without pause.

"Was she photographed to prove receipt?"

Fulgoni shrugged like he didn't know and didn't care.

"Was she?"

"Look, I don't know. I was up here, Haller. What's so—"

"If there's a photo, I want it. Tell your son."

"Fine. Okay."

"When did you paper her?"

"I don't know the date. Last year sometime. Obviously before she got killed by her pimp."

I leaned further across the table.

"How long before she got killed?"

"About a week, I think."

I hammered my fist down on the table.

"She wasn't killed by her pimp."

I pointed across the table at him.

"You got her killed. You and your son. They found out about the subpoena. They couldn't trust that she wouldn't talk."

Fulgoni was shaking his head before I was finished.

"First of all, who is 'they'?"

"Marco, the ICE team. Do you think they would risk this coming out? Especially if planting firearms was common practice with that team. Think of all the reputations, careers, and cases that would be jeopardized. You don't think that's motive for murder? You don't think they'd risk taking out a hooker if it meant securing their operation?"

Fulgoni held up a hand to stop me.

"Look, I'm not stupid, Haller. I knew the risks. The subpoena was filed under seal. Marco couldn't have known about it."

"So she ended up dead a *week* later and you thought, what, that the pimp did it and it was all just coincidence?"

"I thought what the police thought and what my son read to me out of the newspaper. That her pimp killed her and we missed our chance to have her help Moya."

I shook my head.

"Bullshit. You knew. You must have known you set things in motion. How many days *before* the deposition was she killed?"

"I don't know. I didn't sched—"

"That's bullshit! You knew. How many days?"

"Four, but it doesn't matter. It was under seal. No one knew but her and us."

I nodded.

"Yeah, only you and she knew, and what did you expect—that she wouldn't tell someone who might tell somebody else? Or that she might not call up Jimmy Marco, who she used to snitch for, and say, what should I do about this?"

Suddenly I realized something that gave an answer to one of the questions I had been carrying since handling the phony subpoena served on Kendall Roberts. I pointed at Fulgoni's chest.

"I know what it was. You thought Marco had somebody inside the clerk's office. Somebody who told him about the sealed subpoena. That's why your son dummied up the subpoena he had Valenzuela serve on Kendall Roberts. You two didn't want to do it again—get somebody killed. You wanted her to come in so Junior could find out what she knew about Gloria and Marco, but you were afraid a real subpoena would get back to Marco, even if it was under seal."

"You don't know what you're talking about, Haller."

"No, I know exactly what I'm talking about. One way or another, your subpoena got Gloria killed. You both knew it and you decided to keep quiet about it and lie low while some poor schmuck went down for it."

"You're way off base on this."

"Really? I don't think so. Why the subpoenas this week? To me and Marco and the phony one to Kendall Roberts. Why now?"

"Because the petition was filed almost six months ago. We had to move on it or it would be dismissed. It had nothing to do with Gloria Dayton or—"

"That's such bullshit. And you know something, Sly? You and your son are no better than Marco and Lankford in all of this."

Fulgoni stood up.

"First of all, I don't know who Lankford is. And second, we're done here. And you can forget about Moya. He's ours, not yours. You're not seeing him."

He turned and started shuffling toward the door.

"Sit down, Sly, we're not finished," I said to his back. "You walk out of here and the state bar is going to come down all over you and Junior. You're not an attorney anymore, Sly. You are operating a writ mill in here and feeding cases to a kid who sits in an office in a Dodgers jersey and doesn't know the first thing about being a lawyer. The bar will tear him up and throw him away. You want that for him? For you? Who will you feed cases to when Junior's out of business?"

Fulgoni turned around and kicked at the door with his heel to alert the guard.

"What's it going to be, Sly?" I asked.

The guard opened the door. Fulgoni glanced back at him, hesitated, and then said he needed five more minutes. The door was closed and Fulgoni looked at me.

"You threatened my son yesterday but I didn't think you'd have the balls to threaten me."

"It's not a threat, Sly. I'll shut you both down."

"You're an asshole, Haller."

I nodded.

"Yeah, I'm an asshole. When I've got an innocent man facing a murder count."

He had nothing to say to that.

"Sit back down," I instructed. "You're going to tell me how to handle Hector Moya."

27

The wait between interviews with Fulgoni and Moya was twenty-five minutes and two more teeth-rattling sonic booms. When the door finally opened, Moya stepped in calmly and slowly, his eyes steady on me. He walked with a grace and ease that belied his situation and even suggested that the two men behind him were personal valets, not prison guards. His orange jumpsuit was vibrant and had crisp creases. Fulgoni's had been faded from a thousand washes and frayed at the edges of the sleeves.

Moya was taller and more muscled than I had expected. Younger, too. I put him at thirty-five tops. He had wide shoulders at the top of a torso that tapered down like a V. The sleeves of his jumpsuit stretched tightly against his biceps. I realized that despite my interaction with his case eight years before, I had never seen him in person or in a newspaper photograph or television report. I had built a visual image based on fantasy. I had him as a small, round man who was venal and cruel and had gotten what he deserved. I wasn't expecting the specimen standing before me now. And this was a concern because, unlike Fulgoni, Moya was not chained at the ankles and waist. He was as unencumbered as I was.

He accurately picked up on my concern and addressed it before even sitting down.

"I have been here much longer than Sylvestri," he said. "I am trusted and not chained like an animal."

He spoke with a strong accent but was clearly understandable. I nodded cautiously, not knowing whether his explanation contained some sort of threat.

"Why don't you have a seat," I said.

Moya pulled back the chair and sat down. He crossed his legs and held his hands together in his lap. He immediately looked relaxed, as if meeting in a lawyer's office instead of a prison.

"You know," he said, "six months ago my plan was to have you killed in a very painful manner. When Sylvestri spoke of the part you played in my case, I became very angry. I was upset and I wanted you dead, Mr. Haller. Glory Days, too."

I nodded as though I was sympathetic to his situation.

"Well, I'm glad that didn't happen. Because I'm still here and I may be able to help you."

He shook his head.

"The reason I tell you this is because only a fool would think I had no motive to have you and Gloria Dayton eliminated. But I did not do this. If I had, you and she would have simply disappeared. This is the way it is done. There would be no case and no trial of an innocent man."

I nodded.

"I understand. And I know it means little to you, but I also have to tell you that eight years ago I was doing my job, which was to do my best in the defense of a client."

"It does not matter. Your laws. Your code. A snitch is a snitch, and in my business they disappear. Sometimes with their lawyers."

He stared coldly at me through the darkest eyes I think I had ever seen besides my own half brother's. Then he broke away and his voice changed as he engaged in the business of the day, the tone moving from dead-on threat to collegial cooperation.

"So, Mr. Haller, what must we discuss here today?"

"I want to talk about the gun that was found in your hotel room when you were arrested."

"It was not my gun. I have said this from the very beginning. No one has believed me."

"I wasn't there at the beginning—at least on your side. But I'm pretty sure I believe you now."

"And you'll do something about it?"

"I'm going to try."

"Do you understand the stakes that are involved?"

"I understand that the people who did this to you will stop at nothing to keep their crimes secret—because I'm pretty sure you're not the only one they did it to. They already killed Gloria Dayton. So we will have to be very cautious until we can get this into open court. Once we are there, it will be harder for them to hide behind their badges and the cover of night. They'll have to come out and answer to us."

Moya nodded.

"Gloria—she was important to you?"

"For a time. But what is important to me now is that I have a client in the county jail accused of killing her and he didn't do it. I have to get him out and I need you to help me. If you help me, I will certainly help you. That all right with you?"

"It is all right. I have people who can protect you."

I nodded. I expected that he might make such an offer. But it wasn't the kind of protection I was interested in.

"I think I'm all right," I said. "I've got my own people. But I'll tell you what. I've got a client in the pink module at Men's Central down in L.A. You think you can get somebody in there to sort of watch over him? He's in there alone, and I'm worried they're going to see this thing moving toward a trial in which a lot of these secrets are going to come out. They'll know that the best way to avoid that is to avoid having a trial."

Moya nodded.

"If there is no client, there is no trial," he said.

"You got that right," I said.

"Then I will see to it that he is protected."

"Thank you. And while you're at it, I'd double up on whatever protective measures you have for yourself in here."

"That will be done as well."

"Good. Now let's talk about the gun."

I flipped a few pages back on my legal pad to get to the notes I had written off the trial transcript. I refreshed myself on the facts and then looked at Moya.

"Okay, at your trial the arresting officer from the LAPD described coming into the room and arresting you, and then finding the gun. Were you still in the room when they found it or had you already been pulled out of there?"

He nodded as if to say he could answer this one.

"It was a two-room suite. They handcuff me and make me sit on the couch in the living room. A man with a gun stood over me while the others began to search through the room. They found the cocaine in a drawer in the bedroom. Then they said they find the gun. He come out of the bedroom and show me the gun in a plastic bag and I said it was not my gun. He said, 'It is now.'"

I wrote a few notes down and spoke without looking up from the pad.

"And he was the LAPD officer who testified at the trial? An officer named Robert Ramos?"

"That was him."

"You're sure he said, 'It is now,' when you said it wasn't your gun?"

"This is what he said."

It was a good note to have. It was hearsay and therefore might not even be allowed as testimony in a trial, but if Moya was telling the truth—and I believed he was—then it meant Ramos might have had some knowledge of the gun having been planted in the room. Maybe he had been coached to look under the mattress.

"There was no video of the search introduced at your trial. Do you recall seeing anybody with a video camera?"

"Yes, they take a video of me. And the whole room. They humiliate me. They make me take off my clothes for the search. And the video man was there."

This made me curious. They had video but didn't use it at trial. Why? What was on the video that made it a risk to show to a jury? The humiliation of Hector Moya? Possibly. But possibly something else.

I made another note on my pad and then moved on to the next thing I wanted to cover.

"Have you ever been in Nogales, Arizona?"

"No, never."

"You're sure? Never in your life."

"Never."

According to Marco's testimony at trial, he received an ATF report tracing the gun. According to this report, the weapon was a .25 caliber Guardian manufactured by North American Arms. It was originally purchased in Colorado by a man named Budwin Dell, who then sold it at a gun show in Nogales five weeks before it was allegedly found in Moya's hotel room. Dell was not a federally licensed firearms dealer, so he was allowed to sell the gun without a background check or a waiting period. An ID check would be the only thing required in a cash deal. An ATF agent assigned to the ICE team was dispatched to Littleton, Colorado, to interview Dell and show him a photo lineup. Dell chose the photo of Hector Moya as the customer he believed had bought the weapon in Nogales. His receipt book credited the sale to a customer named Reynaldo Sante, which happened to be one of the names contained in the numerous false identification packages found in the room where Moya was arrested.

Dell proved to be a key witness at the trial, locking Moya to the gun and the phony ID found in his possession. Though Moya claimed the gun and ID were planted by the police, it must've sounded preposterous to the jury.

But now with the knowledge that Glory Days and Trina Trixxx were informants to the DEA agent heading the ICE team, I didn't think this was preposterous at all.

"Hector, I need you to tell me the truth about something. Don't lie, because I think the truth will actually help you."

"Ask me."

"The false ID in the name of Reynaldo Sante. In trial you said the gun and the ID were planted in the room by the cops. But that wasn't true, was it?"

Moya thought a little bit before answering. He first nodded his head.

"The ID was mine. Not the gun."

I nodded. I thought so.

"And you used that ID on previous trips to Los Angeles, didn't you?"

"Yes."

"Those trips, when you were checking into hotels under the name Reynaldo Sante, did you also meet Glory Days and Trina Trixxx in your rooms?"

"Yes."

I wrote a few notes down. My adrenaline was kicking in my bloodstream. I was clearly seeing a path in which to take the La Cosse case as well as Moya's. I was on the road to finding something out.

"Okay," I said. "Hector, this is all good so far. I think we can do something with this."

"What else do you want to know?"

"For the moment, nothing. But I'll be back to see you. The main thing I wanted today was your cooperation and to know we could work together. I'm going to need you to testify at my other client's trial. We will build a record in that trial that will support your habeas petition. One case will help the other. You understand?"

"I understand."

"And testifying is not a problem? Your people will understand what you are doing?"

"I will make them understand."

"Then we're good here. The last thing I want to mention is a word of advice on Sylvester Fulgoni."

"Sylvestri, yes."

"Sylvestri, then. He was a very good lawyer but he is not a lawyer anymore. So you have to remember that anything you tell him is not protected like it is with anything you tell me. Be circumspect with what you say to him. Understand? Be careful."

He nodded.

"Okay, and speaking of which, to make things all legal between you and me, you need to sign an authorization that allows me to represent you."

I had the document ready to go, folded lengthwise in my inside pocket. I slipped it and a pen across the table to him and he signed it.

"Okay, then, I think we're finished here," I said. "Stay safe, Hector."

"And you too, Miguel."

28

Once in the Lincoln again I told Earl he could take us back to the city.

"How'd it go in there, boss?"

"You know, Earl, I've visited a lot of different people in a lot of different prisons and I'm not sure if I've ever had a better visit."

"That's good."

"Yeah, real good."

I opened the contacts file on my phone and scrolled down to the Vs. I might not have had Fernando Valenzuela on speed dial anymore but I knew I still had his cell on my contacts list. I made the call and wondered if he'd answer when my name came up on the screen. I was about to hang up before it went to message when he finally picked up.

"Yo, Mick, don't tell me you're calling me with all of this work you promised me."

"As a matter of fact, Val, I thought you should know that I've partnered up with Fulgoni, so it looks like we'll be working together again after all."

"Ain't that a shame. I'll believe it when I hear it from Fulgoni, not you."

"That's fine. You call him. But there's something I need from you right now."

"Of course there is. But I'm not falling for this shit, Haller. I'll call Fulgoni and if he clears it, then I'll see what you need."

"You can do whatever you want, Val. But I need you to text

me the photo you took of Giselle Dallinger when you papered her back in November. You got that? Giselle Dallinger. If I don't get it in the next ten minutes, you're fired."

"We'll see what Sly says about that."

"Sly and his old man are working for me. I don't work for them. You've got nine minutes now, Val."

I disconnected the call. Something about Valenzuela always got under my skin. He always acted like he knew something I didn't, like he had something on me.

"That true?" Earl asked from the front seat. "You and Fulgoni partnering up?"

"Just on one case, Earl. That's about all I could take with those guys."

Earl nodded.

I looked around and saw that he had us back on the 15 Freeway heading south. Traffic was sparse and it gave me hope that we might get into L.A. before the afternoon traffic crunch. That would allow me to keep rolling with the momentum the prison visit had brought.

I called Cisco to once again redirect his activities.

"I'm going to need you to go to Colorado."

"What's in Colorado?"

"A guy named Budwin Dell. He was a witness against Moya at his trial. He's an unlicensed gun dealer from Littleton who testified that he sold the gun to Hector Moya at a gun show in Nogales. I think he lied. I think somebody from the ICE team maybe put him up to it. The ATF probably had something on him. I want you to go talk to him and see if he's going to hold up when I get him on the stand."

"I'm working five different things here, Mick. You want me to drop it all and catch a plane?"

Sometimes momentum can move you too far too quickly. Cisco had a good point.

"I want you to go when the time is right. But I think this guy's going to be key."

"Okay. I'll get out there by the end of the week. But first I'll make sure he's in Colorado. If he's still on the gun show circuit, he might be anywhere. They're all the rage these days."

"Good point. I'll leave it in your hands, then. You know what to do."

"Okay, what else you get up there?"

"Sly Fulgoni Jr. subpoenaed Gloria a week before she was murdered. I think that's what triggered the whole thing. They killed her before she could talk."

Cisco whistled. He did that whenever a piece of the puzzle fell into place.

"There was no subpoena found in her place. I studied the inventory."

"Because they took it. That's why she was killed in her home. They had to find the subpoena or the locals might ask questions."

"How did they know?"

"Fulgoni filed it under seal, so I'm thinking Gloria told the wrong person about it."

"Marco?"

"That's who I'm guessing. But I don't want to guess. I want to nail it down."

"Phone records?"

"If there are any. La Cosse said he and Gloria used burners that they changed all the time."

"I'll see what I can find. You might have to ask a judge for Marco's records and we'll try to match her numbers from the burners."

"That'll be a fight to the finish."

"What else did you get up there, Mick? Sounds like a good trip."

"Yeah, well, I think I got our case. We just need to nail down this guy Budwin Dell and a few other things…"

Prompted by thinking about the fight that would ensue if I sought Marco's phone records, I was suddenly struck by where the case's true battle would most likely be.

"It's going to be a subpoena case," I said. "Getting these people into court. Dell, Marco, Lankford—none of them are going to willingly testify. Their agencies will fight it tooth and nail. The feds will even fight my putting Moya on the stand. They'll cite public safety, the cost to taxpayers, anything to prevent him from being brought down to L.A. to testify."

"They might have a point on the public safety angle," Cisco said. "Moving a cartel guy? This could be Moya's whole plan— to get moved out into the open so his people can make a run at grabbing him. A lot of space between L.A. and Victorville."

I thought about Moya and the conversation we'd just had.

"Could be," I said. "But something tells me that's not the case. He wants out fair and square. And if he wins his habeas, he'll prob- ably walk on time served. He's already been in eight years on two ounces. The only thing holding him is the gun enhancement."

"Well, either way," Cisco said, "you're going to need a strong judge. One who will stand up."

"Yeah, not many of those left."

It was true. Many judges were already fronts for the state. But even those who weren't would be hard-pressed to allow me to present the defense I was envisioning. The true battleground of the case would be in the hearings before a single juror was seated. Unless I came up with another strategy to get my witnesses in.

I decided not to think about it for now.

"So how are you making out?" I asked.

"I'm getting close to connecting Lankford and Marco," Cisco said.

That was good news.

"Tell me about it."

"It's a little tentative now, so give me a day on it. It involves a double murder in Glendale. A drug rip-off going back ten years. I'm waiting on records—it's a cold case, so not a problem getting the docs."

"Let me know when you know. You heard from Bullocks to- day?"

"Not today."

"She—"

"Hey, boss!" Earl said from the front seat.

I looked at his eyes in the mirror. They weren't on me. They were on something behind us. Something that was scaring him.

"What is—"

The impact was loud and hard as something with what felt like the power of a train plowed into us from behind. I was belted in, but even so, my body was hurled forward into the fold-down tabletop affixed to the back of the seat in front of me, and then thrown against the door as the Lincoln went into a sideways slide to the right. Fighting the centrifugal force of the slide I managed to raise my head up enough to look over the right side doorsill. I saw the freeway guardrail a microsecond before we hit it flush and our momentum took us over it.

The car started tumbling down a concrete embankment, the crunching of steel and shattering of glass sharp in my ears as it flipped once, then twice, then three times. I was whipped around like a rag doll until the car finally came to a metal-grinding stop upside down and at the forty-five-degree angle of the embankment.

I don't know how long I was out, but when I opened my eyes I realized I was hanging upside down by the seat belt. An old man on his hands and knees was staring at me through the broken window on the high side of the car.

"Mister, you all right?" the man said. "That was a bad one."

I didn't answer. I reached to the seat belt and pushed the release button without thinking. I crashed down to the ceiling of the car, embedding broken glass in my cheek and aggravating a dozen sore spots on my body.

I groaned and slowly tried to raise myself, looking to the front seat to check on Earl.

"Earl?"

He wasn't there.

"Mister, I better get you out of there. I smell gas. I think the tank ruptured."

I turned back to my would-be rescuer.

"Where's Earl?"

He shook his head.

"Is Earl your chauffeur?"

"Yeah. Where is he?"

I reached up to pull a piece of glass out of my cheek. I could feel the blood on my fingers.

"He got thrown out," the rescuer said. "He's lying over there. He looks bad. I don't think—well, the paramedics will be able to tell. I called them. I called nine-one-one and they're coming."

He looked at me and nodded.

"Thank you," I said.

"Here, let me help you out. This thing could catch on fire."

It wasn't until I crawled out and struggled to my feet, hand on my rescuer's shoulder, that I saw Earl lying facedown on the embankment above the Lincoln. Blood was running down the concrete in a thick stream from his neck and face area.

"You got lucky," the man said.

"Yeah, I'm Mr. Lucky," I said.

I took my hand off his shoulder and leaned forward until my hands reached the concrete. I crawled up the embankment to Earl. I knew right away that he was dead. He must've been thrown clear and then the car rolled over him. His skull was crushed and his face was misshapen and ghastly to look at.

I sat down on the concrete next to him and looked away. I saw the rescuer looking up at me, an expression of horror on his face. I knew my nose was broken and blood was dripping down both sides of my mouth. I guess I was ghastly to look at as well.

"Did you see what happened?" I asked.

"Yeah, I saw it. It was a red tow truck. The thing hit you like you weren't even there and then it kept going."

I nodded and looked down. I saw Earl's outstretched hand, palm down on the bloody concrete. I put my hand on top of it.

"I'm sorry, Earl," I said.

Part 3

THE MAN IN THE HAT

MONDAY, JUNE 17

29

The prosecution took eight days to present its case against Andre La Cosse, strategically finishing on a Friday so the jurors would have the whole weekend to consider its case in full before hearing a single word from the defense. Bill Forsythe, the deputy D.A., had been workmanlike in his presentation. Nothing fancy, nothing over the top. He methodically built his case around the videotaped interview of the defendant and attempted to solidly wed it to the physical evidence from the crime scene. On the tape La Cosse said he grabbed Gloria Dayton by the throat during their argument. Forsythe coupled this with testimony from the medical examiner, who said that the hyoid bone in the victim's neck had been fractured. This coupling was the center of the case, and all other aspects, testimony, and evidence emanated from it like the concentric circles of waves from a stone thrown into a lake.

Yes, Judge Leggoe had allowed the admittance of the damning video, dismissing my motion to suppress the day before the start of jury selection with the single comment that the defense had failed to show that the police had used coercive tactics or had operated in bad faith in any way during the interview. The ruling was not unexpected and I immediately chose to see the silver lining in it; I now believed I had the first solid grounds for appeal should the verdict ultimately go against my client.

Through the video Forsythe gave the jury motive and opportunity, using the defendant's own words to establish them. In my many trials over nearly twenty-five years as a practicing attorney I had found nothing more difficult than undoing the damage inflicted upon defendants by their own words. So was the case here. Jurors always want to hear from the defendants, whether in direct testimony, videotape, or audiotape. It is in the instinctual interpretation of voice and personality that we form our judgments of others. Nothing beats that. Not fingerprints, not DNA, not the pointed finger of an eyewitness.

Forsythe threw only one curve ball at me, but it was a good one. His final witness was another escort for whom La Cosse had formerly provided digital services and management. The prosecutor claimed that he had come forward only the day before after learning of the trial for the first time while reading the newspaper. I argued against his being allowed to testify, accusing the state of sandbagging, but to no avail. Leggoe said testimony of prior bad acts of a similar nature was admissible and allowed Forsythe to put him on the stand.

Brian "Brandi" Goodrich was a small man no more than five three. He wore tight stonewashed jeans and a lavender polo shirt on the witness stand. He testified that he was a transvestite who worked as an escort managed by Andre La Cosse. He testified that Andre had once choked him into unconsciousness when he thought Goodrich was withholding money from him. When Goodrich came to, he was handcuffed to a floor-to-ceiling pole in his living room and he watched helplessly while La Cosse ransacked his home looking for the missing cash. Brandi brought all the usual histrionics to the stand with him — he tearfully recounted that he had feared for his life and felt lucky he hadn't been killed.

At the defense table, I leaned to Andre and smiled and shook my head as though this witness was just a nuisance and not worth taking seriously. But what I whispered to him wasn't so lighthearted.

"I need to know right now, did this happen? And don't hang me out there with a lie, Andre."

He hesitated, then leaned in close to whisper back.

"He's exaggerating. I handcuffed him first to this stripper pole he had in the living room so I could search the place. I didn't choke him out. I grabbed him by the neck one time so he would look at me and answer my questions. He was never unconscious and it didn't even leave a mark. He went to work that night."

"He didn't quit or go with someone else?"

"He didn't quit for six months. Not until he found a sugar daddy."

I leaned back away from Andre and waited for Forsythe to finish his direct. When it was my turn, I countered initially with a few questions I hoped would remind the jurors that Brandi was a prostitute and that he had never made any report of this near-death experience to the police.

"Which hospital did you go to to have your neck treated?" I asked.

"I didn't go to the hospital," he answered.

"I see. So the hyoid bone in your neck was not crushed as it was with the victim of this case?"

"I don't know about the specific injuries in this case."

"Of course not. But you say you were choked into uncon-sciousness by the defendant and you never went to the police or to seek medical attention."

"I was just happy to be alive."

"And to work, too, correct?"

"I don't understand the question."

"You went to work as an escort the same night after this sup-posed life-and-death struggle took place, didn't you?"

"I don't remember that."

"If I produced Mr. La Cosse's business records regarding his bookings for you as a prostitute, would that help you remember?"

"If I worked that night, it was only because he made me and threatened me if I didn't."

"Okay, let's go back to the alleged incident. Did the defendant use one hand or two?"

"Both hands."

"You're a grown man, did you defend yourself?"

"I tried, but he's a lot bigger than me."

"You said you then woke up handcuffed to a pole. Where were you when he allegedly choked you into unconsciousness?"

"He grabbed me from behind as soon as I let him in the apartment."

"So he choked you from behind then?"

"Yes, sort of."

"What do you mean, 'sort of'? Did he choke you or not?"

"He put his arm around my neck from behind and tightened it and I tried to fight because I thought he was going to kill me. But I blacked out."

"So why did you just testify that he used two hands to choke you?"

"Well, 'cause he did. Hands and arms."

I let that hang out there for a few moments for the jury to consider. I thought I had successfully dented Goodrich's credibility in a few places. I decided I should get out while I was ahead and took one last shot in the dark. It was a calculated risk, but I operate under the belief that voluntary witnesses usually want something in return. In this case, Goodrich obviously wanted revenge, but I had a hunch there was something more.

"Mr. Goodrich, are you currently facing any criminal charges, misdemeanor or felony? Anything at all?"

Goodrich's eyes flicked toward the prosecution table for a split second.

"In Los Angeles County? No."

"In any county anywhere, Mr. Goodrich."

Goodrich reluctantly revealed that he had a solicitation case pending in Orange County but denied he was testifying in exchange for help with that.

"No further questions," I said, my voice dripping with disdain.

Forsythe tried to clean things up on redirect, hammering

home that he had made no overture or promise to do anything to help Goodrich in Orange County.

Goodrich was allowed to step down after that. I felt I had gotten a few good swings in, but still, the damage was done. Through the witness the prosecution had added a history of similar actions to the solid pillars of motive and opportunity already established. Forsythe's case was complete then and he rested it at four p.m. Friday, guaranteeing me a weekend of fitful sleep and panicked preparation.

Now it was Monday and it would soon be my turn in front of the jury. My task would be clear. To undo what Forsythe had done. To change the minds of the twelve jurors. In past trials my goal had been to change just one mind. In most cases, hanging a jury is as good as a not-guilty verdict. The DA often chooses not to retry and to soften its stance on a disposition. The case is a sick dog and it needs to be put down as quickly and as smoothly as possible. In the defense trenches that is a victory. But not this time. Not with Andre La Cosse. I was convinced that my client was many things but not a killer. I felt certain that he was innocent of the charges, and so I needed all twelve of the gods of guilt to smile upon me on the day of the verdict.

I sat at the defense table, waiting for the deputies to bring La Cosse in from lockup. Those of us in the courtroom had already been alerted that the bus carrying him from Men's Central was delayed in traffic. Once the defendant arrived the judge would come out from chambers and the defense's case would begin.

I passed the time by studying a page of notes I had jotted down for my opening statement. I had reserved the opener at the start of the trial, exercising my option to address the jury before the presentation of the defense. This is often a risky move because it means the jurors may go several days before hearing any sort of counterargument to the prosecution's theory of the case and presentation of evidence.

Forsythe gave his opening statement to the jury twelve days

earlier. So much time had passed, it would seem that the state's side was deeply and unalterably entrenched in the minds of the twelve. But I also felt that the jurors had to be dying to finally hear something from the defense, to hear the response to Forsythe, the video, and the scientific and physical evidence. They would start to get all of that today.

At last, at nine forty, La Cosse was brought through the lockup door and into the courtroom. I turned and watched as the deputies led him to the defense table, removed the hip shackles, and sat him down next to me. He was wearing the second suit I had bought for him. I wanted him to have a different look than he'd had last week as we started the defense. Both suits had come off the rack in a two-for-one deal at Men's Wearhouse. Lorna chose them after we'd checked out La Cosse's own clothing and found nothing that presented the conservative, business-like appearance I wanted him to have in court. But the new suits did little to disguise his ongoing physical decline. He looked like someone suffering in the latter stages of terminal cancer. His weight loss had gone unchecked during his six-plus months of incarceration. He was gaunt, had developed rashes on his arms and neck in reaction to the industrial detergent used in the jail laundry, and his posture at the defense table made him look like an old man. I constantly had to tell him to sit up straight because the jury was watching.

"Andre, you doing okay?" I asked as soon as he was seated.

"Yeah," he whispered. "The weekends in there are long."

"I know. They still giving you medicine for your stomach?"

"They give it and I drink it, but I don't know if it's doing anything. I still feel like I'm on fire inside."

"Well, hopefully you won't be in there too much longer and we'll get you into a first-rate hospital as soon as you get out."

La Cosse nodded in a way that indicated he couldn't quite believe he would ever leave the shackles and the jail behind. Long-term incarceration does that to an individual—eats away at hope. Even in an innocent man.

"How are you doing, Mickey?" he asked. "How is your arm?"

Despite his own circumstances, Andre never failed to inquire about me. In many ways I was still recovering from the crash of the Lincoln. Earl had died and I was battered and broken—but mostly on the inside.

Physically, I'd suffered a concussion and needed surgery to reset my nose. It took twenty-nine stitches to close various lacerations and twice-a-week physical therapy sessions since then to help restore full motion to my left arm where ligaments were torn in the elbow.

To put it bluntly, I got off easy. People might even say I walked away. But the physical injuries didn't even approach the intensity of the internal damage that still lingered. I grieved every day for Earl Briggs, and the sorrow was only equaled by the burden of guilt I carried with it. A day didn't go by that I didn't recheck the moves and decisions I'd made in April. Most damning was the decision to keep the tracker on my car and to taunt those monitoring my movements by boldly driving to Victorville to see Hector Moya. The consequences of that decision would be with me forever, the image of a smiling Earl Briggs attached to them in my mind's eye.

By the time the wreckage of the Lincoln was examined, the GPS tracker was gone, but it had been there the afternoon before when Cisco had checked out the car. There is no doubt in my mind that I was followed to Victorville. And there is no doubt in my mind about who made the decision to send the Lincoln into the guardrail, if not did the deed himself. I had only one true purpose with this trial. That was to free Andre La Cosse and clear his name. But I considered destroying James Marco in the process to be an integral part of the trial strategy.

When I looked back on what happened up on the 15 Freeway, only one thing came out of it that could even remotely be considered good. A rescue helicopter transported both me and Earl to Desert Valley Hospital back in Victorville. Earl was dead on arrival and I was admitted to the ER. When I came out of surgery, my daughter was there at my bedside, holding my hand. It went a long way toward healing things inside me.

The trial was pushed back almost a month while I recovered, and that cost had been borne most heavily by Andre. Another month of incarceration, another month of withering hope. He never once complained about it. He only wanted me to get better.

"I'm good," I said to him now. "Thank you for asking. I can't wait to get started because now it's finally your turn, Andre. Today we start telling a different story."

"Good."

He said it without much conviction.

"You just gotta concentrate on one thing for me, Andre."

"Yeah, I know, I know. Don't look guilty."

"You got it."

I gave him a playful punch on the shoulder with my good arm. It had been the mantra I had given him from day one. Don't look guilty. A man who looks guilty is found guilty. In Andre's case it was easier said than done. He looked destroyed, and that wasn't too far off from looking guilty.

Of course, I knew something about looking guilty and feeling guilty. But like Andre, I was trying to play my part. I hadn't had a drink since the night before jury selection began. Not even on the weekends. I was sharp and I was ready. For Andre, today was the first day of the rest of his life. Mine, too.

"I just wish David was here," Andre said in a whisper so low I almost didn't hear him.

Reflexively prompted by what he'd said, I turned slightly and my eyes swept across the rear of the courtroom. As had been the case since the start of the trial, the gallery was almost empty. There was an accused serial killer on trial in Department 111 and that was drawing most of the media. The La Cosse case had gotten scant attention in the news, and the cynic in me decided this was because the victim here had been a prostitute.

But I did have a cheering section. Kendall Roberts and Lorna Taylor sat in the first row directly behind the defense table.

Lorna had been making periodic visits throughout the trial. This was Kendall's first day watching. Wary of coming to the courthouse and possibly seeing someone from her past, she had stayed away until I had pointedly asked her to come for at least my opening statement. We had grown close since April and I wanted her there for the emotional support.

And in the back row were two men who had been in attendance every day since the start of jury selection. I did not know their names but I knew who they were. They wore expensive suits but looked out of place in them. They were muscular and had deeply tanned skin from lives seemingly spent outdoors and not in courtrooms. They had the same build as Hector Arrande Moya, with wide, sharp shoulders, and I had come to think of them simply as *Moya's Men.* They were part of the contingent of protectors Moya had dispatched to watch over me after the car crash in the mountains. I had turned down his offer of protection that day in the visiting room. It was too late for Earl Briggs now, but I didn't turn down the offer a second time.

But that was it. No one else was watching the trial. La Cosse's life partner, David, was missing from the benches. He had split, having staged a full withdrawal of La Cosse's remaining gold and leaving town on the eve of the trial. More than anything else, that loss contributed to Andre's demeanor and downward spiral.

In a way, I understood it. Having Kendall in the courtroom was a special thing for me. I felt supported and less alone. Like I had a partner in the fight. But my daughter had so far not set foot in the courtroom and that hurt. The hospital room reunion had only gone so far in rekindling the relationship. And school was no longer an excuse, as it had let out for the year halfway through the prosecution's case. I think my reflexive act to check the gallery was actually one more hopeful search for her.

"You can't worry about that now," I whispered to Andre— and myself. "You have to look strong. Be strong."

Andre nodded and tried to smile.

When David had taken the gold and run, La Cosse wasn't the

only one he had left high and dry. By then I had already taken receipt of a second bar of gold as continuing payment. A third bar was due at the start of trial, but the gold was gone by then. So a case that I had earlier viewed as a potential financial bonanza had turned pro bono as the trial began. Team Haller was no longer getting paid.

At exactly ten o'clock the judge emerged from chambers and took the bench. As was her custom, Judge Leggoe eyed Forsythe and me and asked if there was any business to consider before she brought in the jury. This time there was. I stood, holding a set of documents, and said I had an amended witness list for the court to consider and approve. She waved me up to the bench and I handed her a copy of the new list and then dropped another one off with Forsythe on my way back. I was barely seated again when Forsythe stood to object.

"Your Honor, Counsel is engaged in an age-old practice of deception by trying to hide his real witnesses in a sea of names. His pretrial list was enormous and now he's added what I estimate to be twenty to twenty-five more names and it is evident most of these will not be actually called."

He gestured with the pages behind him to where Lee Lankford sat in a row of chairs against the rail.

"I see he has my own DA investigator on here now," Forsythe continued. "And let's see, he's got not one but now two federal prisoners on here. He's got one…two…three prison guards. He's got what looks like every resident in the victim's building—"

He abruptly cut off the litany and dropped the pages on his table as though depositing them in the trash.

"The people object, Your Honor. It would be impossible to respond beyond that without being allowed the time to look at these names and determine their relationship, if there is any at all, to the case."

Forsythe's objection wasn't a surprise. We had counted on it in the defense plan and strategy we had dubbed "Marco Polo" at the top of the whiteboard Lorna had gotten installed on the brick wall of the boardroom back at the loft. The witness list was the opening move in that gambit, and so far Forsythe was playing his part, though he had not yet—at least vocally—paid attention to the one name on the list that was most important. The name we called our depth charge, sitting there beneath the surface and waiting to be detonated by the first false move by the prosecution.

I stood to respond to the objection, taking another quick glance behind me as I rose. Still no daughter but a small smile from Kendall. As my eyes swept forward they caught and locked for a moment on Lankford. He looked at me with an expression that was sixty percent *What the fuck is this?* and forty percent the usual *Fuck you.* That sixty percent was what I was hoping for.

"Your Honor," I said, looking finally at the judge. "It seems obvious from his objection that Mr. Forsythe already does in fact have knowledge of who these people are and how they would relate to the case. Nevertheless, the defense is happy to allow him time to review the new names and respond. There is no need to interrupt the trial, however. I am planning to regale the jury with my long-delayed opening statement and then begin with witnesses who were on the original witness list and already approved by the court."

Leggoe seemed pleased to have been handed an easy solution.

"Very well," she said. "We will take this up first thing tomorrow morning. Mr. Forsythe, you have until then to study the list and have your response ready."

"Thank you, Your Honor."

Leggoe called for the jury. I stayed standing and read over my notes while the jurors were seated and the judge explained that I had reserved my opening statement at the start of the trial and would deliver it now. She reminded them that the words I would speak were not to be construed as evidence and then turned the floor over to me. I stepped away from the defense table, leaving my notes behind. I never used notes when I was directly addressing a jury. I maintained maximum eye contact the whole time.

The judge had earlier ruled that during openers each attorney would be allowed to stand in the space directly in front of the jury box. This is known by lawyers as the well of the courtroom but to me it has always been the proving ground. I don't mean proving in a legal way. I am talking about proving yourself to the jury, showing them who you are and what you stand for. You have to first gain their respect if you want any hope of proving your case to them. You have to be fervent and unapologetic about standing for the accused.

The first juror I locked eyes with was number four. She was Mallory Gladwell, age twenty-eight, and a script reader for a movie studio. Her job was to analyze scripts submitted to the studio for purchase and development. As soon as she was seated and questioned during voir dire, I knew I wanted her on the jury. I wanted her analytical skills when it came to storytelling and logic. I wanted the jury to ultimately choose my story over Forsythe's, and my gut feeling was that Mallory Gladwell could be the one who led them there.

Throughout Forsythe's presentation of the state's case I kept my eyes on Mallory. It was true that I watched all of the jurors, trying to read faces and pick up tells and cues as to what testimony or evidence had the strongest impact on them, what they were skeptical about, what got them angry and so on. But I had Mallory down as the alpha. My guess was that her skills at breaking down a story would lead her to be a voice, if not *the* voice, during deliberations. She could be my Pied Piper, and therefore she was the one I made the first eye contact with and she would be the last. I wanted her invested in the defense's case.

The fact that she returned the eye contact and did not look away was a strong signal to me that my instincts were on target.

"Ladies and gentlemen," I began. "I don't think any introduction is needed here. We are well into this trial and I am pretty sure we know who everybody is. So I am going to be pretty brief here because I just want to get to the case. To the truth about what happened to Gloria Dayton."

As I spoke, I unconsciously moved two steps forward, spread my hands, and put them down on the front rail of the jury box. I leaned forward, trying to make the communication between one man and twelve strangers as intimate as a one-on-one with a priest or a rabbi. I wanted each one of them to think I was talking only to them.

"You know, lawyers have all sorts of nicknames for things, including juries. We call you people the 'gods of guilt.' Not in any sort of disrespect for religion or faith. But because that's what you are. Gods of guilt. You sit here and you decide who is guilty and who is not. Who goes free and who does not. It is a lofty and yet weighty burden. To make such a difficult decision you must have all the facts. You must have the whole and true story. You must have the proper interpretation of the story."

I glanced again directly at Mallory Gladwell. I lifted my hands off the rail and moved back into the well so I could cover the entire twelve and the two alternates in a tight back and forth sweep. As I spoke I casually moved to my right so that most of the jurors were looking at me on their left.

"I ask that over the next few days or week you pay close attention to the defense's case. You've heard only one side of the story so far—the prosecution's side. But now you are going to hear and see another side. You are going to see that there are two victims in this case. Gloria Dayton, of course, is a victim. But so, too, is Andre La Cosse. Like Gloria he was manipulated and used. She was murdered and Andre has been set up to take the fall for it.

"Realistically, my job here is to sow the seeds of doubt in your mind. If you have reasonable doubt when it comes to Andre's guilt or innocence, then it is your job to find the defendant not guilty. But over the next few days I will go beyond that, and you will come with me. You will come to know that Andre is completely innocent. And you will come to know who really committed this terrible crime."

I paused here but kept my eyes moving across the faces of the jurors. I had them. I could tell.

"Now, before closing, let me just address something that I'm sure has bothered you throughout the presentation of the prosecution's case. That is Mr. La Cosse's means of making a living. To tell you the truth, it bothers me, too. Essentially, he's a digital pimp. And, like many of you, I am a parent, and it disturbs me to think about someone profiting from the sexual exploitation of young women and men. But the verdict you will deliver in this case is not to be influenced by what Andre La Cosse does for a living. You cannot judge him guilty of murder simply because of what he is. I ask you to think of the victim in this case, Gloria Dayton, and ask yourself, did she deserve to be murdered because she was a prostitute? The answer of course is no, and so, too, is the answer to the question should Andre La Cosse be convicted of murder simply because he is a pimp?"

I paused, put my hands in my pocket, and looked down at the floor. It was time for the big finish. When I looked up, my eyes came directly to Mallory's.

"In closing, I make you a promise that you can hold me to. If I do not make good on what I say here, then go ahead and find my client guilty. It's a gamble I am willing to take, and that Andre is willing to take, because we know where the truth is. We have the righteousness of the innocent."

I paused again, hoping Forsythe would throw out an objection. I wanted the jury to see him challenging me, trying to stop me from speaking the truth. But the prosecutor wasn't off the first bus from law school. He knew what he was doing and he held back, not giving me what I wanted.

I moved on.

"The defense will put forth evidence and testimony that proves Mr. La Cosse is nothing more than a patsy. An innocent patsy in the worst kind of scheme. A scheme in which those we trust the most have conspired to frame an innocent man. This is a story about how a conspiracy to protect a hidden truth ultimately led to murder and cover-up. It is my hope"—I turned and used a hand gesture to indicate Andre La Cosse—"as it is Mr. La

Cosse's hope, that you will find the truth with us and return the appropriate verdict of not guilty. Thank you very much."

I returned to my seat and immediately checked my notes to see if I had forgotten anything.

It looked like I had hit all the highlights, and that pleased me. Andre leaned over and whispered his thanks. I told him he hadn't seen anything yet.

"I think we will now take the morning break," the judge said. "When we come back in fifteen minutes we will begin the defense's presentation."

I stood as the jury got up, and watched them move single file through the door to the assembly room. I watched Mallory Gladwell move with her head down. Then, at the last moment, just as she was about to slip through the doorway and out of sight, she turned to look back into the courtroom. Her eyes landed on mine and held for the split second before she was gone.

As soon as the judge adjourned, I headed out to the courthouse hallway to check the status of my first witness.

30

The real reason I had fled the courtroom the moment the judge adjourned and the jury left was to get to the restroom. I had been up since four, thinking about the trial and readying myself for my opener. I had kept the fire stoked with copious amounts of coffee and now it was time to purge.

I saw Cisco sitting on a bench in the hallway next to Fernando Valenzuela.

"How we doing?" I asked as I walked by.

"We're great," Cisco replied.

"Yeah, sure," Valenzuela said.

"I'll be right back," I said.

A few minutes later relief was flooding through me as I stood at the urinal. I even had my eyes closed as I replayed some of the opening statement in my mind. I didn't hear the restroom door open and didn't realize someone had come up behind me. Just as I was zipping up, I was pushed face-first into the tiled wall over the urinal. My arms were pinned and I couldn't move.

"Where's your cartel protection now?"

I recognized the voice as well as the breath of coffee and cigarettes.

"Lankford, get the fuck off me."

"You want to fuck with me, Haller? You want to do the dance?"

"I don't know what you're talking about. But if you ruin this

248

suit, I'm going to see the judge about it. My investigator's sitting out there. He saw you come in."

He yanked me off the wall and twirled me into the swinging door on a toilet stall. I recovered quickly and looked down at my suit to check for damage and buckle my belt. I did it nonchalantly like I wasn't concerned in the least about Lankford's menacing me.

"Go back to court, Lankford."

"Why am I on the list? Why do you want me on the stand?"

I walked over to the row of sinks and calmly washed my hands.

"Why do you think?" I asked.

"That day in the office," he said. "You said you saw me wearing a hat. Why the fuck would you say that?"

I looked up from my hands to the mirror and looked at him.

"I mentioned a hat?"

I reached over and pulled down a handful of paper towels to dry my hands.

"Yeah, you mentioned a hat. Why?"

I threw the wet towels in the trash can, turned, and then hesitated as though I was recalling something from the distant past. Then I looked at him and shook my head as though confused.

"I don't know about the hat. But I know if you touch me again like that, you're going to have more trouble than you can handle."

I opened the door and stepped out into the hallway, leaving Lankford behind. I could barely contain a smile as I approached Cisco, who was still on the bench with Valenzuela. The first rule of Marco Polo was to keep them guessing. Lankford would soon have more than his hat to worry about.

"Everything okay?" Cisco asked.

"Lankford try to grab your dick in there?" Valenzuela added.

"Yeah, something like that," I said. "Let's go in."

I opened the door to the courtroom and held it for them. As they passed by me, I checked the hallway for Lankford and didn't see him. But I did see my half brother walking down the hall, a thick blue binder under his arm.

"Harry."

He turned without breaking stride and saw me. He smiled when he recognized me and stopped.

"Mick, how are you, man? How's the arm?"

"It's good. You in a trial?"

"Yeah, in one eleven."

"Hey, that's the one stealing all the media from my trial."

I said it mock protest and smiled.

"It's a cold case from 'ninety-four. A guy named Patrick Sewell—one sick puppy. They brought him down from San Quentin where he was already doing life for another murder. They're going for the death penalty this time."

I nodded but couldn't bring myself to say good luck. He was, after all, working for the other side.

"So anything new on your driver?" he asked. "They hook anybody up yet?"

I looked at him for a moment, wondering if he might have heard something about the investigation on the law enforcement circuit.

"Not yet," I said.

"That's too bad," he said.

I nodded in agreement.

"Well, I gotta get back in. Good to see you, Harry."

"You, too. We should try to get the girls together again."

"Sure."

We had daughters the same age. But his apparently still talked to him on a regular basis. After all, he put bad people in jail. I got them out.

I entered the court, privately chiding myself for the negative thoughts. I tried to remember Legal Siegel's admonishment to let the guilt go so I could be at my best in defending La Cosse.

After the jury was reseated I called the first witness for the defense. Valenzuela walked to the witness stand, bouncing his palm along the top of the front rail of the jury box as he went. He acted as though testifying at a murder trial was as routine as buying smokes at the 7-Eleven.

He took the oath and spelled his name for the clerk. I took it from there, asking him first to tell the jury what he did for a living.

"Well," he responded. "You might say I'm a man of many talents. I'm the oil that keeps the justice system moving smoothly."

I almost corrected him by suggesting that he actually meant he was the grease that kept the system moving, but I held back. He was my witness, after all. Instead, I asked him to be more specific about his work.

"For one thing, I'm a state-licensed bail bondsman," he said. "I also got my PI license and I use that for process. And if you go down to the second-floor coffee shop in this building, then I'm the leaseholder on that. I'm with my brother on that deal. So—"

"Let's go back for a moment," I interrupted. "What is a PI license?"

"Private investigator. You gotta have a state license if you want to do that kind of work."

"Okay, and what do you mean when you say you use your license 'for process'?"

"Uh, process. You know, process serving. Like when people get sued and stuff and the lawyer has to put out a subpoena if he wants to call somebody to come in to give a statement or a deposition or come to a trial so they can testify. Like what I'm doing right now."

"So you deliver the subpoena to the witness?"

"Yes, like that. That's what I do."

For all his years spent being the oil in the machine, it was pretty clear that Valenzuela did not have much experience testifying. His answers were choppy and incomplete. Whereas I thought he would be one of the easier witnesses to question, I found myself having to work extra hard with him to get a complete answer to the jury. It was not the perfect way to start the defense case, but I pressed on, annoyed more with myself than with him for not conducting a practice run-through beforehand.

"Okay, now did your work as a process server bring you in contact with the victim in this case, Gloria Dayton?"

Valenzuela frowned. What I believed was a straightforward question had thrown him for a loop.

"Well…it did, but at the time I didn't know it. What I mean is, her name wasn't Gloria Dayton at the one and only time I came in contact with her, you see."

"You mean she was using a different name?"

"Yes, she was. The name that was on the subpoena I delivered to her was Giselle Dallinger. That's who I served paper on."

"Okay, and when was that?"

"That was on Monday, November fifth at six oh six in the evening at the lobby entrance of the apartment building on Franklin, where she lived."

"You seem pretty precise about the time and place you did this. How can you be so sure?"

"Because I document every service in case somebody doesn't show up for court or for a depo. Then I will be able to tell the lawyer or the judge that, see, sure enough, the person was served and should've been there. I show them the record and I show them the picture which has the date and time stamp on it."

"You take a photo?"

"Yep, That's my policy."

"So you took a photograph of Giselle Dallinger after you served her with a subpoena last November fifth?"

"That's right."

I then produced an eight-by-ten copy of the date- and time-stamped photo that Valenzuela had taken of Giselle née Gloria and asked the judge to accept it as the first defense exhibit. Forsythe objected to the inclusion of the photo and was willing to stipulate that Valenzuela had served a subpoena on Gloria Dayton. But I fought for the photo because I wanted the jurors to see it. The judge sided with me and I handed the photo to juror number one so it could be examined and then passed from juror to juror.

More than anything else, this was what I wanted to accomplish with Valenzuela on the stand. The image was key because it did more than bring validity to Valenzuela's story. It also captured a look of fear in Gloria's eyes that had to be seen and not testified to. The photo was taken at precisely the moment she looked up from having read the subpoena. She had seen the name Moya in the styling of the case—*Hector Arrande Moya vs Arthur Rollins, warden, FCI Victorville*—and in that instant she had been struck with fear. I wanted the jury to see that look and to surmise that it was fear without me or a witness having to tell them.

"Mr. Valenzuela, who were you delivering that subpoena for?" I asked.

"I was working for an attorney named Sylvester Fulgoni Jr.," he responded.

I half expected Valenzuela to add to his answer the improvisation about Fulgoni being the attorney who put the F-U in litigation, but luckily he spared the jury that. Maybe he was finally getting the hang of being a witness.

"And what was the case the subpoena was attached to?"

"It was called *Moya versus Rollins.* A convicted drug dealer named Hector Moya was trying to —"

Forsythe objected and asked to approach the judge's bench. He obviously didn't want the jury hearing any part of what Valenzuela wanted to say. The judge waved us up and turned on the noise-canceling fan.

"Judge, where is this going?" Forsythe asked. "With his very first witness Mr. Haller is trying to hijack this murder case and take us into another, completely unrelated litigation. I've held back on my objections, but now...we have to stop this."

I noted his use of *we,* as though he and the judge shared the responsibility of keeping me in check.

"Your Honor," I said, "Mr. Forsythe wants to stop this because he knows exactly where I am going with it—and it's a place that he knows is going to derail his whole case. The case Gloria Dayton was served on is exceedingly germane to this case and this trial, and the entire defense theory is built on it. I am asking you to let me proceed and soon enough you will understand why the state wants to block this."

"'Exceedingly,' Mr. Haller?"

"Yes, Your Honor, exceedingly."

She gave it a moment's thought and then nodded.

"Overruled. You may proceed, Mr. Haller, but get there soon."

We returned to our positions and I asked Valenzuela the question again.

"Like I said, *Moya versus Rollins.* Rollins is the warden of the prison in Victorville where Hector Moya's been for, like, seven or eight years. He's trying to get out on account that the DEA set him up by planting a—"

Forsythe objected again, which seemed to annoy the judge. He asked for a sidebar once more but the judge said no. He had to state his objection in open court.

"As far as I know, Judge, the witness is not an attorney, but he is giving a legal interpretation of a habeas case and about to offer as fact the allegations that are merely contained in a lawsuit. We all know that anybody can say anything in a lawsuit. Just because it is said doesn't—"

"Okay, Mr. Forsythe," the judge said. "I think you've made your objection clear to the jury."

Now I wished he had gotten the sidebar. Forsythe had expertly used the objection to undercut Valenzuela's testimony before he had even given it. He reminded the jury in real time that *Moya vs. Rollins* was just a lawsuit that contained allegations, not proven facts.

"I'm going to overrule the objection and let the witness finish his answer," Leggoe said.

In a slightly deflated tone I told Valenzuela to give his answer again and he summarized the main charge of Moya's habeas petition—that the gun that ended up putting him away for life had been planted by the DEA.

"Thank you," I said when the answer was finally out and in the record. "What did you do after you served Giselle Dallinger with that subpoena?"

Valenzuela looked confused by the question.

"I, uh…I guess I told Mr. Fulgoni that it was done," he said.

"Okay, and did you ever see Ms. Dallinger again?" I asked.

"No, not at all. That was it."

"When did you next hear about Ms. Dallinger after November fifth?"

"It would've been about a week later, when I heard that she'd gotten murdered."

"How did you hear that?"

"Mr. Fulgoni told me."

"And did you learn anything else about her death?"

"Well, yeah, I read the paper and I saw that a guy had been arrested."

"You're talking about Andre La Cosse being arrested for her murder?"

"Yeah, it had it in the paper."

"And how did you react to that news when you read it?"

"Well, it was like I was relieved, because it meant that we didn't have nothin' to do with it."

"What do you—"

Forsythe objected again, citing relevance. I argued that Valenzuela's reaction to news of the murder and arrest were relevant because the defense's case was based on the fact that the subpoena that was served on Gloria Dayton was what motivated her murder. Leggoe allowed me to proceed subject to her determining relevancy after the witness's testimony was completed. This was a win with an asterisk for me. Even if the judge later struck Valenzuela's answers from the trial record, she wouldn't be able to strike them from the memories of the twelve jurors.

"Go ahead, Mr. Valenzuela," I said. "Tell the jury why you

were relieved when you heard that Mr. La Cosse had been arrested in the murder."

"Well, because it meant it had nothing to do with this other thing. You know, the Moya case."

"Well, why would you have been worried about that in the first place?"

"Because Hector Moya is a cartel guy, and I thought, you know, that—"

"I think I'm going to stop the witness there," Leggoe said. "Now we are getting into an area beyond the witness's expertise and knowledge. Ask a different question, Mr. Haller."

But I had no more questions. For all his unpolished delivery, Valenzuela had been an A-plus witness, and I felt good about how we had come out of the gate. I turned the floor over to Forsythe for cross-examination but he was wise enough to pass. There wasn't much he could get out of questioning Valenzuela without one of them repeating things that supported the defense theory.

"I have no questions, Your Honor," he said.

The judge excused Valenzuela and he made his way out of the courtroom. Leggoe told me to call my next witness.

"Your Honor," I said. "This might be a good time to break for lunch."

"Really, Mr. Haller," Leggoe said. "Why is that? The clock says it is twenty minutes to twelve."

"Uh, Judge, my next witness is not here yet, and if I could have the lunch hour, I am sure I can have him here to start the afternoon session."

"Very well. The jury is excused until one o'clock."

I moved back toward the defense table while the jury filed out of the courtroom. Forsythe gave me a look and shook his head as I moved by him.

"You don't know what you just did, do you?" he whispered.

"What are you talking about?" I asked.

He didn't answer and I kept moving. At the defense table I

started gathering my legal pads and documents together. I knew better than to leave anything on the table during court breaks. The moment the door closed on the last juror, the judge's voice boomed through the courtroom.

"*Mr. Haller.*"

I looked up.

"Yes, Your Honor."

"Mr. Haller, how would you like to join your client for lunch in lockup?"

I smiled, still not aware of any trespass that I had committed.

"Well, I wouldn't mind the company, but cheese sandwiches aren't on my list of culinary favorites, Your—"

"Then let me put you on notice, Mr. Haller. You never *suggest* a lunch break or any break in front of my jury, do you understand that?"

"I do now, Judge."

"This is *my* courtroom, Mr. Haller, not yours. And I decide when we break for lunch and when we don't."

"Yes, Your Honor. I apologize and it won't happen again."

"If it does, there will be consequences."

The judge then left the bench in a huff, her black robes flowing behind her. I gathered myself and looked over at Forsythe, who had a sneaky smile on his face. He'd obviously worked in Leggoe's courtroom before and knew her personal rules of decorum. *Big deal,* I thought. At least she waited until the jury was gone before she brought out the hammer.

When I got out of the courtroom and into the hallway, I found Cisco pacing near the elevators. He was holding his cell phone to his ear but not talking.

"Where the fuck is Fulgoni?" I demanded.

"I don't know," Cisco said. "He said he'd be here. I'm on hold with his office."

"He's got one hour. He'd better be here."

31

Kendall had left before the lunch break to head up to the Valley and her shift at Flex. Lorna and I walked down Spring and then over to Main to a place called Pete's Café. Along the way I occasionally looked back over my shoulder to make sure we had security with us. Moya's men were always there.

We'd chosen Pete's because it was good and fast and it served an excellent BLT, which for some reason I was craving. The only issue I ever had with eating at Pete's was that it was always full of cops, and this time was no different. Just a couple blocks from the Police Administration Building, the restaurant was a favorite with command staff suits and detectives from the elite Robbery-Homicide Division squads. I exchanged awkward nods and stares with a few guys I recognized from prior trials and cases. We got a table that was cut off from the view of most of the restaurant by a wide support column, and that was fine with me. I was beginning to feel like I had wandered into an enemy encampment when all I wanted was a BLT on whole wheat toast.

Lorna was smart enough to ask me if I wanted her to be quiet while I thought about the case and the day's after-lunch session. But I told her there was no sense in my strategizing a plan for the afternoon until I knew whether Sly Jr. was going to be in court as he was supposed to be. So after ordering we spent the time studying my calendar and looking for billable hours. The firm was running out of money. Before it was

known that there would be no more gold bars coming from
Andre La Cosse, I had spent liberally on P&I—trial preparation and investigation. More was going out than was coming in,
and that was a problem.

This was one reason that Jennifer Aronson was not in court
this morning. I could not afford to take her off the work for
the few other paying clients we had. She spent the morning at a
bankruptcy hearing regarding the owner-landlord of the loft we
used for our team meetings.

At least the credit card I used to pay for lunch went through. I
could only imagine the humiliation that would have come from
my card being confiscated and cut in half in front of an audience
of cops.

The good news was then doubled when I got a text from Cisco
on our way back to the courthouse.

He's here. Good to go.

I shared the news with Lorna that Fulgoni was in the courthouse and was then able to relax the rest of the way back. That
is, until Lorna brought up the thing we had steadfastly avoided
bringing up for nearly two months.

"Mickey, do you want me to start looking around for a
driver?"

I shook my head.

"I don't want to talk about it right now. Besides, I don't have a
car. What do I want a driver for? Are you saying you no longer
want to drive me?"

She had been picking me up each morning and taking me
to court. Usually it was Cisco who drove me home, so he could
check the house to make sure it was clear.

"No, it's not that," Lorna said. "I don't mind driving you at all.
But how long are you going to wait before you try to get back to
normal?"

The trial had been a good salve on the internal wounds left by the crash. The attention it required kept my mind from wandering back to that day we had gone up into the Mojave.

"I don't know," I said. "Besides, we can't afford normal. There's no money for a driver and there's no money for a car until I get the check from the insurance company."

The insurance check was held up by the investigation. The California Highway Patrol had classified the crash as a homicide caused by the intentional hit-and-run by the tow truck. The truck was found a day after the accident, parked in a field in Hesperia and burned to a charred hulk. It had been stolen from a tow lot the morning of the crash. The CHP investigators, as far as I knew, had no line on who had been driving the truck when it had rammed into my Lincoln.

As Sylvester Fulgoni Jr. made the long walk from the rear entrance all the way to the witness stand at the front, he swiveled his head back and forth as if seeing the inside of a real courtroom for the first time. When he got to the stand, he started to sit down and the judge had to stop him so he could remain standing while taking the oath to tell the truth, the whole truth, and nothing but the truth.

After the preliminary questions that established who Fulgoni was and what he did, I zeroed in on Hector Moya's habeas case, asking Fulgoni to go through the steps that led him to subpoena Gloria Dayton to appear for a deposition.

"Well, it started when Mr. Moya told me that the gun that was found by police in his hotel room was not his and that it had been planted," Fulgoni answered. "Through our investigation we concluded that there was a strong possibility that the gun was already hidden in the room when the police arrived to make the arrest."

"And what did that tell you?"

"Well, that if the gun was planted as Mr. Moya insisted, then it was planted by somebody who had been in that room before the police arrived."

"Where did that lead you?"

"We looked at who had been in that room during the four days Mr. Moya was staying there before the bust. And through a process of elimination we narrowed our focus to two women who had been to the room multiple times in those days. They were prostitutes and they used the names Glory Days and Trina Trixxx—that's spelled with three *x*'s. Trina Trixxx was easy to find because she was still working under that name in Los Angeles and had a website and all of that. I contacted her and arranged to meet her."

Fulgoni stopped there, waiting for further direction. I had told him when we discussed his testimony not to take big bites out of the story, to keep his answers short. I also told him not to volunteer anything about paying Trina Trixxx for her cooperation. I didn't want to drop that piece of information into Bill Forsythe's lap.

"Will you tell the jury what happened at that meeting?" I asked.

Fulgoni nodded eagerly.

"Well, first she revealed that her real name is Trina Rafferty. She also acknowledged knowing Mr. Moya and being in his room back at that time. She denied ever planting a gun in the room but admitted that her friend Glory Days had told her she did."

I did my best to feign confusion, raising one hand in an I-don't-get-it gesture.

"But why would she plant the gun?"

This set off an objection from Bill Forsythe and a five-minute exchange of arguments at sidebar. Eventually I was allowed to proceed with my question. This is one of the few places in a criminal trial where the defense has an advantage. Everything about a trial is stacked against the defense, but the one thing no judge wants is a reversal on appeal due to judge's error. So the wide majority of jurists, and this included Judge Nancy Leggoe, bend over backwards to allow the defense to proceed as it

wishes as long as it stays close to the lines of evidentiary proce-
dure and decorum. Leggoe knew that every time she sustained
an objection from Forsythe, she risked being second-guessed and
reversed by a higher court. By contrast, rejection of prosecutorial
objections rarely carried the same risk. In practice this meant that
giving the defense wide latitude in mounting its case was the
safest judicial route to take.

Once I was back at the lectern, I again asked Fulgoni why
Glory Days would plant a gun in Hector Moya's hotel room.

"Trina Rafferty told me that both she and Glory Days were
working for the DEA and they wanted to put Moya away
for—"

Forsythe practically became airborne when he jumped up to
object.

"Your Honor! Where is the foundation for that? The state
strenuously objects to the witness and defense counsel using this
trial to wander aimlessly through this valley of innuendo."

The judge was swift in her response.

"I think Mr. Forsythe is correct this time. Mr. Haller, lay the
foundation or move on to another topic with the witness."

So much for the defense advantage. I took a few seconds to
pull back and retool the examination. I then led Fulgoni through
a series of questions that established the parameters of Moya's arrest and conviction, paying careful attention to the federal code
that allowed prosecutors to enhance the charges and seek a life
sentence because he was found in possession of a firearm and
two ounces of cocaine—a quantity deemed by federal code to be
more than for personal use.

It took me nearly a half hour but eventually I got back to the
question of why Glory Days—who we had now established was
Gloria Dayton—would plant a gun in Moya's room. Forsythe
objected again, saying the groundwork I had just covered was insufficient, but finally the judge agreed with me and overruled the
objection.

"We believed, based on facts brought forward in our investigation, that Gloria Dayton was a DEA informant and that she planted the gun in Mr. Moya's room on the orders of her DEA handler."

There. It was on the record. The cornerstone of the defense. I glanced over at Forsythe. He was writing furiously, even angrily, on a legal pad and not looking up. He probably didn't even want to see how the jury was reacting to this.

"And who was her DEA handler?" I asked.

"An agent named James Marco," Fulgoni replied.

I looked down and acted like I was checking notes on my own legal pad for a few moments so the jurors could let that name— James Marco—sink in deep.

"Mr. Haller?" the judge prompted. "Ask your next question."

I looked at Fulgoni and thought about which way to go, now that I had Marco's name before the jury.

"Mr. Haller!" the judge prompted again.

"Yes, Your Honor," I said quickly. "Mr. Fulgoni, where did you get the name James Marco as Gloria Dayton's supposed DEA handler?"

"From Trina Rafferty. She said that both she and Gloria worked for Marco as snitches."

"Did Trina Rafferty say whether Marco asked her to plant the gun in Mr. Moya's hotel room?"

Before Fulgoni could answer, Forsythe objected angrily, calling the whole line of questioning hearsay. The judge sustained it without allowing argument from me. I asked for a sidebar, and the judge reluctantly signaled us up to the bench. I got right into it.

"Your Honor, the defense finds itself between a rock and a hard place. The court has sustained the objection against hearsay testimony from the witness. That leaves me no alternative but to at least try to get the testimony directly from Agent Marco. As you know, Marco was on the original witness list submitted nearly four weeks ago to the court. However, we have been unable to make service of a subpoena to Agent Marco or the DEA in general."

Leggoe shrugged.

"And what is the remedy you want from the court? To allow hearsay evidence? That's not going to happen, Mr. Haller."

I started nodding before she was finished.

"I know that, Judge. But I was thinking that a direct order to appear from you and carrying the blessing of the prosecution could go a long way toward getting Agent Marco into this courtroom."

Leggoe looked at Forsythe and raised her eyebrows. The ball was now Forsythe's.

"Your Honor, I am happy to give my blessing," he said. "Whether it works or not, all Agent Marco will do is show up and deny these outlandish accusations. It will be a highly decorated agent's word against the word of a whore and I'll—"

"Mr. Forsythe!" the judge broke in, her voice well above a whisper. "You will show a little more decorum and respect in my courtroom."

"I apologize, Your Honor," Forsythe said quickly. "Prostitute. What I meant to say is that this will come down to the agent's word against the prostitute's, and the state has no worries when it comes to that."

Prosecutorial arrogance is a deadly sin when it comes to a criminal court trial. It was the first time I had really seen it in Forsythe and I knew that he might end up eating those words before the case was over.

"Very well, let's proceed," the judge said, "I will adjourn for the day fifteen minutes early so that we can fashion the order to appear."

We returned to our positions and I looked at Fulgoni, waiting for me on the witness stand. He had so far come off as cool, calm, and collected. I was about to change that and take him in a direction we had not discussed or rehearsed in the days building up to the trial.

"Mr. Fulgoni," I began, "how much of this gun-planting theory did Gloria Dayton confirm for you?"

"None," Fulgoni said. "I subpoenaed her for a deposition but she was murdered before I ever spoke to her."

I nodded and looked down at my notes.

"And how long have you been practicing law?"

The abrupt change in direction surprised young Sly.

"Uh, two and a half years next month."

"And have you been involved in a trial before?"

"You mean in court?"

I almost laughed out loud. If Fulgoni had not been my own witness, I would have destroyed him with that answer. As it was, I needed to damn near leave him for dead before I was finished with my direct.

"Yes, in court," I said drily.

"None so far. But I know lawyers who say the object is to stay out of the courtroom and to take care of business before it comes to that."

"Viewing it from where I stand now, that's not bad advice, Mr. Fulgoni. Can you tell the jury how you, just two years out of law school and never in a courtroom before, landed Hector Moya as a client?"

Fulgoni nodded.

"He was a referral."

"From whom?"

"My father, actually."

"And how did that come about?"

Fulgoni gave me a look that I interpreted as a warning that I was crossing into a territory that he had deemed off-limits when we had last discussed his testimony. I gave him a look back that said too fucking bad. I have you under oath. I own you.

I had to prompt him to answer.

"Please tell the jury how your father came to refer Mr. Moya to you."

"Uh, well, my father is incarcerated in the same federal prison where Hector is. They know each other, and my father referred him to me."

"Okay, so you took on the case two years out of law school and filed the habeas petition, hoping to have Mr. Moya's life sentence vacated, correct?"

"Yes."

"Because the firearm that got him that life sentence was planted."

"Yes."

"And you believed it was planted by Gloria Dayton, correct?"

"Correct."

"Based on what Trina Rafferty told you."

"Correct."

"And before filing this habeas petition, did you study the transcript from Mr. Moya's trial in 2006?"

"Most of it, yes."

"Did you read the transcript of the sentencing hearing when the judge sent him to life in prison?"

"I did, yes."

I asked the judge to allow me to approach the witness with a document I entered as the second defense exhibit, the transcript of Hector Moya's sentencing on November 4, 2006.

The judge approved and I came forward to hand the document to Fulgoni. It was already folded back to a page with highlighted material I wanted him to read to the jury.

"What is that you have there, Mr. Fulgoni?"

"It's the transcript from the sentencing hearing in federal court. It's the judge's comments."

"Is that what you read when you were preparing to file the habeas on Mr. Moya's behalf?"

"Yes."

"Okay. What is the judge's name?"

"The Honorable Lisa Bass."

"Can you please read to the jury the quotes from Judge Bass that I have highlighted on the page?"

Fulgoni leaned forward and began reading.

"'Mr. Moya, the presentencing report on you is abysmal. You

have conducted a life full of crime, attaining a high rank in the murderous Sinaloa Cartel. You are a cold and violent man and you have lost all aspects of humanity. You sell death. You are death. And it is my good fortune to be able to sentence you to life in prison today. I wish I could do more. To be honest, I wish you were eligible for the death penalty because I would have used it.'"

He stopped there. The judge's comments continued but I figured that the jury had a good enough taste of them.

"Okay, so you read that sentencing transcript sometime last year as you prepared the habeas petition on Mr. Moya's behalf, correct?"

"Yes."

"Therefore, you knew when you prepared the subpoena for Gloria Dayton what kind of history Mr. Moya had, correct?"

"Yes."

"So then, Mr. Fulgoni, did it ever cross your mind as a young, inexperienced attorney that it might be dangerous to subpoena Gloria Dayton to a deposition in which you would undoubtedly ask her about planting the gun in Hector Moya's hotel room?"

"Danger from whom?"

"Let me ask the questions, Mr. Fulgoni. That's how it works in a real trial."

There was a slight murmur of laughter from the direction of the jury but I acted as though I hadn't heard it.

"Didn't you, Mr. Fulgoni, understand that, by issuing a subpoena and naming Gloria Dayton as the person who planted a gun in Hector Moya's hotel room, you were placing her in great danger?"

"That's why I did it under seal. It was not public information. Nobody knew."

"What about your client? Didn't he know?"

"I didn't tell him."

"Did you tell your father, who lived in the same prison with Moya?"

"But it doesn't make sense. He wouldn't have killed her."

"Who wouldn't?"

"Hector Moya."

"Mr. Fulgoni, you need to answer the questions I ask you. That way we don't have confusion. Did you or did you not tell your father that you had identified as Gloria Dayton the woman who you believed planted the gun in Mr. Moya's room?"

"Yes, I told my father."

"And did you ever ask him if he had told Mr. Moya before Gloria Dayton's death?"

"I did, yeah, but it didn't matter. She was Moya's ticket out. He would not have killed her."

I nodded and looked down at my notes for a moment before continuing.

"Then why did you ask your father if he had given her name to Mr. Moya?"

"Because I didn't understand at first. I thought maybe it was possible that he had acted out of vengeance or something like that."

"Do you think that now?"

"No, because I understand. He needed her alive in order to win the habeas. We needed her."

I hoped the alternative to the scenario I had just explored was obvious to the jurors. At the moment, I was being subtle about it. I wanted them to come to the understanding on their own, and then I would reinforce it with further testimony. When people think they have discovered or earned a certain knowledge on their own, they are more apt to hold on to it.

I glanced at Mallory Gladwell in the jury box and saw her writing in one of the notebooks each juror is given. It looked to me like my alpha juror had gotten the subtlety.

I looked back at Fulgoni. It would have been the perfect moment to finish, but I had Fulgoni on the stand and under oath. I decided not to miss any chance of hammering home the basic theory of the defense.

"Mr. Fulgoni, I am trying to get a fix on the timing of your habeas petition involving Hector Moya. You filed the case and subpoenaed Gloria Dayton in early November, correct?"

"Yes."

"She was then murdered on the night of November eleventh going into the twelfth, right?"

"I don't know the exact dates."

"It's okay, I do. By the morning of November twelfth Gloria was dead, and yet it was another five months before anything happened on the habeas, correct?"

"Like I said, I don't know the dates. I think that is right."

"Why did you wait until April of this year to get things going on the case and to subpoena DEA Agent James Marco among others? What caused the delay until then, Mr. Fulgoni?"

Fulgoni shook his head like he didn't know the answer.

"I was just…strategizing the case. Sometimes the law moves slowly, you know?"

"Was it because you realized that if Hector Moya actually needed Gloria Dayton alive, there might be someone else out there who needed her dead?"

"No, I don't think that's—"

"Were you afraid, Mr. Fulgoni, that you had opened a can of worms with your habeas petition and that you yourself might be in danger?"

"No, I was never afraid."

"Were you ever threatened by someone in law enforcement to stall or shut the Moya case down?"

"No, never."

"How did Agent Marco react to being subpoenaed in April?"

"I don't actually know. I wasn't there."

"Has he ever fulfilled the subpoena and sat for a deposition with you?"

"Uh, no, not yet."

"Has he personally threatened you if you continue the habeas case?"

"No, he has not."

I stared at Fulgoni for a long moment. He now looked like a scared little boy who would lie his way out of anything if he could.

Now was the time. I looked up at the judge and said I had no further questions.

32

Forsythe kept Fulgoni on the stand for a full ninety minutes of hardball cross-examination. If I had made the young lawyer look foolish at times, then the prosecutor made him look downright incompetent. Forsythe clearly had a mission to accomplish with his cross and that was the total destruction of Fulgoni's credibility. I had used young Sly to get several salient points on the record. Forsythe's only hope of undermining those points with the jury was to undermine their source. He had to leave it so the jurors would dismiss Fulgoni's testimony in its entirety.

He came close to mission accomplished by the end of the ninety minutes. Fulgoni looked wrung out. His clothes seemed somehow wilted, his posture was slumped, and he was answering questions monosyllabically, agreeing to almost anything the prosecutor suggested in the form of a question. It was the Stockholm syndrome—he was trying to please his captor.

I tried to intervene and help where I could with objections. But Forsythe deftly kept his questioning inside the lines, and one after the other the objections went down overruled.

Finally, at four fifteen, it was over. Fulgoni was excused and he left the witness stand like a man who never wanted to set foot in a courtroom again, despite being a lawyer. I stepped back to the rail and whispered to Cisco in the first row, telling him to make sure young Sly didn't leave. I still needed to talk to him.

The judge sent the jury home and adjourned court for the day. She invited Forsythe and me back to her chambers to work on the order to appear that would hopefully bring James Marco to court. I told Lorna that drawing up the order would not take too long and she should go down and get her car out of the underground parking garage where she left it every morning.

I caught up to Forsythe in the hallway behind the courtroom that led to the judge's chambers.

"Nice job on Fulgoni," I said. "At least now he has some courtroom experience."

Forsythe turned and waited for me.

"Me? You were the one who started it—and he was your witness."

"A sacrifice to the gods. It had to be done."

"I don't know what you're hoping to get out of this Moya angle but it's not going to fly, Mick."

"We'll see."

"And what's with all the names on the new list? I've got kids I'd like to spend time with tonight."

"Give it to Lankford. He has the time. I think he ate his kids."

Forsythe was laughing as we entered the chambers. The judge was already at her desk, turned to the computer terminal on the side.

"Gentlemen, let's get this done so we can beat some traffic."

Fifteen minutes later I left through the courtroom. The judge had issued the order to appear. The sheriff's department would be charged with delivering it to the DEA's office the next morning. It ordered the DEA to show cause as to why Agent James Marco should not appear in court by ten a.m. Wednesday. That meant either Marco or a lawyer for the DEA would need to show up. If that didn't work, then Judge Leggoe would issue a bench warrant for Marco's arrest and things would really get interesting.

I found Cisco and young Sly sharing a bench in the hallway. One of Moya's men was on his own bench across the hall. The other had trailed Lorna as she went down to get the car.

I walked over to Cisco and Fulgoni and told young Sly that I knew it had been a rough day but that I greatly appreciated the help he had given my client's case. I told him I was still looking forward to working with him on the habeas case in federal court.

"I was right about you, Haller," he said.

"Yeah, when was that?" I asked.

"When I said you were an asshole."

He stood up to leave.

"I nailed it."

Cisco and I watched him stride to the elevator bank. The good thing about working late into the day in the courthouse was that the elevator crowds thinned out and the wait wasn't so bad. Fulgoni caught a ride quickly and was gone.

"Nice guy," Cisco said.

"You should meet his father," I said. "Even nicer."

"I shouldn't speak ill, though. A guy like that, I'll probably end up working for him someday," Cisco said.

"You're probably right."

I handed him my copy of the judge's order. Cisco unfolded the document and looked it over.

"Somebody up there at Roybal will probably use this to wipe his ass with."

"Probably, but it's all part of the game. Just in case, we need to be ready for Marco on Wednesday."

"Right."

We stood up and started heading toward the elevators. Moya's man followed.

"You going to the loft?" I asked Cisco.

Team Haller had been meeting regularly at the loft after court each afternoon. We recounted the occurrences of the day as well as talked and brainstormed about the next one. It was a way of sharing successes and failures. Today I thought we had been more successful than not. It would be a good meeting.

"I'll be there," Cisco said. "I just have one stop to make first."

"Okay, then."

Outside the courthouse, I walked over to Spring Street and saw Lorna's Lexus parked at the curb in front of two Lincoln Town Cars that were also waiting for lawyers from the courthouse. I walked down the sidewalk and past the Lincolns and almost opened the back door of Lorna's car but decided not to embarrass her. I got in the front.

"I guess this makes me the Lexus Lawyer now," I said. "Maybe the movie guys will make a sequel."

She didn't smile.

"Are we going to the loft?" she asked.

"If you don't mind. I want to make sure we're all set for tomorrow."

"Of course."

She abruptly pulled away from the curb without checking the traffic lane and got blasted by a motorist she'd cut off. I waited a few moments, deciding whether I should wade in. I had been married to her once briefly. I knew her moods and that the quiet, clipped dialogue version could boil over if left simmering on the stove too long.

"So what's up? You're upset."

"No I'm not."

"Yes you are. Tell me."

"Why did you make Sylvester Jr. wait for you after court today?"

I squinted, trying to see the connection between making Junior wait and her being upset.

"I don't know, I guess because I wanted to thank him for testifying. It was a rough day for him."

"And whose fault was that?"

Now I realized why she was flatlining me. She felt sorry for young Sly.

"Look, Lorna, that kid is a complete incompetent. I had to expose that because if I didn't, I was going to look just as incompetent when Forsythe mopped the floor with him. Besides,

274

someday he's going to thank me for that. It's better he get his shit together now than somewhere down the line."

"Whatever."

"Yeah, whatever. You know something, Earl never gave me any shit about how I run my cases."

"And look what happened to him."

That hit me like an arrow in the back.

"What? What's that supposed to mean?"

"Nothing."

"Come on, Lorna, don't lay that shit on me. Don't you think I already carry enough guilt about it?"

I was actually surprised it had taken her two months to get to this.

"You knew you were being followed. They put a tracker on the car."

"Yeah, a *tracker*. So they would know where I was going. Not so they could *kill* us. That was never on our radar. They put a tracker on the car, not an IED, for chrissake."

"You should've known when you went up to see Moya they would know you figured everything out and were a danger."

"That's crazy, Lorna. Because I didn't figure everything out. Not then and not now. I'm still flying by the seat of my pants on this case. Besides that, the day before, Cisco said they weren't seeing anything, and I'd made an executive decision to pull the Indians back because they were costing us a lot and you were on my back all the time about the money."

"So you're blaming me?"

"No, I'm not blaming you. I'm not blaming anybody, but obviously somebody missed something because we were not in the clear."

"And Earl got killed."

"Yeah, Earl got killed and so far they've gotten away with it. And I have to live with making the call to pull back on the surveillance, not that it would have changed anything."

I raised my hands in an I-give-up gesture.

"Look, I don't know why this all comes to the surface right now, but can we stop talking about it? I'm in the middle of a trial and I'm juggling chain saws. All of this doesn't really help. I see Earl's face every night when I try to go to sleep. If it helps you to know he haunts me, well, he does."

We rode in silence for the next twenty-five minutes until finally we pulled into the parking lot behind the loft on Santa Monica. I could tell by the number of cars in the lot, including three beat-up panel vans, that our staff meeting would have musical accompaniment. Under the house rules, bands were allowed to practice in their lofts after four p.m.

Lorna and I said nothing as we rode the freight elevator up. Our shoes made angry sounds on the wood floor. They echoed across the empty loft as we headed to the boardroom.

Only Jennifer Aronson was already there. I remembered that Cisco had said that he had something to do first.

"So how did it go?" Aronson asked.

I nodded as I pulled out a seat and sat down.

"Pretty good. Things are in play. I was even able to suggest to Forsythe that he let Lankford vet the new witness list."

"I meant the trial. How was Fulgoni?"

I glanced at Lorna, aware of her sympathies for Sly Jr.

"He served his purpose."

"Is he off yet?"

"Yeah, we're finished with him for now."

"And so you gave the new list, and what happened?"

Jennifer had prepared the new witness list, making sure that every new name had some connection to the case so that we could argue its place on it. That is, every name but one.

"Forsythe objected all over the place and the judge gave him till tomorrow morning to respond. So I want you there, since you know the names better than me. Are you clear in the morning?"

Jennifer nodded.

"Yes. Will I be making the response or just whispering to you?"

"You respond."

She brightened at the thought of going up against Forsythe in court.

"What about if he brings up Stratton Sterghos?"

I thought for a moment before responding. I heard someone riffing on an electric guitar somewhere in the building.

"First of all, there is no if about that. Sterghos is going to come up. When he does, you start to answer and then you sort of look at me as if to ask if you're saying too much. I'll step in then and take it from there."

The new witness list I had submitted was a carefully constructed part of our defense strategy. Every person we had added had at least a tangential connection to the Gloria Dayton case. We could easily argue for his or her inclusion and testimony. However, the truth was, we would actually call few of them to testify. Most of them had been added to the list in an effort to cloak a single name: Stratton Sterghos.

Sterghos was the depth charge. He was not directly or indirectly connected to Dayton. He did, however, live for the past twenty years across the street from a house in Glendale where two drug dealers were assassinated in 2003. It was in the investigation of those murders that I believed an unholy alliance was somehow struck between then–Detective Lee Lankford and DEA agent James Marco. I needed to root that alliance out and find a way to tie it in with Gloria. It was called relevance. I had to make the Glendale case relevant to the Dayton case or I would never get it to the jury.

"So you're hoping Lankford does the vetting and comes up with Stratton Sterghos's connection," Jennifer said.

I nodded.

"If we get lucky."

"And then he makes a mistake."

I nodded again.

"If we get luckier."

As if on cue, Cisco entered the boardroom. I realized that the big man hadn't made a sound as he had crossed the loft. He went to the coffeepot and started pouring a cup.

"Cisco, that's old," Lorna warned. "From this morning. It's not even hot."

"It will have to do," Cisco said.

He put the glass pot down on the cold burner and swallowed a gulp from the cup. We all made faces. He smiled.

"What?" he said. "I need the caffeine. We're setting up on the house and I could be up all night."

"So everything is set?" I asked.

He nodded.

"I just checked it out. We're ready."

"Then let's hope Lankford does his job."

"And then some."

He started pouring more of the dead coffee into his cup.

"Let me just make a fresh pot," Lorna said.

She got up and came around the table to her husband.

"No, it's fine," Cisco said. "I can't stay long anyway. Have to get up there with the crew."

Lorna stopped. There was a pained expression on her face.

"What?" Cisco asked.

"What is this you're doing?" she asked. "How dangerous?"

Cisco shrugged and looked at me.

"We've taken precautions," I said. "But...they are men with guns."

"We're always careful," Cisco added.

I now realized where the heated discussion between Lorna and me in the car had come from. She was worried about her husband, worried that the fate that had befallen Earl Briggs would come to her house next.

33

Cisco called me at midnight. I was in bed with Kendall, having snuck out my back door and once again taken a cab over the hill to meet her. The protection of Moya's men was twenty-four/seven, but I left them behind whenever I met Kendall because she objected to them and didn't want them near her. As had become our routine during the trial, we'd eaten a late dinner at the sushi bar after she closed her studio and then returned to her place. I was deeply asleep and dreaming of car crashes when Cisco called. It took me a moment to adjust to where I was and what the call meant.

"We've got them on tape," Cisco said.

"Who exactly?"

"Both of them. Lankford and Marco."

"Together, same frame?"

"Same frame."

"Good. Did they do anything?"

"Oh, yeah. They went inside."

"You mean they broke in?"

"Yep."

"Holy shit. And you've got it?"

"We've got it all and then some. Marco planted drugs in the house. Heroin."

I was almost speechless. This couldn't be any better.

"And you got that on tape, too?"

"Got it. We got it all. Do you want us to break it all down now? Pull out the cameras?"

I thought for a moment before answering.

"No," I finally said. "I want it to stay. We paid Sterghos for two weeks. Let's keep it all there. You never know."

"You sure? Do we have the money for that?"

"Yes, I'm sure. No, we don't have the money."

"Well, you don't want to stiff these guys."

I almost made a joke about how we had been stiffing the Indians since Columbus got here, but decided it was not the time for an attempt at humor.

"I'll figure something out."

"Okay."

"I'll see you in the morning. Will there be something I can see?"

"Yeah, I'll download it all to Lorna's iPad. You can watch on your way in."

"Okay, good."

After we disconnected, I checked my text file to see if I'd gotten anything from my daughter. I had been sending trial updates each night, telling her how things were going and the major highlight of each day. They had mostly been negative reports until the defense phase began. Now the highlights would be my highlights. The dispatch I had sent her while riding over the hill in the taxi had been about the points I'd scored with Valenzuela and Fulgoni on the stand.

But as usual there was no return text or acknowledgment of any kind from her. I put the phone down on the bedside table and laid my head back down on the pillow. Kendall's arm came around my chest from behind.

"Who was that?"

"Cisco. He got some good stuff tonight."

"Good for him."

"No, good for me."

She squeezed me and I felt how strong she was after many years of yoga.

"Go to sleep now," she said.

"I don't think I can," I said.

But I tried. I closed my eyes and tried to avoid returning to the dream I'd just come out of. I didn't want that. I tried to think about my daughter riding a black horse with a lightning bolt running down its nose. In the vision she wore no helmet and her hair was flowing behind her as the horse she rode galloped across an unfenced field of tall grass. I realized just before drifting off that the girl in the vision was my daughter of a year earlier, at a time when we still spoke regularly and saw each other on weekends. My last thought before succumbing to exhaustion and sleep was to wonder if she would always be frozen at that age in my dreams. Or if I would get experiences with her upon which I could build new dreams.

Two hours later the phone buzzed again. Kendall groaned as I quickly grabbed it off the bedside table and answered without looking at the screen.

"What now?"

"What now? What the hell you think you're doing treating my son like that in open court?"

It wasn't Cisco. It was Sly Fulgoni Sr.

"Sly? Look, hold on."

I got up and walked out of the room. I didn't want to disturb Kendall any further than I already had. I sat at the counter in the kitchen and spoke in a low voice into the phone.

"Sly, I did what I had to do for my client, and now's not the time to talk about it. Fact is, he got what was coming to him, and it's too late and I'm too tired to talk about it."

There was silence for a long moment.

"Did you put me on the list?" he finally asked.

That was what he was really calling about. Himself. Sly needed a vacation from federal prison, so he demanded that his name be put on the amended witness list. He had decided that he wanted to take the bus ride down from Victorville and spend a day or two in L.A. County Jail just for the change of pace and scenery. It didn't matter that there was no need for testimony from him in the La Cosse trial. He wanted me to manufacture an argument for his inclusion on the list and transfer down. If I succeeded, I could then always tell the judge I changed my mind and strategy and no longer needed him. He'd be sent back to Victorville after his little vacation.

"Yes," I said. "You're on the list. But it has not been accepted yet. It comes up first thing today, and it doesn't help you waking me up like this. I need my sleep, Sly, so I can be sharp and win the argument."

"Okay, I got it. You get your beauty sleep, Haller. I'll wait to hear from you and you better not fuck me over on this. My son doesn't know any better. He got a good lesson today. Me, I don't need any lessons. You get me down there."

"I'll do my best. Good night."

I disconnected before he could respond and went back into the bedroom. I was going to apologize to Kendall for the second intrusion but she had already fallen back asleep.

I wished I could so easily do the same. But the second call irreparably broke the sleep cycle and I moved restlessly in the bed for most of the remainder of the night, only nodding off an hour before I was supposed to awaken for the day.

That morning I called a taxi so Kendall could sleep in. Luckily, I had started leaving clothes at her house and I dressed in a suit that wasn't that fresh but at least was different from the one I'd worn the day before. I then snuck out of the house without waking her. Lorna was already waiting for me in the Lexus when the taxi pulled up to my house shortly after eight. Moya's men were there, too, in their car, waiting to escort us downtown. I took two minutes to go up to the house to get my briefcase and then came back down and jumped into the car.

"Let's go."

Lorna abruptly pulled away from the curb. I could tell she had not yet given up her anger with me.

"Hey, I'm not the one who showed up ten minutes late," she

said. "I was the one who was on time and had to sit and wait—
not to mention waiting with the two cartel goons that give everybody the creeps."

"Okay, okay. Let's just drop it, all right? I had a rough night."

"Aren't you lucky."

"I don't mean it that way. I had Cisco waking me up and then
Sly Sr. called to chew me out and I ended up with, like, three
hours total. Did Cisco put the video on your iPad for me to look
at?"

"Yes, it's in the bag in the back."

I reached between the seats to the backseat, where her purse
was on the floor. It was the size of a grocery bag and it weighed a
ton.

"What the hell do you have in this thing?"

"Everything."

I didn't ask for further explanation. I managed to pull the bag
up to the front seat, open it, and find her iPad. I put the bag on
the floor between my feet, lest I pull a muscle leveraging it into
the back again.

"It should be right on the screen and ready to go," Lorna said.
"Just hit the play button."

I opened her iPad case, lit the screen, and saw the frozen
image of the front door of a house I knew to be the home of
Stratton Sterghos. The camera angle was from below and the
quality was not great, as the only illumination came from a
porch light next to the door. I assumed Cisco's people had used
a pinhole camera hidden in a potted plant or some other porch
ornament. The view was from a side angle so that if anyone approached and knocked on the door the camera would capture
their profile.

I hit the play button and watched for a few seconds as nothing
moved or happened on the screen. Then a man stepped onto the
porch, hesitated, and glanced behind him. It was Lankford. He
then turned back and knocked on the door. He waited for the
door to be answered. I waited, too.

Nothing happened. I knew no one would answer the door but it was a tense moment just the same.

"Which way do you want me to go today?" Lorna asked.

"Just hold on a minute," I said. "Let me watch."

The video was without sound. Lankford knocked again with more force. He then looked back off camera and shook his head. Seemingly at the direction of someone offscreen, he turned and knocked again, even harder.

No one answered. A second man stepped up on the porch and moved to Lankford's right side so he could look in through the window next to the door. He cupped his eyes as he leaned against the glass. His face was hidden until he leaned back, turned to Lankford, and said something. It was James Marco.

I froze the screen so I could just look at them. It was an image I knew would cause a sea change in the case. It was perfectly reasonable and acceptable that Lankford would show up at the front door of a man listed as a defense witness on a case he was assigned to for the District Attorney's Office. But the confluence of Lankford *and* DEA agent James Marco on that front porch changed things exponentially. I was looking at digital evidence that tied Marco to Lankford and the events surrounding the murder of Gloria Dayton. At minimum, I felt I was looking at reasonable doubt.

I spoke to Lorna without taking my eyes off the screen.

"Where's Cisco now?"

"He came home, gave me that, and went to sleep. He said he'd be in court by ten."

I nodded. He deserved the the chance to sleep late.

"Well, he did good."

"Did you watch the whole thing? He said watch it to the end."

I pushed the play button. Lankford and Marco grew tired of waiting for the door to be answered and walked off the porch. I waited. Nothing happened. No action on the porch.

"What am I looking—"

Then I saw it. It was barely a shadow on the other side of the porch, but I saw it. One or both of the men walked down the side of the house.

The video then jumped to another view—this one from a camera in the backyard pointed toward the rear of the house. I noticed that the time count jumped backwards ten seconds. I watched and waited and then I saw two figures emerge from both side yards of the house and meet at the rear door. Under the light over the door I could make out their faces. Again it was Lankford and Marco. Lankford knocked on the door but Marco didn't wait for an answer. He squatted down and went to work on the doorknob, obviously attempting to pick the lock.

"This is amazing," I said. "I can't believe we got it."

"What exactly is it?" Lorna asked. "Cisco wouldn't tell me. He said it was top secret but a game changer."

"It is—a game changer, I mean. I'll tell you in a minute. It's not top secret."

I silently watched the rest of the video. Marco got the door open and looked back at Lankford and nodded. He then disappeared inside while Lankford waited outside, his back to the door, and kept watch.

The video jumped inside the house to an overhead camera in the kitchen. It was a fish-eye lens, most likely housed in a smoke detector. Marco walked beneath the camera from the back door to a hallway but then turned around and came back to the kitchen. He crossed the floor and went to the refrigerator, opened the freezer, and reached in. He started checking through the various frozen food containers until he selected a package that contained two pieces of French bread pizza. Living alone, I knew the brand and the pizza well. Marco carefully opened the box without tearing the flap. He then took out one of the plastic-wrapped pizzas and secured it under his arm while he reached into the pocket of his black-leather bomber jacket and removed something. His hand moved too fast for me to identify what he held, but whatever it was, he shoved it into the pizza box and then put the pizza back in on top of it. He returned the box to the freezer under several other packages and turned to the back door.

The video jumped outside again and I saw Marco step out of the house, lock the door, and close it. He had been inside under a minute. He nodded to Lankford and they separated, each walking down the side of the house they had come from. The video ended there.

I looked up to see where we were. Lorna was about to turn onto the 101 from Sunset. I could see down the ramp that the freeway was the usual morning parking lot. I felt the first slight tightening in my chest that always came with thoughts of being late for court.

"Why'd you go this way?"

"Because I asked you and you told me to be quiet. You try so many different ways every day, I didn't know what you wanted."

"Earl always took pride in beating the traffic. He always tried different ways."

"Well, Earl isn't here."

"I know."

I put it aside and tried to think about what I had just seen on the video. I wasn't sure yet how I would use it, but I knew without a doubt it was courtroom gold. We had captured on film a rogue drug agent and his accomplice planting drugs in Stratton Sterghos's house as some sort of scheme to eliminate or control him as a witness. This took things far beyond anything I was expecting.

I whistled low as I closed the iPad and then started putting it back into Lorna's bag.

"Okay, now can you tell me what that is and what you're so excited about that it has you whistling?"

I nodded.

"Okay, you saw that we amended our witness list yesterday, right?"

"Yes, and the judge wants to talk about it today."

"Right. Well, that was part of a play."

"You mean like one of Legal Siegel's moves?"

"Yeah, but it's my move. We're calling it 'Marco Polo.' The amended list had lots of new names on it. You heard Forsythe complain about them."

"Yes."

"Okay, one of the names on the list was Stratton Sterghos. The list was designed to make it look like we were cloaking him, sort of hoping to slip him through with all the others. He was listed right in the middle of all the names of the tenants from Gloria's building. But the play is that we wanted the prosecution team to think that we were up to something and to look for the name that we were hiding in plain sight."

"Stratton Sterghos."

"Right."

"So who is Stratton Sterghos?"

"It's not really who he is. It's where he lives. This video is from his house in Glendale. It is directly across the street from a house where ten years ago two drug dealers were murdered."

"And what's that have to do with Gloria Dayton?"

"Nothing directly. But we've been trying to make the connection between Lankford, the DA investigator who was following Gloria *before* her murder, and Agent Marco with the DEA, who she snitched for. For our defense theory to work, those two have to be connected somewhere down the line. That's what Cisco has been working on and we thought we found it in that unsolved double-murder case. The lead investigator on it was then–Glendale police detective Lee Lankford. And the two victims were connected to the Sinaloa Cartel— the same group Hector Moya is connected to. We know Marco had a hard-on for Moya back then, so it stands to reason he and his unit—the Interagency Cartel Enforcement team, ICE-T for short—were aware of and maybe even working on the two guys that got whacked in that house."

"Okay…"

That was her way of saying she still didn't get it.

"We thought that the double murder was the connection, but Cisco got copies of Lankford's old investigative files on the case and nowhere in any report is Marco or ICE-T even mentioned. So we set up a play with the witness list that we thought would draw them out if there was a connection."

I pointed down to her bag where the iPad was stashed.

"The video proves it. Lankford and Marco are connected, and I'm going to turn this trial upside down with it. It's a game changer. I just have to decide when to change the game."

"But what was the play? How is Sterghos connected?"

"He isn't connected. He just lives across the street from the house where those dealers were killed. We knew we could use him to smoke out Lankford and Marco."

"I'm sorry. Don't get angry but I still don't understand."

"I'm not angry. Look, Lankford now works for the DA. He got himself assigned to the La Cosse case so he could watch over it because, remember, he was following Gloria the night she was killed. So it's his job now to work with Forsythe and help prepare for whatever moves the defense makes. As soon as court was over yesterday, you better believe he and Forsythe sat down with that new witness list and tried to figure out what I was up to. Like, who was important and who I was really going to call."

"And they see the name Stratton Sterghos."

"Exactly. They see that name, and it means absolutely nothing to them. So Lankford goes to work. He's an investigator. He has a computer and a whole array of law enforcement access and data at his fingertips. He finds out pretty quickly that Stratton Sterghos lives on Salem Street in Glendale, and that would have rung a pretty big bell for him because he worked that two-bagger on Salem ten years ago."

"The double murder he never cleared."

"Right. So either on his own or at Forsythe's request, he needs to check out Mr. Sterghos and see what his connection is to the Dayton case. This is what Cisco and I thought would happen.

We also thought—or more like hoped—that if that double murder was the point of connection between him and Marco, Lankford might call up his buddy the DEA agent and say, 'I gotta check this guy out. You want to back me up in case we are going to have a problem?'"

"So you set up the cameras. I get it now. But what happened to Sterghos?"

"A week ago we knocked on his door and said we wanted to rent his house for two weeks for a film production."

"You mean like location scouts or something?"

"Exactly."

I smiled because the ruse we had used wasn't actually a ruse. We had indeed produced a film. Only this film's premiere wasn't going to be a red-carpet affair on Hollywood Boulevard. It was going to premiere in Department 120 of the Criminal Courts Building on Temple Street downtown.

"So Sterghos took our money and then took his wife on a little vay-cay to see their daughter in Florida. We set up cameras around his house and put the name Stratton Sterghos on the witness list as a depth charge. Now we have this."

I pointed to her bag on the floor between my feet.

"You can tell from the video that Marco was hanging back," I continued. "Lankford went to the door by himself. If Sterghos had been home and answered, he would have started with the legit interview. You know, 'I work for the DA, your name is on the witness list, what do you know about this,' and so on. Marco would stay back but be ready if Lankford determined that they had a problem with Sterghos."

"Be ready to do what?" Lorna asked.

"Whatever was necessary. Look at Gloria. Look at Earl. This guy doesn't have boundaries. Look what we have on video. Sterghos wasn't there, so Marco breaks in and plants drugs in the freezer. That was so they could come back and pop Sterghos if they needed to. It would keep him from testifying or ruin his credibility if he did."

"The whole thing is incredible."

"And it's going to be pure gold in court. We just need to figure out when to spring it."

I could barely contain myself while thinking about the possibilities for use of the video.

"You don't have to turn it in to the police?" Lorna asked.

"Nope. It's our video. I'm thinking we use it to play them off against each other, see if we can get one of them to turn against the other. The weaker one. Nothing works better with a jury than an insider spilling his guts. It's better than video. It's better than fucking DNA."

"What about Sterghos? What are you going to do to protect him? You pulled him into this and he doesn't—"

"Don't worry about him. First of all, I'm sure Cisco took care of the drugs Marco planted. Second, we have the video. Nobody's going to lay anything on Stratton Sterghos. He's lying on a beach somewhere in Florida and four grand happier."

"Four grand! Where did that come from?"

"I used my own money."

"Mickey, you better not be tapping Hayley's college fund. That would be all you need to have go wrong with her."

"I'm telling you, I didn't."

She didn't respond and she didn't seem mollified, probably because she could tell I was lying. But I had more than a year before I needed that money to pay for college.

I checked my watch and then looked at the slowly moving river of steel in front of me.

"See if you can get over and get off at Alvarado," I instructed. "We're never going to get there at this pace."

"Whatever."

It was her annoyed tone again. She was still fuming about my being ten minutes late for pickup. Or maybe about where I had been that made me ten minutes late. Or maybe it was a holdover from our angry words the day before. Whichever didn't matter. I missed Earl. He never added any tone to his commentary. He never got lost and he knew better than to sit in the middle of an unmoving freeway when I was due in court.

"What if Marco Polo hadn't worked?" Lorna asked.

"What do you mean?"

"What if they hadn't zeroed in on Stratton Sterghos? What would have happened then?"

I thought for a moment.

"We had other strategies," I finally said. "And I'm not doing too bad as it is in trial. Only one day of defense and I was chipping away at the DA's case. We're in pretty good shape without this."

I nudged her bag again with my foot.

"But now...everything changes."

"Let's hope."

34

Somehow, I made it into Department 120 at one minute before nine. Forsythe was already at his table, with Lankford sitting dutifully behind him in his seat against the rail. At the defense table Jennifer Aronson sat alone. There had been no need for the deputies to bring La Cosse out from lockup, because the jury wasn't coming out until after the hearing on the amended witness list.

I traded looks with Lankford before pulling out my chair and sitting down.

"I thought you weren't going to make it," Jennifer whispered to me in a panicked tone.

"You would have done fine. But listen, things have changed since last night. I need to handle this. I'm sorry, but there isn't enough time to explain the change in strategy. Things have happened."

"What things?"

Before I could answer, the court clerk noticed that all attorneys were present and told us the judge wanted to discuss the new witness list in chambers. We got up and the clerk opened the half door to her corral, which gave us access to the hallway behind the courtroom.

Judge Leggoe had been expecting two lawyers. She saw Jennifer and told me to pull a chair over from a conference table to the arrangement in front of her desk. We sat down in front of her, Jennifer between Forsythe and me. I had smoothly grabbed the chair on the right so the judge would be looking at me on her left.

"I thought it better to hold this hearing in chambers so maybe we can speak a little more freely," Leggoe said. "Rosa, we can go on record now."

She was talking to the court reporter who sat off the rear left corner of the judge's desk with her steno machine in front of her. I noticed that the judge didn't go on the record until after making her comment on her desire to keep the media away from the court business at hand.

I could have objected to the in-camera hearing but I didn't think it would get me anything and it certainly would not score me any points with the judge. So I went along to get along, even though I felt Jennifer staring at me and waiting for me to object. As a general rule, it is better for the defendant to hold hearings in open court. It guards against public suspicions that backroom deals are being made and information is being hidden.

The judge named all those present for the record and proceeded.

"Mr. Forsythe, I assume you've had time to study the defense's amended list of witnesses. Why don't we start with your response?"

"Thank you, Judge. My investigator and I have had barely enough time to review the list of names. And, Your Honor, calling it an amended list is a misnomer. Adding thirty-three names is not amending. It is reinventing and it is unreasonable. The state can't be expected to—"

"Your Honor," I said. "I need to interrupt Mr. Forsythe here because I think the defense can offer a compromise that will cut through a lot of this and might even make him happy."

From my inside coat pocket I withdrew a copy of the list I had worked on in the car that morning after Lorna had exited onto Alvarado and started making good progress toward the courthouse. We had stopped talking about the previous night's activities in Glendale and I had gone to work on the list and what I planned to present to the judge.

"Go ahead, Mr. Haller," the judge said. "What is your proposal?"

"I have a copy of the amended list here, and I have struck all the names I think we can compromise on."

I handed the page to her. I did not have a duplicate to share with Forsythe. It only took the judge five seconds of study for her eyebrows to shoot up in surprise.

"Mr. Haller, you've scratched off all but one, two…four of the names. How could twenty-nine names that were so important to you yesterday be so easily and expeditiously dismissed?"

I nodded like I agreed with the absurdity of my actions.

"All I can say, Judge, is that in the past twenty-four hours the defense has experienced a sea change in its thinking about how best to present the defense of Mr. La Cosse."

I looked at Jennifer. She knew about the Marco Polo play but had no idea what had happened the night before in Glendale. Still, she recognized her cue and nodded in full agreement with me.

"Yes, Your Honor," she said. "We think that we can proceed with just the four remaining names added to our original witness list."

The judge squinted her eyes suspiciously and handed the document across the desk to Forsythe. He scanned it quickly, obviously zeroing in on the names I wanted to keep rather than those I was willing to jettison. Soon enough he frowned and shook his head. I hadn't expected him to just give in.

"Judge, if counsel had made this offer yesterday, I could have saved my investigator a night's work and the taxpayers of this county the overtime cost associated with his efforts. That aside, the people appreciate that counsel is willing to cut down the number of additional witnesses. However, the people still have issue with the names that remain on the list and so I must object to the outstanding amendments."

The judge frowned and looked at her watch. She had probably thought the issue would be settled quickly and she could get the jury back into the box before nine thirty. No such luck.

"Okay," she said. "Let's go through the names. Quickly— we've got a jury waiting. State your objections."

Forsythe checked the list and chose his first battle, ticking the paper with a finger.

"Counsel has put my own investigator on his list, and the people plainly object. This is simply a ploy to get my investigator on the stand and attempt to learn the prosecution's strategies."

I faked a laugh and shook my head.

"Your Honor, defense stipulates that no question will be asked of Investigator Lankford that involves Mr. Forsythe's so-called strategies. I also want to note that we have entered the defense phase of the trial and the prosecution phase has ended. Any strategy employed by the state is clearly already on record or at the very least is obvious. But I also must add that Mr. Lankford is one of the main investigators on this case and the defense is allowed to vigorously question how the state gathers and analyzes evidence and the statements of witnesses. Lankford is an important witness and there is no precedent that would preclude him from being called by the defense."

The judge looked from me back to Forsythe.

"What's your next objection, Mr. Forsythe?"

By not making a ruling on a witness-by-witness basis, the judge was revealing that she likely would make a ruling that took all four names into account and would have something in it for both the prosecution and defense. She would attempt to split the baby in a Solomonic approach. I had anticipated this when I had scratched names off the list earlier. Lankford was the one witness I wanted. Stratton Sterghos's name was simply a plant on the list designed to get a reaction—which I had gotten in spades on the video. I never intended to actually call him and therefore could lose him now. The other two names were a neighbor in the building where Gloria Dayton had lived and Sly Fulgoni Sr. I could lose them all as well, though Sly Sr. would be quite upset about his vacation being cancelled.

"Thank you, Judge," Forsythe responded. "Next the people object to the inclusion of Stratton Sterghos. Our efforts last night have turned up not a single connection between him and this case. He lives in Glendale, far from the events that comprise this case. I am told he is a retired obstetrician who appears to be on vacation at the moment and out of contact. We could not talk to him and therefore we are hampered in our understanding of what Mr. Haller is hoping to achieve by calling him as a witness."

I jumped in before the judge even had time to turn to me and ask for a response.

"As Your Honor knows, the defense is presenting an alternate theory in the motivation behind Gloria Dayton's murder. This has already been argued at length in regard to our inclusion of Agent James Marco, Trina Rafferty, and Hector Moya on our original witness list. Same thing here, Judge. We believe Stratton Sterghos may be able to provide testimony that links the Dayton murder to a double homicide that occurred across the street from his home ten years ago."

"What?" Forsythe cried. "You have got to be kidding me. Your Honor, you cannot allow this wild fishing expedition to infect this trial. For lack of a legal term, this is nuts. A double murder ten years ago is somehow connected to this murder of a prostitute? Come on, Judge, let's not turn your courtroom into a circus, and that is exactly what the court will be doing if it—"

"Your position is clear, Mr. Forsythe," the judge said, cutting in. "Any other objections to names on the list?"

"Yes, Your Honor, I object to bringing Sylvester Fulgoni Sr. down from FCI Victorville. Anything he could contribute would surely be hearsay."

"I have to say I agree," Leggoe said. "Anything further, Mr. Haller?"

"I would like to turn our last response over to my colleague, Ms. Aronson."

I nodded to her and could tell my offer had taken her by surprise. Still, I knew she could respond.

"Judge Leggoe, with all due respect to the court as well as to Mr. Forsythe, appellate courts from across this land have repeatedly held that efforts to thwart the defense from exploring all angles and footholds of alternate theories are perilous and subject to reversal. The defense in the instant case is presenting just such an alternate defense and it would be in error if the court hampered it in doing so. Submitted, Your Honor."

Jennifer had skillfully gotten the words *reversal* and *error* into her final argument. Two words that made a judge think twice. Leggoe nodded her thanks to all three of us, then folded her hands together on the desk. If she took even a minute to consider her decisions, then it was a quick minute.

"I am going to overrule the objection to the calling of Investigator Lankford. He will testify. In regard to Stratton Sterghos, at the moment I agree with Mr. Forsythe. So he is struck. I am, however, willing to take this up again if and when the defense has built a credible path to him. The remaining two names are struck as well until such time that Mr. Haller can make a renewed argument for their inclusion."

Outwardly, I frowned. But the ruling was perfect. Sly Fulgoni Sr. wasn't going to get his vacation, but I got exactly what I wanted—Lankford. The fact that the judge left the door open a crack on Sterghos was a bonus. Now Forsythe and, by extension, Lankford and Marco, had to keep in mind that he was out there, waiting to possibly come into the trial and turn things upside down. If nothing else, it might serve to distract them while I worked other angles that were real and more damaging to the prosecution's case.

"Anything else?" the Judge asked. "We have a trial to get started."

There was nothing else. We were excused and headed back to the courtroom. On the way, Forsythe sidled up to me as I expected he would.

"I don't know where you're going with this, Haller, but you should know that if you drag the reputations of good people through the mud, there are going to be consequences."

I guessed that the gloves were now off between Forsythe and me. He was no longer acting as though he was above the fray. He was down in it. It was the first time I could remember him addressing me by my last name only, a sign that we were no longer going to be collegial about things.

That was okay with me. I was used to it.

"Is that a threat?" I asked.

"No, that's the reality of where we're at," he said.

"You can tell Lankford that I don't react to threats well. He should know that from the last time we crossed paths on a case."

"This isn't coming from Lankford. This is coming from me."

I glanced at him.

"Oh, then I guess I should just shut everything down, have my client plead open to the charges, and beg the court for mercy. Is that what you think? Because that's not going to happen, Forsythe, and if you think you can scare me off, then you didn't ask enough of your colleagues about me before we started down this path."

Forsythe picked up speed and left me behind as we pushed through the door into the courtroom. There was nothing else to say.

I scanned the courtroom and saw Lorna sitting alone in the front row. I knew that Kendall would not be in court because of at least one of the witnesses I planned to call. It was five minutes before ten, according to the clock on the rear wall of the courtroom. I walked up to the rail to talk to Lorna.

"Have you seen Cisco yet?"

"Yes, he's out in the hallway with the witness."

I looked back at the judge's bench. It was still empty and they hadn't brought La Cosse in from the lockup. I knew that with Jennifer at the defense table, things could start without me. I looked back at Lorna.

"Will you come get me in the hall when the judge comes out?"

"Sure."

I went through the gate and walked quickly out to the hall-way. Cisco was there, sitting next to Trina Rafferty. She was dressed much more conservatively than the last time I had seen her. The hem of her dress even came down over her knees and she had taken my advice to wear a sweater to keep her warm in the courtroom because Judge Leggoe had a habit of keeping the temperature down so jurors would stay awake and alert.

Costume-wise Trina Trixxx would be no problem. But I picked up the first inkling of an issue when she pointedly didn't look at me when I approached and spoke to her.

"Trina, thank you for being here today."

"I said I would. I'm here."

"Well, I am going to try to make this as easy as possible for you. I don't know how much the prosecution will have for you, but I won't take long myself."

She didn't respond or look at me. I looked at Cisco and raised my eyebrows. Problem? He shrugged like he didn't know.

"Trina," I said, "I hope you don't mind, but I'm going to take Cisco down the hall a bit so we can talk about private matters. We won't be long."

Cisco walked with me over to the elevator alcove. From there we could keep Trina in sight while we talked.

"So what's going on with her?" I asked.

"I don't know. She seems spooked about something but she isn't saying. I asked."

"Great, that's all I need. Do you know if she talked to anybody last night? Somebody from the other side?"

"If she did, she isn't saying. She might just be nervous about coming to court."

Over his shoulder I saw Lorna waving to me from the court-room door. The judge was on the bench.

"Well, whatever it is, she'd better get over it quick. She'll be on in five minutes. I gotta go."

I started to make a move to go around him, then remembered something and stepped back.

"Great work last night."

"Thanks. You looked at the tape, right?"

"Yeah, on the way in. How much did they plant in the pizza box?"

"About three ounces of black-tar heroin."

I whistled the way Cisco usually whistled.

"You took it out of there, right?"

"Yep. But what do I do with it? If I give it to the Indians, they'll sell it or use it themselves."

"Then don't give it to them."

"But I don't like having it in my possession."

It was a dilemma but the one thing I knew for sure was that we couldn't get rid of it. I might need it as part of my presentation of the video that went with it.

"Okay, then I'll take it. Bring it by the house tonight and I'll put it in the safe."

"You sure you want that kind of risk?"

"This will all be over in a few days. I'll risk it."

I clapped him on the shoulder and moved off toward the courtroom door.

"Hey," he called after me.

I turned and walked back to him.

"Did you pick up on how Lankford was acting in the video?"

I nodded.

"Yeah, like he was taking orders from Marco."

"Exactly. Marco is the alpha."

"Right."

35

The defense strategy was simple: Blaze a path that would lead the jury to James Marco and the unalterable conclusion that he was a rogue drug agent who was entirely corrupt and willing to kill to avoid exposure. Trina Rafferty was one of the steps on that pathway, and I called her as my first witness Tuesday. She had been associated with Gloria Dayton and both had come under Marco's influence and control.

No matter how conservatively she had dressed, there was something about Trina that still displayed an undeniable tawdriness. The stringy blond hair and hollow eyes, the pierced nose and bracelets tattooed around her wrists. These were all features found in many respectable women, but the combination of these and her demeanor left no doubt about who she was when she made her way to the witness stand. As she stood to be sworn in, I remembered that there was a time when Kendall, Trina, and Gloria all covered for one another on jobs because they looked so similar. Not anymore. There wasn't even a remote resemblance between Kendall and Trina. Looking at Trina, I knew I was looking at what could have been for Kendall.

After Trina was sworn in, I didn't delay in confirming the obvious to the jurors.

"Trina, you also have a professional name, do you not?"

"Yes."

"Can you share it with the jury?"

"Trina Trixxx, spelled with a triple x."

She smiled coyly.

"And what is the profession you use that name for?"

"I'm an escort."

"You mean you have sex with people for money, correct?"

"Yeah, that's it."

"And how long has this been your profession?"

"Going on twelve years, on and off."

"And did you know another escort named Gloria Dayton, who used names like Glory Days and Giselle Dallinger?"

"I knew Glory Days, yes."

"When would that have been?"

"I probably met her ten years ago. We used the same answering service."

"And did you also have some sort of work arrangement with her?"

"We covered for each other, if that's what you mean. There were three girls and we covered for each other. If one was busy with a client or had a full schedule and a call came in for her, then one of the other two would take it. And sometimes if a customer wanted two girls or even three girls, then we would all work together."

I nodded and paused for a moment. That last part had not come up previously and it was distracting to me, since the third girl who had not yet been named was Kendall Roberts.

"Mr. Haller?" the judge prompted. "Can we get through this?"

"Yes, Your Honor. Uh, Ms. Rafferty, did you have contacts within the law enforcement community during these times?"

Trina acted puzzled by the question.

"Well, I got busted a couple times. Three times, actually."

"Did you ever get busted by the DEA?"

She shook her head.

"No, just LAPD and the sheriff's."

"Were you ever detained then by the DEA, by an agent named James Marco?"

In my peripheral vision I saw Forsythe lean forward. He always did it before objecting. But for some reason he didn't object. I turned to look at him, still expecting the objection, and saw that Lankford had reached forward from his seat at the railing and touched Forsythe's back. I read it as Lankford, the investigator, telling Forsythe, the prosecutor, not to object.

"I don't think so."

I turned back to the witness, unsure about what I just heard.

"I'm sorry," I said. "Can you repeat that?"

"I said no," Trina said.

"You're saying you don't know a DEA agent named James Marco?"

"That's correct. I don't know him."

"You've never even met him?"

"Not as far as I know—unless he was undercover or something and using a different name."

I turned and glanced back at Cisco in the first row. Obviously, Marco had somehow gotten to Trina Rafferty, and in that moment I wanted to know how. But what was more pressing than the explanation was what I was going to do right now. I could turn on my own witness, but the jury might not like that.

I decided that I didn't have much of a choice.

"Trina," I said, "didn't you tell me previous to your testimony here today that you were a confidential informant who worked for Agent Marco and the DEA?"

"Well, I told you a lot of things because you were paying my rent. I told you whatever you wanted me to tell you."

"No, that's—"

I stopped myself and tried to remain composed. Not only had Marco and Lankford gotten to her, but they had turned her into a weapon of mass destruction. If I didn't salvage this, she could blow up the entire defense.

"When was the last time you spoke with Agent Marco?"

"I don't know him, so I didn't speak to him."

"You're telling this jury that you have no idea who Agent James Marco is?"

"I'm sorry. I don't. I needed a place to stay and some food. I might have told you things so you would give me things back."

It had happened to me before, a witness shifting sides like this. But never so dramatically and with so much damage inflicted on my case. I glanced over at my client at the defense table. He looked bewildered. I looked past him at Jennifer and she had an expression of embarrassment on her face—embarrassment for me.

I turned and looked at the judge, who was equally perplexed. I did the only thing I could in the situation.

"Your Honor, I have no further questions," I said.

I slowly returned to the defense table, passing Forsythe on his way to the lectern to further the damage. As I moved through the narrow channel between the empty prosecution table and the chairs running along the railing I had to pass Lankford. I heard him make a low humming sound.

"Mmm mmm mmmmm."

Only I would have heard it. I stopped, took a step back, and leaned down to him.

"What did you say?" I asked in a whisper.

"I said, keep going, Haller," he whispered back.

Forsythe began his cross-examination by asking Trina Rafferty if the two of them had ever met. I moved to my seat and sat down. The one good thing about Forsythe jumping on his cross so fast was that it saved me for the moment from having to tell my client how badly things had just turned. The Rafferty fiasco was a one-two punch to the guts of our case. Already, without Forsythe piling on—which he was about to do—I had lost a key piece of testimony connecting Marco and Gloria Dayton. Adding insult to that injury, she was more than implying that I was suborning perjury—paying a witness with rent money to lie.

Forsythe seemed to think that by destroying me he was destroying the case. Almost all of his cross centered on Trina's testimony that I fed her the lines she was supposed to speak in testimony in exchange for the apartment just a few blocks away behind the Police Administration Building. And in his zeal to take me down, I saw the way to possibly salvage things. If I could show her to have lied, I stood a good chance of undercutting—in the eyes of the jury, at least—the accusations she was making about me.

Forsythe finished after fifteen minutes, curtailing his cross when I started objecting to nearly every question on the basis that it had already been asked and answered. You can beat a dead horse only so many times. He finally gave up and sat down.

I slowly got up for redirect, walking to the lectern like a condemned man to the gallows.

"Ms. Rafferty, you gave the address of this apartment I am supposedly paying for. When did you move in there?"

"In December, right before Christmas."

"And do you recall when you first met me?"

"It was after. I think March or April."

"Then, how is it that you think I was paying for this apartment for you when I did not meet you until three to four months after you moved in?"

"Because you were meeting with the other lawyer, and he was the one who moved me in."

"And which lawyer was that?"

"Sly. Mr. Fulgoni."

"You mean Sylvester Fulgoni Jr.?"

"Yes."

"Are you saying that Sylvester Fulgoni Jr. along with me is representing Mr. La Cosse?"

I pointed to my client as I spoke, and I asked the question with a reserved astonishment in my voice.

"Well, no," she said.

"Then who was he representing when he supposedly moved you into this apartment?"

"Hector Moya."

"Why did Mr. Fulgoni move you into an apartment?"

Forsythe objected, arguing that Fulgoni and the Moya case were not relevant. I, of course, took the opposite view of this in my response, citing once again the alternate defense theory I was presenting. The judge overruled and I asked the question again.

"Same thing," Trina answered. "He wanted me to say Gloria Dayton told me that Agent Marco asked her to plant a gun in Hector's hotel room."

"And you're saying that never happened, that Mr. Fulgoni made it up."

"That's correct."

"Didn't you testify a few minutes ago that you never heard of an Agent Marco, and now you say Mr. Fulgoni was feeding you testimony regarding him?"

"I didn't say I never heard of him. I said I never met him and I never snitched for him. There's a difference, you know."

I nodded, properly chastised by the witness.

"Ms. Rafferty, have you received a phone call or a visit within the last twenty-four hours from a law enforcement officer?"

"No, not that I know of."

"Has anyone attempted to coerce you into testifying the way you have today?"

"No, I'm just telling the truth."

I had gotten it out to the jury as best I could, even if it was in the form of denials. My hope was that they would instinctively know that Trina Rafferty was the liar, that she had been pressured by someone to lie. I decided it was too risky to continue and ended the questioning.

On my way back to my seat, I whispered to Lankford as I went by.

"Where's your hat?"

I kept moving along the rail until I got to Cisco. I leaned over to whisper to him as well.

"Have you seen Whitten?"

He shook his head.

"Not yet. What do you want me to do with Trina?"

I glanced back at the front of the courtroom. Forsythe had no re-cross, so the judge was dismissing Rafferty from the witness stand. Cisco had picked her up that morning at her apartment building and taken her the three blocks to court.

"Take her back. See if she'll say anything."

"You want me to be nice?"

I hesitated but only for a moment. I understood the threat and pressure people like Marco and Lankford could bring to bear. If the jury picked up on that, then her flip on the stand might be more valuable than if she had testified truthfully.

"Yeah, be nice."

Over Cisco's shoulder I saw Detective Whitten enter the courtroom and take a seat in the back row. He was right on time.

36

As the lead investigator on the Gloria Dayton murder, Detective Mark Whitten had attended most of the trial, often sitting along the rail next to Lankford. However, I had not noticed during the course of the proceedings the two acting much like prosecution teammates. Whitten seemed to keep to himself, almost aloof when it came to Forsythe, Lankford, and everyone else associated with the trial. During trial breaks I had seen him walking by himself back to the PAB. Once I had even seen him in Pete's eating lunch by himself.

I called Whitten as my next witness. He had already testified for a day and a half during the prosecution phase of the trial. He had primarily been used by Forsythe to introduce evidence such as the video of the La Cosse interview. In a way, he was the narrator of the prosecution's story, and as such, his testimony had been the longest by far of any witness in the case.

At the time, I had limited my cross-examination to aspects of the video, repeating many of the questions I hit Whitten with during the unsuccessful motion-to-suppress hearing. I wanted the jury to hear him deny that La Cosse had been a suspect the moment Whitten and his partner knocked on Andre's door. I knew no one would believe that and hoped it would plant a seed of mistrust in the official investigation that would blossom during the defense phase.

I had reserved the right to recall him as a witness, and now was that time. I didn't need to get a lot from him, but what I was going for was vitally important. It would be the fulcrum on which the case would pivot to the defense's side of the equation. Whitten, who was in his midforties with twenty years on the job, was an experienced witness. He had a calm demeanor and spoke in a matter-of-fact tone. He was skilled at not revealing the hostility that almost all cops carry for the defense. That was reserved for times when the jury was not present.

After a few preliminary questions that would serve to remind the jury of his role in the case, I moved on to the areas I needed to explore. Defense work is about building foundations for the evidence and angles you want to introduce. That's what I needed Whitten for now.

"Detective, when you testified last week, you spoke at length about the crime scene and what was found there, correct?"

"That's right, I did."

"And you had an inventory of that crime scene and what was found there, correct?"

"Yes."

"And these were the victim's belongings and property, right?"

"Yes."

"Can you refer to that inventory list now?"

With the judge's permission, Lankford brought the so-called murder book to Whitten. If he had been called by the prosecution, he would have normally taken the witness stand with the thick compendium of all investigative records tucked under his arm. Not bringing it with him to the stand when I called him was a little glimmer of that hostility he was so skilled at hiding.

Working off a copy of the list I had received in discovery, I continued.

"Okay, referring to the inventory list, I see no cell phone. Is that correct?"

"We did not recover a cell phone from the crime scene. That is correct."

"Now, Mr. La Cosse explained to you, did he not, that he'd

been on a call with the victim earlier that evening and that that conversation was the reason he went to her place in person?"

"Yes, that is what he told us."

"But you found no phone in the apartment, right?"

"Right."

"Did you or your partner try to find an explanation for this discrepancy?"

"We assumed that the killer took her phones as a means of hiding his trail."

"You say 'phones.' There was more than one phone?"

"Yes, we determined that the victim and the defendant used a variety of throwaway phones to conduct their business. The victim also had a cell phone for private use."

"Can you tell the jury what a throwaway phone is?"

"These are inexpensive phones that come with a limited number of minutes of call time. When you burn up the minutes, you throw the phone away or in some cases you can reload them with new minutes for a fee."

"These were used because call records would be difficult to obtain by investigators if the phone was thrown away and you didn't know where to start looking."

"Exactly."

"And this is how Mr. La Cosse and Ms. Dayton communicated in the course of their business, correct?"

"Yes."

"But you found none of these phones in the apartment after the murder, correct?"

"Correct."

"Now, you mentioned that the victim also had a cell phone for private use. What did you mean by that?"

"This was an iPhone that she owned and that she used for calls unrelated to her escort business."

"And this iPhone was also missing after the murder?"

"Yes, we never found it."

"And whoever killed her, you think he took it."

"Yes."

"What was the theory behind that?"

"We believed it was an indication that the killer knew her and that they might have communicated by cell phone or his name and number might be in a contact list on the phone. So the killer took all of the phones as a precaution against being tracked in that way."

"And the phones have never been found?"

"They have not."

"So, did this cause you to go to the phone company and order the call records from these phones?"

"We ordered records for the iPhone because we found some bills in the apartment and knew the number. As far as the throw-aways went, there was no way to order records when we didn't have the phones or the numbers. There was nowhere to start."

I nodded like I was learning all of this for the first time and coming to a deeper understanding of the difficulties Whitten faced on the case.

"Okay, so going back to the iPhone. You ordered records and you had some records you'd found. You studied these records for clues, correct?"

"We did."

"Did you find any calls to or from Mr. La Cosse on that iPhone?"

"No, we didn't."

"Did you find any calls that were significant or of note in those records?"

"No, we didn't."

I paused there and made a face as I looked down at my notes. I wanted the jury to think I was troubled by the detective's last answer.

"Now, these records that you ordered, they contained all incoming and outgoing calls on that phone, correct?"

"Yes."

"Even local calls?"

"Yes, we were able to obtain local records."

"And you studied these?"

"Yes."

"And did you find any calls, either coming in or going out, that were significant to your investigation?"

Forsythe objected, saying I was repeating my questions. The judge told me to move along. I asked Whitten to find in the murder book the three-page printout of calls on Gloria's iPhone.

"Are those your initials on the bottom right corner of this document's front page?"

"Yes."

"And you wrote the date of November twenty-sixth there, correct?"

"Yes, I did."

"Why is that?"

"That would be the date that I received the document from the phone company."

"That would have been fourteen days after the murder. Why did it take so long?"

"I had to secure a search warrant for the records. That took some time and then it took the phone company some time to put it all together."

"So by the time you got these records, Andre La Cosse had already been arrested and charged with the murder, correct?"

"That's correct."

"You believed that you had the killer in jail, correct?"

"Yes, correct."

"So then, what good were these phone records?"

"The investigation always continues after an arrest. In this case, all leads were followed and we continued all valid avenues of investigation. The report on the phone records was one of them."

"Well then, did you find any numbers on this list that were connected to Mr. La Cosse?"

"No."

"None?"

"None."

"Then did any of the numbers listed here—there must be about two hundred—have investigative value to you?"

"No, sir, they didn't."

"And, by the way, how are the numbers ordered here?"

"By frequency of calls. The numbers she called the most often are at the top and then they go down in descending frequency from there."

I turned to the last page and told Whitten to do so as well.

"So on the last page here, these are numbers she called just once?"

"Correct."

"For how long a period?"

"The search warrant asked for records going back six months."

I nodded.

"Detective, let me draw your attention to the ninth number down on the third page. Can you read that out to the jury?"

I heard rustling as Forsythe decided I might be doing more than wasting the court's time and turned the pages of his copy of the document.

"Area code two-one-three, six-two-one, sixty-seven hundred," Whitten read.

"And when was that number dialed on Gloria Dayton's iPhone?"

Whitten squinted as he read.

"At six forty-seven p.m. on November fifth."

Forsythe now understood where I was going with this and stood up and objected.

"Relevancy, Your Honor," he said with an urgent tone in his voice. "We've allowed defense counsel great latitude, but where does it end? He is going far off the reservation here, stringing out the details of one three-minute phone call. It has nothing to do with the case at hand or the charges against his client."

I smiled and shook my head.

"Your Honor, Mr. Forsythe knows exactly where this is headed, and he does not want the jury to go there because he knows the house of cards that is the prosecution's case is in great peril."

The judge made a motion with her hands, bringing her fingers together.

"Connect it, Mr. Haller. Soon."

"Right away, Your Honor."

I looked back at my notes, got my bearings again, and pressed on. Forsythe's objection was nothing more than an attempt to break my rhythm. He knew it didn't stand a chance on its merits.

"So Detective Whitten, this call went out at six forty-seven on the evening of November fifth, just seven days before Ms. Dayton's murder, correct?"

"Yes."

"How long did the call last?"

Whitten checked the document.

"It says two minutes, fifty-seven seconds."

"Thank you. Did you check that number out when you got this list? Did you call it?"

"I don't recall if I did or not."

"Do you have a cell phone, Detective?"

"Yes, but I don't have it on me."

I reached into my pocket and pulled my own phone. I asked the judge to allow me to give it to Whitten.

Forsythe objected, calling what I was about to do a stunt and accusing me of grandstanding.

I argued that what Forsythe called a stunt was merely a demonstration, not unlike the demonstration a week earlier when he asked the deputy medical examiner to demonstrate on Lankford how the victim's hyoid bone was crushed during her strangulation. I added that having the detective make the call to the number in question was the easiest and quickest way to ascertain who Gloria Dayton had called at 6:47 p.m. on November 5.

The judge allowed me to proceed. I walked up and handed my phone to Whitten after turning on its speaker. I asked him to call 213-621-6700. He did so and placed the phone down on the flat railing that ran in front of the witness stand.

The call was answered by a woman's voice after one ring.

"DEA, Los Angeles Division, how can I help you?"

I nodded and stepped forward, picking up the phone.

"Sorry, wrong number," I said before disconnecting.

I stepped back to the lectern, savoring the pure silence that had followed the voice of the woman who had said DEA. I stole a quick glance at Mallory Gladwell, my alpha juror, and saw an expression that soothed my soul. Her mouth was slightly opened in what I took to be an *Oh My God* moment.

I looked back at Whitten as I pulled a photograph I'd had ready from beneath my legal pad. I asked permission to approach the witness with the defense's first exhibit.

The judge allowed it, and I gave Whitten the eight-by-ten shot that Fernando Valenzuela had taken of Gloria Dayton when he served her with the subpoena in the Moya case.

"Detective, you have in your hand a photo that has been marked as defense exhibit one. It is a photo of the victim in this case in the moment she was served with a subpoena in a civil matter styled as *Moya versus Rollins*. Can I draw your attention to the time and date stamp on the photograph, and will you read that out to the jury?"

"It says six oh-six p.m., November fifth, twenty twelve."

"Thank you, Detective. And so, is it correct to conclude from that photo and the victim's phone records that exactly forty-one minutes after Gloria Dayton was served with the subpoena in the Moya case, she called the DEA's Los Angeles Division on her personal cell phone?"

Whitten hesitated as he looked for a way out of his predicament.

"It is impossible for me to know if she made the call," he finally said. "She could have loaned her phone to someone else."

I loved it when cops dissembled on the stand. When they tried not to give the obvious answer and made themselves look bad in the process.

"So then it would be your opinion that forty-one minutes after being served as a witness in a case involving an incarcerated drug dealer, someone other than Ms. Dayton used her phone to call the DEA?"

"No, I'm not saying that. I don't have an opinion on it. I said that we don't know who was in possession of her phone at that moment. Therefore, I can't sit here and say with certainty that it was she who made the call."

I shook my head in a feigned show of frustration. The truth was I was elated by Whitten's response.

"Okay, Detective, then let's move on. Did you ever investigate this call or Gloria Dayton's connection to the DEA?"

"No, I did not."

"Did you ever inquire as to whether she had been an informant for the DEA?"

"No, I did not."

I could tell Whitten was about to blow his cool. He wasn't getting any protection from Forsythe, who, without valid objection in hand, was hunkering down in his seat, waiting for the damage to end.

"Why not, Detective? Doesn't this strike you as one of those 'valid avenues of investigation' you spoke of earlier?"

"First of all, I knew nothing about the subpoena at that time. And second, informants don't call the main number of the DEA. That would be like walking through the front door with a sign on your back. I had no reason to be suspicious about one quick call to the DEA."

"I'm confused now, Detective. So are you now saying you were aware of the call and just not suspicious of it? Or, as I think you just said a few minutes ago, you didn't even recall checking out that number or the call. Which is it?"

"You're twisting what I say around."

"I don't think so, but let me rephrase. Before testifying here today, did you or did you not know that a call from the victim's personal cell phone had been placed to the DEA one week before her death? Yes or no, Detective?"

"No."

"Okay. So then it is safe to say you missed it?"

"I wouldn't say that. But you can say whatever you want."

I turned and looked back at the clock. It was eleven forty-five. I wanted to take Whitten in another direction but I wanted to leave the jurors with Gloria's phone call to mull over at lunch. I knew if I suggested to the judge that we take the lunch break now I would end up in lockup with my client for the next hour.

I turned back to Whitten, needing to string things out at least another fifteen minutes. I looked down at my notes.

"Mr. Haller," the judge prompted. "Do you have any more questions for the witness?"

"Uh, yes, Your Honor. Quite a few, in fact."

"Then I suggest you get on with them."

"Yes, Your Honor," I said. "Uh, Detective Whitten, you just testified that you did not know that Gloria Dayton had been subpoenaed in a case involving Hector Moya. Do you recall when you found out?"

"It was earlier this year," Whitten answered. "It came to light through the exchange of discovery materials."

"So, in other words, you learned of the subpoena she received because the defense told you, correct?"

"Yes."

"What did you do with the information once the defense furnished you with it?"

"I checked it out as I check out all leads that come in."

"And what did you conclude after checking it out?"

"That it had no bearing on the case. It was coincidental."

"Coincidental. Do you still feel that it was coincidental now that you know that Gloria Dayton's personal cell phone was used to call the DEA in Los Angeles less than an hour after she was served with the subpoena in a case that accused her of planting a gun on a DEA target?"

Forsythe objected to the question on multiple grounds, and Leggoe had her pick. She sustained the objection and told me to rephrase the question if I wanted to get it in. I simplified and asked again.

"Detective, if you knew back then on the day of Gloria Dayton's murder that a week earlier she had called the DEA, would you have been interested enough to find out why?"

Forsythe was on his feet again before I finished the question and jumped in right away with his objection.

"Calls for speculation," he argued.

"Sustained," Judge Leggoe said without giving me the opportunity to argue.

But that was okay. I no longer needed Whitten to answer. I liked how the question hung out there like a cloud over the jury box.

Sensing it was the right time to pause, the judge called for the lunch break.

I moved over to the defense table and stood next to my client as the jury filed out of the box. I felt as though I had recovered from the Trina Trixxx fiasco and was back on top. I glanced out to the gallery and saw only Moya's men in the public seats. Cisco had apparently not come back from escorting Trina Rafferty home. And Lorna was nowhere to be seen.

No one had been watching. No one who mattered to me.

37

Jury trials always made me hungry. Something about the energy expended in constant wariness of the prosecution's moves while worrying about my own moves steadily built a hunger in me that started soon after the judge took the bench and grew through the morning session. By the lunch break I usually wasn't thinking about salad and soup. I usually craved a heavy meal that would carry me through the afternoon session.

I made calls, and Jennifer, Lorna, Cisco, and I agreed to meet at Traxx in Union Station so I could indulge my appetite. They made a great hamburger there. Cisco and I gorged on the basics—red meat, French fries, and ketchup—while the ladies fooled themselves into being satisfied with Niçoise salads and iced tea.

There wasn't much talk. A little discussion about Trina Rafferty. Cisco reported only that something or someone had scared her shitless and she wasn't talking, even off the record. But for the most part I stayed in my own world. Like a boxer in his corner between rounds, I wasn't thinking about the earlier rounds and the punches missed. I was only thinking about answering the next bell and landing the knockout blow.

"Do they ever eat?" Jennifer said.

This question somehow bumped through my thoughts, and I looked across the table at her, wondering what I had missed and what she was talking about.

"Who?" I asked.

She nodded toward the great hall of the train station.

"Those guys."

I turned and looked through the doorway of the restaurant and into the massive waiting area. Moya's men were out there, sitting in the first row of stuffed-leather chairs.

"If they do, I've never seen it," I said. "You want to send them a salad?"

"They don't look like salad eaters," Lorna said.

"Carnivores," Cisco added.

I waved our waitress down.

"Mickey, don't," Jennifer said.

"Relax," I said.

I told the waitress we were ready for the check. It was time to get back to court.

The afternoon session started on time at one o'clock. Whitten returned to the witness stand and looked a little less crisp than he had in the morning. It made me wonder if he'd braced himself for the afternoon with a martini or two for lunch. Maybe the whole aloof thing was actually about covering an alcohol habit.

The plan with Whitten now was to use him to set up my next witness. My case was a daisy chain of interlocking witnesses, where one was used to build the path to the next. It was Whitten's turn now to pave the way for a man named Victor Hensley, who was a security supervisor at the Beverly Wilshire hotel.

"Good afternoon, Detective Whitten," I said cheerily, as if I was not the same attorney who had brutalized him in the morning's session. "Let's turn our attention here to the victim of this horrible crime, Gloria Dayton. Did you and your partner, as part of your investigation, trace her movements up until the time of the murder?"

Whitten made a show of adjusting the microphone to buy some time as he thought about how to answer. I was pleased to see this. It meant that he was on alert and looking for the trapdoor in the simplest of questions from me.

"Yes," he finally said. "We composed a timeline for her. The closer it was to the time of the murder, the more details we were interested in."

I nodded.

"Okay, so you checked out the last escort job she went out on that night?"

"Yes, we did."

"You talked to the man who regularly drove her to her assignations, correct?"

"Yes, John Baldwin. We talked to him."

"And her last job was at the Beverly Wilshire, correct?"

Forsythe stood up and objected, saying I was going over a timeline that had already been established by Whitten during his direct examination in the prosecution phase. The judge agreed and asked me to break new ground or to move on.

"Okay, Detective, as testified to earlier, there was a disagreement that night between the victim and the defendant, am I right?"

"If you want to call it that."

"What would you call it, then?"

"You are talking about before he killed her?"

I looked at the judge and widened my hands in a feigned signal of astonishment.

"Your Honor..."

"Detective Whitten," the judge said, "please curtail such prejudicial statements. It is the jury's role to determine the guilt or innocence of the defendant."

"I apologize, Your Honor," Whitten said.

I asked the question again.

"Yes. They had a disagreement."

"And this disagreement was over money, correct?"

"Yes, La Cosse wanted his share from a client and Gloria Dayton said there had been no client, that nobody was in the room he sent her to."

I pointed at the ground as if pointing to the moment he just described.

"Did you and your partner investigate that disagreement to determine who was right and who was wrong?"

"If you mean, did we check out whether the victim was actually holding out on La Cosse, yes we looked into it. We determined that the room La Cosse sent her to was unoccupied and that the name La Cosse said he gave her belonged to the guest who was in that room previously but had already checked out. There was no one in that room when she went to the hotel. He killed her for holding out on money she didn't have."

I asked the judge to strike Whitten's last sentence as unresponsive and prejudicial. She agreed and instructed the jury to disregard it, for whatever that was worth. I moved on, hitting Whitten with a new set of questions.

"Did you check to see if the Beverly Wilshire had surveillance cameras on site, Detective Whitten?"

"Yes, and they do."

"Did you review any of video from the night in question?"

"We went to the security office at the hotel and reviewed their video feeds, yes."

"And what did you glean from your review, Detective Whitten?"

"They don't have video on the guest floors. But from what we did see of the lobby and elevators videos, we concluded that there was no one in the room she was sent to. She even checked at the front desk and they told her no. You can see it on the video."

"Why didn't the state present this video to the jury during the prosecution phase of this trial?"

Forsythe objected, saying the question was argumentative and irrelevant. Judge Leggoe agreed and sustained the objection, but again the question was more important than the answer. I wanted the jurors to wish they had seen the video, whether it was germane to the murder or not.

I moved on.

"Detective, how do you account for the discrepancy between Andre La Cosse setting up the date at the Beverly Wilshire and Gloria Dayton going there and finding the room unoccupied?"

"I don't account for it."

"It doesn't bother you?"

"Sure it bothers me but not every loose end gets tied up."

"Well, tell us, what you think happened that could explain what seems to be some kind of mix-up on Andre La Cosse's part?"

Forsythe objected, saying the answer called for speculation. This time the judge overruled, saying she wanted to hear the detective's answer.

"I really don't have an answer," Whitten said.

I checked my notes to see if I had forgotten anything and then glanced at the defense table to see if Jennifer had any reminders. It looked like I was clear. I thanked the witness and told the judge I had no further questions.

Forsythe went to the lectern to see if he could bandage the wounds I had opened in the prosecution's case during the morning session. He would have been better off passing, because it came off—at least to me—as though he was more worried about semantics than content. He brought out that Whitten had been an undercover narcotics officer in an earlier part of his career. As such he had several confidential sources that fed him tips. None of them, he testified, contacted him through the main number of the police station. That would have been highly unusual and dangerous. They all were given private numbers with which to make contact.

That was all well and good, but it did not speak to Gloria Dayton's circumstances and gave me an easy setup when it was my turn for redirect. I didn't even go to the lectern with my legal pad.

"Detective Whitten, how long ago did you work as an undercover narcotics officer?"

"I did it for two years—two thousand and two thousand and one."

"Okay, and do you still have the same cell phone number from those days?"

"No, I'm in homicide now."

"You have a new number."

"Yes."

"Okay, so what if one of your informants from two thousand and one wanted to call you today because they had information you needed to have?"

"Well, I would direct this person to current narcotics investigators."

"You're missing the point of the question. How would that old source of yours reach out to you, since the old established method of contact is no longer in existence?"

"There are a lot of different ways."

"Like calling the main number of the police station and asking for you?"

"I don't see an informant who wants to stay an informant doing that."

Whitten understood what I wanted and obstinately didn't want to give me the point. It didn't matter, though. I was sure the jury understood. Gloria Dayton had no way after so many years to contact Agent Marco but to call the DEA's main number.

I gave up and sat down. Whitten was dismissed and I called my next witness, Victor Hensley.

Hensley was a Trojan horse witness. His was the sixteenth name on the original witness list that the defense turned in before the start of trial. In keeping with court protocol, each name on the witness list was followed by a brief description of who the person was and what his or her expected testimony would be. This was to help the opposing side decide how much focus and time to apply to vetting and preparing for the witness's testimony. However, in placing Hensley's name on the list, I didn't want the prosecution to know my true purpose—which was to use him to enter the Beverly Wilshire's security videos as defense exhibits. So I listed Hensley's occupation and simply described him as a corroborating witness. My hope was that Forsythe and his investigator Lankford would view Hensley as a witness who would confirm that no one had rented the room that Gloria Dayton had gone to on the night of her death.

As it turned out, Hensley reported to Cisco during a check-in phone call that during the run-up to the trial, he'd had only one brief visit at the hotel from Lankford and had never spoken to Forsythe at all. All of this boded well for me. I realized as Hensley took the stand, carrying with him a smart-looking leather folder with his notes inside, that I stood a good chance of not only maintaining the momentum begun that morning with Whitten but increasing it.

Hensley was in his late fifties and looked like a cop. After he was sworn in, I quickly ran down his pedigree as a former detective with the Beverly Hills Police Department who retired and took the job in security at the Beverly Wilshire. I then asked him if the hotel security staff had conducted its own investigation of the part the premises had played in the hours before Gloria Dayton's murder.

"Yes, we did," he answered. "Once we became aware that the hotel played a tangential part in the situation, we looked into it."

"And did you take part in that investigation yourself?"

"Yes, I did. I was in charge of it."

I then led Hensley through a series of questions and answers that outlined how he had worked with LAPD detectives and confirmed that Gloria Dayton had entered the hotel that evening and knocked on a guest-room door. He also confirmed that the room where she had knocked was empty and that no guest was staying in it.

My Trojan horse was now inside the gate and I got down to work.

"Now, from the very start, the defendant has claimed to police that a prospective client had called from the Beverly Wilshire and said that he was in that room. Is that possible?"

"No, it's not possible that a guest was staying in that room."

"But could someone have gotten in that room somehow and made the call?"

"Anything's possible. It would have to be someone who had a key."

"Is it an electronic key?"

"Yes."

"Did you check to see if someone stayed in that room the night before?"

"Yes, we checked, and someone did stay in that room the night before. That would have been Saturday night. We'd had a wedding reception in the hotel, and the bride and groom stayed in that suite that night."

"When is checkout time?"

"Noon. But they asked for late checkout because they had an evening flight to Hawaii. Since they were newlyweds, we gladly accommodated them. They left at four twenty-five that afternoon, according to our records, meaning they probably left the room at four fifteen or so. We covered this in our investigation."

"So the room was occupied until four fifteen or so and then not rebooked for Sunday night."

"That's correct. Because of the late checkout, it was not put on the availability list because housekeeping wouldn't have it ready until much later."

"And if someone somehow got access to that room—got in somehow—then he would have been able to use the phone to call out, is that right?"

"That is correct."

"Would a call from outside the hotel be put through to that room if the caller requested it?"

"The policy at our hotel is that no call is transferred to a room without the caller asking for the guest by name. You cannot just call up and ask for room twelve-ten, for example. You have to know the name, and it has to be a registered guest. So the answer is no. The call would not have been put through."

I nodded thoughtfully before continuing.

"What were the names of the newlyweds who had the suite the night before?"

"Daniel and..."

He opened his yellow folder and checked his notes from the investigation.

"...Laura Price. But they were checked out and on their way to Hawaii when all of these events were supposedly happening."

"Earlier in this trial, the prosecution introduced a video of the police interrogation of the defendant, Andre La Cosse. Are you familiar with it?"

"No, I have not seen it."

I got permission from the judge to reshow a portion of the interrogation on the overhead screen. In the segment, Andre La Cosse told Detective Whitten that he received a blocked call from someone named Daniel Price at about four-thirty the afternoon before the murder. As a security measure, he then asked for a callback number and the caller provided the phone number and a room number at the Beverly Wilshire. La Cosse said he called the hotel back, asked for Daniel Price's room, and was put through. They made arrangements for escort service at eight p.m., with Giselle Dallinger being the provider.

I turned the video off and looked at Hensley.

"Mr. Hensley, does your hotel keep records of incoming calls to guest rooms?"

"No, only outgoing calls, because those are charged to the guest account."

I nodded.

"How would you explain that Mr. La Cosse had the right name and room number when he called the hotel?"

Hensley shook his head.

"I can't explain it."

"Is it possible that because of the late checkout given the newlyweds, the name Daniel Price was still on the guest list that the hotel operator uses?"

"It's possible. But once they checked out, the name would have been removed from the current guest list."

"Is that a human process or a computerized process?"

"Human. The name is deleted from the current guest list at the front desk when someone checks out."

"So if the person handling the assignment at the front desk got busy with other work or other guests, that process might have been delayed, correct?"

"It could have happened."

"It could have happened," I repeated. "Isn't three o'clock check-in time at the hotel?"

"Yes, it is."

"Is the front desk generally busy at that time?"

"It all depends on the day of the week, and Sunday check-ins are usually slow. But you're right, it could have been busy at the desk."

I didn't know what any of this got me, but I felt that the jury might be getting bored. It was time to open the trapdoor in the Trojan horse's belly. Time to come out of hiding and attack.

"Mr. Hensley, let's move on a bit. You said in your earlier testimony that the hotel's own investigation confirmed that the victim, Gloria Dayton, had entered the hotel on the evening of last November eleventh. How did you confirm that?"

"We looked at video from the cameras and pretty soon we found her."

"And you were able to track her by different cameras and video as she moved through the hotel, correct?"

"That's right."

"Did you bring a copy of the video from the cameras with you to court today?"

"Yes, I did."

He pulled a disc out of one of the pockets of his leather folder and held it up for a moment.

"Did you ever give a copy of that video record to the LAPD investigators who were working on the case?"

"The detectives came by early in the investigation and reviewed our raw feeds—this was before we put together a single video that tracked the woman they were interested in through the hotel. We later put that together and made all the material available, but nobody came to pick it up until a couple months ago."

"Was that Detective Whitten or his partner?"

"No, it was Mr. Lankford from the DA's Office. They were prepping for the trial and he came around to collect what we had."

I wanted to turn and look at Forsythe, to try to get a read on whether he ever saw the video—because it sure never showed up on any discovery list I had seen.

But I didn't look at the prosecutor, because I didn't want to give anything away. Not yet, at least.

"Do you see Mr. Lankford here in court today?" I asked Hensley.

"Yes, I do."

I then asked the judge to tell Lankford to stand, and Hensley identified him. Lankford looked at me with eyes that were as cold and gray as a January dawn. After he was reseated, I turned to the judge and asked if the attorneys could approach. The judge waved us up and she knew exactly what I wanted to talk about.

"Don't tell me, Mr. Haller. You didn't get copied on the videos."

"That's right, Judge. The witness says the prosecution has had this material for two months and not a single frame of video was turned over in discovery to the defense. That's a direct violation of—"

"Your Honor," Forsythe broke in. "I have not even seen these videos myself so—"

"But your investigator took delivery of them," the judge said in a tone of incredulity that told me she was going to come down on my side on this.

"Your Honor," Forsythe sputtered, "I can't explain this. If you wish to question my investigator in camera, I am sure there is an explanation. The bottom line is all parties are in agreement that the victim visited that hotel in the hours before her death. It's not in dispute, so the trespass here is minimal. No harm, no foul, Judge. I make a motion we press on with the case."

I shook my head wearily.

"Judge, there is no way of knowing whether there is no harm and no foul without looking at the videos."

The judge nodded in agreement.

"How much time do you need, Mr. Haller?"

"I don't know. There can't be a lot of material. An hour?"

"Very well. One hour. You can use the conference room down the hall. My clerk has the key. Step back, gentlemen."

As I walked back to the defense table, I raised my eyes to the railing and found Lankford staring back at me.

38

I borrowed Lorna's iPad back from her after the judge broke for the hour. Since I had already studied the Beverly Wilshire videos at length, my purpose in complaining about the prosecution's discovery violation was actually an effort to conceal my own violation in not providing the same videos to Forsythe. Either way, I didn't need an hour to study them again. Instead, I used the time to watch the surveillance video from the Stratton Sterghos house once more and to strategize its best use in bringing down Marco and Lankford on the way to a not-guilty verdict for Andre La Cosse. The video was indeed the depth charge I had hoped for. It was waiting below the surface for the prosecution to sail over. When I detonated the charge, Forsythe's ship would sink.

My case plan was to take things right up to the bell on Friday and rest my case just before the jury was discharged for the weekend. That would give them two full days to consider things before we moved to closing arguments. This meant I was most likely looking at Friday morning as the introduction point of the Sterghos video. I had plenty of witnesses to present between now and then.

At three twenty-five, there was a single knock on the door and Leggoe's courtroom deputy looked in. It said HERNANDEZ on his name tag.

"You're up," he said.

When I got back to the defense table, the video remote and laser pointer were waiting for me at my place.

And my defendant was, too. I realized that Andre's downward spiral could now be measured by the hours instead of days. He had actually deteriorated in the hour I had spent in the conference room and he had spent in the courthouse lockup.

I squeezed his arm. It felt as thin as a broomstick under his sleeve.

"We're doing well, Andre. Hang in there."

"Have you decided if I get to testify?"

This was an ongoing conversation we'd been having during the trial. He wanted to testify and tell the world he was innocent. He believed — not without some merit — that guilty men remain mute and the innocent speak out. They testify.

The problem was that, while Andre wasn't a murderer, he was a man engaged in a criminal enterprise. Additionally, his deteriorated physical condition would likely not garner sympathy from the jury. I didn't want him to testify and didn't think he needed to. I had come to believe, contrary to my earlier instincts, that our best shot at a not-guilty verdict was to keep him in his seat.

"Not yet," I said. "I'm hoping that it will be so obvious that you're innocent that it won't matter."

He nodded, disappointed in my answer. I realized that he had lost so much weight in the two weeks since jury selection started that I needed to think about getting him a better fitting suit. There were only four or five court days left before the jurors began deliberations, but I thought it was the right thing to do.

I wrote a note about it on my legal pad, tore the page out, and then handed it back over the rail to Lorna just as the judge came out from chambers and took the bench.

Victor Hensley was recalled to the witness stand and Judge Leggoe gave me permission to position myself in the well while I showed the composite Beverly Wilshire security video and asked Hensley questions.

I first established through Hensley the date and time of the video that we would watch and had him explain how video from several different cameras was edited together so Gloria Dayton could be tracked in her movements through the hotel. I also had Hensley explain that there were no cameras on the guest-room floors because it was a privacy issue. The hotel management apparently thought it was bad for business to film who entered what rooms and when.

I handed Hensley the laser pointer so he could keep the red dot on Gloria as she made her way and he narrated. I realized that the video gave the jurors their first glimpse of Gloria in motion. During the prosecution phase they had seen autopsy photos, mug shots, and screen shots from her Giselle Dallinger websites. But the video was Gloria as a living person, and when I glanced at the jury, I saw that they were fully engaged in watching her.

That was what I wanted, because my next set of questions to Hensley would take them in a new direction. I retrieved the remote and the laser and stood back in the well. I started playing the video trail from the beginning and then froze the image when Gloria was passing through the lobby and in front of the man in the hat.

"Now, Mr. Hensley, can you look at the screen and tell the jury if you have any members of your staff there in the lobby?"

Hensley said the man standing at the elevator alcove was part of the security staff.

"Anyone else that you can see?"

"No, I don't believe so."

"What about this man here?"

I put the laser dot on the man in the hat, who was sitting on the divan and looking at his phone.

"Well," Hensley said. "We can't see his face in this frame. If you play it until we see his face…"

I hit the play button and the video advanced. I had drawn eyes toward the man in the hat. But he never changed the position of his head and his face was not seen. The video jumped when Gloria went into the alcove and then stepped onto an elevator. There was a black screen for a few seconds and then the video showed Gloria getting back on the elevator on the eighth floor and going down to the lobby.

When the video jumped again to her exit walk through the lobby, I hit the slow button on the remote and put the laser dot on the man in the hat once again to orient the jurors. I said nothing while all eyes were on the screen. I held the red dot on the man in the hat as he got up and left behind Gloria. I then froze the image a moment before he left the screen.

"Does that man work for the hotel?" I asked.

"I could never see the face but, no, I don't think so," Hensley said.

"If you could not see his face, how do you know he isn't an employee?"

"Because he would have to be a floater and we don't have floaters."

"Can you explain to the jury what you mean by that?"

"Our security is post-oriented. We have people at posts—like the man at the elevator alcove. We are posted and we are visible. Name tags, green blazers. We don't have undercovers. We don't have floaters—guys who float around and do whatever they want."

I started to pace in front of the jury box, first walking toward the witness stand and then turning back to cross the well. With my back turned to Hensley and my eyes on Lankford sitting against the rail, I asked my next question.

"What about private security, Mr. Hensley? Could that man have been working security for someone staying in the hotel?"

"He could have. But usually private security people check in with us to let us know they're there."

"I see. Then, what do you think that man was doing there?"

Forsythe objected, saying I was calling for speculation from the witness.

"Your Honor," I responded. "Mr. Hensley spent twenty years as a police officer and detective before spending the past ten in security for this hotel. He's been in that lobby countless times and dealt with countless situations there. I think he is more than qualified to render an observation on what he sees on the video."

"Overruled," Leggoe said.

I nodded to Hensley to answer the question.

"I would bet that he was following her," he said.

I paused, wanting to underline the answer with silence.

"What makes you say that, Mr. Hensley?"

"Well, it looks like he was waiting for her before she even got there. And then when she comes back down, he follows her out. You can tell when she makes the sudden turn to go to the front desk. That catches him off guard and he has to correct. Then he follows when she leaves."

"Let's watch it again."

I ran the whole video again in real time, keeping the laser dot on the hat.

"What other observations do you have about the video, Mr. Hensley?" I asked afterward.

"Well, for one, he knew about our cameras," Hensley said. "We never see his face because of the hat, and he knew just where to sit and how to wear it so he would never be seen. He's a real mystery man."

I tried hard not to smile. Hensley was the perfect witness, honest and obvious. But calling the man in the hat a "mystery man" was beyond my expectations. It was perfect.

"Let's summarize, Mr. Hensley. What you've told us here today is that Gloria Dayton came into the hotel on the evening of November eleventh and went up to the eighth floor, where she presumably knocked on the door of a room where no one was staying. Is that correct?"

"Yes, correct."

"And that when she went back down the elevator and left the hotel, she was followed by a 'mystery man' who was not an employee of the hotel. Correct?"

"Again, correct."

"And just over two hours later she was dead."

Forsythe weakly objected on the grounds I was asking a question that was outside the scope of Hensley's knowledge and expertise.

Leggoe sustained the objection but it didn't matter.

"Then I have no further questions," I said.

Forsythe stood for his cross-examination but then surprised me.

"Your Honor, the state has no questions at this time."

He must have decided that the best path out of the "mystery man" debacle was to pay it no mind, give it no credibility, act like it didn't matter—and then retreat with Lankford and engineer some kind of response in rebuttal.

The problem for me was that I didn't want to put another witness on the stand but it was only four ten and probably too soon in the judge's estimation to end court for the day.

I walked to the railing behind the defense table and leaned over to whisper to Cisco.

"Tell me something," I said.

"Tell you what?" he answered.

"Act like you're telling me about our next witness and shake your head."

"Well, yeah, I mean we don't have another witness unless you want me to go to the hotel where we stashed Budwin Dell and bring him over."

He shook his head, playing along perfectly, and then continued.

"But it's four ten now and by the time I got back it would be five."

"That's good."

I nodded and returned to the defense table.

"Mr. Haller, you can call your next witness," the judge said.

"Judge...I, uh, don't exactly have my next witness ready. I thought Mr. Forsythe would have at least a few questions for Mr. Hensley and that would take us through until four thirty or five."

The judge frowned.

"I don't like quitting early. I told you that at the start of the trial. I said have your witnesses ready."

"I understand, Your Honor. I do have a witness but he is in a hotel twenty minutes away. If you want, I can have my investigator—"

"Don't be ridiculous. We wouldn't get started until almost five. What about Mr. Lankford? He's on your witness list."

I turned and looked back at Lankford as if I was considering it. Then I looked back at the judge.

"I'm not prepared today for Mr. Lankford, Your Honor. Could we just break for the day now and make up the lost time by shortening our recesses over the next couple days?"

"And penalize the jury for your lack of preparedness? No, we're not going to do that."

"Sorry, Judge."

"Very well, I am adjourning court for the day. We will be in recess until nine o'clock tomorrow morning. I suggest you be prepared to begin then, Mr. Haller."

"Yes, Your Honor."

We stood as the jury filed out, and Andre needed to grab me by the arm to pull himself up.

"You okay?" I asked.

"Fine. You did good today, Mickey. Real good."

"I hope so."

The deputies came for him then. He would be taken back to the courtside cell, where he would change from his baggy suit into an orange jumpsuit. He would then be put on a bus and shipped back to Men's Central. If there were any delays in the process, he would miss chow time in the jail and go to sleep hungry.

"Just a few more days, Andre."

"I know. I'm hanging in."

I nodded and they led him away. I watched them take him through the steel door.

"Isn't that touching?"

I turned. It was Lankford. He had come up to the defense table. I looked over his shoulder at Forsythe. The prosecutor was standing over his table, trying to fit a thick stack of files into his thin attaché case. He was not paying attention to Lankford and me. Behind him, the courtroom had emptied. Lorna had gone down to get the car. One of Moya's men had followed her while the other had moved out into the hallway to wait for me. Cisco and Jennifer had already left the courtroom.

"It is touching, Lankford," I said. "You know why? Because that's an innocent man, and you don't see too many of those around here."

I raised my hand in a who-am-I-kidding gesture.

"But of course you know that better than almost anybody, don't you? I mean the part about him being innocent."

Lankford shook his head like he didn't get it.

"You really think you're going to get him off with this mystery man defense?"

I smiled as I started putting my own files and notes into my briefcase.

"We're actually calling it the 'Cat in the Hat' defense. And believe me, it's a lock."

He said nothing in response and I paused my efforts to look at him.

"One-Echo-Robert-five-six-seven-six."

"What's that, your mother's phone number?"

"No, Lankford, it's your license plate number."

I saw a split-second change in his eyes. It was recognition or maybe fear. I kept going, improvising but following some instinctual path to an unknown destination.

"It's a city of cameras. You should have lost the plate before you started following her. That next witness the judge wanted to hear today? He's bringing video from outside the hotel, and he's going to identify you as the cat in the hat."

The look in Lankford's eyes wasn't fleeting anymore. It was the vicious look of a cornered animal.

"And then you're going to have to explain to the jury why you were following Gloria Dayton before she was murdered and before you were on the case."

Lankford suddenly moved into me, grabbing my tie to jerk me away from the table. But the tie came off in his hand and he stumbled backwards off balance.

"Hey! Is there a problem?"

Forsythe had taken notice. Lankford recovered and I looked at Forsythe.

"No, no problem."

I calmly took my tie back from Lankford. His back was to Forsythe. He stared at me with those black-marble eyes. I started clipping my tie back on and leaned in to whisper.

"Lankford, I'm going to go out on a limb here. I don't think you're a killer. I'm guessing you got into something way over your head and you got pushed. Used. You found her for somebody and he did the rest. Maybe you knew what was coming, maybe not. Either way, you're going to let an innocent man go down for it?"

"Fuck you, Haller. Your client is scum. All of them are."

Forsythe walked up to us then.

"I'm leaving now, gentlemen. I ask again, is there a problem here? Do I have to stay here and babysit you two?"

Neither of us broke our stares to look at the prosecutor. I answered.

"We're fine. I'm just explaining to…Investigator Lankford the reason I wear clip-ons."

"Fascinating. Good night."

"Good night."

Forsythe went out through the gate and down the middle aisle of the empty courtroom. I picked up with Lankford where I had left off before the interruption.

"You've got less than twenty-four hours to figure out how you want to play this. Tomorrow your buddy Marco is going to go down. You can go down with him or you can get smart and get out of this in one piece. There is a way, you know."

Lankford slowly shook his head.

"You don't know what the fuck you're talking about, Haller. You never do. You don't know who you're dealing with. In fact, you don't know shit."

I nodded as though I felt I had been properly rebuked.

"Then I guess I'll see you tomorrow."

I clapped him on the arm like I was saying good-bye to a good friend.

"Don't fucking touch me," he said.

39

Under directions from Lorna, Cisco brought wine and pizza from the takeout at Mozza to the loft for the postcourt staff meeting that night. She said it was warranted because for the first time in two weeks of trial and more than seven months of prep, it felt like there was something to celebrate.

It was unexpected to have a midtrial celebration, but the bigger surprise was seeing Legal Siegel in a wheelchair at the end of the table. He had a mobile air tank on the chair and was happily munching on a piece of pizza.

"Who sprung you?" I asked.

"Your girl here," Legal said, pointing with his pizza at Jennifer. "She rescued me from those people. Just in time, too."

He toasted me with his slice, holding it up with two bony white hands.

I nodded and looked at everyone. I guess the reluctance to celebrate anything showed on my face.

"Come on, we finally had a good day," Lorna said, handing me a glass of red. "Revel in it."

"I'll revel in it when it's over and we put the big NG on the scoreboard," I said.

I pointed to the whiteboard, which had our defense strategy outlined on it. But I took the glass and a slice of sausage pizza, and smiled at the others as I made my way to a chair by Legal Siegel. Once everyone was seated, Lorna initiated a toast to me, and with great embarrassment I held up my glass. I then hijacked the moment and added my own toast.

"To the gods of guilt," I said. "May they release Andre La Cosse soon."

That turned the happy moment somber, but it couldn't be helped. Getting a not-guilty verdict was a long shot. Even when you knew in your gut that you were sitting next to an innocent man at the defense table, you also knew that the NGs came grudgingly from a system designed only to deal with the guilty. I had to satisfy myself with knowing, no matter the outcome, that I had done all I could do for Andre La Cosse.

I then cleared my throat, held up my glass, and offered another toast.

"And to Gloria Dayton and Earl Briggs. May justice be done by our work."

The others chimed in and an impromptu moment of silence followed. It seemed that we all were reminded that the victims in this case were many.

I broke the spell by steering everyone back to the business at hand.

"Before we all get too drunk, let's talk about tomorrow for a few minutes."

I went down the line, pointing to each as I gave orders and asked questions.

"Lorna, I want to go in a little bit early. So pick me up at seven forty-five, okay?"

"Hey, I'll be there if you'll be there."

A not-so-veiled reference to my showing up late that morning.

"Jennifer, are you with me tomorrow or do you have things on your calendar?"

"I'm there in the morning. In the afternoon I've got a loan-modification hearing."

Another foreclosure case, which were still the only cases bringing in any money.

"All right. Cisco, where are we with the witnesses?"

"Well, you have Budwin stashed at Checkers. Just let me know whether to bring him to the courthouse. You got my guy from the Ferrari dealership standing by and ready to authenticate. Then you've got the big question. Marco. Will he show up or not?"

I nodded.

"He has till ten, so I'd better be able to put someone in the chair at nine when the judge comes out. So bring Budwin over first thing."

"You got it."

"When does Moya come in?"

"They won't divulge an exact time for security reasons. But they are transporting him from Victorville tomorrow. I don't think you can count on him in court till Thursday."

"That'll work."

I nodded. Things seemed to be in place. I would have rather held back Budwin Dell, the gun dealer, until after I knew whether Marco was going to testify, but I had no choice. A trial was always a work in progress and it almost never rolled out the way you initially planned or envisioned it.

"What about going with Lankford ahead of Marco?" Jennifer asked, eyeing the witness order I had written along one side of the whiteboard. "Would that work?"

"I have to think about it," I said. "It might."

"There are no maybes and might-bes in trial," Legal Siegel announced. "You gotta be sure."

I put my arm on his shoulder and nodded my thanks for his counsel.

"He's right. Legal's always right."

Everyone laughed, including Legal. The work questions finished for the moment, we went back to eating. I took a second piece of pizza and soon the wine worked its way into everybody in the room, and the banter and laughs continued. All seemed well in the Haller & Associates universe. No one seemed to notice that I was not actually drinking my wine.

Then my phone started vibrating. I pulled it from my pocket, checking the caller ID before answering because I didn't want to intrude on the moment.

LA COUNTY JAIL

Normally, I wouldn't take a call after hours from the jail. Most of the time it's a collect call from somebody who got my name and number from somebody else. Nine out of ten times it's somebody who says he has money for private counsel but ultimately proves to be lying about that and everything else. But this time I knew there was a good chance it was Andre La Cosse. He had taken to calling me from the jail after court to discuss what had happened that day and what to expect the next. I stood up and worked my way around the table so I could walk out into the loft and be able to hear the call.

"Hello?"

"I'm looking for Michael Haller."

It wasn't Andre and it wasn't a collect call. I instinctively closed the door to the boardroom to further insulate myself from the noise.

"This is Haller. Who is this?"

"This is Sergeant Rowley at the Men's Central jail. I am calling to tell you there has been an incident involving your client Andre La Cosse."

He had pronounced "La Cosse" wrong.

"What do you mean? What incident?"

I started pacing across the empty wooden floor, putting more space between me and the boardroom.

"The inmate was assaulted early this evening in the transportation center at the Criminal Courts Building. Another inmate is being investigated."

"Assaulted? What does that mean? How bad is it?"

"He was stabbed multiple times, sir."

I closed my eyes.

"Is he dead? Is Andre dead?"

"No, sir, he was transported in critical condition to the jail ward at County/USC Medical Center. No other details on his condition are available at this time."

I opened my eyes, turned, and unconsciously raised my left hand in an impotent gesture. A sharp pain shot through my elbow, reminding me of my injury, and I dropped my arm to my side.

"How could this happen? What exactly is the transportation center at CCB?"

"The TC is the staging area in the courthouse basement where custodies are loaded on buses for transport back to our different holding facilities. Your client was about to be transported back to Men's Central when the assault took place."

"Aren't these people in shackles? How could—"

"Sir, the incident is under investigation and I can't—"

"Who is the investigator? I want his number."

"I'm not at liberty to give you that information. I am only calling as a courtesy to tell you there has been an incident and your client is at County/USC. Yours is the only name on his sheet here."

"Is he going to make it?"

"I don't know that information, sir."

"You don't know shit, do you?"

I disconnected before I heard a reply. I started walking toward the boardroom. Lorna, Cisco, and Jennifer were standing behind the glass window, watching me. They knew something was up.

"Okay," I said after entering. "Andre got stabbed in the courthouse before they put him on the bus tonight. He's at County/USC."

"Oh my god!" Jennifer exclaimed.

Her hands went to her face. She had sat next to Andre through several days of the trial, often whispering in his ear explanations about what I was doing when I dealt with witnesses. I was too busy with the trial. She had become the chief handholder, and that had drawn them close.

"How?" Cisco said. "Who?"

"I don't know. They said another inmate is under investigation. This is what I want to do. I'm going to go to County/USC and see what his status is and if I can get in to see him. Cisco, I want you on the investigation. They wouldn't tell me the name of the suspect. I want to know who it is and what connections he could have to Marco and Lankford."

"You think they're behind this?" Lorna asked.

"Anything's possible. I spoke to Lankford today after court. I tried to rattle him but he didn't rattle. Maybe he knew what was going to come down."

"I thought you had Moya's people protecting him," Jennifer said.

"In the jail module, yeah," I said. "But it would be impossible to cover the buses and the courthouse. It's not like I could get him a bodyguard."

"What do you want me to do?" she asked.

"I want you to take Legal back first. Then I want you to blueprint an argument against mistrial."

Jennifer seemed to come out of the shock of the moment and focus for the first time on what I had just said.

"You mean—"

"I was told he was in critical condition. I don't know if that means he's going to live or die. But either way I doubt he's going to court in the foreseeable future. The default setting on that is to go to mistrial and start over when he's recovered. If Leggoe doesn't come to that on her own, then Forsythe will make the motion because he saw his case start to go sideways today. We have to stop it. We're about to win this case. Let's proceed with the trial."

Jennifer pulled a pad and pen up from her bag that was on the floor.

"So we want to continue the trial with Andre in absentia? I'm not sure that will fly."

"They proceed with cases when defendants escape during

trial. Why not here? There's got to be a precedent. If not, we need to make one."

Jennifer shook her head.

"In those escape cases, the defendants forfeit the right to be present by their own actions in escaping. This is different."

Not interested in the legal discussion, Cisco stepped out into the loft space so he could start working his phone.

"No, it's different but the same," I said. "It's just going to come down to the judge and judicial discretion."

"Judicial discretion is a big fucking tent," Legal said.

I nodded and pointed at him.

"He's right, and we have to find space in that tent."

"Well, I would say that at the very least we are going to need a waiver from Andre," Jennifer said. "The judge won't even consider it if Andre hasn't signed off, and we don't know if he's in a condition to sign or understand any of this."

"Pull out your computer and let's write up the waiver right now."

There was a printer on the counter beneath our whiteboard. We had set things up for printing in the loft after my car was wrecked and the printer I had was destroyed.

"You're sure he'll be able to knowingly sign?" Jennifer asked.

"Don't worry," I said. "You write it up, I'll get it signed."

I spent six hours in a family waiting room on the lockdown floor at County/USC. For the first four hours I was repeatedly told that my client was in surgery. I was then told he was in recovery but that I could not see him because he had not regained consciousness. During the whole time, I never lost my cool with anyone. I did not complain and I did not yell.

But by two o'clock in the morning I had reached the limits of my patience and started demanding to see my client at ten-minute intervals. I pulled out the full arsenal, threatening legal action, media attention, even FBI intervention. It got me nowhere.

By then I had received two updates from Cisco on his investigation of the investigation. In his first call, he confirmed much of what we had suspected; that a fellow inmate who had been in the courthouse for his own trial had attacked Andre, using a shiv fashioned from a piece of metal. Though shackled at the waist like all the men waiting in lines to load onto jail buses, the suspect dropped to the ground and managed to slip the waist chain down over his feet, freeing his movements enough to attack Andre and stab him seven times in the chest and abdomen before he was overpowered by jail deputies.

In his second call, Cisco added the name of the suspect—Patrick Sewell—and said he had found no connection so far by case or other means to either DEA agent James Marco or DA investigator Lee Lankford. The name of the assailant was familiar to me, and then I remembered that Sewell was the defendant in the death-penalty case my half brother was in trial with. I recalled that Harry had said Sewell was brought down from San Quentin, where he was already serving a life sentence. This told me Sewell was the perfect hit man. He had nothing to lose.

I told Cisco to keep working it. If he came up with even a slim connection between Sewell and Marco or Lankford, then I'd be able to create enough smoke to make Judge Leggoe think twice about calling a mistrial.

"I'm on it," Cisco said.

I expected nothing less.

At three ten in the morning, I was finally allowed to see my client. I was escorted by a nurse and a detention deputy into the high-dependency unit of the medical wing. I had to gown up because of the risk of infection to Andre, and then I was able to enter a surgery recovery room where Andre's frail body lay attached to a concert of machines, tubes, and hanging plastic bags.

I stood at the end of the bed and just watched as the nurse checked the machines and then lifted the blanket over him to look at the bandages that wrapped Andre's entire torso. His upper body was propped at a low angle on the bed, and I noticed that next to his right hand was a remote for setting the bed's incline. His left wrist was handcuffed to a thick metal eyelet attached to the bed's side frame. Though the prisoner was barely clinging to life, no chances were being taken with the possibility of escape.

Andre's eyes were puffy and half open, but he wasn't seeing anything.

"So...is he going to make it?" I asked.

"I'm not supposed to tell you anything," the nurse said.

"But you could."

"The first twenty-four hours will tell the tale."

At least it was something.

"Thank you."

She patted my arm and left the room, leaving the deputy standing in the doorway. I walked over to the door and started to close it.

"You can't close that," the deputy said.

"Sure I can. This is an attorney-client conference."

"He's not even conscious."

"Right now he isn't, but it doesn't matter. He's my client and we are entitled by the U.S. Constitution to private consultation. You want to stand in front of a judge tomorrow and explain why you failed to provide this man—who is now the victim of a vicious crime—his inalienable right to confer with his attorney?"

In the Sheriff's Department, all academy graduates are transferred directly into the detention division for their first two years on the job. The deputy in front of me looked like he was twenty-four at the most and maybe even still on probation. I knew he would back down and he did.

"All right," he said. "You have ten minutes. After that, you're out of here. Doctor's orders."

"Fine."

"I'll be standing right out here."

"Good. I feel safer already."

I closed the door.

40

Judge Leggoe brought the attorneys into chambers first thing the next morning. Lankford was invited in with Forsythe so he could brief the judge on what was known in regard to the stabbing of Andre La Cosse. Lankford, of course, couched it in terms of the kind of random violence that happens often between incarcerated men.

"Most likely it will be determined to be a hate crime," he said. "Mr. La Cosse is a homosexual. The suspect is already convicted of one murder and is on trial for another."

The judge nodded thoughtfully. I could not counter Lankford's insinuations because so far Cisco had not come up with any link between Patrick Sewell — La Cosse's suspected assailant — and Marco and Lankford. My response was weak at best.

"There's still a long way to go in the investigation," I said. "I would not jump to any conclusions yet."

"I'm sure they won't," Lankford said.

He didn't have the judgmental smirk that was customary on his face. I read that as an early indication of something changing in Lankford. Maybe it was the weight of knowing he wasn't in the clear. If the attack on La Cosse was, as I believed, an attempt to end the case by eliminating the defendant, then it had failed. The question now was how badly it had failed.

"Your Honor," Forsythe said. "In light of these events and

the recovery time the victim will certainly need, the state moves for a mistrial. I really don't see any alternative. We will not be able to guarantee the integrity of the trial or the jury if the case is continued until the defendant reaches a condition in which he can come back to court—*if* he ever reaches that condition."

The judge nodded and looked at me.

"Does that make sense to you, Mr. Haller?"

"No, Your Honor, not at all. But I would like my colleague Ms. Aronson to respond to Mr. Forsythe. She is better prepared than me. I spent the night at the hospital with my client."

The judge nodded to Jennifer, and she responded with a beautiful and unrehearsed argument against mistrial. With every sentence I grew prouder of the fact that I had picked her for my team. Without a doubt she would someday leave me in the dust. But for now she was working for me and with me, and I could not have done better.

Her argument had three concise points, the first being that to declare a mistrial would be prejudicial to the defendant. She cited the cost of mounting the defense and the continuation of Andre La Cosse's incarceration; the physical toll it would take; and the simple fact that with the prosecution team having seen most of the defense's case, it would be allowed with a mistrial to retool and be better prepared for the next trial.

"Your Honor, that is not fair in any perception," she said. "It is prejudicial."

In my opinion that argument was good enough on its own to win the day. But Jennifer hammered it down with her next two points. She cited the cost to taxpayers that a new trial would certainly entail. And she concluded that the administration of justice was best served in this case by allowing the trial to continue.

These last two points were particularly genius because they hit the judge where she lived. A judgeship was an elected office, and no jurist wants to be called out by an opponent or a newspaper for wasting taxpayer dollars. And the "administration of justice" was a reference to the discretion the judge had in making this decision. Leggoe's ultimate goal was the administration of justice in this matter and she had to consider whether cutting and running on the case allowed for it or precluded it.

"Ms. Aronson," the judge said after Jennifer submitted, "your argument is cogent and persuasive, but your client is in a hospital bed in a critical care unit. Surely you're not suggesting that we bring the jury to him. I think the court is faced with a dilemma here with only one solution."

This was the only part that was rehearsed. The best way to get what we wanted was to lead the judge to it, not come out of the gate with it.

"No, Judge," Jennifer said. "We think you should proceed with the case without the defendant present, after admonishing the jury not to consider the defendant's absence."

"That's impossible," Forsythe blurted out. "We get a conviction and it will be reversed on appeal in five minutes flat. The defendant has the right to face his accusers."

"It won't be reversed if the defendant has knowingly waived his right to appear," Jennifer said.

"Yeah, that's great," Forsythe responded sarcastically, "but last I heard, your client is lying unconscious in a bed and we have a jury sitting out there in the box ready to go."

I reached into my inside jacket pocket and pulled the waiver I had taken to County/USC the night before. I handed it across the desk to the judge.

"That is a signed waiver of appearance, Judge," I said.

"Wait a minute, wait a minute," Forsythe said, the first notes of desperation creeping into his voice. "How can that be? The man's in a coma. I doubt he could sign anything, let alone *knowingly* sign it."

The judge handed the waiver to Forsythe. Lankford leaned over from his chair to look at the signature.

"I was at the hospital all night, Judge. He was in and out of consciousness, which is not the same as being in a coma. Mr. Forsythe is throwing around medical terms he doesn't know the meaning of. That aside, during my client's periods of consciousness he expressed to me the strong desire to continue the trial in his absence. He doesn't want to wait. He doesn't want to have to go through this again."

Forsythe shook his head.

"Look, Judge, I don't want to accuse anyone of anything but this is impossible. There's just no way that this—"

"Your Honor," I said evenly, as though it didn't bother me that Forsythe was calling me a liar. "If it will help with your decision, I have this."

I pulled my cell phone and opened up the photo app. I went to the camera roll and expanded the shot I had taken in my client's hospital room. It showed Andre in his bed, propped at a forty-five-degree angle, a bed table positioned across his midsection. His right hand was on the table, holding a pen and signing the waiver. The shot was angled down from Andre's right side. The angle and the swelling around his eyes made it impossible to tell if his eyes were open or closed.

I handed the phone to the judge.

"I had a feeling Mr. Forsythe would object, so I took this quick shot. Something I learned from my process server. There was also a deputy on the room named Evanston. If necessary, we can wake him up and bring him to court to attest to the signature."

The judge pointedly handed the phone back to me instead of letting Forsythe look.

"The photo isn't necessary, Mr. Haller. You're an officer of the court and I take you at your word."

"Your Honor?" Forsythe said.

"Yes, Mr. Forsythe?"

"I would like to request a brief delay to allow time for the state to consider and formulate a response to the defense."

"Mr. Forsythe, this is your motion, and on top of that, you

were the one just moments ago reminding the court that there was a jury waiting to proceed."

"Then, Your Honor, the state requests that the court conduct a thorough examination of the defendant and assure that the waiver Mr. Haller purportedly has was indeed voluntarily and knowingly signed by the defendant."

I had to head this off before one of Forsythe's desperate attempts to stop the trial took hold.

"Your Honor, Mr. Forsythe is a desperate man. He obviously will say anything to stop this trial. You have to ask yourself why and I think the answer is that he knows he is going down. We are proving that Mr. La Cosse is innocent in there, and the jury, the gallery, everyone, knows it, including Mr. Forsythe. And so he wants to stop it. He wants a court-sanctioned do-over. Judge, are you really going to allow this? My client is an innocent man and he has been jailed and abused and deprived of everything, including possibly his very life. The administration of justice demands that this trial continue. Right now. Today."

Forsythe was about to bark back, but the judge held up her hand to stop him. She was set to make the call but was interrupted by a buzzing from the phone on her desk.

"That's my clerk."

Meaning that she had to take the call. I winced. I felt that I had her and that she was about to deny the motion for mistrial.

She picked up the phone and listened to something briefly, then hung up.

"James Marco is in the courtroom with an attorney from the DEA," she said. "He's ready to testify."

She let that sink in for a few moments and then continued.

"The motion for a mistrial is denied. Mr. Haller, you will call your next witness in ten minutes."

"Your Honor, I must strenuously object to this," Forsythe said.

"Strenuously noted," Leggoe responded, a harshness in her voice.

"I request that these proceedings be stayed while the state takes the matter up on appeal."

"Mr. Forsythe, you can file your notice to appeal anytime you want, but there is no stay. We're back in session in ten minutes."

She gave Forsythe a moment to come back at her. When he didn't, she ended the session.

"I think we're finished here."

On the way back to the courtroom, the defense team kept a steady separation of fifteen feet behind the state team. I bent over to whisper to Jennifer.

"You hit it out of the park," I said. "We're going to win this thing."

She smiled proudly.

"Legal helped me with the talking points when I was driving him back last night. He's still sharp as a razor."

"You're telling me. He's still better than ninety percent of the lawyers in this courthouse."

Up ahead in the hallway I saw Lankford holding the door to the courtroom open and waiting for us after Forsythe had gone through. We held each other's eyes as I approached, and I took the door gesture as a signal. As an invitation. I touched Jennifer on the elbow and nodded for her to go ahead into the courtroom. I stopped when I got to Lankford. He was a smart guy. He knew the effort to stop the trial and stop me had failed. I gave him an opening because I still needed one side of the conspiracy to cave. And as often as I had crossed swords with Lankford, I wanted Marco to go down even more.

"I've got something you should take a look at," I said.

"Not interested," he said. "Keep moving, asshole."

But there was no conviction in it. It was just his starting point in a negotiation.

"I think this is something you'll be very interested in."

He shrugged. He needed more in order to make the decision.

"And if you're not interested, your pal Marco will be."

Lankford nodded.

I went through the door and entered the courtroom. I saw Forsythe at the prosecution table. He had pulled out his phone and was making a call. I assumed it was to a supervisor or to somebody in the appellate unit. I didn't much care which.

Lankford passed me and went to his seat at the rail. I went to the defense table and picked up the iPad I had borrowed from Lorna. I engaged the screen and cued up the video from the Sterghos house, then stepped over to the railing and put the device down on the empty seat next to Lankford as I brought my right foot up to tie my shoe. I whispered without looking at Lankford.

"Watch it to the end."

As I stood up, I scanned the crowded courtroom. Word that Department 120 was where the action was had already spread through the courthouse. In addition to Moya's men, who were in their usual spot, there were at least six members of the media in the first two rows, a variety of suited men I identified as fellow lawyers, and the highest concentration I'd seen in a long time of professional trial watchers—the retired, unemployed, and lonely who wander courthouses every day in search of human drama, pathos, and anguish. I wasn't sure whether the draw was Marco's appearance or the fact that the defendant had been nearly stabbed to death the evening before in the CCB's basement, but the message had been transmitted and the people had come.

I spotted Marco four rows back. He sat next to a man in a suit who I assumed was his lawyer. Marco hadn't bothered to dress for the occasion. He was wearing a black golf shirt and jeans again, the shirt tucked in so the gun holstered on his right hip was fully on display. The gunslinger look.

I decided that I needed to try to do something about that.

I looked down and saw that Lankford had already viewed the silent video and returned it to the empty seat. He sat there in what appeared to be a daze, perhaps understanding that his life was unalterably going to change before the end of this day. I brought my other shoe up onto the chair to tie. I bent down again, my eyes on Marco in the gallery as I whispered to Lank-ford.

"I want Marco, not you."

41

The judge took the bench as promised and briefly eyed the number of people in the gallery.

"Are we ready for the jury?" she asked.

I stood to address the court.

"Your Honor, before we call the jury, I would like to address a couple of matters that have just now come up."

"What is it, Mr. Haller?"

She said it with exasperation clearly in her voice.

"Well, Agent Marco is here presumably to testify as a witness called by the defense. I would like to request that I be allowed to treat him as a hostile witness and I would also ask that the court direct Agent Marco to remove the firearm he is wearing openly on his belt."

"Let's take these one at a time, Mr. Haller. First, you have called Agent Marco as a defense witness and he has so far not answered a single question. On what basis should you be allowed to treat your own witness as a hostile witness?"

Classifying a witness as hostile would allow me more freedom in questioning Marco. I could ask leading questions needing only a yes or no response.

"Your Honor, Agent Marco has sought to avoid testifying at this trial. He has even brought his lawyer with him today. Additionally, the one and only time I have met Agent Marco, he threatened me. I think that makes him, well, hostile."

Forsythe stood to respond, as did Marco's attorney, but the judge waved them off.

"Your request is denied. Let's start the testimony and see how it goes. Now, what troubles you about Agent Marco's sidearm?"

I asked if she could direct Marco to stand in the gallery so that she could see his gun. She agreed and ordered him to stand.

"Your Honor," I said, "I believe that his wearing his weapon in such an open way is threatening and prejudicial."

"He *is* a law enforcement officer," Leggoe said. "And that will be established, I'm assuming, when he begins his testimony."

"Yes, Judge, but he's going to walk by the jury on his way to the stand looking like he's Wyatt Earp. This is a courtroom, Judge, not the Old West."

The judge thought for a moment and then shook her head.

"I'm unconvinced, Mr. Haller. I'm denying that request as well."

I had hoped the judge would read between the lines and understand what I was seeking. I was going to push Marco out of his comfort zone and, depending on how things went, possibly even accuse him of murder. You never know how people are going to react, even law enforcement officers. I would have been far more comfortable knowing Marco was unarmed.

"Anything else, Mr. Haller? The jury has been most patient waiting on us."

"Yes, Judge, one more thing. This morning I will call Agent Marco, followed by Investigator Lankford. I would ask that you instruct Mr. Lankford to remain in the courtroom so that I can ensure his testimony."

"I will do no such thing. Mr. Lankford is expected to be where he should be, but I will not restrict his movements in the meantime. Let's bring the jury in now."

I glanced back at Lankford after the ruling and saw his cold-eyed stare trained fully on me.

The jury was finally seated, and the judge took five minutes to explain to them that the defendant would likely not be present for the rest of the trial. She said this was due to a hospitalization that had nothing to do with the trial or the case at hand. She admonished them not to let the defendant's absence affect their deliberations or view of the trial in any way.

I then took my place at the lectern and called James Marco to the stand. The federal agent stood in the gallery and stepped forward with an undeniable confidence and ease in his stride.

After the preliminaries that identified him as a DEA agent and member of the ICE team, I quickly got down to the script I had worked out in my head during the sleepless night before.

"Agent Marco, please tell the jury how you knew the victim in this case, Gloria Dayton."

"I did not know her."

"We have heard testimony here that she was your informant. Is that not true?"

"It is not true."

"Did she call you on November sixth to inform you that she had been subpoenaed in a habeas corpus case involving Hector Arrande Moya?"

"No, she did not."

"Are you familiar with Hector Arrande Moya?"

"Yes, I am."

"How so?"

"He's a drug dealer who was arrested by the LAPD about eight years ago. The case was eventually taken over by federal prosecutors and it landed in my lap. I became the case agent on it at that time. Moya was convicted of various charges in federal court and sentenced to life in prison."

"And in the course of your work on that case, did you ever hear the name Gloria Dayton?"

"No, I did not."

I paused for a moment and referred to my notes. So far, Marco had been nothing but cordial in his responses and seemed unconcerned by being forced to testify. His denials were what I had expected. My job was to somehow open a crack in the facade and then exploit it.

"Now, you are currently involved in a federal case involving Hector Moya, are you not?"

"I don't know the details because the lawyers are handling it."

"Mr. Moya is suing the federal government, alleging that you set him up in that bust eight years ago, is he not?"

"Mr. Moya is in prison and is a desperate man. You can sue anybody for anything, but the fact is, I was not there when he got busted and it wasn't my case. It came to me afterward and that's all I know about the whole thing."

I nodded as though I was pleased with his answer.

"Okay, let's move on. What about other players in this case? Do you know or have past experience with anyone?"

"Players? I am not sure who you mean?"

"For example, do you know the prosecutor, Mr. Forsythe?"

I turned and gestured toward Forsythe.

"No, I don't know him," Marco said.

"How about the lead investigator on the case, Detective Whitten?" I asked. "Any past association with him?"

Forsythe objected, asking where I was going with this meandering examination. I asked for the judge's indulgence and promised to get to the point quickly. The judge let me carry on.

"No, I don't know Detective Whitten either," Marco answered.

"Then how about the DA's investigator, Mr. Lankford?"

I pointed at Lankford, who was sitting face forward, staring at the back of Forsythe's head.

"He and I go back about ten years," Marco said. "I knew him then."

"How so?" I asked.

"There was a case when he was with the Glendale PD, and we crossed paths."

"What was the case?"

"There was a double murder, and the victims were drug dealers. Lankford caught the case and he consulted with me a couple, maybe three, times about it."

"Why you?"

"DEA, I guess. The dead guys were drug dealers. There were drugs found in the house where they got killed."

"And Detective Lankford wanted to know what? If you knew anything about the victims or who might have killed them?"

"Yes. Things like that."

"Were you able to help?"

"Not real—"

Forsythe objected again, citing relevancy.

"We are trying a case involving a murder seven months ago," he said. "Mr. Haller has shown no relevancy to this case ten years ago."

"Relevancy is coming, Your Honor," I responded. "And Mr. Forsythe knows it."

"Soon, Mr. Haller," the judge responded.

I nodded my thanks.

"Agent Marco, did you just say you were unable to help Detective Lankford?"

"I don't think I was. As far as I know, they never made a case against anyone."

"Were you familiar with the victims in that case?"

"I knew who they were. They were on our radar but they weren't the subjects of an active investigation."

"What about in this case, Agent Marco? The Gloria Dayton case. Has Investigator Lankford consulted you on it?"

"No, he has not."

"Have you consulted him on it?"

"No, I have not."

"So, no communication between you two?"

"None."

There was the crack. I knew I was in.

"Now this double murder you spoke of from ten years ago, was that the one on Salem Street in Glendale?"

"Uh…yes, I believe so."

"Are you familiar with the name Stratton Sterghos?"

Forsythe objected and asked for a sidebar. The judge signaled us up to the bench, and then, as expected, the prosecutor complained that I was trying an end-run move to bring Sterghos in as a witness when the judge had already struck him from the witness list.

I shook my head.

"Judge, that is not what I am trying to do now, and I will go on record right here and say I will not be calling Dr. Sterghos as a witness. He's not even in Los Angeles. All I want to do here is establish whether the witness knew that I had put Sterghos on the witness list. He said he's had no contact with anyone associated with this case, but I will be introducing evidence to the contrary."

Forsythe shook his head like he was exhausted by my antics.

"There is no evidence, Judge. This is just a sideshow. He's trying to hijack the case while he chases after rainbows."

I smiled and shook my head. I looked back at the courtroom and happened to see Lankford walking down the center aisle to the rear door.

"Where's your investigator going?" I asked Forsythe. "I'm going to put him on the stand in a few minutes."

The question to Forsythe alerted the judge. She raised her head to look over us.

"Mr. Lankford," she called.

Lankford stopped five feet from the door and looked back.

"Where are you going?" the judge asked. "You are going to be called soon as a witness."

Lankford held his hands out like he was not sure of an answer.

"Uh, the men's room."

"Be back soon, please. You will be needed shortly and we have already lost enough time this morning. I want no more delays."

Lankford nodded and continued out of the courtroom.

"Excuse me a moment, gentlemen," the judge said.

She rolled her chair to her left and leaned over the edge of the bench to converse with her clerk. I heard her ask the clerk to tell one of the courtroom deputies to make sure Lankford came back promptly to the courtroom.

That made me feel better about things.

The judge rolled back and returned her focus to the subject of the sidebar. She warned me that her patience had grown exceedingly thin and that I needed to draw the string on the net she had allowed me to cast.

"Yes, Your Honor."

I went back to the lectern.

"Agent Marco, did anyone tell you that the name Stratton Sterghos had appeared on the defense's amended witness list this week?"

Marco showed the first signs of discomfort, shaking his head wearily.

"No. I don't know that name. I never heard of the man before you just brought him up."

I nodded and made a notation on my legal pad. It read *Got you, motherfucker.*

"Can you tell the jury where you were on the night of November eleventh of last year?"

Forsythe stood.

"Your Honor!"

"Be seated, Mr. Forsythe."

Marco shook his head casually.

"I can't remember exactly what I was doing that far back."

"It was a Sunday."

He shrugged.

"Then I was probably watching *Sunday Night Football.* I don't know for sure. Does that make me guilty of something?"

I waited, but nothing more came.

"The way it usually works is that I ask the questions," I said.

"Sure," he said. "Ask away."

"What about two nights ago on Monday? Do you remember where you were that night?"

Marco didn't answer for a long moment. I think he realized that he might be standing in the middle of a minefield. In the silence, I heard the rear door of the courtroom open and turned to see Lankford returning, one of the courtroom deputies behind him.

"I was on a surveillance," Marco finally said.

I turned back to the witness stand.

"A surveillance of whom?" I asked.

He shook his head.

"That's a case. I'm not going to talk about it in open court."

"Was that surveillance on Salem Street in Glendale?"

Again he shook his head.

"I'm not going to talk about open investigations in court."

I stared at him for a long time, wondering how far I should push him.

I finally decided to wait and looked up at the judge.

"Your Honor, I have no further questions at this time but I request that the court hold Agent Marco as a witness so that I can recall him later today."

The judge frowned.

"Why can't you finish your direct now, Mr. Haller?"

"I need to take testimony from another witness this morning, and from that testimony I will draw the final questions I'll have for Agent Marco. I appreciate the court's ongoing indulgence of the defense's presentation."

Leggoe asked Forsythe if he had an issue with my plan.

"Judge, the people have grown very weary of defense counsel's flights of fancy but once more we are willing to take the ride. I know this will be another crash-and-burn and forgive me but I just can't look away."

The judge asked Forsythe if he wanted the opportunity to cross-examine Marco before he stepped down. This would be in addition to the opportunity he would have after I brought the DEA agent back to the stand in the afternoon. Without much thought, he opted to wait to conduct one uninterrupted cross-examination. And as a safety measure, he reserved the right to call Marco back to the stand even if I didn't.

The judge told Marco he could step down but ordered him to return to the court at one p.m. She then told me to call my next witness.

"The defense calls Lee Lankford."

I turned to look at Lankford. He was slowly starting to stand.

"And, Your Honor, we're going to need the audio-visual remote for a video demonstration."

I made sure I requested it before Marco and his attorney got out of the courtroom. I wanted them thinking about the video I planned to play.

42

Lankford walked with a steady but slow pace to the witness stand, his eyes staring at a fixed point on the wall behind it. I watched him closely. He looked like a man who was running equations internally while running on autopilot externally. I thought this was a good sign, that he was realizing his one way out was through me. I decided I would know pretty quickly into his testimony which path he had chosen.

As the DA's investigator assigned to the case, Lankford had been granted a standard exception that allowed him to remain in court even though he had been listed as a witness by the defense. This meant that going all the way back to jury selection he had been a familiar presence to the jurors as he sat each day against the railing behind Forsythe. But he had never been introduced before the moment I made him stand and be identified during Hensley's testimony the day before. So I walked him through who he was and what he did, and I included his background as a former Glendale homicide detective, even though that information had been revealed earlier by Marco.

I then moved into matters intrinsic to the defense case. It seemed to me that all the tendrils of the case had led me to this one witness. It all came down to this moment.

"Okay," I said. "Now let's talk about this specific case. How did it work? Were you assigned to this prosecution or did you request it?"

Lankford sat with his eyes cast downward. His posture and demeanor indicated he had not heard the question. He remained motionless and said nothing for several seconds. The silence stretched to the point that I felt the judge was on the verge of prompting him when he finally spoke.

"We normally have a rotation when it comes to murder cases."

I nodded and was formulating a follow-up when Lankford continued.

"But in this case I personally requested the assignment."

I paused, waiting for Lankford to say more, but he was silent. Still, I interpreted his full answer as a strong indication that we had come to a tacit agreement earlier.

"Why did you request it?"

"I had been assigned previously to a murder case in which the prosecutor was Bill Forsythe and we had worked well together. At least, that was the reason I gave."

Lankford looked directly at me when he added the last sentence. I believed there was some kind of message in it. There was almost a pleading look in his eyes.

"Are you saying you had an ulterior motive for requesting the case?"

"Yes. I did."

I could almost feel Forsythe tightening up as he sat at the table next to the lectern.

"What was that motive?"

"I wanted to be on the case so I could monitor it from the inside."

"Why?"

"Because I was told to."

"You mean by a supervisor?"

"No, I don't mean a supervisor."

"Then by who?"

"James Marco."

I don't think in all the thousands of hours I have spent in courtrooms that I had ever had such a moment of clarity. But I knew the moment that Lankford said the name *James Marco* that my client, if he was to survive his injuries, would be set free. I looked down at the top sheet of my yellow legal pad and composed myself for a moment before continuing.

And in that moment, Forsythe rose in slow motion, as if knowing by reflex that he had to stop this but being unsure of how to do it. He asked for a sidebar and the judge told us to come forward. As we assembled in front of the judge, I actually felt sorry for Forsythe because of the predicament the prosecutor was in.

"Judge," he said, "I would like to request a fifteen-minute recess so I can confer with my investigator."

"That's not going to happen, Mr. Forsythe," Leggoe responded. "He's a witness now. Anything else?"

"I'm being sandbagged here, Judge. This—"

"By Mr. Haller or your own investigator?"

Forsythe stood frozen.

"Go back, gentlemen. And Mr. Haller, continue with the witness."

I went back to the lectern. Forsythe sat down and stared straight ahead, bracing for what was coming.

"You said that Agent Marco told you to monitor this case?" I asked Lankford.

"Yes," he said.

"Why is that?"

"Because he wanted to know whatever we could find out about Gloria Dayton's murder investigation."

"He knew her?"

"He told me she was his informant a long time ago."

I made a mark on my legal pad, checking off one of the points I had wanted to make through Lankford's testimony. I glanced over at the jury box. Twelve for twelve, plus two alternates, they were riveted. And so was I. I had chosen Lankford over Marco as the weaker part of the conspiracy. He saw the Sterghos house video and, of course, knew he was the man in the hat. He knew that his only way out was to carefully attempt to pick his way through his testimony without snagging himself on perjury or self-incrimination. It was going to be hard to do.

"Let's back up for a minute," I said. "You're familiar with the video taken through security cameras at the Beverly Wilshire hotel that showed Gloria Dayton on the evening she was murdered, are you not?"

Lankford closed his eyes for a long moment and then opened them.

"Yes, I am."

"I am talking about the video first shown to the jury yesterday."

"Yes, I know."

"When did you first see that video?"

"About two months ago. I don't remember the date."

"Now yesterday during testimony, Victor Hensley, a security supervisor at the hotel, said he believed that the video showed Gloria Dayton being followed when she left the hotel. Do you have an opinion on that?"

Forsythe objected, saying the question was leading and beyond the scope of Lankford's knowledge and expertise. The judge overruled it and I asked Lankford the question again.

"Do you think Gloria Dayton was being followed the night of her death?"

"Yes, I do," Lankford said.

"Why is that?"

"Because I was following her."

What followed that answer may have been the loudest silence I had ever heard in a courtroom.

"Are you saying that is you on the video—the man in the hat?"

"Yes. I'm the man in the hat."

That got another check mark on my pad and another roaring silence. I realized that Lankford might be exorcizing his demons by confessing, but he so far had not admitted to anything that was actually a crime. He continued to give me that same pleading look. I came to believe in those moments that he and I were making an unspoken agreement. It was the video, I realized. He didn't want it played. He wanted to tell the story as a cooperating witness, not have the Sterghos video shoved down his throat while on the stand.

I was willing to take that deal.

"Why were you following Gloria Dayton?"

"I had been asked to find her and to find out where she lived."

"By Agent Marco?"

"Yes."

"Did he tell you why?"

"No. Not at that time."

"What did he tell you?"

Forsythe objected again, saying I was asking for hearsay testimony. The judge said she was going to allow it, and I thought about what Legal Siegel had said the night before about judicial discretion being a big fucking tent. No doubt I was living in the tent now.

I told Lankford to answer the question.

"He just said he needed to find her. He said she was a snitch who had left town many years ago and now she was back but he couldn't find her, so he thought she was using a new name."

"So he left it up to you to find her."

"Yes."

"When was this?"

"Last November, the week before she was murdered."

"How did you find her?"

"Rico gave me a picture he had of her."

"Who is Rico?"

"Rico is Marco. That was his nickname because he worked racketeering cases."

"You're referring to RICO as in the Racketeer Influenced and Corrupt Organizations Act?"

"Yes."

"What was the picture he gave you?"

"He texted it to me. He took it the night he turned her. It was old—like from eight or nine years before. He had busted her but made a deal not to book her if she snitched for him. He took her photo for his snitch file and he still had it."

"Do you still have that photo?"

"No, I deleted it."

"When?"

"After I heard that she was murdered."

I gave that answer a pause for effect.

"Did you use the photo to find her for Marco?"

"Yes, I started looking at locally based websites for escorts and eventually I found her using the name Giselle. The hair was different but it was her."

"Then what did you do?"

"Contact with escorts on this level is usually buffered. They don't just give out their home addresses and cell numbers. On Giselle's page, there was mention of a 'Pretty Woman Special' at the Beverly Wilshire. I asked Rico—Marco—to get me into a room there using one of his UC aliases."

"By 'UC,' you mean undercover?"

"Yes, undercover."

"What was the name, do you remember?"

"Ronald Weldon."

I knew this could be checked with Hensley and hotel records if I needed to corroborate Lankford's story later. The case had suddenly changed dimensions with Lankford's testimony.

"Okay, what happened next?"

"Marco got the room and gave me the key. It was on the eighth floor. I went there, and when I was opening the door, one of the bellmen arrived with a cart to the room across the hall."

"You mean it looked like the people in that room were checking out?"

"Yes."

"What did you do next?"

"I went into my room and watched through the peephole. There was a couple in the room opposite mine. The bellman left with their luggage first and then they left. They didn't pull the door closed all the way. So I went across and into the room."

"What did you do in there?"

"I looked around first. And I got lucky. In the trash can, there were several envelopes, and it looked like wedding cards had come in them. They were addressed to Daniel and Linda or Mr. and Mrs. Price and things like that. I figured out that his name was Daniel Price. So I used that name and that room number to set up Giselle Dallinger to come that night."

"Why did you go through such elaborate efforts?"

"Because first of all, I know everything can be traced. Everything. I didn't want this coming back on me. And second, I worked vice when I was a cop. I know how prostitutes and pimps work it to avoid law enforcement. Whoever the setup person was for Giselle would call me back at the hotel. It was their way of hopefully confirming I wasn't law enforcement. I could've done it from the room Marco got me, but I saw that open door and thought it would be better and completely untraceable to me. And Marco."

With his answer Lankford walked across the line from plausible deniability to conspiracy to commit. If he had been my client, I would have stopped him by now. But I had my own client to clear. I pressed on.

"Are you saying that you knew what was going to happen to Giselle that night?"

"No, never. I was just taking precautions."

I studied Lankford, unsure if he was elaborately covering his own culpability in a murder or actually telling the truth.

"So you set up the liaison for that night and then you waited for her in the lobby, correct?"

"Yes."

"Using your hat as a shield against the cameras?"

"Yes."

"And then you followed her home to Franklin Avenue."

"I did."

The judge interrupted at that moment and addressed the jury.

"Ladies and gentlemen, I know it seems as though we just got started but we are going to take a quick five-minute break. I want you to go to the jury room and stay close by. I want all counsel and the witness to remain in place, please."

We stood as the jury filed out. I knew what was coming. The judge couldn't just sit there without warning Lankford of his peril. As soon as the jury room's door closed, she turned to my witness.

"Mr. Lankford, do you have counsel present?"

"No, I don't," Lankford responded calmly.

"Do you want me to pause your testimony here so you can seek the advice of counsel?"

"No, Your Honor. I want to do this. I've committed no crime."

"You are sure?"

The question could be taken two ways. Was Lankford sure he didn't want a lawyer, or was he sure he had committed no crime.

"I would like to continue to testify."

The judge stared at Lankford for a long moment as if taking some sort of measure of him. She then turned away and signaled for the courtroom deputy to approach the bench. She whispered to the deputy and then he immediately walked to the side of the witness stand and took a position next to Lankford. He put his hand on his sidearm. It looked as if he was about to make an arrest.

"Mr. Lankford, will you please stand."

Looking puzzled, Lankford stood. He glanced at the deputy and then at the judge.

"Are you wearing a firearm, Mr. Lankford?" Leggoe asked.

"Uh, yes, I am."

"I want you to surrender your weapon to Deputy Hernandez. He will secure it until your testimony is completed."

Lankford didn't move. It became clear that Leggoe was concerned that he was armed and might attempt to harm himself or others. It was a good move.

"Mr. Lankford," the judge said sternly. "Please hand your weapon to Deputy Hernandez."

Hernandez responded by unsnapping his holster with one hand and keying his shoulder mike with the other. I assumed he was broadcasting an emergency code of some sort to others in courthouse security.

Lankford finally raised his hand and reached inside his sport coat. He slowly removed his gun and handed it to Deputy Hernandez.

"Thank you, Mr. Lankford," the judge said. "You may sit down now."

"I have a pocket knife, too," Lankford said. "Is that a problem?"

"No, Mr. Lankford, that is not a problem. Please be seated."

There was a collective exhale of relief in the courtroom as Lankford sat down and Hernandez took the gun to his desk to lock it in a drawer. Four deputies flooded into the courtroom through the rear door and the holding area entrance. The judge immediately told them to stand down and called for the jury to be returned to the box.

Three minutes later, things seemed to have returned to normal. The jury and witness were in place and the judge nodded at me.

"Mr. Haller, you may proceed."

I thanked the judge and then tried to pick up at the point where I had been interrupted.

"Investigator Lankford, did you tell Agent Marco to meet you there at the Franklin address?"

"No, I called him and gave him the address. Shortly after that I left. I was done. I went home."

"And two hours later, Gloria Dayton, the woman using the name Giselle Dallinger, was dead. Isn't that right?"

Lankford cast his eyes down and nodded his head.

"Yes."

I once again checked the jury and saw that nothing had changed. They were mesmerized by Lankford's confession.

"I'll ask you again, Investigator. Did you know she would die that night?"

"No, I did not. If I had..."

"What?"

"Nothing. I don't know what I would have done."

"What did you think would happen once you gave Gloria Dayton's address to Marco?"

Forsythe objected, saying the question asked for speculation, but the judge overruled it and told Lankford he could answer. Like everyone else in the courtroom, Leggoe wanted to hear the answer.

Lankford shook his head.

"I don't know," he answered. "Before I gave him the address that night, I asked him again what was going on. I said I didn't want to get involved if she was going to get hurt. He insisted that he just wanted to talk to her. He admitted that he knew she was back in town because she had called him from a blocked number and told him that she'd gotten a subpoena in some civil case. And he said he needed to find her to talk to her about it."

I underlined that answer with some silence. Essentially my case was made. But it was hard to end Lankford's testimony.

"Why did you do this for Agent Marco?"

"Because he had a hold on me. He owned me."

"How?"

"Ten years ago I worked that double-homicide case in Glendale. On Salem Street. I met him on that and I made a mistake..."

Lankford's voice trembled slightly. I waited. He composed himself and continued.

"He came to me. He said there were people...people who would pay for the case to remain unsolved. You know, pay me not to solve it. The truth was, my partner and I probably weren't going to close it. Not a shred of evidence was left in that place. It was an execution and the hitters had probably come across the border and then gone right back. So I thought, what difference would it make? I needed the money. I had gotten divorced and my wife—my ex-wife—was going to take our son away. She was going to move to Arizona and take him, and I needed money for a good lawyer who would fight it. My boy was only nine. He needed me. So I took the money. Twenty-five thousand. Marco made the deal and I got the money and after that…"

He paused there and seemed to go off on some internal flight of thought. I thought the judge might step in again here because, statute of limitations notwithstanding, Lankford had certainly now confessed to a crime. But the judge remained as still as every other person in the courtroom.

"After that, what?" I prompted.

It was a mistake. It brought Lankford back angry.

"What, you want me to draw you a picture? He had me. You understand what I'm saying? He *owned* me. This little hotel thing wasn't the first time he used me or told me what to do. There were other times. A *lot* of other times. He treated me the way he treated his snitches."

I nodded and looked down at my notes. I knew the case was over. I didn't need to bring back Marco or put any of the other witnesses on. Moya, Budwin Dell—none of them were needed, none of them mattered. The case ended right here.

Lankford had his head down so no one could see his eyes.

"Investigator Lankford, did you ever ask Agent Marco what happened that night to Gloria after you gave him her address?"

Lankford nodded slowly.

"I asked him point-blank if he killed her, because I didn't want that on my conscience. He said no. He said he went to the apartment, but when he got there she was already dead. He said he set the fire because he didn't know if she had anything that would link him to her. But he claimed she was already dead."

"Did you believe him?"

Lankford paused before answering.

"No," he finally said. "I didn't."

I paused. I wanted to hold the moment for the rest of my life. But then finally I looked up at the judge.

"Your Honor, I have no further questions."

I passed behind Forsythe on the way to the defense table. He remained in his seat, apparently still deciding whether to mount a cross-examination or simply ask the judge to dismiss the case. I sat down next to Jennifer and she whispered urgently in my ear.

"Holy shit!"

I nodded and leaned toward her to whisper back when I heard Lankford speak from the witness stand.

"My son is older now and he'll be okay."

I turned back to see who he was talking to, but he was bent over in the witness stand and obscured by the wood paneling. It looked like he was reaching down to something that had fallen to the floor.

Then, as I watched, Lankford sat up straight and brought his right hand up to his neck. I saw his fingers wrapped around a small pistol—a boot gun. Without hesitation he pressed the muzzle into the soft skin under his chin and pulled the trigger.

The muffled pop from the gun brought a shriek from the jury box. Lankford's head snapped back and then forward. His body listed slowly to the right and then dropped down behind the front panel of the witness stand out of sight.

Screams of horror and fear came from all over the courtroom, though Jennifer Aronson never made a sound. Like me, she sat there speechless, staring at what now appeared to be the empty witness stand.

The judge started shouting for the courtroom to be cleared, though even her high-pitched and panicked tenor drifted into the background for me. Soon it was as though I couldn't hear a thing.

I looked over at the jury box and saw my alpha, Mallory Glad-well, standing with her eyes closed, hands pressed against her open mouth. Behind her and to either side of her, other jurors were reacting to the horror of what they had just witnessed. I will always remember the composition of that scene. Twelve people—the gods of guilt—trying to unsee what they all had just seen.

Part 4

THE GODS OF GUILT

MONDAY, DECEMBER 2

Closing Argument

The Gloria Dayton case is long over. Six months later, its ripples on the surface of my life still move with a current all their own. The trial ended, of course, when Lankford pulled his backup gun and took his own life in front of the jury. Judge Leggoe declared a mistrial, and the case went no further than Department 120. Unsurprisingly, the District Attorney's Office chose to dismiss all charges against Andre La Cosse, citing the "likelihood" of his innocence and other extenuating circumstances. Of course, no one at the DA's Office or the LAPD admitted they flat out got it wrong from the start.

After his release, Andre was transferred to Cedars-Sinai, where he was treated by the best of the best, underwent more surgeries, and recuperated for six weeks in state-of-the-art medical surroundings. I sent every invoice that came from a doctor or the hospital to Damon Kennedy at the DA's Office. I never heard back.

When Andre finally left the hospital, he walked with a cane, and he likely always will. Grateful for the outcome of the criminal case, he agreed to allow me to handle a civil claim against the city and county, seeking damages for his wrongful arrest and incarceration and the physical and mental harm to him that resulted. Neither of the defendant governments wanted to go anywhere near a courtroom with the case, and we negotiated a settlement. I started by demanding a million dollars for every stab wound my client suffered but ultimately we settled for $2.4 million on top of all the medical bills.

My cut amounted to the biggest single paycheck in the history of Michael Haller & Associates. I gave bonuses to everyone on the defense team and sent a check for a hundred thousand to Earl Briggs's mother. I thought it was the least I could do.

That still left me more than enough for a three-week Hawaii vacation with Kendall and to buy a pair of Lincoln Town Cars. One was to use immediately, one to save for the years ahead. They were both low-mileage 2011 models, the last production year of the luxury model's thirty-year run.

For a while after the trial, I couldn't catch a break in the public relations department. I was once again vilified in the media and the courthouses, this time as the guy who went after a witness so hard and viciously that he killed himself on the stand. But eventually my reputation was saved by a three-part series that ran in the *Times* in September under the headline "The Trials of an Innocent Man." The stories exhaustively detailed the trial, the attack, and the ongoing rehabilitation and recovery of Andre La Cosse. I came out looking pretty good in the stories as the lawyer who believed in his client's innocence and did what he had to do to win his freedom.

The articles went a long way toward securing the financial settlement with the city and county. They went even further with my daughter. After reading the newspaper series, she tentatively opened communication with me again. We talk and text a couple times a week now and I have driven out to Ventura to watch her ride in equestrian competitions.

Where the articles didn't help me was with the California bar. An investigator with the professional ethics unit opened a file on me shortly after publication of part two in the *Times*. That report interviewed the doctors who treated Andre after the stabbing and raised serious questions about whether Andre could have possibly been conscious and of clear mind when he supposedly signed the waiver of appearance I had brought to his bedside at County/USC. The bar investigation is ongoing but I'm not worried. Andre came through with a notarized statement attesting to my legal acumen and recounting how he knowingly signed the document in question.

My other one-time client Hector Arrande Moya was both a winner and loser in the course of the year. Sly Fulgoni Jr., with tutoring from me as well as from his father, won the habeas case, and Moya's life sentence was vacated by the U.S. District Court. But upon his release from the prison in Victorville, he was immediately taken into custody by immigration officials and deported as an undesirable to Mexico.

Meanwhile, the fate and whereabouts of James Marco officially remain a mystery. He left the courthouse that day in June, slipping out in the confusion and alarm immediately following the Lankford suicide. He has not been seen since, and his face now graces Wanted posters in the same federal building where he once worked. He is the subject of wide-ranging investigations by the FBI and his own DEA. According to unnamed sources quoted in the *Times* series, the crimes and corruption of the ICE team he headed for over a decade run deep, and a federal grand jury will be hearing evidence well into next year. The unnamed sources said Marco was believed to have sided with one faction in a long-running war within the Sinaloa cartel and had been doing that faction's bidding in Southern California. It was even suggested that the effort to put Hector Moya in prison for life came on orders from Marco's bosses in Mexico.

Among the other things the grand jury is probing, according to the *Times,* is an alleged relationship between Marco and the female attorney who represented Patrick Sewell, the man charged with attacking Andre in the courthouse transportation center.

The U.S. Marshal's Office is primarily focusing its search for Marco in southern Mexico, where it is believed he may have escaped to with the aid of the cartel leaders who long ago corrupted him. But I am pretty sure they will never find him. Hector Moya told me once about how his enemies disappear, never to be found. Two weeks ago I received an e-mail from an address unknown to me but with a subject line that simply said Saludos Del Fuego. I opened the e-mail to find an embedded video and nothing else. It was only fifteen seconds long, but the video provided a lifetime's worth of horror. It depicts a man hanging by his neck from a tree. He is obviously dead, his badly beaten face swollen and bloody, his skin and clothes burned black in places.

I am pretty sure the dead man is Marco. I forwarded the video to the deputy marshal heading the search for him. Once it is authenticated, I expect there to be an announcement that Marco is believed dead, though it is unlikely they will ever find a body.

I have deleted the video from my computer but it will never be erased from my mind. I have no doubt that it came from Moya and no doubt that he wanted me to know what became of Marco. When I think about the rogue agent's fate, I remember the night in June at the loft when I was surrounded by my team and raised a glass to justice for Gloria Dayton and Earl Briggs. Some forms of justice are more horrible than others. But in this case I think justice has been rightly served.

Officially, Gloria Dayton's murder remains open because no one has been or will ever be convicted of the crime. The memory of Glory Days now resides in a city's consciousness as she takes her place in the pantheon of public victims.

In the meantime, not so much attention has been paid to Earl Briggs. His case remains open and the subject of the grand jury's ongoing investigations. But I mourn him more than Gloria or any other. I often think of the miles we rode together, the ground we covered on the road and in life.

Everybody has a jury, the voices they carry inside. Earl Briggs sits on my jury, Gloria Dayton, too. They are there with Katie and Sandy, my mother, my father, and soon Legal Siegel as well. Those I have loved and those I have hurt. Those who bless me and those who haunt me. My gods of guilt. Every day I carry on and I carry them close. Every day I step into the well before them and I argue my case.

ACKNOWLEDGMENTS

The starting point for this story came alive during a discussion with Tom Rosenberg and Gary Lucchesi, producers of *The Lincoln Lawyer*. To them the author will always be grateful.

The author also relied upon the help of many others in the research and writing of this book. They include Asya Muchnick, Bill Massey, Daniel Daly, Roger Mills, Dennis Wojciechowski, John Romano, Greg Kehoe, Terrill Lee Lankford, Linda Connelly, Alafair Burke, Rick Jackson, Tim Marcia, John Houghton, Jane Davis, Heather Rizzo, Pamela Marshall, and Henrik Bastin. Many, many thanks to all.

ABOUT THE AUTHOR

Michael Connelly is the author of twenty-five previous novels including the #1 *New York Times* bestsellers *The Black Box, The Drop, The Fifth Witness, The Reversal, The Scarecrow, The Brass Verdict,* and *The Lincoln Lawyer,* as well as the bestselling Harry Bosch series of novels. He is a former newspaper reporter who has won numerous awards for his journalism and his novels. He spends his time in California and Florida.